Dear Reader,

Duets was first launched in May 1999 and has proved to be a fan favorite. Each month we set out to bring you four sparkling romantic comedies in two separate volumes. You met many new authors in the lineup and revisited longtime Harlequin stars. Your letters and e-mails told us how *much* you enjoyed Duets!

Here at Harlequin we are always striving to reinvent ourselves, and so is the case with Duets. This is our last month of publication. Beginning in October 2003, look for Flipside, our brand-new romantic comedy series. In response to reader interest, we will be publishing two single books a month that are even longer than Duets novels. Look for #1 *Staying Single* by *USA TODAY* bestselling author Millie Criswell. Joining her in the launch month is Stephanie Doyle with #2 *One True Love?*

I think you will love these stories and all the fun books in Flipside in the months to come. Don't forget to check us out online at eHarlequin.com for news about all your favorite authors and books.

Yours sincerely,

Ms Birgit Davis-Todd
Executive Editor
Harlequin Books

A Baby…Maybe?

"Let's make a run for the truck."

Rex grabbed Cara's hand. "Come on, before we drown in this rain."

"I can't run. Not in these shoes." She looked down at her cute, strappy and ridiculously impractical sandals.

"Take them off, then."

"I will not! There's yucky stuff in this field." There was no way she was going to chance putting her bare foot in whatever it was that covered the ground.

He sighed, clearly frustrated with her. What did he expect? She was a city girl, not a cowgirl. Then, without warning, he lifted her off her feet and ran toward the fence.

Cara knew she was in heaven—although she'd never imagined heaven would be so wet and sloppy. Rex's arms were strong, holding her firmly and easily against his hard chest. With each long stride she snuggled deeper in his embrace. She barely felt the rain that was now pounding down on them.

He stopped beside the truck and pulled on the door handle. Nothing. He pulled again, harder, and still the door didn't open.

"Cara, please tell me you didn't lock the doors."

For more, turn to page 9

How To Hunt a Husband

"Bull."

"That's right, ma'am, just call me Bull. And of course I like steak. A real manly meal, that is. I was afraid we'd be eating some highbrow food, like couscous or sushi."

The minute Shannon's mother was out of the room Shannon started laughing. "You're good, Nate, uh, I mean Bull. Very good."

"I thought she was going to pass out," he said.

"Me, too. I bet she's gone to get reinforcements, namely my dad. You must have her really flustered."

When Shannon's parents returned, she noted how they kept shooting looks at each other. It was that strange couple-speak that truly connected people—people who were meant for each other—had. Those kinds of looks carried more meaning than words. She wondered if Nate would agree.

Bull, aka Nate, sidled up to Shannon quietly as her parents busied themselves setting the dinner table. He whispered softly in her ear, "I totally agree."

For more, turn to page 197

HARLEQUIN DUETS

ISBN 0-373-44174-6

Copyright in the collection:
Copyright © 2003 by Harlequin Books S.A.

The publisher acknowledges the copyright holders
of the individual works as follows:

A BABY...MAYBE?
Copyright © 2003 by Bonnie Tucker

HOW TO HUNT A HUSBAND
Copyright © 2003 by Holly Fuhrmann

Visit us at www.eHarlequin.com

Printed in U.S.A.

A Baby...Maybe?

Bonnie Tucker

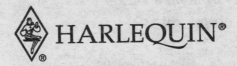

HARLEQUIN®

TORONTO • NEW YORK • LONDON
AMSTERDAM • PARIS • SYDNEY • HAMBURG
STOCKHOLM • ATHENS • TOKYO • MILAN • MADRID
PRAGUE • WARSAW • BUDAPEST • AUCKLAND

Dear Reader,

My friend and co-worker Christine Lewis and I were partaking in our favorite activity—eating lunch—when I said, "I'm writing a book about a guy, Rex Noble, who owns a bull sperm bank." Christine said, "Really? That's no bull?" From that moment on, "Noble Sperm Bank and That's No Bull" became the theme for the story.

A Baby...Maybe? is a special book. Cara and Rex meet at a time in their lives when they need each other most. Like Cara and Rex, I, too, have been fortunate to be surrounded by friends who have been there when I needed them the most. Cathy Maxwell and Barbara Daly—what can I say about sisterhood? Kevin Duvall, a brilliant man who offered me a job opportunity that changed my life. I have been privileged to work with some of the greatest and most compassionate people I will ever know. I hope more than anything *A Baby...Maybe?* will bring home how special friends are and how wonderful love can be.

Happy reading!

Bonnie Tucker

Books by Bonnie Tucker

HARLEQUIN DUETS

2—I GOT YOU, BABE
50—GOING IN STYLE
64—A ROSEY LITTLE CHRISTMAS
84—THE GREAT BRIDAL ESCAPE

HARLEQUIN LOVE & LAUGHTER

18—HANNAH'S HUNKS
52—STAY TUNED: WEDDING AT 11:00

For my daughter,
With love, pride and utmost respect
Elizabeth Tucker FC3
United States Navy

Prologue

EVERY TUESDAY MORNING at exactly ten o'clock, Cecilia Romano, Brigit O'Malley, Rachel Turner and Jessica-Marie Leigh sat down at the card table in the Erie, Pennsylvania, Recreation Center and went about the business of playing very serious pinochle.

On this particular Tuesday, Cecilia and Brigit had drawn each other as partners. Anyone just observing these fifty-something women would think: *Cecilia and Brigit, best friends.*

The truth was, while they didn't completely hate each other, they didn't like each other much either.

Cecilia would say it was all that O'Malley woman's fault, because of her hussy daughter, Mary Kathryn, who, right under the nose of everyone and God Almighty himself, ran out on her wedding with the best man. The best man being none other than one Tony Donetti.

That same Tony Donetti, who, by all rights, should be married right now to Cecilia's daughter, Cara.

Her poor, sweet baby girl, Cara. Dumped like yesterday's pasta. Cecilia sighed.

A normal person would think that a sigh like the one she just let out—a beautifully, totally despondent sigh—would elicit a question from someone sitting two feet away as to what was wrong that would bring on such a lovely sigh. One would think.

While Rachel and Jessica-Marie looked at her in a questioning manner, other people, namely that cold-hearted witch sitting across the table, didn't ask what was wrong. In fact, that Brigit O'Malley woman totally ignored Cecilia. So Cecilia did what she had to do, which was sigh again, longer and with a little more oomph this time.

Finally, that mother-of-a-groom-stealer woke up from her stupor, fanned the cards, then placed them close to her chest, a move that made Rachel ask Jessica-Marie, "Do you think they're passing codes?"

Brigit rolled her eyes at Rachel, then said with a holier-than-thou attitude, "What is it now, Cecilia?"

Well! Cecilia would show her. With a long, torturous moan, she, the mother of all mothers who deserved martyrdom at the very least, said, "Nothing. I'm fine. Just fine." However, for good measure, she released another moaning sigh, even longer and more despondent than those that had come before.

"I'm not stupid, Cecilia," Brigit said in her soft Irish brogue. "None of us are." To which the other two women nodded. "You're trying to tell me something. I've been trying to ignore you, which has become impossible."

"I don't know what you're talking about," retorted Cecilia.

"You might as well spit it out and get it off your chest."

"You wouldn't understand."

Brigit went back to studying her cards. "Never mind then."

That wouldn't do. Brigit should have known that according to the *Rules of Female Friendships* she was to press Cecilia to reveal all. Therefore, Cecilia ignored Brigit's feigned noninterest and said her piece. "Because your man-stealing daughter, that… that…whatever she calls herself now, is married. Whereas my darling Cara, the victim of your…

whoever she is…will suffer the rest of her life by never fully trusting a man again.''

''Mary Kathryn, that's her name and you know it.''

Cecilia shrugged, dismissing the woman's daughter. ''That doesn't change a thing.''

Brigit slammed her cards facedown on the table and glared at Cecilia. ''What are you talking about?''

''The pain my Cara's going through after having lost her Tony.'' Cecilia tsked. ''She hasn't left her apartment except for obligatory commitments. Her job, for instance. Although she can barely crawl out of bed to get to work in the morning.'' She placed a hand over her heart. ''She is suffocating so, in a quagmire of depression. Has lost untold weight. All because of your hussy daughter.'' Cecilia glared at Brigit, all the while thinking that the college professor scientist had better damn well be impressed by her use of the word *quagmire*. After all, Brigit should understand scientific language and be able to relate a swamp to a mother's sorrow.

''Mary Kathryn is not a hussy.'' Although to Cecilia's ears, Brigit didn't sound so sure of herself. ''I'm sorry Cara's depressed.''

Cecilia didn't think she had to share with the women at the table that there was a slight chance—okay, a one-hundred-percent chance—that she might be exaggerating a bit. Okay, a lot. The fact was, much to Cecilia's horror, Cara wasn't depressed. In fact, she was downright cheery about not being married, and that bit sharply into a mother's soul.

For that reason, too, Cecilia felt with all her heart and soul that Brigit O'Malley, mother of Mary Kathryn—who now went by the name of Kate, as if to hide her shame for stealing Cara's man—would pay, and pay dearly.

Cecilia would figure out a way to take care of

Brigit. But she was simply at a loss as to what to do about a daughter who liked being single.

Last night she had awakened at three o'clock with horrid dreams dancing through her head. Dreams of growing old with a spinster daughter who was happy in her spinsterhood. And even worse, no grandchildren. She would be the laughingstock of the Italian community. The church. This couldn't possibly be happening to her. Now she was on a mission. To see her daughter happily married, no matter how miserable being happily married made Cara.

But now Brigit was pointing a finger at her. At her! How dare she? "You think you've got it bad?" she was saying. "I've got it worse."

Cecilia slammed her own cards on the table. "How do you figure that? Your daughter is married."

"Shannon."

"Shannon?" Shannon was the younger O'Malley daughter. A free spirit from what Brigit had said, although she had never talked much about Shannon.

It was Brigit's turn to do the moaning and sighing. "Oh, if you only knew."

That woman's display of grief didn't sit well with Cecilia. If anyone was going to be doing the moaning and sighing around here it would be her. She asked Brigit in a clipped tone, "Only knew what?"

"Don't get me wrong," Brigit answered. "I love Shannon, she's a wonderful daughter. But it worries me, you know..."

"No, I don't know."

"Well, she's so attractive. Much more so than your Cara, if you know what I mean."

Cecilia wondered if there would still be a place for her in heaven if she had murderous thoughts about Brigit. So as not to ruin her chances for a place up there, Cecilia said diplomatically, "I guess she could be considered more attractive than my Cara if you were a man who happened to like pale, skinny women with stringy hair, instead of slender, bosomy women with beautiful creamy complexions and luxurious, thick hair down to the waist.'' She gave a little snort. ''There's no accounting for taste.'' She made sure she conveyed to all that Brigit had no taste, either.

''Well, I've got news for you, Cecilia Romano. When it comes to beauty and brains my Shannon has it hands down.''

''Oh, please,'' Cecilia scoffed. This conversation had gotten totally out of hand. All Cecilia had wanted was to get Brigit to admit that Cecilia was the wronged party. Because from the time Mary Kathryn, or Kate, or whatever she called herself, had walked out of her wedding to Seth straight into the arms of Tony Donetti, Brigit had acted as if she was the one who needed a pity party.

Not once in all the time that had passed since the wedding that didn't happen, had Brigit offered an ounce of sympathy to Cecilia or Cara, the true victims of Tony Donetti's dumping.

And now that woman had the gall, the absolute gall, to sit there across the table and tell her that Cara wasn't the most beautiful young lady in the whole universe. Where were the woman's eyes? Cecilia held up her hand. ''How many fingers do I have up?''

''Are you crazy?''

''Are you blind?''

''You know, Cecilia, I feel sorry for you. Having Cara for a daughter. I mean, my Mary Kathryn may have walked out on one wedding, but she was married to someone else within a month.'' Brigit wasn't letting anything come in the way of her self-righteous glow, least of all Cecilia's sorrow.

Cecilia's eyes turned into buttonhole slits as she glared at her nemesis.

''Now, I have Shannon—'' Brigit sighed so beautifully that Cecilia felt plagiarized "—and she's so lovely."

"Humph."

"Despite what your bitter heart spews forth," she said in a rhythmic, singsong way.

"My heart is not bitter."

"And I know she will be married soon, too. Why, men are banging down her door."

"You're such a liar."

"Oh, really?" Brigit raised an eyebrow, picked up her cards and made a big production of tapping them on the table into some kind of uniform order.

Cecilia might have disliked Brigit in the past, but from this moment on, she hated her with a passion. "Your skinny little daughter? Don't make me laugh."

Brigit leaned across the table, and, with her face composed in some kind of know-it-all expression, her breath smelling like a cross between cloves and mint, she said, "That's right, Cecilia. I guarantee that my lovely Shannon will be married before your homely Cara."

Brigit had that smug expression on her face that Cecilia would like nothing better than to wipe off. Permanently. She could barely focus on the woman who now leaned back in her chair, tapping her cards against her teeth, getting her horrid germs all over them. "You know I'm right." Brigit hammered in another nail.

"You're so wrong." The fact that Brigit truly believed Cara couldn't get a husband was ridiculous and Cecilia had to get that misconception straightened out posthaste. "My Cara will be married first. All she has to do is choose one suitor among many."

"I thought you said she couldn't get her butt out of bed."

"I said she could only get out of bed for obligatory demands. Dating is one of those. Why, she has been known to have one date for dinner and another date, on that very same day, for a midnight movie.''

''Shannon has had three dates in one day.''

''No, she hasn't.''

''On more than one occasion, in fact.''

''Wanna bet?''

''Bet on what? That Shannon has had three dates on the same day or that she will be married first?''

Cecilia had to stop and think about that for a second. Ooh. Choices. So many juicy choices.

She waited a little too long, since her silence opened the door for Brigit to continue her rant. ''In fact, if you're so sure about your daughter—'' her voice dripped sarcasm ''—then why don't you put your money where your mouth is?''

''How much are we talking about here?'' Cecilia was so certain that Cara would be married first that she wanted to make sure the bet was going to be big enough to cover the cost of the wedding.

''I'm not sure I mean money.''

''Backing out already, eh?'' She let out a self-righteous snort.

''No.'' Brigit paused. ''What if it weren't money, but something better? Something tangible?''

What could be better than a sum large enough to pay for a wedding? Maybe a honeymoon, too. ''What do you have in mind?''

''A trip.'' Brigit lost her edge, and her voice became soft. ''Maybe to Ireland.''

''I can't afford that and you know it. You're only saying that to get out of your own bet because you know you're going to lose.''

''How about somewhere local,'' Jessica-Marie suggested. ''Or almost local. Like the Catskills.''

Brigit scowled. ''That's not anything like Ireland.''

''No, but it's a vacation, and that's what you both need. Desperately,'' Rachel added.

"For how long? A day? A week?" Visions of her dirty dancing with Patrick Swayze after he dumped the too-skinny kid with kinky hair twirled with lust through Cecilia's mind. Kind of dreamy-like she asked, "A month?"

"If it's here in the States, it can only be a weekend. After all, *some* of us work," Brigit said.

"If you can call giving a lecture on the topic of slime twice a week work." Cecilia laughed at the very idea that Brigit considered herself a working woman. Maybe when she was younger and hungry for tenure, but certainly not now.

"I'm ignoring you and your stupidity," Brigit said.

"Good, you ignore, I have things to work out here." She tapped her head, ignoring Brigit's eye-rolling. That woman would learn soon enough the error of her ways.

Cecilia quickly figured what it would cost Brigit to send her to the Catskills. Hotel, food, ski rental, lift fees, dance lessons, an afternoon at the new spa that had just opened at the most luxurious hotel. It was adding up, and the thought of emptying Brigit's bank account made her smile. "Let's do it."

She stuck out her hand and Brigit grabbed and shook it without a moment's hesitation. "You're such a sucker," she said.

Cecilia laughed at that one. "My Cara will be engaged within a month, and married within two. Or sooner."

"Sucker, sucker, sucker."

"It's only a matter of her picking out which beau from the vast parade of beaus who've been breaking down her door."

"Dream on, Cecilia."

And dream she did. She had seen a bathing suit at the mall that had her name written all over it. She'd head over there this very afternoon and put it on layaway.

The women continued to play their Tuesday games, only Cecilia's mind was miles and miles away. She began to make a mental list of all the work she had to do to win the bet. Finding a groom for Cara—who was happy without a man, poor misguided soul that she was—would take a lot of work and a major attitude adjustment on her daughter's part. It could be done, but there wasn't a moment to lose.

1

Noble Sperm Bank Association
Where Pedigree Counts and That's No Bull

REX NOBLE SAW the first billboard, slammed his foot on the brake, skidded into the right lane to avoid being rear-ended and ended up on the shoulder.

He flung the door open and jumped out of the car. An entire lane of speeding vehicles honked at the maneuvers but Rex barely noticed the havoc he'd wreaked. His eyes were fixed on the other billboard, the one across the freeway. Once he'd taken in both of them, he got back into the car and sank in total despair onto the steering wheel.

He'd been anticipating the debut of the billboards with a bit of pride and excitement that he hadn't expected, and under no circumstance would admit to having. He didn't need the billboards to advertise Noble Sperm Bank. His service was so specialized that ranchers and farmers across the country already knew or had heard about him and his prize-winning Galloway bull. Any advertising he did was through livestock and fatstock shows, cattle magazines and word of mouth. He didn't need an advertising agency to promote his business.

Then, about a month ago his good friend Dan Sullivan had asked him to help his brother Clay out as a favor. Clay had moved to Houston from Chicago and was starting up an advertising business. Because of Dan, Rex had agreed to be Clay's first client.

Rex had no problem helping Clay get his business going. He didn't even mind spending the money on the billboards to help his friend. What he had a problem with, though, was the billboards. They were nothing at all like what he and Clay had agreed upon.

The supports for the mammoth, anatomically correct bovine structures had been sunk deep inside concrete cylinders buried along the barbed-wire fence. The first billboard had been cut out in the shape of an enormous bull complete with a huge—make that very huge—reproductive organ. The bull proudly stood watch above old Mabel Sturgeon's cornfield.

On the opposite side of the freeway, in Hector Herman's hay field—which butted up against Mama Jo's Bar-B-Q, known to the locals as margarita heaven— was the cow. Her big brown eyes stared adoringly across the freeway at the bull. The cow's eyelashes blinked slowly and her udder swung seductively. Her tail didn't move. It was permanently shaped to resemble a heart.

The sexually explicit billboards were double-sided, so anyone traveling the Southwest Freeway either coming or going from Pegleg, Texas, could see the manly bull and swooning cow.

Clay's ideas had sounded good in theory, and had even looked good when he presented the mock-up. But except for being from the right species, what was displayed across the freeway was nothing even remotely similar to the mock-up.

Rex had suggested the billboards use solar power for the cattle's moving parts. But he certainly hadn't expected the bull to be moving in such obscene glory or the cow to have such a provocative sway. And move and sway they did. The bull's tail slowly swayed back and forth while its front right hoof stomped up and down. Thick smoke blew out of its nostrils. He could swear the cow's udders rippled with excitement.

Even for the short time he stood in front of the bull billboard, passengers in cars and trucks traveling in both directions honked horns or rolled down windows, shouting out greetings that were not, by any stretch of the imagination, G-rated. The ''woo-woos,'' and ''hubba-hubbas,'' were harmless enough. However, one woman—her car went by pretty darn fast, but Rex got a good enough look to be certain it was Clara Dempsey—yelled out, ''I want a man that has what that bull has, Dr. Noble.'' Her arm pointed through the wind in the general direction of the bull's, er, jewels. If Clara's mama knew what her daughter had said, she'd have herself a stroke.

One of the worst things about the porno-bovine billboards, as far as Rex was concerned, was the distraction they created on the busy freeway. Someone was sure to get in an accident. He didn't want to be responsible for anyone getting hurt or killed. Especially not over obscene cattle. He didn't want to explain to some teenager's parents why those billboards were up there in the first place. He didn't want to be responsible for a family's anguish. He certainly didn't want to give any of those smarmy ambulance-chasing lawyers a reason to come after him. And as long as the words *Noble Sperm Bank Association* were painted larger than life along the cow's back, and *Where Pedigree Counts and That's No Bull* was up there on the bull's back for all the world to see, there would be no doubt who to serve with the subpoena. Him. Rex Noble.

He took the cell phone from his pocket and punched in Clay's number. ''I'm out on the freeway looking at the billboards,'' he said. ''You need to get out here now.''

"I'm having a massage."

"Massage?"

"It's been a stressful month, getting those ready. Need to get the kinks out." Rex heard a muffled "Hey, Patty, baby, not so rough." Then Clay said into the mouthpiece, "They look great, don't you think?"

"We have to talk."

"I can be out there tomorrow morning. Got a date tonight."

Rex stomped to his truck. He normally wasn't an angry man, only his patience was being sorely tested. He threw the phone into the truck and climbed in after it. He gunned the engine, eased his way onto the freeway and headed toward his office.

When he walked through the door he saw his lab technician, Cathy, sitting behind the receptionist's desk talking on the phone. That meant only one thing—Barbara hadn't shown up again today. "The billboards must have gone up either in the dark last night or early this morning," Cathy said. If it were possible to be shot dead by looks alone, the look Cathy sent him would have him dead on the floor.

The other phone lines were ringing incessantly. She said goodbye to the caller, then punched the other lines to put everyone on hold. "Where have you been?" She was scowling at him. For no reason as far as he was concerned.

"I went to see the billboards. You knew that."

"Where's your cell phone? I've been calling you for the last twenty minutes."

"In the truck."

"Did you have it on?"

"Sure I did. I called Clay."

"Why didn't you answer?"

"I didn't hear it." He remembered throwing it in the cab of the truck. Maybe he overthrew and it went out the other window and was there in the grass somewhere near Mama Jo's. He wasn't going to admit that to Cathy though. "Did Barbara call?"

"Of course. She said she wasn't coming in today. She has a sore toe."

"Fire Barbara." He had hired her as a favor to his mother. Every time he'd done someone a favor lately, he ended up getting burned. Barbara was absent more than she was in the office. "Forget that, I'll call my mother and have her fire Barbara." He was done doing favors for people. He was done being nice. From now on he was going to be a bastard. Then he wouldn't have to worry about obscene billboards and receptionists who didn't show up for work.

"Oh, nuts," Cathy moaned when the phone lines started ringing again, the time limits on the hold buttons up. She picked up the receiver and shoved it in Rex's chest. "You answer it," she whispered.

"Yes, Mrs. Taggert. I saw them this morning," he said. "They'll be taken care of as soon as possible."

Before he could hand the phone back to Cathy, it rang again. She punched in another button, pushed his hand and phone back toward his face and he got another earful, this time from his own mother. When he was off the phone with her, he pulled the plug out of the wall. Silence. Blissful, peaceful silence.

Until Cathy broke it. "Do you know how many phone calls I've gotten this morning about that bull you have hung over the freeway?" Cathy asked. "And I'm using the word *hung* in the literal sense, as in hanging the billboard, not the hung bull."

He glared at her. "I know what you're talking about and since I just saw them, I have a pretty good idea what you've been going through."

"Mama Jo called and she wants you to keep them up forever," she said. "Apparently her business is booming."

"It's only midmorning." Although he had noticed the parking lot had been nearly full.

"Maybe it's the breakfast crowd."

"The billboards are obscene."

"I haven't seen them yet. I'll drive over there later and tell you what I think. Just so you know, though," she added, "a couple of the calls were serious. The president of the Pegleg High School Future Farmers of America wants to know if the bull's penis is proportionate. He wanted to know if there were special hormones you were feeding LuLu that he could experiment with on his bull before the livestock show next year."

"I'll get back to him on that." He took a deep breath. "Plug the phone back in. I'm ready."

Rex went back to his office, sat down and spent the rest of the morning fielding calls. If the calls had been serious ones like that of the high-school kid, geared toward information about the insemination process, or extracting semen, or what the cost of inseminating a cow with his prize bull, LuLu, might be, that would have been fine. But many calls were all about the size of a bull's penis and whether or not Rex also provided growth hormones for men who wanted to become as large as the bull on the billboard.

Later that afternoon, he went back out to the billboards. Maybe he had only imagined what they looked like. After all, it had been pretty early in the morning when he had first seen them. He couldn't even remember if he'd had his first cup of coffee yet.

No, it was just as he remembered. A bull with an over-inflated penis and a sex-starved cow in the first throes of bull-love. Rex saw red all over again. He searched for his most recent missing cell phone. He searched between the front seats of the cab, under the seats, the back seats. The phone he finally found inside a Burger Bay bag was from three cell phones ago.

He powered it up and punched in Clay's number for the second time that day. "Get your sorry ass out here at ten tomorrow morning."

He drove the truck to the car wash and gave them explicit instructions to search every fast-food bag, every container, every nook and cranny for cell phones. He spent the rest of the time in the car-wash waiting room fielding sly innuendoes about the size of his bull, while women old enough to be his grandmother were sliding their gazes down the front of his jeans.

It was too much for a man to take.

CARA DROVE to her parents' house after a horrible day at school. She didn't want to go, she only wanted to go home and get into a hot bath. A lavender bubble bath laden with rosemary bath oil. She'd slather her face with a cucumber facial mask and relax for a while. That's all she wanted to do. She wanted to wash away the meeting she'd had with Mr. and Mrs. Simpson about their son, Carl. Sometimes being a kindergarten teacher wasn't all it was cracked up to be. She loved teaching, but dealing with a set of parents who thought their destructive son was cute and who felt his biting and hitting other children should be ignored, made her more determined than ever to have her own child and raise him the right way. Show other parents how the job should be done.

But instead of going home and washing her horrible day away, she headed toward her mother's, like the good daughter she was. Right now she regretted calling her mother at lunchtime just to say hello. She should know by now there was never any simple hello when it came to her mom.

"I bought you the most adorable white blouse,"

Cecilia had gushed. "Come by after school and pick it up."

"Not today, some other time."

"It's so pretty. It would look beautiful with your complexion."

"It can wait until next week. You know I'll be on spring break and will be able to spend so much more time with you."

"I suppose it can." Cecilia had sounded hurt and put out. The classic *I do everything for you, my ungrateful daughter, and this is the thanks I get.* "Even though this is Friday night, and technically your spring break starts after school gets out this afternoon."

There was no winning with her mother. The pitfalls of being an only child meant that Cara had no sibling who could share Cecilia's overenthusiastic mothering techniques. It meant that she was the only one Cecilia lavished all her attention on. It meant that she had to be accommodating whether she wanted to or not, because Cecilia had a way of laying on the guilt if Cara even tried to assert some independence.

With only the rearview mirror as a guide, Cara did the best she could to freshen her makeup. She pulled her hair out of its band, and redid the ponytail before she went inside. The one thing she didn't want to hear was another lecture about the way she looked and how it would affect her chances of getting a husband. If her mother brought up that stupid bet one more time, Cara swore she'd go absolutely crazy.

With a deep sigh, she closed her powder case and stuck it back in her purse. There was no hope of looking any better than she did right now. And right now she looked as if she'd been through ten kindergarten relay races and was on the losing team. She might be able to powder her nose, put lipstick on and redo her hair, but there was nothing she could do about the rainbow of finger-paint colors on her skirt and the red ink on her pointer finger she'd tried to scrub off but couldn't.

She had barely gotten her foot over the threshold when her mother descended on her, scolding her. "You look terrible."

"Mom, it's been a long day," she started explaining, but had to stop talking when Cecilia pulled her by the arm so forcefully that she almost lost her balance and had to concentrate just to stay upright. Her mother dragged her into the living room and stopped right in front of the man who struggled to get himself out of the deep cushions of the couch and onto his feet.

Cecilia quickly turned sugary-sweet and beamed like a proud mother hen when she did the introductions. "This is Billy Atkins, darling. He has a very promising career in waste disposal."

Cara smiled at the same time she grabbed her mother by the fleshy part of the arm, and said in a fierce whisper, "I can't believe you brought another man here to meet me. I can't believe I fell into this trap. Again."

"Say hello to our guest."

Cara bit down on her tongue and did what was expected of her. She said, "Hello." Cara could never be accused of not being polite. She listened as her mother waxed poetic about Billy's wonderful disposition, which, Cecilia stated, she had personal knowledge of since he always left the trash cans upright on the curb and not thrown into the street.

Finally, after Cecilia had expounded all his wonderful attributes, they went into the kitchen and sat around the table. Her father, lucky man that he was, had long since disappeared with his paper, not to be seen again.

Cara could hardly keep her eyes open, and her

yawns were getting more and more difficult to hide behind her hand.

"Snap to, Cara." Her mother pinched her knee under the table. "You can sleep late tomorrow. You'll be on vacation, remember?"

"Believe me, I remember." This time she didn't bother to stifle the yawn. Nine whole days of more surprise fix-ups. Who could possibly forget? The knowledge of what her mother would probably try to do would have sent her into a deep depression, were she susceptible to depression, which she wasn't.

But what she was tired and hungry. "Are we going to eat, Mom?" she asked.

"Later, dear. We have plenty of time."

Both her mother and Billy ignored her growling stomach and her mother certainly didn't offer to supply her only daughter with fortification. So while those two droned on like long-lost friends who had suddenly found one another, Cara lapsed into her favorite daydream.

She had started having this dream about five years ago after seeing her co-workers get married, become pregnant, have baby showers and then the babies. There had to be something about some people who reached a certain age, and the yearning to have a baby became overwhelming. Cara would shop for the baby gifts or see babies in strollers, or mothers sitting in the park holding infants in their arms, and the need to have her own baby would be so profound that it hurt. Ached. Deep inside her where a baby should be growing.

Problem was, her mother's offerings of husband material made Cara nauseous. The idea of bedding down with any of these men, even to have a child, was simply out of the question. And for her, marriage and children went together. She didn't see any other way. For some people, a baby out of wedlock was fine. But it wouldn't work for her. She had to have it all. And right now, everything seemed so far out of reach.

Before her mother had made the bet with Brigit, Cara still had hopes of finding a perfect husband. Now with all of the Erie eligibles being paraded before her, her hopes dimmed to zero.

And if the sampling of the parents from her kindergarten class were an example, something must happen to couples between the time they got married and the time their children head off to kindergarten. It was as if they lost all power to their kids and stopped being a couple. True, she only had meetings with the parents whose kids were having problems. Still, she had never come across more men and women who took little or no responsibility for the wrongdoings of their five-year-olds.

Cara only wanted a baby to hold, and cuddle, and raise the right way, to be a good citizen, a credit to his or her country. She knew she could do it right. She certainly had plenty of examples of how *not* to do it.

But the men her mother was pushing off on her did nothing for her, and there was no way she'd contemplate having children with any of them. She wanted a husband who would be her partner in raising their kids, not just any old guy, which seemed to be her mother's criterion. There had been the grocery deliveryman, Harold Sutcher—shy, balding and definitely not her type. Then there was Boomerang Jones, the high-school football coach who, as part of his contract, had to teach math, only he didn't know how to add one and one much less multiply one times one. There had been the used-car salesman, the bus driver, the travel agent, the lawyer, the accountant. The list went on and on. It seemed every single day and every single night Cecilia found some poor guy who wasn't married—or at least said he wasn't married, who really knew?—and searched Cara out wherever she was to do the introductions. The grocery store, the beauty shop, it didn't matter. One morning, she even brought a man to school, and in front of the whole kindergarten class gushed, "I'm sorry to bring Jack here to school, darling, but I knew you'd want to meet him, because I know he's your destiny." He wasn't, nor were any of the others.

Last week, Cara had been so frustrated she had called her friends Kate and Tony Donetti and told them what Cecilia had been doing. They already knew, since Kate was Shannon's sister, and Shannon was apparently getting the same treatment from her mother, Brigit, as Cara was getting from Cecilia. They'd commiserated then offered her an open invitation to visit them in Texas.

When Billy looked over at her, smiled and belched and didn't even say, "Excuse me," she knew she couldn't go on with this anymore. She had to get away or else she'd go positively nuts. She pushed herself away from the table that had no food on it yet, and said, "I have to go."

"Go where?" her mother demanded, eyes wide in surprise at Cara's sudden burst of independence.

Before her mother could say a word of protest, Cara said, "I need to get home."

"You can't be rude to our guest."

Cara's blood pressure was soaring. She could feel her blood curdling and her face flushing with heat. Her mother didn't have the slightest idea how this parade of men was affecting her daughter. And Cara, the good girl, the child who never made waves, who never did anything to make anyone angry, had reached the boiling point. Maybe her rotten, biting, hitting kindergarten student had the right idea all along. Maybe he, too, was so frustrated by his parents that he did what he did out of frustration. "He's not *my* guest, Mom. He's yours. They've all been yours. You have been using me like some pawn in your silly bet with Brigit, and I can't believe that you would subject me, your only daughter, your only child, to this. What kind of mother are you?"

"How dare you talk to me like that?" The look of hurt on her mother's face was almost enough to make Cara want to take it all back. But not quite.

"I dare because you won't stop bringing these losers to meet me." She looked at Billy. "With the exception of you, of course. You're not a loser."

He nodded and grinned because he believed her. She shook her head and sighed. He didn't get it.

"Everything I've done is for your own good. To help you find your happiness."

"I *am* happy." She was, too, except for the fact that she now knew she would die a shriveled, childless old maid. When the truth sank in, she might be miserable, but it hadn't sunk in yet.

"Oh, my God!" Cecilia crossed herself and spit in her hand. "Don't say such things. You're miserable and you know it."

"Mother, please, look at me. Do I look miserable to you."

"Yes, you do." Cecilia reached up and brushed stray strands of hair from Cara's face. "Of course, if you would only comb your hair, and wash that paint from your hands, and keep your clothes clean—why don't you wear aprons at school when you play with those children?—then maybe someone as wonderful as Billy here would fall in love with you. And you could get married, say, next week," she suggested hopefully.

"Mother!"

"It's really all your fault, you know. It's not as if

I haven't brought you a wonderful selection to choose from.''

"Okay, I've had enough. Bye, Billy. Bye, Mom.''

She headed toward the door with her mother trailing on her heels and shouting behind her, "Be back here tomorrow at noon. There's someone I want you to meet, and I've made lunch reservations.''

Cara didn't even break her stride getting out of that house. When she arrived at her apartment, she called Tony and Kate. She needed their help. "Can I take you up on your invitation? I know this is short notice…in fact, it's extremely short notice. And I know tomorrow is Saturday and you may have plans for the weekend, and I know—''

"Nonsense, you don't know anything.'' Kate laughed. "We'd love to have you, Cara, and the sooner you get here, the better it'll be. This is a perfect place for you to have a retreat,'' she exclaimed. "I can't wait to see you again.''

"We won't tell a soul where you are.'' Tony was on the extension phone. "In other words, Cecilia will never know.''

"And neither will Brigit,'' Kate added.

"Thank you.'' Cara let out a sigh of relief. "I may actually have a peaceful vacation.''

"You'll have a great time. This is a perfect place to hide,'' Tony said.

"Maybe not.'' Suddenly all the doubts stated bombarding her. "Your house is the first place my mother will look for me.'' Cecilia would be relentless in her search. Cara knew her mom.

"Tell you what. Instead of staying here in Houston, you'll go to Pegleg. That's a great place to hide. It's a small town right outside of Houston, there's a great bed-and-breakfast owned by a friend of ours. She'll make sure you have all the privacy you need,'' Tony said. "It's only a few miles from the house and my restaurant."

"You'll love Mandelay," Kate promised. "No one will find you until you decide you want to be found."

After Cara said her goodbyes to Kate and Tony, she called the airline and booked herself on the first flight to Houston the next morning. Nothing was going to stop Cara from getting away from her mother and her marriage-minded meddling.

Cara opened the closet door and stared at the clothes hanging there. What did she have that was appropriate for a vacation in Texas?

There were the calf-length dirndl skirts, wide and loose enough for getting down on the floor to play with the kids. A variety of buttoned-down shirts, high at the neck and modest to the point of being virginal. She had plenty of clothes all right. A closet brimming with modest skirts, slacks, shirts and sweaters—the clothes of a quiet, conservative schoolmarm. Was that the look she wanted for this vacation, or was that actually the look she was escaping? Suddenly afraid to make such a momentous decision, she turned on the weather station and monitored the Houston-area weather—sunny, with the chance of rain, high in the low eighties and humid. The eighties. In March, no less. Wonders never cease.

Hot enough to go naked. Even though she was all alone in her apartment, Cara blushed. Where had that idea come from? Her naked? Well, why not? She was on vacation. She didn't have her mother watching over her, dictating her every move. She not only could sleep naked, she could walk around the room naked. She could answer the doorbell naked. Okay, maybe that was going too far, but still, naked was freedom.

She laid her khakis carefully over the back of the chair along with a powder-blue short-sleeve sweater. She opened her travel bag and packed three more short-sleeved sweaters, and then she reached slowly into the closet for her one tank top, the one she always wore with a shirt over it. No more. At least no more for the next week. Underpants, bras, socks and a belt followed. She was about to throw in her favorite brushed-cotton nightie with the sweet-pea flowers, long Shakespearean sleeves and a high neck trimmed with a heavy lace that practically covered her hands and made sure no cold air got anywhere close to her neck. But something stopped her. She held the gown for barely a second before putting it back in the drawer. This was her breakout trip, and she wasn't going to miss the opportunity to sleep naked by bringing a nightgown.

She totally threw caution to the wind when she climbed up the stepladder to get her strappy white sandals, the ones with the two-inch heels she had bought on sale two summers ago and had never worn. She carefully wrapped each shoe in a plastic grocery sack. She was going to be daring and bold, she promised herself. Wearing white sandals when it was weeks and weeks before Memorial Day would be almost as daring as sleeping naked. She wondered if she should sleep naked with the sandals on, and giggled. That wouldn't be such a bad idea. She could answer the doorbell with nothing on but those white sandals.

Except with her luck, it would be someone like Billy the waste disposal man on the other side of the door. That thought was depressing, until Cara remembered peepholes, and knew she didn't have to open the door to any Billys.

She tucked her toiletries—safely packed in plastic zippered sandwich bags—into all remaining crevices. Cara glanced around the bedroom, making sure she wasn't forgetting anything. Coco Mademoiselle. Still in the box, unopened, the clear plastic wrap a testament to its forlorn status on the dresser. She had tried on the perfume in the department store and loved it. Had bought it on a whim, like the sandals. Hadn't worn it, either.

She unwrapped the package and sprayed the perfume on her neck and wrists, inhaling deeply. Good. Just as she remembered. Into the bag it went. Then she took it out again and sprayed everything she had packed in the bag with Coco Mademoiselle.

She thought she had everything ready to go until she glanced at the top of her dresser. Then again, maybe not.

She called it a jewelry box, but it was more like a chest than a box. Made of solid, heavy oak, it had come to her through her grandmother Romano and all the generations of Romano women before her. Over a hundred years ago, her great-great-grandparents had brought it to America, filled with silver and copper coins, nothing that would seem of real value. Nothing worth stealing.

Only, the coins inside the chest were actually there to distract anyone from finding the real treasure the chest held.

Cara walked slowly over to the dresser. You only live once, she told herself. What was she saving all of the jewelry for? They were there for her to use. She wore the earrings almost every day. They were the smallest of the gold coins her forebears had brought over in the secret compartments built into the chest. The coins had been set in a gold-filigree bracket by a past Romano relative. She looked at her reflection in the dresser mirror. She never thought twice about wearing the earrings. They were so much a part of her. But they were only a small part of the treasure.

She lifted the lid and reached inside, bringing out what remained of the solid-gold coins. Some of the coins had been used to start businesses, to send Romanos to college, to get started in life. She had inherited what remained. That same Romano relative who had done the earrings also had made coins into a necklace, bracelet and brooch. They were solid gold, heavy and priceless.

Cara tried on the necklace and almost collapsed under the weight of the coins, each set in a filigree frame then attached to the gold necklace. The bracelet was the same design, and the brooch was layered with coins in the shape of a crescent moon.

She never wore any of the jewelry except the earrings. Tomorrow all that would change. The coins had brought her ancestors luck. They would bring her luck, too. She didn't know how, she didn't know where, all she knew was that she was going to wear those pieces of jewelry, either separately or together, and her life would work out fine.

She undressed for bed, took the sweet-pea nightgown back out of the drawer and was about to put it on but stopped. No, she wouldn't need it. She set her alarm and slipped naked beneath the sheets, took a few deep breaths, then with eyes wide open stared at the ceiling, waiting for the alarm to go off.

Saturday morning couldn't come fast enough, and when the alarm finally buzzed, she was already set to go. She left her car parked on the street in front of the apartment building and took a cab to the airport. She checked her luggage, walked over to the airport gift shop and stopped in front of the mailbox outside the entrance. She took the goodbye note she had written to her parents out of her purse, unfolded it and read it one last time before licking the envelope shut and sending it on its way.

The note was simple and very, very sweet. It was also to the point, because she felt extremely sympathetic to her parents' feelings.

Dear Mom and Dad,
I didn't take my cell
phone, so don't even try to
call, because it would just
be a waste of time.

                              Love,
                              Cara

2

AT TEN O'CLOCK on Saturday morning Rex parked his pickup about fifty feet from the cow billboard on the shoulder of the freeway, close to the outdoor patio of Mama Jo's Bar-B-Q.

The meat smoking in the massive drums on the backside parking area had probably been cooking for at least twenty-four hours already. The smell of huge slabs of beef saturated with flavors from mesquite and hickory chips made his stomach growl despite that he had finished breakfast only about an hour earlier.

Mama Jo happened to be one slick businesswoman who knew how to bring in the customers. Twenty-four hours a day, seven days a week, those smokers were working, and the sweet-tangy aroma of smoking beef could be inhaled from miles away. It was no wonder Mama Jo's was the busiest restaurant in Texas. Automobiles and trucks were guided to Mama Jo's on the smoky barbecue fumes alone. His friend Tony often joked that it was a good thing Donetti's Irish Pub and Sushi Bar was just outside the fragrant limits of Mama Jo's Bar-B-Q, or he'd be out of business. There was nothing in the world like the aroma of Texas barbecue.

On the other side of the freeway the wind carried the smoke puffing out of the bull's nostrils right toward him. That smoke, on the other hand, didn't leave him with the same feeling as Mama Jo's Bar-B-Q did. Not even close.

Rex peered up at the cow billboard. Either way, up close or fifty feet away, the view was the same. He feared the image of shimmering udders would be branded on his brain forever.

Clay's black Mercedes screeched to a stop behind Rex's truck. Clay, using his hand as a shield against the sun, stood next to his car as he looked up at the sign. "Whaddya think?" he asked, his smile bright, his eyes optimistic. "Great advertising campaign, eh?"

"No Bull?" That was the first thing Rex asked. "When did you come up with that slogan?"

"It just came to me. Pure inspiration at work, that's what it is."

"Inspiration?" He didn't see any kind of divine entities at work here.

"Isn't it great? Noble, no bull. No-ble. Get it? Huh?" Clay nudged Rex in the ribs.

Rex stepped away from Clay's elbow. "I get it. The problem is, I didn't get what I paid for."

That seemed to stop Clay cold. "What are you talking about?"

"I did not pay for bestial pornography."

Clay looked confused.

"You glittered her udders."

"The pièce de résistance. Great, huh?"

"You had the mock-up. This is nothing like the mock-up. The billboards were supposed to look more like that." He nodded at the Noble Sperm Bank Association, A Breed Apart logo painted on his truck. "It's a very simple, very subtle proclamation that tells everyone in Pegleg, Texas, and breeders across the country what I do."

"You have stiff competition." He glanced at the bull. "No pun intended. You said that yourself. How do you expect to get breeders interested in your bull with some pansy-looking logo like that?"

"Let's get something straight. My business is doing just fine. I hired you as a favor to your brother. These billboards may ruin me." And it wasn't just himself that was at stake. He had his investors to think about. This wasn't a one-man operation.

"They're not going to ruin you. They're going to make you. You need a bull that looks like he's got what it takes to make things happen. And that's what I gave you."

"What you gave me is a bull who looks like he's getting ready to hump the cow."

"That's the idea." Clay nodded, as if Rex was finally getting it.

Only Clay was the one who didn't get the program. "Look at what kind of interest these billboards are generating," Rex said as vehicles whizzed past, honking their horns, making catcalls out the windows. "I want some of that," some lady yelled. "Whoo-whoo," another hooted.

"You're not going to be sorry you put your advertising needs in my hands. Your business will boom."

"It's already booming."

"Now it will explode. I see putting these billboards everywhere. Maybe even have cow and bull magnets, the kind that have the lips that come together to kiss. Or we could put the magnets on their—" Clay gave Rex a man-to-man look. When Rex's expression finally appeared to sink into the ad executive's brain, Clay's voice became serious and he mumbled, "Just a thought." He cleared his throat. "We'll add the magnets as inserts to telephone and electric bills."

Rex held up his hand. "Forget it."

"Let me finish. I'm only getting started here. I have plans. Big plans. Wait till you hear about the cow and bull calendar," he said with pride. "Not to mention the huge advertising campaign I've outlined for magazines and newspapers. You'll have to clone your bull just to keep up with the business."

"The billboards have got to come down."

"No way," he said in disbelief.

"All the way down."

"You're killin' me." Clay's voice was strangled.

"Replace them with regular rectangular billboards that look like my logo."

"You're going to ruin an incredible campaign," Clay accused him.

"The bull's penis is so big it's offensive."

"Bulls have big penises."

"Yes, they do, but it doesn't have to be displayed ten feet long on a billboard."

"Men need visuals, you know that. They have to see what they're getting. It's like silicone."

"What?"

"The woman's breast. Silicone breasts aren't real, but that doesn't stop men from fantasizing about them. Same with the bull's bobby. Guys know it's not real, but that's not going to stop them from thinking if their cattle was inseminated with your bull's semen, they could breed a giant."

"That's not what the phone calls we've been getting—"

"Have you been getting calls already?"

"We can't keep up with them."

"It's amazing, isn't it, what a little advertising will do for a business?"

"You don't get it. I'm quickly becoming the laughingstock of this county." Rex's jaw was clenched so tightly it hurt. "These are not phone calls about doing business with me. These calls range from women screaming about the obscene nature of the bull's organ to men wanting to know if I provide growth hormones for them."

"As they say in the advertising world," Clay said flippantly, "any publicity is good publicity."

"Publicity is over. Take the billboards down. Today."

"I can't do that today. No one works on Saturday."

"I work on Saturday."

"You're the customer, but I'm telling you right now, you'll be sorry you didn't go with the plan."

"What I'm sorry about is that I'm going to have to listen to Cathy rag on me about losing another cell phone."

"I can understand the cell phone issue. And maybe that's just what you need. Time without a phone, to think, and you might reconsider the advertising campaign. When you find your phone, call me and let me know if you really want to take the billboards down."

"I do."

Clay was already back at his car. "I'll wait to hear the final decision."

"I told you my final decision," he shouted to Clay, but the man had already slammed the door shut and was heading back on the freeway.

What was with these people? Didn't anyone listen anymore?

CARA ARRIVED at Houston's George Bush Intercontinental Airport around midmorning. In her excitement and rush to leave the apartment and get to the airport, she hadn't eaten breakfast.

She would have had something at the airport, but her gold coins kind of wreaked havoc with the new heavy-duty security in place. Every time she walked through the metal detectors, X-ray alarm buzzers sounded. Off came the earrings, off came the brooch, off came the necklace and finally the bracelet. The buzzers still rang. Her belt was next and then her loafers.

Finally, off came the safety pin she had used in place of the button she hadn't time to sew back on her khakis. That final humiliation and embarrassment was almost worth having to endure when the buzzer was silent. They gave her back the button and kept the safety pin.

It took a full ten minutes and the help of a stranger to get all the jewelry back on. By then there was no time to grab a snack.

She'd been given cheese and crackers on the first plane, and peanuts on the second, but that didn't do much to combat her hunger. By the time she landed, she was absolutely famished. She retrieved her luggage, then she had to wait at the car-rental counter as they processed her paperwork.

"I'm sorry," the rental agent said. "You had ordered an economy sedan, and we don't have any left."

Cara stared at her. "What am I supposed to do?"

The lady smiled, and in the brightest Texas accent she said, "Don't you worry about any little thing. You have your choice—at the same price and terms as the economy car—of either a minivan or a Mustang."

Cara's stomach growled. Normally she would have been embarrassed, except all she could think about was a Mustang. "Mustang," she said before common sense told her to take the minivan.

She signed the papers and was given a map and directions to Mama Jo's Bar-B-Q, the restaurant where she was to meet Kate. The shuttle bus dropped her in front of the car she would call her own for the next nine days. All thoughts of food and hunger instantly fled the moment she saw her Mustang. Not just any Mustang either. A bright red convertible. This was about as close to heaven as a woman could get.

Here she was, a meek, mild kindergarten teacher who always did for others and never made waves. A good daughter who tried to please. Now, she had run away from home, kind of, and she was going to be driving a Mustang convertible. What was happening to her? Cara didn't even feel one little twinge of guilt for running away, leaving only the note to ease her poor mother's mind. That almost bothered her because she should have felt guilty for not feeling guilty. But right now, all she felt was the hot smooth surface of the hood of the Mustang and this incredible excitement about the nine blissful days she'd spend here in Texas. No mother nagging her. No introductions to fixer-uppers as candidates for marriage. Just peace. And boy, did she need peace.

She carefully followed the directions to the restaurant. She had been to Houston once before, and it was just as she remembered. Expansive. The city went on and on. She remembered what Tony had told her once, that Houston was so big, that when you finally reached the end of the city limits, you were in Dallas. If the drive she was taking to Pegleg was any indication, she figured Tony was speaking the truth.

Cara finally passed the town of Stafford, and then Missouri City, and by the time she saw the second Sugar Land exit and the first Pegleg exit, she had been on the road for over ninety minutes. The excitement and anticipation pumping through her was giving way to the overwhelming hunger deep inside her. She could have sworn that she had smelled barbecue miles and miles away. It must have been traveling on a phantom cloud. Yet, as she got closer to Pegleg, the scent of cooking beef became stronger. Maybe it wasn't just a phantom cloud.

Cara took the correct exit and turned into the parking lot. It was like nothing she had ever seen before. The lot took up at least a city block. She had to drive around the perimeter and the aisles at least twice before a car pulled out, leaving her a space to park. She pressed a button and the convertible's top rose up, then dropped into place. She grabbed her purse, got out of the car. There was a button on the key chain to lock the door. Remote locks—it was incredible. She couldn't believe her luck.

A long line of customers were giving their names to the hostess, just hoping to get a table. It took a full five minutes to get to the hostess, who told her the wait for a table would be at least another hour.

"Do you have a phone I can use?" Cara asked.

"Sure." The young woman signaled her to come around the counter and pointed to the black desk phone.

"I'm here. I made it," Cara said when Kate answered the phone.

"I'm about twenty minutes from the restaurant. I'm on my way."

The hostess smiled at Cara as she walked to the front of the counter. "There's iced tea, soda, water and some nibblers." The lady pointed to the table off to the side. "Help yourself, and if you want, you can wait out on the patio."

Cara filled a tall glass with ice and poured tea out of one of the glass pitchers. She placed a pile of spicy-hot chicken wings on a very large plate. They would never have plates that large in Erie. She dabbed ranch dressing over the top layer of wings and, satisfied the dressing had dripped through the layers of chicken, she grabbed a stack of napkins and followed several other customers outside.

The sun shone so brightly here in Texas. Only a few fluffy cottonball-like clouds scattered here and there marred the perfection of the huge expanse of blue sky.

When she had left Erie that morning it had been raining, the temperature close to freezing. The blue worsted-wool overcoat she had worn for the past five winters now rested in the Mustang's trunk. Her hair, usually pulled back in a tight ponytail, hung long and curly down her back, touching below her waist.

For the first time in months, maybe years, Cara felt free, unencumbered, and she loved every second of that feeling. She knew it would be only a matter of time before her old routine would return with a force so great it would knock her over. She had nine days. That was all. The extent of her freedom. Then back to Erie she'd go. Back to her old school, back to her old life. Best not waste her freedom by thinking about her life in Erie.

The patio was crowded. The tables full. That didn't surprise Cara, considering the hour-long wait. She walked around the perimeter of the patio until she found an empty spot along the decorative wrought-iron fence. She balanced her plate on top of one of the spikes on the fence so she could use both hands to wrap a napkin around the condensation of the tea glass. She sipped the tea and looked out toward the freeway. That's when she saw the billboard.

It was a shaped like a cow. Its eyelashes were blinking, and the udders, which seemed to be sparkling in the sunlight, were moving, too. It was so sweet. And then, as if it were a sign from above, across the cow's side were the words Noble Sperm Bank Association.

Thoughtfully, Cara circled her palm over where a baby would grow. She looked at the sign again. A sperm bank. That was it. That was the answer to what she needed. It wouldn't be an illicit affair that created a child, it would be a laboratory. Perfectly innocent, nothing about it would bring embarrassment to her parents.

She had been thinking about having a baby for years, and now for the first time it seemed as if it could be done practically without having to marry one of Cecilia's less-than-stellar choices. Yes, she would have to weigh the pros and cons of being a single mother. And she would—carefully. She'd get all the information first and then make a decision. An informed decision.

She would have to ask a lot of questions. Of course, that posed the next problem. What do you ask? "Hey, I'd like to have a vial of sperm?" Or perhaps, "Brother can you spare a cup?" Would she hand over a container and say, "Fill 'er up"? Maybe that would have been good when there were full-service gas stations, but there weren't any of those anymore. She'd bet there weren't full-service sperm banks either. Not the kind where you could bring in your own gallon container and have them pour in the fuel, so to speak. Oh, who knew? She didn't.

Anyway, all this worrying was silly. Why worry about that now? First things first. She'd go in, she'd ask questions, she'd get the information. After she had the information, she'd leave the sperm bank with her head held high—because there was nothing embarrassing or degrading about using a sperm bank—go back to her hotel room and mull over the pros and cons. She'd even sleep on it for a night or two and then tell them yes.

Cara checked to make sure her plate was still balancing on the railing, and it looked fine. She bent down to get a piece of paper and a pen out of her purse to write down the Noble Sperm Bank's phone number and address. That's when she heard a very deep masculine voice utter a very naughty word.

She straightened up to give that deep voice a talking-to, the way she would to her students. There were certain words a person didn't say in mixed company. When she did, she came face-to-face with a pair of sky-blue eyes and a head and shoulders covered in chicken wings. She glanced down at the railing. "You knocked down my wings," she said.

"I don't think so, lady."

"They were right here. And now they're on you. Where did you come from?"

"Right there." He pointed to the grass on the other side of the patio. "Minding my own business. I was bombed."

"Yes, you were," she said. She didn't know what else she could say except, "But I didn't do it. At least, not on purpose."

He cast her a doubtful glance.

"I didn't." She had to catch her breath. When he stood in a full and upright position he was tall. She figured that out because the patio was a little bit above ground level and he towered over her. Then she notice a cell phone in his hand and the cell phone seemed kind of flattened.

"*I* didn't touch your telephone," she stated, pointing to the crunched accessory, being held together by only a few wires.

"I know that. I was down here looking for the phone when I got pelted." He reached down to the ground and brought up her plate. He held it out to her. "I believe this is yours."

She scrunched up her eyes, and her lips had contoured themselves into a pained expression. She held out her hand. "I believe it is."

He handed her the greasy plate stained with barbecue hot sauce and ranch dressing. She picked off several blades of grass and dropped them on the ground.

"I believe these are mine, too." She plucked one wing out of his hair, then another and another. He did nothing to help her. Just stood there, his lips set in a sardonic leer. She had to pause a moment before she went for the shoulders. Touching him with her fingers made the muscles in her belly jump around, do a dance, make her kind of queasy. Which was strange since her hands and her belly were pretty far apart. The nausea had to be from lack of food. That was probably it. Although it didn't account for her shallow breathing and inability to fill up her lungs.

She took a wing off his shoulder. His muscle tightened beneath her touch. He rotated them, which sent several chicken wings plunging downward.

There was one on top of his belt buckle. She reached for it, but he brushed her hand away, taking care of that area himself.

"I'm so sorry," Cara said softly. "I'll be happy to…"

"I can do this one myself." He may have said that, but he made it sound like a challenge.

"I was going to say I'd be happy to pay."

"Of course you were. That's what I was thinking you were going to say."

"Well, I was."

"The food was yours, not mine."

"I meant for the cleaning bill."

"Don't be silly." His voice, deep and kind of gravelly, made her want to lean forward, closer, made her wish he'd talk in longer sentences. She didn't detect much of a Texas accent.

He was looking beyond her, waving at people. She heard a few comments like, "Way to go, Doc," and "Did you miss your lips?" This man, the doc, waved and took the teasing all pretty good-naturedly considering she had clobbered him with food and everyone knew red sauce never washed out of anything.

Cara peeled the napkins off the side of her tea glass. Although they were thin and would hardly do any good, she still reached out again, brushed his stained shoulders with the limp wet napkins. Not one of her better ideas, she realized too late, after the splatters had spread into smears and the napkins tore into gross little pieces.

"I'm so sorry." She barely could get the words out. "I just want to crawl into a hole and die of embarrassment."

"No, you don't," he countered.

"You're right." She balled what was left of the napkins and put the mess on the plate, crowning the pile of dirty wings. "It seemed like the nice thing, the right thing to say, though." She gave him her best smile as she did a "I'm a woman, I don't care what you think" half shrug. She'd seen it done on TV many times. It looked good.

"Very nice."

"Thank you. Can I ask you a question?" she said.

"Ask away."

"What were you *really* doing down there?" She picked up her glass of iced tea. The glass was wet and her hands were sticky. She wiped the moisture from the sides of the glass. Her hand shook a little and that surprised her. She couldn't possibly be nervous, could she? With a man? That would be silly. "Were you trying to look under my skirt?"

"What? Do you think I'm stupid?"

She shrugged.

"If anyone is being stupid, lady, it's you."

"That's not a very nice thing to say."

"Well, you're not wearing a skirt."

"Oh." She grinned at him. "I'm on vacation."

"And I was on a mission. Which I had already told you about." He waved the broken phone. "My assistant would have killed me if I lost another one."

Rex hadn't needed to be showered with chicken, hot sauce and ranch dressing, thank you very much. Then again, in front of him, separated only by an iron railing was one stunning-looking female, and if he had to be hit on the head with chicken, she was the one he'd like to be doing it. For once, he would consider thanking Cathy and her constant pestering that had sent him back out looking for his lost cell phone.

The lady on the patio was small. Very small. But after a cursory gaze down her figure, he decided she wasn't small everywhere. Not where it counted. Her brown hair looked mighty thick and heavy and hung down past her waist. Strands of hair fell over her shoulders, covering her breasts. She flipped it behind her by shaking her head and using the back of her wrist—the only part of her hand not covered in sauce. When she did that, the sun reflected off the gold around her wrist, neck and ears, almost blinding him with its brightness. All the jewelry seemed to made of coins that jangled with her movements. If the coins were real and not the hollow cheap stuff you could buy at the five-and-dime, then the gold had to weigh more than she did. He was impressed by her ability to stand straight and not be weighed down by hair and jewelry.

And that hair. When she tossed it all behind her, revealing her breasts and all the gold, he had to admit that he liked that. A lot. It was nice. Real nice. The curls, not her breasts. Although her breasts, from what he could tell by their shape under the sweater, were something he could be real comfortable with exploring further. They looked mighty good, too.

Her small nose was straight except at the tip where it turned up very slightly. Her chin was rounded and at this moment quivering, as if she was trying not to laugh. Her brown eyes were big, almond-shaped and fringed with black lashes so long they almost touched her eyebrows.

She tilted her head a little to the right, squinted against the sun, and then her lips moved and she spoke, which by itself wasn't unusual, since lips did move when people spoke.

However, her lips— Man-oh-man, how did a guy put into thought what his body signaled when he watched those lips move? How did he describe a basic need and desire? If he could have grabbed her, lay one on her, and suck the living daylights out of those full pink lips he would have. And if he did that, she'd let him and she'd like it and beg for more. Then again, so would he.

"Where are you from?" he asked.

"I'm not from here."

He didn't need her to tell him that. Her hair, long and mostly straight, gave that away. Pegleg women were known for their big hairdos, not anything as *natural* as what this lady had crowning her head.

"Where?"

"East."

"As in Louisiana?"

"No, east."

He wasn't stupid. "Louisiana *is* east." Females. This one was ornery, but sexy as all get-out. So he set a smile on his face, one he hoped reeked of friendliness and not lust, and tried to picture her naked. He made no apology for that either. He was, after all, first and foremost, a guy. A guy who could tell that the woman standing there looking so cute was very interested in him. "I was wondering," he started, his accent getting a little thicker, a little more Texas, "Miss Person From the East..." His voice trailed off when the lady turned away from him and waved at Kate Donetti.

When she turned back toward him, he fully expected her to offer her name, address, vital statistics and phone number. Instead, she said, "You're a very nice man. Thank you for being so understanding."

She shoved the plate of grassy wings at him, which

he had no choice but to grab or they'd fall again, then she did an about-face and left him standing there.

She might have run away for now, but Rex knew Kate Donetti. If the chicken lady was friends with Kate, he'd find her again in no time at all.

3

CARA'S FIRST THOUGHT was to confide everything to Kate. She wanted to tell her all about how she was thinking about using the sperm bank to get artificially inseminated, to have her heart's desire, a baby—and outwit her mother. It wasn't that she didn't want her mother to win the bet, it was the fact that the bet shouldn't have been made in the first place. Parents were not supposed to place bets on their children's lives. It wasn't done.

Just as she was about to tell Kate her hopes and dreams for the future, something in her head told her, "Stop." Instinct kept her from revealing her plan, at least for a little while. It wasn't that she didn't trust Kate to keep a secret. It had more to do with not wanting to debate the pros and cons of her decision with anyone. She could debate herself down to the ground if she wanted. Cara just didn't want anyone to burst her bubble. Not that Kate had ever been less than supportive, but right now there were so many people wanting to run her life, tell her what to do, make decisions for her. It was taking away the joy a woman should have when making her own choices, even if some of those choices might turn out to be mistakes. Not that having a baby would be a mistake. A baby would probably be the one decision that was right. It was having the baby out of wedlock that wouldn't be right. Unfortunately, in life, sometimes a woman had to sacrifice what was right for what was in her heart.

Still, Cara didn't want to confide her intentions to anyone until she called Noble Sperm Bank, talked to one of the nurses and got as much information as she could. Once she had the information then she would be able to make an informed, not impassioned, decision. If she decided to go ahead with her plan, that would be the time to confide in Kate. So instead of talking about babies and creams, she told Kate about how she accidentally spilled her chicken on some great-looking guy. "Did you see him?" Cara asked. "He was to die for."

"I saw you talking to someone, but I was too far away. What's his name?"

"I don't know. I thought you'd know."

"I probably would have known if I had seen him. What did he look like?"

"He was very tall, dark hair, wearing cowboy boots."

"Oh, I know who that is," Kate said.

"Who?" Cara got so excited she practically jumped off the chair.

"Let's see." Kate tapped her long fingernail on a front tooth. "It could be any one of the thousands of men who live here."

"He had blue eyes," Cara added helpfully.

"And?"

Kate didn't seem to find that piece of information helpful at all, which surprised Cara. She thought it was a good clue. "Piercing blue eyes?" she asked, hoping that would be better.

Kate only shrugged.

Maybe if Kate had seen how crystal clear the blue of his eyes were, how bright, then she would have known who Cara's cowboy was. There was a piece of information that she was leaving out. She closed her eyes and thought hard. Then she remembered the most important piece of information, that's all. "I know he's a doctor." Cara offered triumphantly.

"That limits our scope to about five hundred men in this area alone. We're narrowing him down. Anything else you remember?"

What else was there to notice? Cara had soaked in the doctor's handsome face and the body that looked as if it lifted thousands of pounds of weights. She had noticed everything important. "No. I guess that's all."

Kate started laughing. "You goose."

"Not really. It's probably for the best. I'll be leaving in nine days anyway. No point in getting all flustered and lusty after some cowboy that I'll have to leave behind with a broken heart."

Now Kate was roaring. "That's the spirit. That's what I like to hear. Not like you sounded on the phone last week. You sounded as if your mother had beaten you down."

"She almost has. I'm starting a new lease on life. I'm going to be independent. I'm going to be my own person. I'm going to fly."

"Oh, Cara." Kate's voice softened and her smile seemed bittersweet. "Sometimes making that decision is the hardest thing to do, but the rewards are well worth it."

Kate would know, too. She had walked out of her wedding and left the groom at the altar, a groom picked by her meddling mother, Brigit. Brigit, the woman who had the bet with Cecilia.

Cara held up her fisted hand, only her pinkie sticking out. Kate linked her own pinkie with Cara's and together they said, "Kindred spirits."

"What do you want to do while you're here?" Kate asked, breaking their sisterhood moment.

"Lots of things." Like get pregnant. "Do you have

any suggestions?'' If only she had thought to get the cowboy's name.

''We'll find plenty to do. Starting with shopping.''

By the time they finished a lunch of smoked brisket so tender it melted in Cara's mouth, potato salad made with hard-boiled eggs, sweet relish, green and black olives and onions, fried okra and homemade garlic bread, they were beyond stuffed. Cara and Kate rolled out of Mama Jo's and waddled toward their cars.

''I'll never eat another bite of food,'' Cara said. Her stomach hurt from squeezing so much down, filling up spaces she didn't even know she had. Too many more meals like that one and she'd have to buy a second ticket for the flight home to accommodate the extra bulk in her hips and thighs. The food was too good. Way too good.

''I know. I say that every time I come here. And then I'm right back again.''

''I thought you didn't eat meat.'' Cara remembered Tony and Kate's heated debates about the hazards of eating beef and sushi. Kate was sure everything Tony served at his restaurant was unhealthy and would kill the clientele. This opinion didn't sit well with Tony.

Now however, Kate was blushing. ''Don't mention this to anyone, but Mama Jo's beef is an exception. My one and only dip into meat.''

''I can see why.'' Cara clutched her stomach and nodded in agreement.

''You just don't know,'' Kate whispered conspiratorially, although there was no one around to hear. ''I'm only glad Mama Jo's is miles down the road from Donetti's or we'd go out of business. I'm telling you, that woman can cook.''

Cara dug in her purse for a roll of antacids. She had been carrying an extra-large supply of them since her mother had started the marriage campaign in earnest. She took four, and offered the rest of the roll to

Kate, who unceremoniously dumped all of them into her mouth and quickly chewed.

"Ooh, that was good," Cara said, which was about the biggest understatement of the year.

"Nothing like a big barbecue lunch topped off with antacids for dessert. God, we're pathetic," Kate groaned.

"Next time, I think I'd like to try the fried turkey."

"Ooh, Cara, that's a very good choice. In fact, I'll bring the dessert next time. A roll of antacids apiece. That should cover it."

As they walked to their cars, Cara was absolutely positive that Noble's cow with the flirty eyelashes called out to her, "Mommy, Mommy-to-be. Hurry up. I want to be born."

Cara, as nonchalantly as she could, pointed to the cow, and said, "Cute, isn't it?"

"Did you see the bull on the other side of the freeway?"

"A little."

"Did you see the way he was hung?"

"I don't think so."

"You'd know if it you had. Oh, baby. His thingee—" She held her hands wide apart, then stretched them even wider. "It would give any mortal man a definite inferiority complex."

"I guess I wasn't paying attention." Cara's heart started to beat a little faster. She hadn't been around many naked men, and the few she'd seen hadn't particularly impressed her. Maybe the bull would give her something to judge her next boyfriend by. An instant replay of all the men her mother had paraded before her recently made her doubt she'd ever have a boyfriend again. Not if those were the choices. She thought of the cowboy, her cowboy, covered in barbecue sauce and chicken wings. Those piercing clear blue eyes. She only wished she'd jumped on him—

literally—when she'd had the chance. If she were ever going to do anything daring and out of schoolteacher character, this was the time to do it. Before she had to go back and be Miss Romano again.

"Is this sperm-bank business reputable?" She held her breath, hoping against hope.

"Sure it is, Cara. Rex has one of the finest reputations in the country. If there was a person considering artificial insemination, you couldn't get any better than Noble Sperm Bank. They've been in the business for years."

"Interesting…" Cara's thoughts trailed off to baby powder and booties.

"I have to tell you, Rex is a to-die-for single guy who isn't dating anyone and doesn't want to." She stopped and pulled Cara's arm, stopping her, too. "He's got pretty, blue eyes, too," Kate teased. "Want me to fix you up?"

"You said he didn't want to date."

"Cara, you have so much to learn. They all say that. It's a man's way of playing hard to get, when they all want to be gotten. I'm telling you, these Texas cowboys—" A big smile crossed her lips and she sighed.

"I don't think so." At this point, after all the men her mother had tried to set her up with, and figuring that single men were all the same just with different accents, she had no use for any of them until they grew up a little. Besides, she'd seen the only cowboy she was interested in, and if she couldn't have him she'd have no one. "Anyway, I don't want anyone to know I'm here."

"He wouldn't call your mom and tell her you were hiding out in Texas."

"I've never met the man. How do I know he wouldn't? The fewer people who know I'm here, the safer I'll feel. My mother has ways of finding things out.''

"Just think about it. If you change your mind, you'd like a Texas man. I know they take some getting used to, but these guys have been raised right. They're gentlemen.''

"Okay, Kate. I'll think about it.'' Cara stopped in front of the Mustang. "Here's the car.''

"Hey, if this isn't a guy magnet, I don't know what is.'' She stroked the hood. "Now all you need is a cowboy to give you the ride of your life.''

"You're terrible.'' Cara punched her friend on the arm, wishing all the while that she could find that cowboy one more time and work on getting that ride.

"I know, I know. I'm sorry. I miss that very dry Erie sense of humor,'' Kate said wistfully. "People here in Pegleg are nice, but they just don't get it, you know what I mean?''

"I think so. Kate, I know I'm going to have a great time this week.'' *Life-altering time is more like it.*

"Not without a cowboy of your own.''

"As far as getting fixed up with a cowboy, we'll see.'' Cara laughed.

That seemed to satisfy Kate. She said, "Great. Don't think too long. I'd hate for you to change your mind on the plane ride back.''

"I won't.''

"I'm there.'' Kate pointed several rows over. "Follow me to Mandelay, I'll introduce to you Rosey, and you can get yourself settled in and rested. How's that?''

Cara gave Kate a hug. "Thank you so much. You'll never know how much I appreciate what you and Tony have done for me. I sprang all this on you yesterday and you just…just…'' Tears were suddenly burning in the back of her eyes and she didn't know why. Maybe she was tired, or stressed. Or maybe she just needed a good cry and a good friend. Or maybe her tummy hurt from so much food. Or all of it. "You've been wonderful."

Kate's smile disappeared from her face and she stared intently at Cara. "No. It's me who has to thank you. If it hadn't been for you, Tony and I would never have gotten married. I can never thank you enough. I love him more than life itself." She walked toward her car, stopped and turned around, shouting out to Cara, "Except when he's being a jerk about the food he serves in that restaurant."

Cara followed Kate through the streets of Pegleg, finally turning off one tree-lined country road and onto a long laneway. She could see the red-tile roof from where she was, but little else. Live oak trees lined both sides and were so big and old their branches and leaves met in the middle and formed a majestic canopy over the lane.

When the trees broke, the mansion came to view. Three stories, stained glass, white pillars and a wrap-around veranda made Cara feel as if she had walked back a century into another life.

Rosey Sullivan greeted Kate with a big hug, and when Kate introduced Cara, she received a welcoming hug as well.

It felt like being at home in the middle of her hugging, kissing Italian family.

"I'm giving you the best room," Rosey said. "It's a corner room, with windows on the east, south and west. You'll be able to see the sun rise and set. You'll love it," Rosey said.

"Of course she will," Kate agreed. "Only the best for us Erie people."

"It seems like everyone is moving down here to Pegleg," Rosey said. "And not one of the transplants is a Texan."

"You'll get over it, Rosey." Kate smiled then

turned to Cara. "I've got to get home, but I'll call you later. If you feel like staying here tonight and doing nothing, I'll understand. It's an incredibly peaceful place."

Cara picked up one bag, Rosey took the other and they walked side by side up the huge spiral staircase to the second floor, then down a long hallway until they reached the corner room.

Rosey swung open the door. Cara took one look and knew she had come home. The room was bigger than her whole apartment in Erie. The four-poster canopy bed was covered with a white eyelet quilt, big, fluffy embroidered pillows and a lace dust ruffle. A colorful wedding-ring quilt had been folded over the back of a bentwood rocker.

"It's beautiful," Cara told her.

"It's the way I had always hoped it would look." Rosey went to the door. "Enjoy your stay."

As soon as Cara heard Rosey's footsteps fade away, she pulled the sperm bank's phone number from her wallet and punched in the numbers. When the woman who answered the phone gave Cara an appointment for noon the next day, Cara was stunned. "We're open on Sundays. The doctor sees clients after church," she said.

Cara carefully wrote down the directions then left her room. A few minutes later Rosey had given her directions to the local public library. Cara sat herself at one of the computer terminals and spent the rest of the afternoon on the Internet researching artificial insemination.

The more she read, the more excited she became. It really seemed like a viable idea. That is, if she could get through the not-having-a-husband issue with her family. And since the way she got pregnant wouldn't be through sex, she didn't think that would be a problem.

The procedure itself should be a breeze. The way she figured it, all they would have to do would be to sell her a frozen vial or two. From what she read, she'd be able to fill up a tube, shoot it inside her and voilà, instant pregnancy.

A flash of worry hit her when she thought about buying the semen and not getting pregnant the first time. But, when she thought about it, with her luck she'd become pregnant almost instantaneously, if not sooner. After all, wasn't it true single women became pregnant without even trying, while the married women who were desperate for babies could go on for years and years without ever getting pregnant? Then, instead of taking a vacation and relaxing, letting nature takes its course, they went through in vitro fertilization. That was all well and good for them.

For herself, though, she preferred the home-implant method. She didn't think she should have to go into a hospital and undergo a long procedure, since she had no reason to believe she wasn't fertile.

Cara knew exactly the kind of baby she wanted, too. A cowboy baby. She'd even make sure her baby knew his heritage. She would teach him Texas words like *reckon* and *fixin'* and *ain't,* which everyone who had any kind of schooling at all knew weren't proper words, but there were some, including Texas cowboys, who insisted on using them anyway. This would be so perfect.

She had it all narrowed down. All she needed was to head down to the Noble Sperm Bank and look through their catalog of the eligible cowboys who had donated sperm. She would read their descriptions carefully. She wanted to make sure he had gone to college. On second thought, she didn't know how much stock cowboys put into going to college. After all, would they need a degree to ride the range? She thought not. Okay, she was flexible. High school. He would have to have finished high school. The rest of her child's education she'd take care of herself. Environment was very important. More important than genes.

She wanted her cowboy to be tall and slender, with broad shoulders and blue, blue eyes. Curly hair—or at least wavy—would be most desirable. Dark brown hair.

Cara's insides fluttered with butterflies of excitement. With the cowboy's sperm and her egg, a clear shot into the womb and—bam—nine months later, her new name would be "Mom." She couldn't wait.

When Tony and Kate called later to ask her to dinner, Cara declined. She wanted to go to bed early. She didn't tell them that a good eight hours made her complexion seem brighter and the bags under her eyes—the ones that had appeared since her mother had gone on a find-Cara-a-husband rampage—would disappear.

By nine o'clock she had slipped between the quilts. Naked. With her eyes closed. She should have been able to relax, but she tossed and turned, first to the left and then to the right. One leg stuck out of the quilt. Then she flung the covers aside and lay there, naked, with the ceiling fan blowing over the top of her, cooling down her body that was flushed with heat. She had to stop thinking about that dark-haired, blue-eyed doctor covered in chicken wings. She tried to go to sleep, but the more she tried, the more elusive sleep became. Finally, she decided sleeping with one's eyes open would just have to do, because shut-eye wasn't anywhere nearby.

4

REX HAD EVERY INTENTION of finding the woman who had rained hot wings over him. His reason was simple and basic. In his opinion, she was exceptionally gorgeous. She had made every muscle—and he meant *every* muscle—in his body tense and harden from the second he stood up on the other side of the railing and saw her standing in front of him holding nothing more than a glass of iced tea and a few wet napkins.

Rex hadn't been so sucker-punch-attracted to a woman in longer than he could remember. He wasn't about to let her get away without at least exploring the possibilities of what those feelings could mean.

He didn't bother to question the attraction, which may have been unusual for a guy so determined to remain single. But the desire to see her again was there and that was what he was going with now. If hard-pressed to come up with a more substantial reason, he could say with certainty that it wasn't her eyes. Many women he knew had big brown eyes with long, curly black eyelashes. Wasn't her breasts either. Women all over the place had bigger, lusher breasts. The kind of breasts that made the fingers on a guy like him itch with the possibility of unhooking the back of the bra and releasing the bounty to his touch. To his gaze. He could almost feel her soft skin on his fingertips, the thoughts were so real.

Nope, those weren't the reasons why he wanted to see her again. It was her accent that had gotten his attention. The sound of her voice was soft, but she definitely hit those consonants with a hard edge that didn't fit her looks. He wasn't used to that hard edge in the accent. Texas women dragged out every syllable and there was nothing about their accents could be considered a hard edge. He wanted to hear this stranger's voice again. And he always got what he wanted. Well, most of the time anyway. He picked up the phone and punched in the numbers of the one person who he knew held the secret to the identity of the soft-looking, hard-accented woman.

"What do you mean you don't know who I'm talking about?" Rex laughed because he figured Kate Donetti was joking.

"I don't know who you're talking about," Kate repeated with pure aplomb.

Surely Kate had to be joking. He tried again. "The woman you met for lunch yesterday. Who is she?"

"What woman?"

"You were at Mama Jo's?"

"Yes."

Rex didn't hide his deep, frustrated sigh. The truth was, even though Rex couldn't begin to understand the mind of an eastern woman and had no intention of ever trying, he had never before had any lady tell him no for no good reason. That being the case, he said, "Give me one good reason you can't give me her name."

"It's a secret."

"What do you mean, it's a secret?" She was acting ridiculous. "Are we talking about the same lady? Long hair, slender figure, nice—" he cleared his throat "—nice features."

"Yes, we are."

"What's her name?"

"I can't tell you."

"Why not?" He couldn't believe they were having

this no-conversation kind of conversation. He expected an answer to his question, not this secrecy stuff she was dribbling out.

"I'm telling you, she doesn't want anyone to know she's here. I can't give you her name."

"Is she a wanted woman?" *By someone other than me?* "Maybe the police are looking for her?"

"No police. Some people want her, not for what she's done but for what she hasn't done."

"Kate." He drew out her name, trying to cajole her with his charm.

"Rex." She drew out his name just as long. Even longer for that matter. "If I could tell you I would, but I can't so I won't." She almost sounded sorry. But not quite.

"It's just a damn name." Now he was more intrigued than ever. More determined than a bulldog. He'd find out, there was no doubt about it.

"I know that, Rex. But if I told you, I'd have to kill you." Then she added, almost as an afterthought, "Rosey's not going to tell you either, so don't even try and ask her. Do you understand what I'm saying?"

Rex smiled a big goofy grin. He knew exactly what she was saying and thanked her for the gift she had given him. He hung up the phone, checked his watch and got the truck keys.

REX STOOD, fingers looped through belt loops, staring up at the dark windows of the room where the lady with no name was supposedly sleeping. His old buddy Tigger should have told him her name, but he hadn't. Rex had always considered Tigger a friend, a man who would stand by him. Until now. He had done Tigger a favor, getting him the job at Mandelay. Retirement hadn't been good to the guy because Tigger needed to feel useful, not put out to pasture. Rosey had needed an overnight desk clerk, so the match between Tigger and Mandelay was perfect.

The way Rex figured, if anyone would give him the name of the woman he was looking for, it would be Tigger. Didn't Kate direct him over here in the first place? Why would she have sent him to the B&B if no one would tell him the woman's name?

He had tried to explain that to Tigger, to no avail.

"Can't do it," Tigger had said. "Told it was some kinda secret. Not supposed to give out her name to no one, no-how."

"You're talking to me." This was getting beyond ridiculous.

"Don't matter who you are, Doc. You ain't gettin' her name." He paused. "Can tell you though, since Miss Rosey didn't say nothin' about not tellin' you this. The little lady is stayin' in that corner room on the southeast side. Second floor. She ain't left all night."

So Rex, on a mission to discover her name, and anything else he could, walked outside. Tiny lights lit the path to the back of the mansion where her room would be located, and gas lamps were placed at various locations around the property to provide a measure of light in the darkness of the night.

The only room with a balcony on the southeast corner was completely dark. There was a French door and windows wrapped around the corner, but there was not one light peeking through any curtain. He gathered small pebbles from around the grass area near the patio and halfheartedly threw the first one at the window. It hit with a light ping then dropped. He threw the next one harder, and the ones after that harder still. Lights did not come on.

Rex, knowing Tigger and his propensity for napping, had a pretty good idea that the woman had gone out for the night and Tig had slept through the whole departure. With only two pebbles left in his hand, he took aim for one of the French doors. It hit with a fine sounding pop, then landed on the balcony. Still no response from inside.

As he raised his arm to throw the last pebble, number eleven, the drape covering the door fluttered and was pushed aside. Her face, the face he had been waiting forever to see again, peered through the glass. "It's about time," he called up to her.

She opened the door a tiny crack. "Who's down there?"

"Me."

"Me, who?"

"You know who me is," he said with smug confidence. "You've been waiting for me all night."

"Have I?" The door opened a little more. He could see her nose and chin. "I don't think so," she said with a supreme feminine haughtiness that made him smile.

"Admit it," he ordered with pure male smugness.

Cara could not believe who was standing below her room. If dreams really did come true, this was it. But she'd never tell him that. "I'll admit nothing," she said. She'd admit only to herself that she'd been dreaming of this moment since she had left the restaurant. "How did you find me?" she asked.

"It wasn't easy. No one will tell me your name."

Did she hear right? "Who did you ask?" Maybe he'd asked the wrong people.

"What? I can't hear you. Come outside."

"I can't come outside, Dr.—Dr.— What's your name?"

"I'm not telling you mine until you tell me yours," he said from below. "Come out where I can see you."

That made her smile. The old "I'll show you mine, if you'll show me yours" game. He must have really wanted to find her if he had located her without a name. A sudden warm tingle traveled up her legs and made her shiver.

"Doctor, I have a problem," she called down. "I'm not dressed."

There was silence.

"Doctor?"

"I'm trying to get a visual here."

"How long will that take?"

"I don't know. Help me out." He cleared his throat a few times. "I need a little more information."

"I'll try to help as best I can."

"So, let me get this straight. You're wearing nothing at all?"

"Stark naked."

Silence again.

"Doctor?" she called out playfully.

"Give me a second. A picture is forming."

"You go ahead and form that picture. I'll be right back."

"Don't feel the need to dress on my account," he called after her.

She shut the door right after she heard him say, "Hot damn."

"Now what?" She glanced frantically around the room. No robe. No nightgown. Only street clothes. And suddenly, even the un-teacher-like clothes she'd brought with her didn't seem sexy enough for tonight.

She grabbed the top sheet off her bed and wrapped it around her, tucking the end inside the material above her breasts. She looked in the mirror. Her hair was wild, all over the place and she finger-combed it back, putting it into some kind of order the best she could. Except for her shoulders, arms and face, she was completely covered. She looked like a Greek goddess, Italian style.

Taking a deep breath, she opened the patio door and stepped outside.

He gazed up at her and didn't say a word. Not one single solitary word. All she heard was the rustling leaves and the lone screech of an owl. A second stretched into two. Then three. Maybe she didn't look like a goddess. Maybe she looked more like a mussed-up schoolteacher playing dress-up on Halloween.

"Lady?"

"Yes," she said softly, trying to smile, only not sure if there was anything to smile about. Maybe he was sorry he put forth the effort to track her down.

"The visual just isn't coming together in my mind. You better just take that off," he called up to her.

"Where are you?" Even though the area was fairly well lit, she couldn't see him.

"Here." He came out of the shadow of the big oak growing in front of her room, its branches reached out in all directions, some hitting the roof. He waved his arm, sounding hopeful. "So you taking it off?"

"No."

He reached for one of the lower branches and swung himself up, using the trunk like a ladder and the branches as rungs.

"You can't do that."

"Watch me." He continued climbing.

"I'm naked under this sheet." She was getting panicky. Not because she thought he'd hurt her. But then again, she didn't know anything about him. If Rosey and Kate wouldn't tell him her name there must be a reason. Maybe he was married already, with ten kids and cheated on his wife—the cad.

"That's okay. I've seen naked people before."

"Of course you have." Did he think just because she was from Erie that she didn't know doctors saw naked people? "But you haven't seen me naked." Was that not obvious to a doctor from Texas?

He stopped midclimb and gave her a heart-stopping smile. "We can remedy that."

She shook her head, her hair a massive wave of tangles and curls shifting across her back and shoulders. She wasn't good at the verbal bantering that came so easy to some women, and it showed when he let out a belly laugh. "You're cute, you know that?"

She shook her head again.

"You look like a deer caught in the headlights."

"That's not good. Don't think I want to remind you of Bambi."

"How about Bambi's older, sexy sister?"

She smiled back at him. "Much, much better."

When he had reached the thickest branch that was level with her balcony, he straddled it, leaning his back against the trunk. The light in the room behind her was enough illumination to see his eyes and the smile on his lips. If it had been lighter, she would bet his eyes would be laughing at her. "Why did you come up here?" she asked.

"Would you have gone down there?" He nodded toward the ground.

"Not in this."

"But that—" he pointed to her sheet "—has such possibilities."

"Really? I'm almost afraid to ask."

"You'll find out when I get to know you better."

"Are you sure that's going to happen?" Maybe she wasn't so bad at bantering after all. "Because I might say no." *Not likely.*

"That's a possibility, but I love a challenge."

"I'm a challenge?" That surprised her. She'd never thought of herself that way.

He crossed his arms over his chest. His muscles bulged under his cotton shirt and he seemed to relax against the trunk. "Do you know why no one will tell me your name?" he asked.

She shook her head. She wasn't about to tell him

that because if he wasn't a wife cheater, he could be an ax murderer. Or both.

"I asked Kate because I saw her waiting for you at the restaurant. She wouldn't say. I asked old Tigger downstairs, and he had instructions from Rosey that no one was to give out your name. Why is that?" He was smiling, but the grin was dead-on serious.

Hmm, if he could find her without her name, then her mother and family could probably find her, too. If they knew where to start looking. That was a scary thought.

"Maybe you're a serial killer who hasn't been caught yet. But they know you are, and if you killed me, then it would look bad for Pegleg. So, not only are they trying to protect me, they're saving the name of their town."

"Me?" His voice practically squeaked. A sure sign of guilt in her book. "You can't believe that."

"I don't know. Are you going to kill me?" she asked.

"With kindness. Among other things."

Her eyes squinted at him. "A knife?"

His mouth opened and no words came out. Finally he said, "You're kidding, aren't you?"

"Absolutely not," she answered with great dignity. "I don't know you."

"I could say the same for you." He retorted. "How about this. Let's start to get to know each other better. Hi," he said. He leaned forward, his arm outstretched, his fingers only a foot away from the balcony. She held on to her sheet as best she could, leaning over the railing, reaching toward him, finally feeling her fingertips brush over his, and he captured her hand and held on. Air caught in her lungs and she couldn't exhale. His touch did that to her.

"What's your name?" His voice husky. Sexy. Urging.

"What's yours?" she whispered back.

He let go, leaned back again, his spine returning to its resting place against the trunk. "You go first."

She shook her head.

His stare was turning her on. She almost didn't recognize the feeling, it had been so long, but once she did, that got her even more excited. Moisture had already formed at the juncture between her legs, and now the unfulfilled ache deep in her belly made her want to cry out about the injustice of it all. That this man who she didn't know, and would never see again after this week, would make her feel the way he made her feel.

"So, pretty lady, you won't tell me your name. And I won't tell you mine unless you go first. So we're at an impasse."

"Seems that way."

"I can deal with that." He looked at her, smiling. "Great-looking sheet. Love the way it fits you."

She softly laughed. "You don't think the color is all wrong?"

"White goes great with your hair. Nice hair, too."

She ran her fingers through the tangles. "Thanks," she said. "I'm glad the tousled look appeals to you."

His gaze was downright sexy. "There's a lot about you that appeals to me."

There, he did it again. How was she supposed to answer something like that? She wasn't prepared for this smooth-talking cowboy with the glib tongue.

"Let's cut to the chase," he said. "Are you married?"

"Are you?"

"Can you answer just one question with a simple yes or no? What's the big deal here. First no name, and now marital status is—"

"No."

"What do you mean, no? No, you're not married,

or no, you can't answer a simple question?'' He nodded and didn't look happy. ''You must be married.
Your husband doesn't know you're here and that's
why no one would tell me your name.''

''I'm not married.''

His face went from irate to nonchalant, which made
her want to laugh, but she couldn't. ''I knew that.''

''Of course you did.'' He didn't know anything.
''Are you?''

''Married? No. No kids either. That I know about.
Or that claim me.''

''Me neither. But, maybe soon. I'm hopeful.''

That look came across his face again. The look of
a predator out to defend his woman. She liked that.
''Are you engaged?'' he asked.

''No, much to the horror of my mother. She's trying her best to lure them in.''

''Are you here to land yourself a husband?''

Before she could answer, he went on, ''Because if
you are, as much as I think you're cute as all get-out,
don't look to me to fulfill those dreams. It ain't gonna
happen.''

''Why would I want to get married?'' She gestured
with both hands, which made the sheet slip a bit, but
she pulled it right back up.

''All women do,'' he said with certainty.

''That is not true. All mothers want their daughters
to get married, but not all women want to be in that
institution.'' And even if she did, she'd never let him
know it now. He was nothing but a smooth-talking
playboy out for a good time. Probably another reason
Rosey and Kate had kept her name away from him.

''I know how that goes. My parents are the same
way. They keep throwing these women at me.''

''My mother has this bet with this other lady about
whose daughter will get married first. She's driving
me nuts.'' She spread her arms to better show him

just how crazy her mother was driving her, and that's when the sheet did slip almost right past her breasts. Almost, but not quite. She grabbed on to it before any nipples showed. She gave him her back and retied the sheet, this time knotting it closed. When she turned back toward him, she mumbled, ''Sorry.''

''No problem.''

''I get too excited when I talk about my mother and that bet.''

''If you get that excited—'' his glance slid down the length of her body, then slowly up again ''—I'll talk about your mother more often.''

''I think you're being patronizing.''

''You are wrong. I'm sympathizing. I'm trying to share your feelings.''

''Are you for real?''

''My mother is desperate to get me married. She says I need to soften up a bit, try and understand the woman's point of view.''

''Is it working?''

He gave her a cocky grin and shrugged one shoulder. ''I'll let you make up your own mind about that.''

''Okay then.'' She shimmed a little, making the sheet a bit tighter. ''I'll think about it.''

He watched her with a look of hunger in his eyes, but he didn't say another word, until he asked, ''Any brothers or sisters?''

He changed the subject and she was grateful. She shook her head.

''Me neither. If I had a sister maybe I would have gotten better advice about girls. My mother's advice isn't going over too well.''

Cara smiled at that. ''You're not too bad.'' Actually he was pretty great, but she wouldn't tell him that, because his male ego could get too big.

''I always wanted a brother or sister,'' he said.

"Actually, I wanted three of them. Being an only child is not easy."

"Believe me, I know. There's no one around to defuse the attention you get from your parents."

"There's no one to play with growing up, especially if you're like me and you're a kid on a farm. I had a dog, I had a cow, cats were everywhere, but it would have been nice to have a brother to do stuff with."

"Do things? It's impossible to do things if you're an only child. Because there's no older brother or sister who had been there before, to smooth the road. We're charting the unpaved highways through life."

"That's right. No one has gone before us to make it easier to get away with things."

"It would have been less strict," Cara said. "Because in my house, everything had a 'no' answer. Even before the question was asked, the answer was no. Then I got to ask the question and the answer was still no. Even if it was a matter of something simple like washing my hair."

"Your parents wouldn't let you wash your hair?" he asked, surprised.

She leaned over the railing again. "No, that was just a hypothetical example of how strict they were. The problem started when I cut my hair."

"I get a haircut every couple of weeks, I never had to ask."

"I got it cut once. You would have thought I had committed a crime, the way they acted. Not my father. It was my mother." The memories still hurt. Only, Cara knew the hell she got for cutting her hair was nothing like what she was going to get when she returned home from Texas. It would make the haircutting incident look like an ice-cream sundae.

"You have beautiful hair," the doctor said softly. "It was the first thing I noticed about you."

"I thought it was the way I delivered food that you first noticed." She smiled at him.

He smiled right back. "I can never forget that. Your hair though, it's not like Texas hair." He was shaking his head in awe of something so different. "Can I touch it?"

"Why not?" Cara leaned even farther forward over the railing, her breasts straining against the sheet, struggling for release. She couldn't hold everything in, and figured he would be concentrating on her hair and not looking at her chest. Only one quick glance in his direction and that theory was blown out of the water. Somehow though, the thought that he found her attractive enough to look everywhere, and that he wanted to touch her hair, made her feel powerful in a way. Like a real woman. She found strength in that.

She grabbed hold of the ends of her hair. The strands reached below her waist and even with her arm stretched out, she could still hold on to a good portion of it.

The doctor leaned forward, hands brushing against hands as he took possession of her hair. "Soft," he said. "I thought it might be soft, but I wasn't sure."

"Who's out there?" a rusty voice sliced through the darkness. Cara jumped back at the same instant the doctor let go of his hold. Her sheet almost came down again, but this time her impulses were working a little swifter and she stopped it just in time.

"Who is that?" she asked. A ripple of fear went through her. "He has a gun. A big gun."

"Tigger, is that you?" the doctor called out. "It's a rifle," he said for her benefit.

"I knew it was a rifle, Doctor. But it still shoots things. You know him?" Maybe the doctor was an escapee from jail, associating with people who carried big rifles. Or maybe the man with the rifle was a police officer and had come to arrest the doctor. Or maybe the doctor wasn't a doctor at all, only playing at being a doctor. She'd seen that movie, *Catch Me If You Can,* and she knew all about people who faked their identities.

"Don't move, or I'll shoot." The rifle was bigger and longer than the small man holding it. He staggered under the weight, the long barrel swung first toward her, then toward the tree, then back toward her.

"Tigger, put it down."

The gun aimed at the tree again. "Doc, is that you up there?"

"It's me," the doctor said. "Lower it, Tig. It's okay."

"Get your carcass out of that tree. Right now, ya hear? You know you ain't supposed to be up there."

The doctor's laugh was deep and oh so lovely. And if the rifle-bearing man called him a doctor, then he must be a doctor after all.

"I'm on my way down," the doctor said.

"What's the doctor's name?" Cara called out to Tigger.

"Don't you dare tell her, Tig. Not until she tells me her name."

"Won't say a word, Doc." The rifle had been lowered. Tigger grinned up at her. "That's a right nice dress you've got on there, ma'am. My wife had one just like it."

"Thanks." She waited for a brief second before she asked, "Can you see okay?"

"I sure can," Tigger said. "Rosey's got it well lit out here, but just in case, I brought me this flashlight." He shone the beam on her, then on the doctor's face.

The doctor towered at least a foot over Tigger, and from behind him, shook his head. Cara understood immediately. "Mr. Tigger, thank you so much. I hope your wife was able to get as much enjoyment out of her dress as I'm getting out of mine.''

The doctor gave her a big smile and she knew then she had done the right thing, going along with what Tigger thought he had seen. He put his arm around the smaller man and urged him back toward the front of Mandelay. They stopped for only a second when the doctor wrested the rifle away from Tigger. He looked back one more time, found her still standing on the balcony and waved.

When they were out of sight, she went back into her room, shut the door and let the sheet drop like a puddle to the floor. This time when she climbed into bed, she reveled in all the sensations—the cool air hitting her skin, the way her breasts tightened, her nipples puckered, her skin against the bed linens. As she tucked the covers around herself, she knew she wouldn't have any trouble falling asleep. She only wished she had the long, lean and very naked body of that doctor cuddling right there next to her.

5

IT TOOK A FEW MINUTES for Cara to fully wake up on Sunday morning. The pillow she hugged was a poor substitute for the cowboy doctor who she really wished she was hugging right now. She flipped the pillow behind her head and sank deep into its feathers. She rubbed sleep from her eyes, yawned, then stretched her stiff muscles under the down quilt.

It was a beautiful morning. She could see that from the sun trying to shine into her room. She knew the sun would win and the cloudy gray sky would melt away.

Not that gray skies mattered, because they didn't. Not one bit. Her world right now was full of sunshine because, despite being pelted with chicken, her cowboy doctor had found her.

That chicken incident had been right up there as one of her most embarrassing moments, second only to walking down the aisle at her high-school graduation, very conscious of Tommy Rompart walking behind her, watching her, or so she'd wished. He had been captain of the soccer team, a hunk to die for, with shoulders out to here, narrowing to slim hips down to there.

He was her very own high-school secret crush. Not once in all the years they had been in school together, despite coming right behind her in alphabetical order, had Tommy ever acknowledged that she existed. Cara was invisible to him. Which is why Tommy walking behind her had made concentrating on the simple act of putting one foot in front of the other entirely too complicated. Which is why she'd tripped over her own feet and fell, first on one knee and then, not able to catch her balance, ended up sprawled on her stomach, face to the floor. Her cap flew off in one direction, the heel of her shoe broke and went behind her. Tommy tripped on the heel, or her feet, she was never sure what caused his fall. Cara only knew he landed right on top of her. She felt every single part of his body across her back and buttocks. Their programs had scattered. When Tommy tried to get himself off her, he'd dug his elbow into her kidney. Ignoring her moan of pain, he'd used her back for leverage to stand.

By the time Tommy was back on his feet, she had righted herself to a sitting position. She had taken his extended hand, accepting his help to rise, all the while apologizing profusely, which he brushed aside. The whole episode couldn't have taken a minute at the most. The ceremonies hadn't even stopped. Without hardly missing ten beats, Cara and Tommy had returned to their places in the line. As they passed, the guests handed back their programs and caps.

Cara proceeded to the stage, a little lopsided on her broken shoe, and received her diploma. The principal, Mrs. Merish, had whispered to her, ''Are you all right, Cara? It's not like you to make a scene.''

Sadly, that was so true. Plain, white-picket-fence Cara. Nothing wrought iron, ornate or fancy about her. Since Tommy had never spoken to her before or after that embarrassing incident, she really had no reason to think the doctor would have ever wanted to speak to her either, let alone seek her out. But he had. And she was so glad he did.

She knew he had to have gone through a huge process to locate her, since he had done it without knowing her name.

The doctor. Cara got tingly just thinking about him and what he had done. He was so romantic. Throwing pebbles at her window, scaling a giant-size tree to get closer to her. And then, doing the most intimate thing possible, touching her hair. Caressing the waves, gently pulling, sending tingles from her head to her toes. All that and they didn't know each other's names.

Her imagination took flight. What was so wrong with a spring-break fling between two strangers? What could be more romantic or more exciting? A no-strings-attached, nothing-but-sex fling. Something she'd never done before. Had never even thought of doing before because, until now, she had never met any man who made her even want to consider such a wild adventure.

Life was short, she knew that. If she never saw him again after she went back to Erie, and if they never knew each other's names, then it wouldn't be too personal. It would be a kind of fun, wild week of romance and sex. It could be very exciting. Very memorable.

If she thought enough about it, she might even get up the courage to pursue the idea. If he could find her, she could certainly find him.

Right now though, she had things to do, a doctor to see, decisions to make. She flung back the covers and the chill in the room hit her body with an arctic blast. Goose bumps jumped across her skin, her nipples puckered almost painfully, her feet instinctively rubbed each other, urging warmth back.

She wrapped the quilt around her and went to stand at the middle set of windows. Looking at the view from her window, she saw nothing but blue-gray sky and vast amounts of space. A space bigger than any she'd ever been in before.

A perfect day. She closed the drapes, dropped the quilt on the bed and headed for the shower. Later, fresh and clean, she pulled out her clothes. Her outfit had to be perfect. She dressed so carefully—the gray skirt, pink sweater set and gray suede pumps with three-inch heels gave her confidence.

She gathered her purse, made sure she had the directions to the clinic and left the room.

She was almost at the main door when Rosey called out, "Good morning."

Cara said good morning back, had her hand on the door handle ready to leave, when Rosey asked, "Don't you want breakfast?"

"No, I'm not hungry, thanks." Cara was so used to being questioned about every move she took, every decision she made, that she was almost ready to launch a defense on the pros of artificial insemination for single women. It took a moment to realize Rosey hadn't asked her anything more personal than if she wanted to eat. The idea that someone wasn't examining her every move was almost unheard of in her life. It threw her for a loop. She almost wanted to give the woman a hug just for the simple act of minding her own business.

"Are you okay?" Rosey asked. "You've got this little pained look on your face. Maybe you better get something to eat after all."

"I'm fine, really." Suddenly, Cara realized that she wanted to talk about her plan, she wanted to tell someone. Rosey would be a perfect person, because, like the doctor, Cara would never see Rosey again. She wouldn't pass judgment because, the truth was, Rosey didn't care one bit what Cara did. The thought was reassuring. Rosey would be a perfect test case on the reaction of the general public. "I'm going to the

Noble Sperm Bank.'' She watched the woman carefully for any sign of a negative reaction.

''Cara, that's wonderful!'' Rosey practically gushed as she ran around the check-in counter and gave Cara a bear hug. ''I'm so happy for you.''

''You are?'' That was not what she'd expected.

''Oh, yes. I was hoping something like this would happen. I hope it works out for you.''

''You do?'' What was going on here?

''Don't be so surprised. It's what everyone wants.''

''Everyone?''

''Yes.''

Cara couldn't help but be surprised. She had never thought anyone's reaction would be so excited. ''I want it more than most,'' she confessed.

''Then you will get it. If you want something or someone bad enough, it will happen.''

''I hope so.''

''Let me know how things go, okay?''

''Okay, but, Rosey, please don't tell Kate or Tony. I want to surprise them.''

Rosey's thumb and pointer finger clamped together, and she waved them over her mouth. ''My lips are zippered. We keep our secrets here.''

''I know you do.''

''I bet they'll be so happy when you tell them,'' she said.

''I hope so.'' She could only hope her family would be, too. Maybe that was one hope too many.

It wasn't until Cara was in the car and on the road that she realized Rosey had been the other person who knew the doctor's name. Without having a cell phone, there wasn't anything Cara could do about getting that information now.

The drive out to Noble Sperm Bank was a long one. Or maybe it just seemed long because she was so anxious to be there.

She had expected it to be inside the little town of Pegleg, but it was farther out in the country. Actually, to anyone from Erie, the whole town of Pegleg would have been considered "in the country." To people from Pegleg, the country meant about a half mile past the last four-way stoplight.

Cara zigzagged down blacktop roads, barbed-wire fences bordering either side, and behind them, cows and horses grazed.

The way to the doctor's office was clearly marked, as was the route to a middle school, the French Toast Restaurant, post office, library and a subdivision called Tranquillity Park. Despite the signs, though, she didn't see any of these establishments. All she saw for miles and miles was grass, livestock, big trees and a creek that seemed to meander along the same road she drove.

But she kept on going. As long as there were signs saying she was driving in the right direction, she wasn't about to stop until she reached what she now considered to be the House of Conception.

REX WAS WHISTLING as he drove up to the office Sunday afternoon. He was still angry as all get-out about those billboards, and he still intended for them to come down. But right now he wanted to concentrate on one little lady. He didn't want anything to interfere with how he remembered her wrapped in a very revealing white sheet.

When she had come out on the balcony last night with only that ridiculous sheet for cover, he almost fell out of the tree. The light had been shining behind her, so he could clearly see the outline of her legs, and that alone had made him want to jump off the branch and onto the balcony. Her breasts though, they had been right there for him to feast his gaze on. Okay, so maybe they hadn't been *right there*. Maybe *right there* was in his imagination. He'd even go so far as to admit they were well hidden under the sheet, except for how her nipples had stood erect, evidence of her excitement that not even the sheet could cover. Now, him being a guy, he had to believe her excitement was for him. If he thought any other way, he wouldn't be a true guy, he'd be a wimp guy.

Which is exactly why Rex had stayed in the tree. If he had gotten onto her balcony, that sheet wouldn't have stayed on her. It would have been on the floor with them on top of it, using the sheet the way a sheet was intended to be used. For lovin'.

His fingertips itched with the desire to touch her, to feel her, to smell her. Last night, when she let him touch her hair, he'd gotten hard. Excited over hair? He had, and the sensation had been very uncomfortable. He wanted to do it all over again. Only more.

He would have gone back this morning if he'd had the time. He definitely planned on climbing that tree again tonight. He figured he'd move a little closer to the balcony this time and see how she took his advancement. He didn't want to move too fast now, didn't want to scare her.

Rex waved at the old regulars sitting on the porch waiting for him to unlock the door. Tigger—the traitor—was there, acting as if he was some superior being, having information the others didn't know but wished they did.

Rex parked in the employee lot at the back of the building, then walked around to the front. All the men had keys and could go inside without waiting for him, but they never did.

"You're late again, Doc," Tigger said, tapping his watch with his finger. "You go back and see the little lady after you left me at the office last night?"

He heard snickers from the other men, which meant Tigger didn't keep Rex's evening adventures a secret for long. Rex did what he had to do when it came to the old guys, he ignored them.

He held the door open for them as they shuffled inside. "You know everything, Tig. Did I?"

"I'll never tell. Your secret's safe with me."

That was a joke and they both knew it. "The only safe secret seems to be the lady's name."

"What you say?" Tigger held a hand to his ear.

"Get inside." As frustrating as the men were, Rex loved each and every one as family.

"You need to get your damn watch fixed," Jasper Carter told him, hustling to make sure he got his favorite chair. "You're late gettin' here."

"No, I'm not," Rex said. They had the same argument every week. He had expected the men to take it from there, and start their bickering, the same bickering they did every Sunday, only this day, they stood around in a half circle looking at him. "What?" he asked.

"Who is she?"

"Who is who?"

"The girl you was chasin' when you got caught up in the tree with your pants down yesterday," Jasper said.

"What are you telling them?" Rex turned to Tigger. "I didn't have my pants down."

"I ain't told them nothin'." Tigger turned to his friends and winked.

"I did," Barbara said as she walked into the office.

"Where have you been?" Rex asked.

She glared at him, as if to say, "Who are you to ask me where I was?" But she didn't say that, she only said, "It's none of your business. I called in sick. That's all you need to know."

Tigger coughed.

The men shuffled toward their chairs.

Rex said, "My mother's going to fire you, Barbara."

She didn't say a word. She didn't have to. The look she sent him said it all.

Barbara left the reception area and walked toward the back of the building. Rex turned on the lights and computer, then went into the small kitchen to brew a pot of coffee. Cathy had Sundays and Mondays off, and always urged him to do the same. Or at the very least take Sunday off. He couldn't though. Livestock and ranchers worked seven days a week, and he worked the same hours as his clients.

Besides, if he closed up on Sundays, the old men sitting in his waiting room would have to find somewhere else to park their asses and argue. Frankly, Rex would miss them. Except for Tigger. Right now he'd like to punish the old guy and ground him from the office for a week.

But he wouldn't. The old men meant a lot to him. They also had a stake in his business. In LuLu to be exact. LuLu the prize bull. The bull that had been owned by one Jeb Stevens, formerly of Montana and lately of Miami Beach. The bull that had gone on the auction block and sold for seven hundred fifty thousand dollars—if he said three-quarters of a million dollars, it made LuLu sound even more valuable. The bull that Rex now owned in partnership with his father and the seven men in his waiting room, who all had staked their retirement savings on LuLu and the semen he'd produce. Not because they thought the bull was a great bargain. Hell no. They all thought Rex had paid too much. But they believed in Rex, believed in his dream, and wanted Rex to succeed. If it took some overpriced bull to do that, well, then that's what it took.

LuLu was fed organically grown grain. No impurities had ever passed the bull's lips. The cattle on

Rex's ranch were fed the same mixture. All top-quality beef and first-rate breeding stock. Now, Tony Donetti was breeding Angus cattle for his own restaurant, and he also used the same mix of feed. It was superior feed for superior beef.

An Angus was an Angus, but LuLu was a Galloway. Before he had come into Rex's possession, LuLu had sired hundreds of championship stock cattle. Rex had had him about a year now, and the bull was well on his way to topping that record. Not the old-fashioned way though, but through the artificial insemination process.

Not that Rex prevented LuLu from having his way with a cow. LuLu just wasn't interested in cows. He was a million-dollar—or damn close to it—gay bull. Which didn't matter to anybody as long as he had what it took to produce championship calves for those willing to pay the price.

Jasper, Tigger and the rest of the guys were all sitting around, chewing the fat along with their tobacco and pretending they had nowhere to go, nothing to do. Everyone knew, however, they were there in the waiting room for one reason and one reason only. To protect their bull and make sure there would be a return on their investment while they were still around to enjoy it.

Only today, they were seeming to get a big kick out of Rex and the mystery lady—a mystery to everyone but Tigger, that is.

After the coffee finished brewing, Rex put the pot on the warmer in the waiting area. The men slowly creaked out of their chairs and took their place in line for a little jolt of caffeine to keep them going.

Rex sat in Barbara's chair to start working. He checked the calendar. None of the three appointments either Barbara or Cathy had scheduled canceled, which meant he was booked for most of the day. The first was with a woman, Cara Romano, a name he didn't recognize. The other two, Herman Jakes and Georgiana Rodgers, he had done business with before.

"Hey, boys, we've got us a new lady coming to visit." There weren't many women ranchers in the area. Georgiana, widow of Roger, had recently turned the ranch that had run in the red during Roger's lifetime to pure black when she started breeding Galloway cattle using Noble semen, so they knew her.

As far as the prospect of a new lady went, all he got was abstract grumbling from the old men. They were more interested in the woman over at Mandelay than anyone coming to talk about semen.

Still, Rex let them know, "A new customer means more profit, boys."

"True, true," Clyde, always the philosopher, agreed. "Tigger said she wore a sexy dress. I forget what that means."

"Get out." Roy chopped him on the shoulder.

"It's been a long time," Clyde whined.

"Time for my nap." Ted Clark placed his already-empty coffee mug on the table next to him, slumped in his chair with his bony shoulders against the wall and covered his face with his Stetson. "Wake me if anything exciting happens."

He said that every week, and the boys had yet to wake him.

Barbara came up behind Rex, slapping him on the back. "Get up outta there, that's my chair."

"This is your chair? Are you sure? I think it forgot who you were. Chair, this is Barbara, she works here, full-time on a temporary basis."

"Rex, dear, I was sick yesterday." The pink-haired lady smiled sweetly, then slid her gaze over to Tigger, who watched her the same way that LuLu eyed the semen machine.

"I heard some interesting news last night," she said to Rex.

"We all know about Rex climbing the tree to that young lady's room," Pete said.

"That's old news," Barbara scoffed.

"Old already?" Rex didn't know whether to be happy or disappointed. "How did you now about that?"

She shook her head in disgust. "Everyone knows about what a fool you made of yourself over that girl. She's not even from Texas. What are you thinking?"

He was thinking that while he couldn't find "that girl's" name, everyone knew about him climbing the tree. Go figure.

"I need to tell you about a call I got yesterday from my dear friend Irma, who talked to her friend Jamie, who just happens to be first cousin to none other than Chad Ottaway from the Ottaway Ranch in Tucson. Isn't this a coincidence?" She was all excited. "Did you hear?"

"Hear what?" Tigger asked.

"Where's your hearing aid?"

"I hear fine."

"Then listen. Did you hear what happened at the Ottaway Ranch yesterday?" She poked Rex in the chest.

"I was busy yesterday, fielding phone calls because my receptionist, that being you, wasn't here. So no, I didn't hear anything."

"Well." Barbara made sure she had everyone's attention, ignoring the jab about her not-so-great work habits, and focusing on Tigger, she said in a know-it-all voice, "The semen—courtesy of none other than Tony Donetti's big bull, Rufus—was hijacked."

"Yesterday?" Clyde asked.

"Tony?" Rex couldn't believe it.

The others got loud and vocal, calling for the FBI,

CIA, army, navy and every other military branch, including the Texas Rangers, to be brought in on the case and capture the person who was hijacking the semen. "But for the grace of God and semen go I," Tigger said. "This is war. Arm yourselves."

The old men shouted out a hearty amen.

"Calm down, everyone." Rex shuffled through the stack of mail until he found *Proliferation,* the cattle breeding industry magazine. There was an article in there about this very subject.

What happened to Tony could affect them, too. No longer were cattle rustlers stealing the old-fashioned way by rounding up calves and branding them with a competitor's mark before herding them onto a waiting truck. Now they'd gone high-tech. They intercepted frozen semen through the mail, or hired a mole to infiltrate an operation and walk away with hundreds, if not thousands, of vials. Stealing the frozen semen of championship bulls like LuLu and starting their own breeding production would be cheap to start and could earn them millions down the road, considering each straw of semen could fetch upward of two hundred and fifty thousand dollars.

So far he had been lucky and had avoided these modern-day rustlers. But he didn't know how much longer his luck would hold out. Not if Tony was getting robbed. This brought everything too close to home.

WHEN CARA APPROACHED the Noble Sperm Bank her first thought was that it was a mistake. This couldn't be a clinic or a medical office. Maybe she'd been watching too much TV and that's why she thought sperm banks were supposed to be in big medical centers. She certainly hadn't expected the entrance to be an ornate picket fence, with wide-open gates to allow a car to drive through.

She hadn't expected the building to be a one-story white structure, with ten windows along the front that were framed by forest-green shutters. A porch, painted white like the building, went from end to end. A double door was in the middle, green like the shutters, and on each side of the door were five rocking chairs, vacant, swaying gently in the slight breeze. She almost sighed at the rocking chairs. So maternal. She wondered if mothers who had success with the sperm bank brought their babies back and sat on the chairs, nursing the infants. If she lived here, she'd do that. The whole environment was so peaceful, so beautiful. Even though it wasn't what she'd expected, it was perfect.

Cara drove to the gravel area that said Guest Parking. The lot was almost full, mostly with pickup trucks, some old and decrepit-looking, some shiny and new. She was surprised to see that every truck and car had its windows rolled down. The Mustang's top was down, but she pressed the button to return it to its closed and locked position. When she got out of the car she locked the doors behind her. That's what she always did and she didn't think visiting a town like Pegleg was going to change that. Just because everyone else around wasn't careful about their belongings didn't mean she could let down her guard or become careless.

Cara removed the clip she had kept her hair in for the drive and brushed it out, refreshed her lipstick and powder and put on the long-sleeved sweater that matched her pink shell. She touched her earrings, patted down her necklace and finally jiggled the bracelet. She frowned at it. One of the gold brackets that framed a coin was empty and pulled away from the bracelet. The idea that one of the coins was gone upset her. It wasn't just a missing coin. It was a missing piece of her heritage. She checked the rest of the bracelet as best she could and thought it seemed secure, but she wasn't sure.

As soon as she got back to Erie, she'd take everything to a jeweler, get it all appraised and make sure all the coins were securely fastened. Until she did that, she knew she probably shouldn't be wearing her entire heritage at once. Right now though, she had to, because she was sure the coins were going to bring her luck. She just wasn't sure which piece of jewelry would bring her the most luck, and she was afraid that if she left one at Mandelay, that would be the piece that she would have needed.

Even if she convinced these people she would be a fit and loving mother without a spouse, she still had her own family to contend with. That, she thought as she rubbed the coins on her wrist, would take all the luck each coin could give.

With her head held high, doing her best to look worldly and sophisticated, Cara walked up the steps, opened the door and jingled into the lobby of the Noble Sperm Bank Association and came to a stop so suddenly that every coin clashed ferociously against the next and her heart was pounding even louder than her jewelry.

It was him. Her cowboy. Sitting over there near the pink-haired lady. Could he be the doctor? She quickly glanced around the room, taking in the elderly men. Tigger was there, too, kind of drooling at her, holding a cup. They all held little cups, held out kind of expectantly. Could all those old men be donors?

"Oh, no." The words slipped out before she could stop them. She couldn't help it. Right now she felt as if she were a peach on the receiving end of a paring knife.

If this was the crop of sperm she had to choose

from, the pickings were not good at all. In fact, some of her mother's selections were starting to look good by comparison. And *that* was something Cara thought she'd never have to say.

6

SOMEWHERE IN THE BACK of Cara's mind she remembered, albeit dimly, that she'd been determined to act sophisticatedly northeastern. Worldly and knowledgeable. Although her knees had almost buckled out from under her, she said, ''Fancy meeting you here, Doctor.'' All the manners her mother had drilled into her came to the fore.

So, standing very straight, she smiled as she walked toward him. What if he'd volunteer to be her sperm donor? That thought almost brought her to a halt again. Then everything would be so right in her world. The very idea of him with his hand covering his male member and doing what it took to relieve himself in a cup...why, the thought sent flames rushing through her. She could hardly breathe. As if those blue eyes of his held some magnetic force, which she was sure they did, she moved toward him, not able to stop the forward motion despite her thoughts about him. She didn't know that wanting to help him donate sperm was what a prospective mother-to-be should be thinking about.

She took notice of the expressions that had crossed his face. First he'd seemed surprised to see her, then almost joyful. But now he was frowning. She'd just walked in. How could she possibly have disqualified herself for motherhood in such a short time? Surely the memory of a few piddly little chicken wings couldn't have that effect.

Then there was last night. When the top of her sheet fell down, did that disqualify her? Maybe he thought she had done it on purpose and she was promiscuous. She wasn't. And her thoughts a moment ago, he couldn't possibly know what she was thinking.

Could he?

She stuck out her hand and said, "Cara Romano."

Rex grabbed her hand and held on. He could not believe his good fortune. Cara Romano and his mystery woman were one and the same. She had never said a word about breeding Galloways.

"And you are?" she asked, not even attempting to remove her hand. He wanted to tell her he was her dream come true. Instead, he told her his name.

"You couldn't tell me last night?"

"You didn't either."

She scowled at him. Such a beautiful scowl. Except the way he figured it, after last night, she should be sending him looks of lust. This wasn't going the way he'd imagined it would go when he would see his mystery woman again. Cara. Beautiful name.

If he had been writing the script, she would have said something along the lines of, "Oh, my dream lover, I have missed you so. The hours spent away from you were agony." Or, even a more neutral, "You handsome, sexy devil, let's go to my house and count my coins."

Instead, she had a look of terror and shock on her face—a face even more beautiful than he'd remembered from yesterday. And if he'd heard her correctly, the words of passion she'd uttered when she walked through the door and saw him, were, "Oh, no."

Barbara came up behind Rex and whispered in his ear, "Batting under five hundred, are you?"

"Not for long," he murmured, massaging Cara's hand, taking great pleasure in watching her blush. Not many women blushed anymore.

He had an idea for tonight that she was sure to agree to. He'd entice her to dinner and a walk in the park. Maybe a few kisses, or more, before the evening ended. If it ended at all. Hey, they were old friends by now, having seen each other twice. Only, instead of coyly flirting as he had expected, she said, "What a surprise to see you again so soon."

She leaned a little closer, all that gold stuff around her neck and wrist clinking like mad, and he knew she was trembling at the very sight of him, trembling with desire, which was a much more positive sign than her words would indicate.

Maybe she'd said "Oh, no" because she'd realized just how much he'd seen last night, and the idea that she'd been so exposed to him, when she hadn't intended to be, embarrassed her. He wasn't embarrassed though. All he had to do was look at her beautiful hair, gorgeous face and luscious body, and it was enough to make him have a wet dream right here in the middle of his place of business.

After expending all that energy trying to find out her name with absolutely no luck, it was an act of Providence that Cara and his mystery lady were the same person. That she had come to him. He tried his best to smile in a friendly, professional manner because, after all, he was at work, even if the work he wanted to do was on her. He had a feeling his smile bordered on a leer of appreciation and lustful longings.

"I'm serious, why are you here?" she asked, her voice soft, shaky.

"I'm here because you're here," he said.

Why did she look so surprised to see him? He didn't get it. "Come on, Kate or Tony must have told you where to find me. You made an appointment."

"With you?"

"Who do you think?"

They both knew the sexual energy between them was enough to light a fire. He had to ask, in a low voice, "Why do you sound so shocked to see me?" Because he knew she must have known where he was. "Is it for the benefit of the people in the room?"

"Yes," she breathed. Then she said much more firmly, "No," in the same breath. "You're my chicken cowboy." Her gold things jangled even louder. "You're my tree-climbing Romeo." That firm voice got a little fainter.

"I'm the doctor," Rex corrected her, feeling his smile slip a little. This was not right. Not right at all. "I'm not a chicken cowboy. Have nothing to do with poultry." He was a cattleman all the way and proud of it. "This is exactly where I'm supposed to be."

"You're the doctor?" Taking one step back, she covered her mouth with her hand, but he still heard another, "Oh, no," even if it was muffled.

Damn. That was the third time. Maybe the fourth. Who was counting? What was wrong with the woman? Her attitude was downright emasculating. Rex glanced at the old boys sitting in the lobby. He didn't need to look at Barbara—he heard her snickering.

Ted had woken up enough to say, "That's the gal he climbed the tree for?" Six others confirmed, still sitting where they always sat, each under the champion-bull picture he felt best evoked his own personality. Only now, instead of leaning back against the wall, which was their way, they were leaning forward. While their eyesight may not be as good as it once was, their hearing was another matter. They were craning their ears to hear what was being said. Ted, being the tallest and the one who did things his own way, gave the others a scornful look and he pulled out his hearing aid. The others might be too vain to wear one, but Ted clearly wasn't going to miss a thing.

"You're the doctor who does the sperm?" She pointed a gold-coin-bearing arm at him, then swung it to the wall where Noble's Sperm Bank Association declared what the business was all about. "Rex Noble?"

"That's me."

"I see." If her voice got any fainter it would fade completely away.

"Purty hair, young lady," Tigger called out. "Reminds me of Beulah's. You remember Beulah, don't you, Arthur? The old chestnut mare I had. Beulah's tail had the same red in it as that young'un's." He used his pointer finger to circle the air. "See the way red kinda sparks through the brown with the sun comin' through the window like it is?"

"Shut up, Tigger. She ain't no horse," Arthur growled.

That's for sure, Rex thought, but Tigger had it right about the lady's hair. While she was wearing a very conservative sweater and skirt, the gold coins hanging around her neck, wrist and ears, coupled with that long, silky-looking hair that reached below her waist—the hair that felt like silk when he wove it through his fingers last night—spoke volumes about the wild streak he knew now she had, even if for the most part it was buried inside her. Because if she knew she had a wild streak, she would never have said, "Oh, no." She would just have screamed, "Oh, yes!"

Even imagining her saying "Oh, yes" was enough to intrigue Rex to no end. Not to mention the desire he had to run his fingers through her hair once again. This lady was a breath of fresh air after the few Georgiana Rodgers–type of ranching women who frequented his business.

"Let me ask you a question. Why didn't Kate want me to know your name? Why did Rosey want to keep your name a secret? It's just a name. Is there something going on here that I'm not aware of?"

She turned away from him for a moment and glanced at the men sitting in the lobby. Rex followed her gaze. He almost laughed at the old coots as they scooted their chairs away from the wall, getting closer to the action. When they saw the lady watching them, all movement stopped. Some of the guys looked at the ceiling, humming; Harry pretended to clean his fingernails.

"I really don't know. I was thinking the same thing yesterday, and the only thing I could come up with was that a, you're married, or b, you're a serial killer."

"He's a killer all right, sweetie," the pink-haired lady chimed in. "He kills them with kindness. And rumor has it, he's a good kisser, too." She walked over to Cara and held out her hand. "I'm Barbara. I'm the office manager." She turned to Rex, as if daring him to deny it.

"You can call yourself what you want, Barbara, there's no raise in it for you."

"I'm Cara, from Erie."

"I don't know where Erie is. Is it near Dallas?"

"No." Cara laughed. "It's in Pennsylvania."

"That's too far away. They talk funny over there, you know, east of the Mississippi, no one can understand them." She leaned forward and said confidentially, "That's why there's so much crime up there in the East."

"There's no crime here?" Cara asked.

"Oh, just semen rustling, nothing we can't take care of with a few shotguns."

Rex put his arm around Barbara and pulled her

away. "You're scaring her. Leave the poor girl alone."

"What's on the floor there?" Barbara moved toward a shiny gold object by the door. She came back and handed Cara one of the gold coins from her bracelet. "Be careful about these, honey. Don't want you to lose something so pretty."

After thanking her profusely, Cara confessed that she hadn't felt the coin drop. "That worries me."

"Don't wear them then, until you get them fixed," Rex said.

"I have to. They bring me luck. And anyway, I have a feeling, with the cost of what I'm going to do, I'm probably going to have to turn the coins over to you for payment."

"We'll talk about it."

"There's something else. Kate and Tony." Cara fidgeted with the bracelet, then looked up at him, dead serious. "They have no idea I'm here at your clinic today. Do you understand my being here *is* a secret?"

"I'm a doctor. It's unethical for me to tell anyone about anything that goes on between a client and me."

"What about them?" She tilted her head in the direction of LuLu's benefactors who were in the process of moving toward them once again.

"Get back!" he ordered.

The *clip-clop-clunk* of boot heels and chair legs again stopped.

"Ah, Doc," Ted whined.

"This is a private conversation."

There were more grumblings as they scraped back toward the wall. "It's harder going in reverse," Jasper complained.

Spindly wooden legs stalled in the grout. Chairs with old bones seated on them dipped precariously backward. "We ain't gonna tell no one no how," Arthur shouted to the lady.

"No one will know your secret," Rex promised, looking at the other men. He then whispered so only she could hear, "They're hard-of-hearing." Then shouted, "Right, boys?"

They nodded. "We're crazy about pickled herring," Arthur agreed, speaking for the group.

Rex winked at her. "Believe me now?"

"Thank heavens." The look of relief that came over her face was priceless.

"Okay then. You're here and you don't want anyone to know you're here."

She smiled. "That's right. Thank you, Dr. Rex Noble."

Rex, however, was happy again. With the woman of his dreams standing right there in front of him with no food in her hands, and the memory of her wrapped in a sheet burning in his mind, he saw nothing but a lot of possibilities ahead.

He said, "So, how can I help you?"

Cara moved another step closer. Her long hair peeked out from behind her as it waved from side to side. The gold coins around her neck clanged against each other. That high-pitched noise, plus the brightness of the gold, caught the attention of the old men who had started scraping their chairs closer again. At least they all stayed in their chairs. All except Arthur. He got up and approached her. First, he leaned his craggy face close to her ear and touched the coins dangling from the lobe. When he was satisfied with the earring, he lifted her right hand and looked at the bracelet hanging loosely from her wrist. Before Rex realized what Arthur had in mind and could stop him, Arthur nabbed a coin from her necklace, trapped it between his teeth and bit down. She gasped and he let go.

Arthur didn't apologize. What he did do was hand down his verdict. "You got yourself a right fine dowry hangin' round your neck, li'l lady."

"I haven't thought of these as a dowry." She touched the necklace. "Why, my grandma, may she rest in peace, would flip over in her grave if she thought I'd ever use these coins for monetary advancement."

"You're not married, then?" Arthur asked, sliding a glance toward Rex.

She got a strangely defensive look on her face, Rex thought, as she said, "No." Arthur blew out air and grunted some unintelligible words, but "good catch" and "fine baby-carrying loins" were among the ones Rex understood. Judging from Cara's red cheeks, so did she, but for some reason Rex couldn't fathom, the statements seemed to please her. She was blushing, but she actually looked sort of relieved.

"Sit down," Rex ordered Arthur. "Behave."

"I'm goin', but I'm not promising nothin' else." He did an about-face, going back to his chair. When he had his butt seated once again, he leaned forward, like the rest of the old men, elbows on knees, chins supported by the palms of their hands, and watched Cara and Rex with great intensity. Not one of those geezers so much as blinked.

CARA KNEW, deep in her heart, there was no reason on earth to be embarrassed about having an artificial-insemination conversation with a doctor. Only, that was before she found out the doctor was her cowboy, her very own Romeo.

She had done her research. She knew she would ask intelligent questions. Except now she was all flustered, so she doubted anything she said would sound intelligent.

What worried her most was giving the impression of being desperate, as if this was the only way she could have a baby. Some people might take that to mean that no man found her desirable or marriageable. She was afraid she would sound lonely and needy, as if she thought a baby would fill her life because there wasn't a man to do it.

None of that was been true, but how could she explain without sounding as if it were all true?

She knew she had to bite the bullet and keep going. She would pretend Rex was ugly and old and undesirable. It would be hard to do. She wondered if he ever conducted interviews where the woman kept her eyes closed. If she had hers closed, she might be able to get through the process without jumping out of the chair, wrapping her arms around him and begging him to donate to her cause.

She was trying hard to think of the words she needed to get the conversation about sperm and eggs rolling, when his blue eyes captured her gaze and all rational thought momentarily left her. Without him saying a word, she was drawn toward him, as if his eyes had some kind of magnetic force impossible to resist. Which they did.

"Come here with me," he said, and she followed him to the reception desk. The desktop was neat and orderly, nothing that looked out of place except for some girlie magazine called *Proliferation*. Whether the doctor saw her looking and was embarrassed by being caught reading that kind of rag, or whether he was only straightening the desk, she couldn't know, but he pushed the magazine aside and put another piece of paper across the top. She could still read most of the big bold letters on the cover though. The title of the lead story, as much as she could see, said, "Ustling A Profitable Business."

All right, so she'd admit she was a tiny bit disappointed. But, well, it wasn't as if Cara didn't know men were flawed. She'd been subjected to Erie's less than finest over the last month. She should be used to it by now.

Not that the doctor's liking pornography mattered anyway. She was here today, not on a personal matter, but on business, strictly business. Although as far as sperm went, when she looked at him, she wanted to get downright personal.

"Are you okay?" He sounded concerned.

"Why?"

"Your breathing seems forced."

She put her hands in front of her, palms facing toward him. The bracelet tinkled. "I'm fine. I promise."

"I hope we can help you." His grin was warm and friendly.

Not we, *you*, she thought as she slowly lifted her gaze from the desk and looked up at him.

"I'm sure you can help me," she said. *I've been waiting for someone like you my whole life. Oh, Mama, if you could see me now.* On second thought, she wanted to keep her mother out of this. "But I have a lot of questions."

"I'm here to answer every one of them."

She knew she couldn't keep staring at his face, his beautiful, handsome face, so she looked around the room. The men in the lobby were all talking about her and the fact that the doctor had climbed a tree to see her last night. She picked out those words very easily.

Some of the men were chewing gum. Some were

chewing their toothless gums. They still held on to their little cups. Then one of them spit into the receptacle. *Oh, God. That's gross. Unsanitary.* ''I don't want that one's.'' She pointed.

''That one's what?''

''You know what. In fact, I don't want any of theirs.'' She stared at the candidates for fatherhood by proxy.

Some had balding heads, others wore sweaty cowboy hats, so who knew if there was hair under those hats. She noticed a few with hair growing out of their ears. And chewing tobacco. Filthy, dirty habit.

They couldn't possibly be a sampling of the men who donated sperm to the Noble Sperm bank. Could they? She had to ask. ''I gather these gentlemen are donors.'' Her hand swept the air, pointing randomly at the waiting room and its occupants.

''Every one of them,'' the doctor replied with such obvious pride and affection that it took her back. ''I wouldn't have a business if not for them.''

That was a little bit discouraging. She didn't want them. She wanted Dr. Noble. He was so handsome. So downright sexy in his jeans that fit over muscled legs, and those legs, she knew, could perform miracles. She'd seen him climb a tree, after all.

He was everything a girl dreamed a man could be, and then some. One glance into the waiting room and she also knew that one day he, too, would be old, potbellied and bald, with hair growing out of his ears.

She had to wonder if the sperm stock from the Noble Sperm Bank was old and decrepit, like the men in the waiting room. If so, was it hard to find donors that were young and handsome like the doctor himself?

Rex handed her a clipboard. A form was there to

fill out and a pen hung from a string tied to the clip. "Do you know what your needs are? We stock many different varieties, and all come from championship lineage."

Cara made a sudden, surprising and totally out-of-character decision to go straight to the point. So she put on her best smile. "My needs are very simple, Doctor." Then, without taking a breath, not wanting to lose her courage, "I want your sperm."

7

SINCE "I WANT your sperm" was the boldest, the most outrageous statement Cara had ever made in her entire life as a good girl, she was braced for a little reaction from Rex. A positive one like, "All right. Let's go for it," or a negative one like, "I'm going to wash your mouth out with soap," which is what her mother would have said. What she didn't expect was for Rex to level those gorgeous blue eyes at her and say with a perfectly serious face, "That's why everybody comes here. For my semen. Or eggs."

She gasped. "You make eggs too?" This she hadn't counted on. He didn't look like a half-male, half-female type. If she were forced to describe him in twenty-five words or fewer, she'd just say, "pure male," and save herself twenty-three words.

His eyes twinkled a little and his mouth quirked at one corner. "Sure. Raw or hard-boiled. Maybe scrambled. You want over easy, you're in trouble."

Cara heaved a sigh of relief and smiled back. He was joking. He was talking about breakfast. "Thanks anyway," she said. "I'll handle my own eggs."

"Fine with me. Seriously, though—" and he did look very serious all of a sudden "—you wouldn't believe how many people think they ought to be cooked first in case they're carrying the E. coli virus."

"I'm certain that my eggs aren't carrying an E. coli virus," Cara said firmly. It had never occurred to her she might have to have her eggs cooked first, nor did she have any intention of cooking them. "You're talking about artificially inserted eggs, aren't you?" she asked hopefully. "Not the ones that appear naturally."

"Well, yes." A puzzled looked crossed his face before he said, "I only mentioned it because many clients who want semen also want eggs. I wanted you to be aware we're a full-service operation here."

Of course. It was beginning to make sense to her. Some women not only didn't have semen handy, but also couldn't make their own eggs. How sad. "I should have realized that."

"You're a first-timer. You can't be expected to know everything. But, let me tell you, we do whatever it takes to make a client happy."

She doubted that included a personal donation—*without* the cup. However, he did touch her arm, and where his fingers touched, she burned. He must feel it, too. He had to feel it. Right this minute she felt hot enough to cook her own eggs. "As far as I know, I'm not having a problem with eggs. So we won't have to worry about whether they have to be cooked or not. Although I would certainly trust your judgment if I did have a problem," she added, to let him know how much trust she had in him. It was also important to her that he know she was in great physical shape, a good candidate despite her marital nonstatus.

"That's good." He nodded in a very friendly, professional way.

That wasn't good. She wanted him to get personal. She wanted him to feel the fire. She wanted him the way he was last night. Only not in the tree. She wanted him on the balcony with her. Under her sheet, not looking at her in the sheet.

With a lot of discipline, Cara, who didn't want to look anywhere else except at him, made herself drag her gaze away from Rex Noble and look around the lobby again—not a great view after Rex. She didn't want to think about these old guys as possible father material for her unborn—unmade—child. If her donor were one of the old guys, she might want her eggs cooked after all, just to be safe.

Rex was so colorful in his red plaid shirt, the sleeves folded above his elbows, his faded blue jeans, his beautiful blue eyes and his dark brown hair. By contrast the lobby area could only be described as sterile with its dove-gray tile and grout. The walls were gray, too, and blended so well with the tile that she would be hard pressed to tell where the floor ended and the walls began.

Hanging on the walls, where she would have expected to see paintings of pregnant women or mothers nursing their babies or even bouncing babies on mothers' laps, anything to indicate the success of the Noble Sperm Bank—instead she saw oil paintings of cattle.

The paintings were lovely. She could never dispute that they weren't. Cows nursing calves, others of big bulls similar to the one on the billboard that Cara had driven over to see that morning. And what a bull that was!

The old men were now sitting together in the middle of the lobby. When she arrived at the clinic, they'd been seated exactly two chairs apart from each other and each sat beneath a picture of a bull, not a cow.

"They're fixtures," Rex said, nodding toward the men.

And yet not quite fixed. Cara slowly moved her gaze back to him. "Are they here all the time?"

"Every day."

"Don't they work?"

"They work at being here."

Everything was so different in Texas. Or maybe it was just Pegleg. Maybe the cow pictures were part of a subliminal message to women because cows produced milk and milk and babies went together. As for the bull pictures…well, every man would want to be built like a bull, especially like the one on the billboard. So the pictures must symbolize fertility. And fertility was the name of the business after all.

"Take the application with you, and you can fill it out in a private room." He smiled at her, that killer smile. "You can ask me anything you want, I'll do my best to answer everything."

Once they were in a private room, how could she possibly pour out her hopes and dreams to this man? He was all mixed up inside her. She wanted him, she wanted his vital bodily fluids, but she also felt an urgent need to kiss him senseless and have her way with him. Correction, he wasn't mixed up. She was.

The bottom line, though, was that she wanted a baby, and how could a man, even a doctor, understand the depth of her longing for a child? She must have had this longing for years but had suppressed it, she realized. The whole idea started to take form and come alive when she saw the billboards and realized there might be a possibility of doing this without marriage.

"This is a very difficult decision," she told him.

"I'm here to help with anything I can," he said. "I know this business like I know the south forty."

She didn't know what he meant by the south forty, but when he said he would help any way he could, she immediately thought a cupful of the doctor would be the best possible thing he could do to help. She'd even be willing to help with the collecting. The thought of the collecting process, her touching him, bringing him to point that he spilled over with joy made her throat dry up, her skin feel clammy. It made tiny tingles zigzag right through her.

Meanwhile, the old men in the lobby were all holding their cups kind of outstretched, looking expectantly at her. No, that would be totally out of the question. She wasn't an equal-opportunity collection processor.

The doctor was grinning. Oh, that grin of his. She wanted to melt her lips right on top of it. "I have a lot of questions. My not being married might make the semen process unattainable."

He looked puzzled. "I can't imagine why," he said slowly, gazing at her with a thoughtful look on his face. "I don't have a problem with it. Not at all."

"She wants your semen, Doc. Quit talkin' so much and go give it to her. Then take the lady out to eat so you won't have to be climbin' trees."

"Don't take the first male you see," Barbara added, pointing out to the lobby. "Choose carefully."

It looked as if she was pointing to the pictures, but she couldn't be. She had to be pointing to the men.

Clyde scraped his chair forward, too, holding out his cup, positively beaming. "You betcha she does. We've got the best. Which one do you think she'll take?"

"There's a lot of choices," Jasper said.

Cara glared at Rex. "I thought you said they were hard-of-hearing," she hissed.

"They are. They just get excited at the thought of a sale."

"You're not funny." Cara's hands were clenched so tight the knuckles turned white. She shook, not from fear but from anger. "I have been open with you and they're making fun of me."

"Cara." He did something totally unprofessional, and something she desperately craved. He wrapped both arms around her, and she almost sank her breasts into his chest. She needed to get that close, or closer. "That's what we're here for. To provide semen. That's our business." His voice was soothing, a typical doctor voice talking to a distraught patient.

"Those old men?"

"An integral part of the business."

"That's disgusting." She pushed out of his arms. "Exploiting old men like that. They need to be retired from service. The products they produce can't possibly be as healthy as young ones."

"Money is money," Rex argued, "and they have every right to participate, every right to make a profit. Or don't you believe in free enterprise?"

"You're being patronizing again."

"No, I'm not. Come on, let's go into the conference room, I'll explain the process, and you can ask me as a many questions as you want."

She nodded. She had nothing to lose. Staring back at the lobby, she doubted right now, with those as her choices, she'd gain a lot either.

"I understand. I want to help you any way I can. I want to make it an enjoyable experience. One you'll remember always. Since this is your first time, it should be all the more special." He draped an arm around her shoulders and looked back at the lobby. "We're going to talk about her options," he threw back to the men. "In private."

"You don't know how hard this whole thing is for me. To have come to this decision to use artificial insemination. It's not an easy decision to make," she told him as they walked down a long hallway toward his office.

"People use this method for all kinds of reasons. It shouldn't be a hard decision to make, though. We do provide the best product."

"Are you sure?" she asked, turning her head to glance again at the men in the lobby. Okay, maybe he was just as delusional about his business as her mother was about the business of getting a daughter married. It was possible. More's the pity.

He stopped in front of a closed door. The wall was

glass, and inside she could see a long wood conference table with at least twelve big leather chairs surrounding it.

Rex opened the door, stretching out his arm, holding it open for her. He stood so tall, with shoulders the size of ten football fields and tanned, muscular, pumped-up biceps that were so steely-looking they seemed to call out to her to touch them, feel them, have them wrap his arms around her and protect her for life.

For life. That could only mean marriage. That's not what she wanted. She wanted a baby and that was it. She knew she'd consider having it the old-fashioned way if he'd agree. They could have fun. It could be a noncommitment kind of thing. What was the difference anyway, whether it was shot through some kind of injector, or whether he personally injected her. She sighed, and he asked what was wrong.

"Nothing," she said. "Just thinking. Big step, that's all."

He nodded. Two long, thick fingers, gently rough, grazed under her chin as he applied gentle pressure to lift her face so she could gaze into his eyes. "I'm sure it is, Cara. I know there are breeders who feel the begetting and the begotting should only be done one way, the old-fashioned way, whether you're talking cattle or humans. But sometimes the old-fashioned way doesn't work, and that's where the Noble Sperm Bank Association comes in. We provide the service when nature, for whatever reason, doesn't."

Not that she didn't love the feel of his fingers on her chin, not that she didn't find gazing into his eyes a dizzying experience, but what went through her head was, "Why is he talking about cattle?"

Suddenly she knew. The evidence ticked by like a movie in her head. The bull and cow billboards. The ancient cowboys in the lobby sitting under pictures of bulls. The magazine *Proliferation.*

She whispered, "May I look at pictures of your donors?"

He gave a soft, sexy chuckle. "Now, if that isn't just like a woman. She wants to see what they look like, not the stats." He turned away from her, went to a bookshelf and pulled a huge, leather-bound volume out. "Here they are, but I'm going to cut to the chase. The donor you want is LuLu."

"Lulu?" Cara felt she was seriously in danger of fainting.

With a flourish, Rex flipped the book open and gestured toward the picture on the page. There he was, Rex's prize donor, bigger than life in every sense of the word.

"That *is* a bull," Cara said. "I've made a terrible mistake."

8

CARA KNEW she was in a situation of her own making. It wasn't as if Dr. Rex Noble had been hiding what it was his company did or the services he provided. The cow and bull billboards right there on the freeway had stated in no uncertain terms exactly what their services were, for heaven's sake. She felt so foolish. She was a gullible dreamer who had seen only what she wanted to see and had missed the obvious.

Now she could only hope her facial expression said, *Bull sperm is exactly the kind of sperm I've been looking for all my life.* But gazing at the beauty of his face only rammed home the intensity of what it was she really wanted. And this wasn't the place she'd get *that*.

She wished he were ugly. Then she wouldn't care what he thought about her and her mix-up. Instead, he was to die for. And she had a funny feeling he knew it. He could have sold not only sperm but anything he wanted to sell with those chiseled features of his.

As far as Cara was concerned, he could have been selling cat food with recipes on how to cook it. She'd have been right there in line to buy enough cans to fill her basket, and she'd not only cook it, she'd eat it with a smile. All Rex would have had to say was, "Ooh, this is good, baby, give it a try."

When she'd walked through the door, she'd thought she'd be able to go to a picture book and find some man who had the looks and personality that she liked and that she'd want to pass on to her child. And she had, but his sperm wasn't for sale. That meant she would have to win it honestly.

How? First, by assuring him she wasn't the flake that she no doubt appeared to be.

"Here's what I had in mind," she said, and paused for inspiration.

"Yes?"

Rex. Great name. Rhymed with sex. She let out a breath and wished she could start peeling off her clothes, she was that hot. When she tried to speak, it came out as a squeak, so she cleared her throat and tried again. This time it was a little better. "I really like it in Pegleg. I've visited here before, you know."

"No, I didn't."

"I came several months ago to see Tony. And Kate. Both of them."

"Tony's quite a guy." He held up a Donetti's Irish Pub and Sushi Bar matchbook for her to see. "Kate, too. Even if they did keep your name a secret."

"That's what friends are for." She smiled at him, and her brain finally leaped into action.

Her smile nearly made Rex start unbuckling his belt, but that would have been jumping the gun. Cara was coming on to him, which was fine. It wasn't as if he hadn't been coming on to her from the moment he climbed the tree. He was glad she found him attractive. He returned her smile. "Friends that are loyal. Loyalty means a lot."

"They're great," she practically gushed, leaning forward, allowing him to see the plump tops of pink breasts. He had seen more last night, but last night she wasn't aware of what she had revealed. Right now, she was showing her assets on purpose, and he liked that. Liked it a lot.

Man, she was pretty. She had scooted a little closer

to the conference table. He followed suit, leaning over, coming a little closer to her, too. He could breathe in her soft, spicy floral perfume, something he hadn't smelled on any other woman before. Made him want to put his lips along the silky skin of her neck and inhale her sweet scent.

As fast as his common sense had left him, it returned. He leaned back in his chair and away from her magical spell. She looked a little confused, as if it took her a minute to register that he wasn't falling for her charms. Only she'd be wrong. He had fallen for her, head over heels, the moment he'd stood up in front of Mama Jo's covered in chicken and seen her standing there. He was afraid that he'd rip off her clothes and take her on the conference table. That wasn't the way he wanted it to be. He wanted to get to know her, to win her over with his personality and charm. But she didn't know it yet. He watched her expressions go from flirtatious to confused, to what he thought looked like hurt. He didn't want her hurting.

She slowly pulled away from the table, leaving nothing behind but that spicy scent, and settled back into her own chair, ramrod straight.

"I haven't eaten at Tony's restaurant yet," she said, her voice low and husky, "but I'm told the food is wonderful. He raises the beef himself, feeds it some kind of special food he mixes himself."

"I know all about it. Who do you think gave him his first cow and bull to breed?"

"You?"

"Yes. He breeds Angus. My LuLu is a Galloway. Those are pictures of Galloways out in the lobby."

"I had a baby rabbit that had the same markings."

"They're something. Look around the room here. The result of fine breeding and championship stock."

"They're amazing." She glanced at the wall to her

left. Hung from chair-rail height to the ceiling were blue ribbons, trophies, plaques and a pair of stuffed bull's balls. She turned away when she realized what they were, her face heating. Maybe she wasn't as sophisticated as she had thought. "I'm impressed."

"It's a top honor," Rex said, the pride in his voice as large as the bull's stuffed organs.

"I think I was talking about the trophies."

Rex glanced at the trophy in question. "That's what I was talking about, too."

Okay, so they both were lying. What else was new? She fanned the corner of the catalog. "I'd like one, you know."

"A bull?"

"I was thinking of a sweet little cow. Like the one on the milk cartons. Or on your billboard. That's why I'm here." She leaned forward again, but this time it looked natural, as if she was really excited about her plan, although the pose still gave him a mind-boggling view of her breasts. "I'd like to pick out a really nice cow, then inseminate her with sperm from your prize bull—" She hesitated.

"LuLu," he prompted her.

"LuLu. And then my cow would have her own beautiful little calf." The woman's eyes actually went all misty.

Rex blinked. This cock-and-bull—or cow-and-bull—story sounded pretty fishy to him. "Where would you put it?"

"On my farm. I want to buy a farm like Tony's, only smaller, I mean really, really smaller." For a second, Rex could glimpse a bit of worry mixed in with her enthusiasm.

"We call Tony's *farm* a ranch," he said.

She tilted her head slightly. "I thought a ranch was for horses."

"Cattle, too. At least here in Texas. And I'm guessing, and it's only a guess, mind you, in Pennsylvania, too.''

Her lower lip stuck out a little. ''You're making fun of me, aren't you?''

''Now, why would I do that?''

''Because I'm from the city and don't know a farm from a ranch, so you think I'm dumb.'' She sniffed.

''That's not true.'' Again he moved forward, the table edge cutting into his ribs. He wanted to feel closer to her, he liked being close to her, and for the first time, it scared him. He felt almost out of control when it came to her, and he had from the moment he saw her. Otherwise he never would have been climbing trees. Sure, she was beautiful. She had skin the color of peaches, and hair that looked like silk. Her fingernails were long and tapered, her hands smooth. ''I'm not making fun of you. Teasing maybe, but never making fun.''

''Thank you,'' she said softly, lowering her gaze, staring at his extended arms, his hands only an inch away from hers. Her fingers stretched out, the tips a fraction of a space from his. And just as quickly, she balled them into fists and moved them away from him.

That was good, he thought, because if something like the perfume she wore, which was so faint that he could barely smell it, was strong enough to entice him and make him want to nuzzle her neck, sink his lips into that soft skin, he needed to know he was having an equally strong effect on her.

He watched her brown eyes, already big, widen even more. Her lips parted, her tongue peeked out, then outlined them, leaving a moist trail behind. He raised his hand, then stopped himself when he realized he had been about to follow where that tongue had been. *Fool,* he called himself. *Idiot.* He didn't know her really, not yet.

But boy, did he want to touch those lips of hers.

He tossed Donetti's matchbook across the table, where it slid off the opposite end, landing on the carpet below. He put his wayward hand under his thigh, rendering it useless against what his male instinct was urging him to do. He had to settle for a knee that was rubbing against her knee. Lucky knee. "Believe you me," he said, "it never occurred to me you were dumb."

"Well, good." Her body relaxed and her shoulders lifted. She gathered that hair, that thick, glossy hair, and threw the whole mass behind her, where it landed over the back of the chair like a waterfall. He'd never seen hair like hers before and he had a longing to dig his fingers right through it. Last night hadn't been enough. He needed more. Much more. For the life of him he didn't know why.

"I'm not dumb. I'm a schoolteacher."

"Really." He didn't care what she did for a living. All he could think about right now was the difference between hair that had been shampooed and left alone versus hair that had been teased and lacquered with maximum-hold hair spray.

"I really liked Pegleg when I first visited. Then when I went home to Erie, all I could think about was how much I wanted to get back here and visit again."

"I'm glad you wanted to come back," he said.

"Me, too. But what struck me most," she said softly, looking at him all innocent-like underneath those long thick eyelashes she had, "was how cute the cows were."

He stopped himself from laughing. He cleared his throat and hoped he looked serious. "Cute?"

"Just absolutely precious," she gushed. "And I tried and tried to figure out a way—a reason to come back and stay in Pegleg, at least for the summers— and finally it dawned on me."

"You did?" he asked. "It did?" She was confusing him.

"Cows." She lifted her shoulders and brought them back down with a beautiful sigh, as if that one word, *cows,* explained it all. It explained nothing.

She must have sensed his skepticism, because she said, "It's the Erie winters," as if he should have known that. "They're positively wicked."

He'd never been farther east than Chicago, and that had been in the spring, but he agreed with her. "Snow and ice." Even he knew that. It had snowed in Pegleg, oh, about twenty years ago. A momentous event. It had to have been if he still remembered.

She looked at him as if she expected more. More of what, he didn't know. But he tried. "That white stuff."

"Absolutely." She glowed. "More than you can possibly imagine. So I thought and thought."

"You did all that thinking. During the snow?"

"During recess."

"I don't understand." She had lost him. Again.

"You know, when the kids go outside and play. Only they couldn't because of the snow. So we tried to think of summertime games, and we came up with the cow game."

In his mind, the only game Cara was serving up was a mass of confusion. "What's the cow game?"

"Moo-moo."

"Am I supposed to know this?"

She at least had the decency to blush. "No. It's like Go Fish, only instead of saying 'go fish,' they say, 'moo-moo.' It's a lot more fun."

"What does this go-fish-moo-moo have to do with cows and bulls?"

Now she was looking at him as if he were dense. "It made me long for Pegleg and to have my own cow."

"Of course." He grabbed her knee and squeezed. "I shoulda known."

Even though he heard her breath catch when he touched her, and that gave him a bit of satisfaction if he did say so himself, she didn't lose her train of thought. If she ever even had one in the first place.

"But then I thought..." She went on without skipping so much as a beat, although she did place her hand on his, which made him catch his breath. She took it away, too quickly in his mind. "...what could I possibly do on a teacher's salary that would let me stay in Pegleg, at least during the summer?"

"Why summer?"

"Because that's when I have vacation. I teach, remember?" She didn't sound exactly exasperated, but she definitely was talking to him as if he had less than a full set of brain cells.

"Are you saying you're not going to live here the rest of the year?"

"I'm from Erie."

"People move from where they're from all the time. What does that have to do with anything?"

"I have a job. I have responsibilities." She paused. "My parents are there. Remember, my mother?" She lowered her voice, "She is going to have a cow, no pun intended, of course."

Understanding almost dawned on him. "Of course. But it was bad, you know."

"The pun or my mother?"

"Both, but I'm talking about your mother."

"You can't imagine."

"Your mother has driven you to raising cattle."

"One cow," she corrected him. "Plus one calf. So—" She leaned forward again. "So, can you help me? Because—"

Ted's voice scratched through the intercom. "Your one o'clock is here."

"Ask him to wait. Offer him a drink. I'll be there soon." He wasn't anywhere near finished with Cara. "Go on." He nodded at her.

"Because I can't do it without your services. See—" and she gazed at him so earnestly he couldn't help but believe her "—I can't afford to buy and feed both a bull and a cow."

"No?"

"Oh, no, and certainly not for the length of time it might take them to do the natural thing." Her cheeks turned a pretty shade of pink. "So I'm only going to buy a cow." She sounded triumphant. "And if you supply the sperm—" she whispered the word *sperm* "—then everything will be perfect."

"The *semen*, you mean. Get the term right." He followed her example and whispered the word *semen*, too. "If I supply the semen, then eventually you'll have two cows anyway."

"But mama cow feeds baby cow, and I'll be saving all my money to feed the baby when she gets older and needs to eat that special formula that Tony makes."

"That will be great. The cow will like that."

"Still," she said, "I have to search the area for some land. Some pretty land with trees and flowers, and maybe a little cottage in the middle. Maybe with a stream. And ducks and chipmunks."

"I don't recall any chipmunks around here. Squirrels, maybe."

She waved a hand. A very lovely hand. "No matter. Chipmunks, squirrels…doesn't matter. They're both cute little rodents."

"That's true." The lady might be a schoolmarm, might even be very smart, but she was putting on a show for him. He didn't know why—he didn't care. He was enjoying her show as much as if he were down at the Alley Theater watching a play onstage.

He was going to go along with her, see how far she took it. He hoped she'd stay all day. He'd work around his other appointments. He didn't want her, or the show, to end. "They also carry rabies," he said very seriously.

"I wasn't going to play with them," she said all huffy.

"Of course not." He knew she didn't believe what she was saying, but her imagination was incredible.

He took moment to reflect upon Cara's arrival in Pegleg. First, she'd dumped chicken wings on him. She couldn't have known him then, but when she sashayed away, swaying her butt, he knew she was making sure she'd gotten his attention. Which she had. Very, very much so. Then she'd sworn Rosey, Kate and Tony to secrecy about her name and location, and now he knew why!

Because she must have wanted to see him again. She had to know that all the mystery would have him going after her, and she'd been right. He hadn't counted on the chemistry. And there was one sizzling glass of chemicals between them waiting impatiently to boil over.

The whole story she'd woven about wanting to raise a cow in the summer was as artificial as that sugar-free powder stuff they put into coffee to cut calories. But now he knew why. She was weaving the tallest tale he'd ever heard because she wanted something out of him. Something that she hadn't wanted last night, that must have dawned on her this morning.

For a moment his eyes narrowed, but then he relaxed a little and smiled. She probably wanted to trap him into marriage, because that's what all women wanted, wasn't it? His claim to singlehood last night must have given her a challenge. She had given herself away when she told him about her mother and the push to get married. So she couldn't find a guy in Erie, and had come to Texas to look.

It wasn't the first time someone had tried to marry Rex off, and it wouldn't be the last. The only reason he didn't call her on her game was that he enjoyed being with her. He was attracted to her.

Marriage, no. But sex with her? That was a definite sure thing.

Now that he'd wised up and established control over himself and the situation, he crossed his arms over his chest and let her go on weaving.

And weave Cara did. "And I will take my cow and let her live on that piece of land, all by herself. She won't have to share with anyone else. Until she has her baby."

"What about the cottage?"

"That's for me."

"Isn't that sharing the land?"

"Hmm." Her eyebrows rose, her forehead creased in concentration. "You're right. I hadn't thought of that."

"Cows are social creatures. It would get lonely without another cow to talk to."

"Are you making fun of me again?"

"No," he quickly denied. She was so easy. "I never made fun of you before, either. Remember?"

She seemed to weigh his protestations and rule in his favor, because she didn't get up and leave. "I hadn't thought of all that...." Her voice trailed off. "I kind of like the idea of having a cow as a pet. Can they be trained? Like a dog?"

"I doubt it." He answered her question very seriously. What he doubted was that she was serious at all.

She had been fiddling with her hair, and now some of the silky strands had swung back over her shoulder and were hiding her breasts. She tossed them back. A sight to behold. Her hair, that is, not her breasts. He wasn't looking at them at all. He wasn't noticing how rounded and soft they looked. He wasn't paying any attention to the way her nipples tightened when the air conditioner came on and the cold blast of air blew from the outlet in the ceiling and rained on top of her. Nope, he wasn't paying a bit of attention to any of that.

"This is what I'm going to do— Rex? Rex?"

"What?" He moved his gaze to her face and almost had the grace to be embarrassed for getting caught. Almost, but not quite.

"Were you listening?" He could tell she knew he hadn't been.

"Of course, you're doing something."

She looked at him in a slanty kind of way, as if she had caught him in the act of doing something bad and she wanted to send him to the principal. Which, of course, she had. But she kept on talking, so he got a reprieve. "First I'm going to scope out the area around here, and search for a perfect piece of land to put my new little—"

"Cows are big."

"—big cow on. It will be a perfectly lovely piece of land. She will be able to roam freely, and have her baby, and it will be a heavenly place for her." Cara let out a big, deep breath. She couldn't believe that she was telling him this story.

Lying was one of those things she had never done before. But she was doing it pretty substantially at the moment. Funny thing was, just like the baby she wanted, this plan sounded good to her, too. Living in the country in a little cottage, a cow roaming the land, mooing for her breakfast, depending on her for sustenance and love. Maybe the whole thing wasn't out of the realm of possibility. She'd get a job teaching at Pegleg Elementary School, if they had one. The

thought terrified her for a split second. Actually it
wasn't that thought, it was the thought of telling her
mother she was moving away from Erie. But since
the idea was only a daydream at this point, why waste
time being terrified? Besides, if she wanted to do this
badly enough, she could probably swing it.

A cow on the outside, her own baby on the inside,
in the country, in Texas, at least for the summers and
maybe even—

"Have you looked at land?"

Men had the most irritating practical streaks.
Couldn't he see she was busy daydreaming? She
shook her head.

"Do you know anything about artificial insemination? Raising cattle?"

Again she shook her head. "But I would love for
you to show me everything, from how you get it, to
how you implant it, to where you keep it. Just everything."

"You want me to show you everything?" He lowered his voice, and she knew it was another one of
his flirty come-ons. He could see right through her.
For some reason, that didn't even bother her. Not one
bit. Although she had the decency to be ashamed of
herself. Almost.

Wait. She was a schoolteacher, living on a schoolteacher's salary. Plus, she had a mother who would
make short work of a daydream involving a cow, calf,
ranch, cottage. As quickly as she'd invented it, the
daydream crashed and burned. As much as she'd love
to live the life she'd just described, it was unrealistic.
She stood up and held out her hand in a gesture that
meant he should hold out his and they should shake.
Only he didn't hold out his hand, so with coins clank-
ing, she dropped hers to her waist.

"Where are you going?" he asked.

"I just realized this idea I have is totally unrealistic." She stared at her toes. "I don't know what I was thinking. There's no way I can do this on my salary. And it would hurt my mother if I moved away."

"There might be a way. How's five o'clock?"

"I don't understand."

"I'll pick you up at five. I'll show you around. Introduce you to LuLu. The prize. Then you can decide if your idea is unrealistic."

She had a date. She couldn't believe it. He had asked her out, and there wasn't any mother intervention involved. She gazed at him, feeling as if she'd slid back into her dream. "All right, then. I'll be ready."

"Do you want me to come through the downstairs lobby, or should I climb the tree to get you?"

"If you climb the tree, I doubt you'll be going down to the lobby anytime soon after that."

He grinned. Really big. She liked that grin, especially when it was directed at her.

She had almost confessed to thinking the Noble Sperm Bank was for humans and not cattle. She had been ready to tell him about her desire to have a baby, not a calf, not a cow, not a bull and not a husband, almost...but she hadn't.

Suddenly it dawned on her, instinct had made her keep her mouth shut. She wanted him, that was a basic need. She wanted a baby, that was a desire so great it almost hurt.

And here he was, offering to climb a tree and visit her in her room, which even if she didn't want a baby, she would have gladly accepted from him.

It all made such sense. It was a no-brainer. Sperm. Semen. Fresh from the source. No plastic cups required.

9

CARA LEFT the clinic feeling excited in more ways than one. She'd get to meet LuLu, the father of her unborn child. Um, calf. Rex was so excited about showing her LuLu, she didn't have the heart to tell him there weren't going to be any unborn calves.

Anyway, she wanted to see the bull. She wanted to see the ranch. And more than anything else, she wanted to be with Rex.

She had a little bit of a problem though. What did a woman wear to meet a bull or look at cows? Or shop for land, for that matter? The closest she had ever come to a cow was reading *Mazy the Lazy Cow* to her kindergarten class. Cows had never been a part of her life.

While Cara didn't consider herself to be a snob or an affected sort of female, she didn't think of herself as unsophisticated either. She might not have traveled the world, but she had been to places in the United States people from all over the world came to visit. Places like New York, Washington, D.C., Chicago, Los Angeles and Rochester, Minnesota. Not that Rochester was a great tourist site, but it did have the Mayo Clinic. And the greatest place of all, Green Bay, Wisconsin, home of the best football team in the world, the Green Bay Packers.

So while she didn't consider herself a person who had seen the world, she felt she was a person who had seen a good portion of her own country. She could carry on a conversation about almost anything. She felt so sure of herself right now, so confident in so many ways, that she knew she could mix in with any person from any walk of life. So why was she having this attack of inadequacy about meeting a bull?

Or was it an attack of inadequacy about going out with Rex?

Whatever it was, there was only one cure for it. Cara headed straight for the mall. She had never been much of a shopper. In Erie, her schoolteacher wardrobe had been fine, and very bland and boring. In Pegleg, at the mall, a whole new world opened up to her.

Victoria's Secret and three-for-ten-dollars thong underwear was the perfect place to start. Decadently wonderful.

She passed by the conservative slacks without a backward glance. Low-slung hip huggers, the kind whose waistband barely covered her bottom and didn't come close to reaching her belly button—that's what she tried on instead, and with a very large gulp, purchased. Her new top skimmed down to almost, but not quite, meet the jeans. A straw purse, slip-on sandals with a cork platform and a very large-brimmed hat with pretty flowers sewn into the band finished off her new outfit. Of course, it also reduced her baby-cow-semen, land-cottage-dog fund by a little bit, but it wasn't as if she really intended to have all those things. Just the baby. And if she really got her courage up, she might get the human semen free.

She wasn't sure about the reaction her new clothes would have on Rex, but for herself, she felt suddenly empowered. If her mother saw her, she'd kill her, which made her feel extremely guilty, but oh, so good.

Cara took everything back to Mandelay. She showered, put her new clothes on, then went back to the mirror and turned to see herself as someone else would see her—namely Rex. She wanted to know if she felt the same way wearing her new clothes as she had while trying them on.

The reflection staring back at her didn't look like the same Cara who had left Erie only a few days before. Now her skin glowed. Her brown eyes had a sparkle in them. Her cheeks were bright and there was a smile on her face that she couldn't possibly wipe off. Even if she wanted to, which she didn't.

She touched the necklace. The bracelet rattled. Her knuckles grazed the bottom of an earring. The jewelry was a dilemma she would have to deal with. When she wore all the coins, she felt as if she had so much luck. As if her decisions were all right. Her confidence level high.

Then she saw something that did wipe that giddy smile off her face. She stared at her bracelet, then brought it up close to her eyes to be sure she was really seeing what she thought she saw. More coins were missing. One empty gold bracket was twisted open as if someone had taken a pair of needle-nosed pliers to it.

She must have snagged it on something. But when?

It wasn't just the loss of another coin. It was the loss of one tiny bit of the luck she was sure came her way when she wore all the jewelry at once.

Luck. How silly. Still, she believed in luck. There was so much she could control in her life. She could shop for clothes in Texas and buy what she really wanted. She could answer questions about the Green Bay Packers, tourist sights to see while traveling in the United States and anything at all about teaching little boys and girls. She felt confident about all these things.

Where her problems cropped up was in the area she had little or no expertise. Romance. That was another matter altogether. Sure, she had dated, a lot. She had been around, a little. But she still had no idea how to make a man see her as the one and only lady to want forever. Or even to lust after for an hour.

Now that she knew she wanted Rex to donate sperm to make her a baby, she had to figure out a way to make it happen. The attraction between them was undeniable. She didn't think the sex part would be any problem. And if she should get pregnant, well… After all he'd said about not wanting to get married, and since she didn't either, she doubted her being pregnant would present much of a problem to him. Just thinking about doing it the old-fashioned way, with him deep inside her, made her knees go weak and her stomach burst with bombing butterflies.

His baby. Her baby. Their baby. A real cowboy baby.

She'd use her feminine wiles to convince him. If she had any to use. She carefully outlined her lips with a ruby pencil and filled in the color with her Red-Hot Mama lipstick. She puckered up for the mirror, leaving her eyes wide open. Her lips puckered didn't look all that bad, but not extremely sexy either. Certainly not like the puckered lips on the models in lipstick commercials.

Maybe if she sucked in her cheeks and puckered. No, all that did was make her eyes bulge out and a strange vacuuming sound come out of her mouth. Of course, in a real situation they would both have their eyes closed and be so caught up in passion Rex wouldn't notice the vacuuming sound.

For the first time in her life she wished she knew how to do the sexy kind of flirting that led up to the passionate kind of romance. Or even knew how to make her lips pucker better.

She picked up the phone, punched zero for the front desk, although there really wasn't a front desk at Mandelay, just Rosey, so it wasn't surprising that Rosey answered. "Do you know how to make lips fuller?" she asked her.

Rosey must have been busy doing something, because she didn't answer for a while. Then she said, "Ah." And then, "Well, I've heard hemorrhoid salve would do it. I don't think I have any around here," she added delicately, "but if it's important to you…"

"No, no, just curious," Cara mumbled and was about to hang up when Rosey added, "But I was about to call you. Rex is here."

Those simple words, "Rex is here," drove all rational thoughts out of her head. She had to tell herself that the right foot went first, then the left, and march two-three-four.

Before she left her room, she had the good sense to take one last look in the mirror. The lipstick was still on and still bright red. After a brief sweep with the brush, her hair looked wild. She had to forcibly stop herself from tying it back into its old ponytail. A tug on her top, a check on her posture, deep breath, smile on face, okay, she was ready to go. Missing some lucky coins, but ready. She placed the hat on her head, grabbed her new purse and headed to the lobby.

REX WAS HOLDING UP a wall and talking to Rosey. "Hey," he said, "when a guest needs something for hemorrhoids, he needs it bad. Cara and I could run up to the store first and bring some back before we—"

"No, no," Rosey said. She had a funny sparkle in her eyes, Rex thought, for an innkeeper with a guest in pain. "It's not, I mean, she'll be, ah, he'll be…"

She babbled on for a few seconds, but then Rosey had always been inclined to babble, and he was just killing time anyway, waiting for his first glimpse of Cara.

And he got it. The first thing he glimpsed were her toes.

Toenails polished a bright red, slender feet slipped into sandals she'd be sorry she'd worn when they headed to the field but that he was mighty glad she had on now. Her stomach came into view next. Flat, her belly button a perfect inny. She wore a white crop top. The collar reached her neck, her necklace bright on top of the white material. The lower part of the shirt barely covered her breasts, and he wasn't even sure they were covered. He could swear he saw a fleshy curve peeking behind the material. If that wasn't a breast, then his body had a very male reaction for no good reason.

She made her way slowly down the stairs. He could tell she was balancing carefully on those shoes, those ridiculous sexy shoes. The shoes were the kind that made him want to grab hold of her legs, fling off the shoes, then suck on those red-painted toes.

"Hi," he said.

"Hi," she said.

He took her by the arm. "Bye." She waved back at Rosey. He walked her out the door, then, having a feeling he'd forgotten something, stuck his head back in.

"Bye," he said to Rosey. She wiggled her fingers at him. She seemed to be laughing. That didn't make any sense whatsoever. Laughing at what? Women.

"You look nice," Rex said.

"I hope I'm dressed okay for meeting LuLu."

"Perfect."

"Because I really didn't know what to wear. I mean, this is sort of like meeting your father-in-law for the first time. I want to make a good impression."

"And then we'll drive around, and I'll show you some property near my ranch that's pretty reasonable."

"What's reasonable to you may not be to me."

"I'm the owner. It'll be reasonable."

She was liking him more and more. He was making everything so easy for her. But it wasn't meant to be, and she'd have to tell him she wasn't buying land or cows. Now would be a good time.

"And on the way we can look at some of the cows and calves. You can see what you're getting into."

Maybe later would be better. She had time.

She smoothed down her already flat belly, which made his own tie into a strong knot of red-hot desire.

"You couldn't have picked anything more appropriate," he complimented her again. She looked as if she were going to a chi-chi luncheon downtown. Not that he was complaining. Not at all. She could expose herself to LuLu anytime she wanted. As long as he was invited to tag along.

He opened the door to the truck, took her arm and guided her in. It was a big step up, and it was as if God himself had answered a prayer when her sandal slipped off, exposing a bare foot. He picked up the shoe. It looked heavier than it was, with its cork platform and thin strip of tan leather across the top. He figured it couldn't weigh more than an ounce. Instead of handing the sandal to her, he circled her ankle—a very slender one at that—and placed the shoe back where it belonged. The need to suck her toes slammed into him again. He ignored the need and slammed the truck door instead.

He headed back toward the clinic and his ranch, which was all part of the same five hundred acres he owned. All along the route he pointed out land that was for sale. "But I don't own that land," he said. She nodded her head, the smile never leaving her face.

"Do you want to take notes?" he asked.

"I'm still weighing my options."

"This would be a nice place to buy."

"I thought you wanted me to look at your land."

"I'm talking about Pegleg." He couldn't believe he had said that. He didn't know if he wanted her to move here. Not yet. Too soon.

"I can't move here permanently. It would only be for vacations and summer."

However, he didn't want her to tell him it wasn't a possibility. He had no choice but to argue. "Why wouldn't you want to move here? Permanently, I mean." Not that her moving here made any difference to him. But the very idea that a person wouldn't want to live in Texas, and Pegleg in particular, seemed a bit odd to him. "After all," he said. "This is Pegleg."

"I'm from Erie." She laughed at him, which didn't sit well. Not well at all. First Rosey and now Cara. What was with females lately?

"Don't you get it?" he asked. "Erie doesn't have a thing on Pegleg."

"Have you ever been to Erie?"

"I don't have to have been there. You're not looking to buy semen from an Erie sperm bank are you?"

"No. But until I saw your billboards, I hadn't intended to buy semen at all."

"I thought you told me you had intended to raise a cow."

She looked out the window. "I did say that, and that's right, I did intend to buy a cow."

"The billboards sold you?" That wasn't good. He didn't want the billboards to sell anything. He didn't want Clay to be right.

"Oh, yes, it did." She sighed, crossing her arms over her chest, pushing her breasts upward and outward.

He could see her nipples under the white cloth, pointed, erect. Not that he was looking, because he wasn't. Much.

Cara said, "As soon as I saw the bull and the cow, I knew I had to have some."

"Some?"

She looked almost embarrassed. Her voice became soft, thoughtful. "A baby. To raise."

"A calf, you mean?" These city women. They had so much to learn.

"Of course that's what I mean." She had this faraway look.

"I told my marketing man to take those billboards down."

"I don't know why. They certainly got my attention."

"But it's not the image I want to project."

"What image is that?"

"One of a serious business venture. Not something like two lovesick cattle looking at each other across the freeway as if they can't wait to get at it." He glanced at her. "I don't mean any offense, Cara."

"I'm not taking offense. But they're so cute."

He liked the sappy look on her face, but it didn't change his mind. "The billboards are coming down. Next week."

"I'm glad I saw them when I did, then, because if this week had been next week, I never would have known to contact you and I never would have met you."

"Are you glad you met me?"

She looked at him. Not that he could see her looking, but he could feel her looking, and when he glanced her way, his feelings were confirmed. She definitely was looking.

"I haven't decided if I'm glad I met you or not." She got all prim and proper, in direct contrast to her perky nipples and luscious-looking breasts that he could almost but not quite see through the short shirt. Not that he was looking.

Her answer had not been the answer he had expected. Not the one he had been looking for. He thought she'd say, "Oh, Rex, I've been looking for you all my life, you sexy thing."

"There's the clinic," she said instead.

"Yep. LuLu lives about a mile from here."

The land where he kept LuLu under lock and key, so to speak, was the kind of place Cara had described to him earlier, right down to the cottage, flowers and squirrels. He knew she'd like it, not that it mattered whether she did or not. He wanted to believe it. And he would have believed it, too, if he didn't like being with her so damn much.

"LuLu used to stay in the field behind the clinic," he said. "We decided to move the cattle once the threat of rustling started."

"Rustling?" Her eyes seemed to get bigger and her red lips went into a perfect little "oh."

"Hasn't happened here yet, but there's always a threat, especially during the livestock shows. Now semen is being stolen. Sometimes out of the storage areas, sometimes during the shipping between the breeding farms and its destination."

"That's pretty incredible. I hope they catch the culprits."

"Like I said, it hasn't happened here yet."

Rex turned into an unmarked driveway and pulled up to an electronic hitching post. He punched some numbers into a keypad and the wrought-iron gate opened to let them continue up the driveway toward the house. After going through the gate, Rex stopped the truck, waiting for the gate to close and lock behind them.

Instead of oohing and aahing over the cottage as most women he had taken here had done, Cara seemed to be watching him watch the gate lock.

"What's going on here?" she said, sounding suspicious.

"Protection."

"Do I need protection?"

"Not from me. I'm harmless," he said, and for the most part he believed it. "It's for LuLu."

She gave him a sidelong glance. "I'm not sure I believe you."

"What don't you believe?"

"That you're harmless."

"Good. Because when it comes to you, I'm not sure I will be."

Those were the most encouraging words Cara could have heard. Maybe her red lipstick and puckered pouty lips were actually working.

From the road, the cute little cottage looked like any ordinary fifty- or sixty-year-old cottage, not unlike the others they'd seen scattered here and there along the road.

Rex circled the house, then stopped the truck again to open a gate through the tall bay laurel hedge that protected the back of the property. Cara let out a gasp. The hedge wasn't the back of the property at all. It hid not only a mean-looking barbed-wire fence, but acres and acres of land that seemed to stretch out forever.

"Surprise," Rex said.

"You're telling me," Cara murmured.

The road they took now led through all those acres and was nothing more than flattened grass that wound through fields of identical grass that wasn't flattened. Behind more barbed-wire fence, cattle dozed under huge oak trees or milled around, chewing their cud and seeming to socialize.

The road didn't seem to lead to any particular destination, but instead, wound around trees, around ponds and over what she suspected passed for a hill in this flat part of Texas.

He finally stopped the truck beside a field where a lone bull stood all by himself, away from the other cattle.

Rex came around to her side of the truck, opened the door and held out his hand. She didn't think twice before placing hers inside of his. She was glad to have his help. Glad to feel his touch. And so glad she was wearing her hat. She had bought it because it was cute, different from anything she'd worn before, and it would block out the sun, which seemed even more fierce as it was setting than it had at high noon. She could hear a rumble of thunder from somewhere far away. Then a few light raindrops landed on her shoulders, but they stopped almost at once. Nothing to worry about.

"I wish I'd brought an umbrella," she said as Rex slammed the truck's door shut.

"It's not going to rain," Rex said.

"I felt a few drops."

"Humidity."

"Sure."

He laughed and took her hand. Cara didn't care if he teased her. She only knew he must never let go of her hand.

He did let her go, though. Just long enough to separate the barbed wire and let her climb between the wires and into the field. Then he took her hand again and led her up the path of doom, toward the bull. She looked down at her clothes, making sure she wasn't wearing red. "I don't know if it's a good idea to get very close to him," she said.

"He loves to meet new people."

"But I'm not from Texas."

"I won't tell if you won't."

She tightened her grip on him, and felt her fear fade away when he tightened his, too.

Even Cara, who knew nothing about four-legged creatures—the hamsters raised in her classroom during the school year being the exception—could see how majestic the bull was. He held his head proudly high, and not even his tail moved, and that surprised her because she could see the flies buzzing around him and would have thought he'd take great pleasure in swatting them away. In fact, the only reason she knew he was alive was that his eyes, big and chocolaty brown, followed her movement.

"That's a big bull," she said.

"A championship bull." Rex looked as proud as a new father who had just given birth. Himself. "Let me introduce you."

He sounded so serious. He tugged her along. Personally, she was in no hurry to get there. Not that the bull scared her, although LuLu was a very big bull. It was Rex's hand in hers. Good. Reassuring. She didn't want him to let go. Furthermore, she felt that she was the one who had to make a good impression, not LuLu. She was already impressed by LuLu. And now she was face-to-face with him. He was looking her over, and his expression was speculative.

"My, my," she said. "Let's go. It's really starting to rain and it's not humidity." It wasn't that the bull scared her. Okay, the bull terrified her. Made her want to run and hide. Despite that, it was hot outside, she could see smoke coming out of his nostrils.

She couldn't restrain a little shriek when he reached out and nuzzled her cheek, but it wasn't a kiss the bull had in mind. He was after her hat. Her new hat, and he was trying to bite it off her head! His mouth was so big—maybe the size of an Olympic-size swimming pool—that if he took the hat, he might take her whole head with it.

"Help," she said in a tiny shriek.

Rex pulled an apple out of his back pocket. Cara had no idea how it had gotten there. She hadn't noticed any bulges, at least not any along his backside.

He held out his hand, palm open, letting the bull smell the apple. LuLu, more gentle than any dog being offered a bone from the butcher, used his lips to nuzzle the apple out of Rex's hand.

"Oh, how cute," Cara said. "Just like a two-ton puppy. Now let's go."

Rex laughed. After downing the apple in one crunch, LuLu sidled back up to Cara and with his enormous snout, nuzzled her shoulder. "What does he want?"

"He's harmless, Cara. He only wants to eat your hat, not you." Rex tugged at the bull's nose ring, and the bull's snout followed. "There," he said, letting go of the ring. "Now everything's fine."

LuLu grunted disdainfully and went right back to Cara's hat. Rex frowned. This time he grabbed the nose ring and tugged LuLu a few steps away. There the bull stopped and looked back at Cara with an expression of lovesickness and longing in his big bull-eyes.

"He likes you," Rex said.

"You think?" She felt odd being liked by a bull. Being on the bull's approved list.

Now that LuLu wasn't trying to eat her hat, Cara grew more courageous. She moved her pace up a notch, moving faster to catch up with Rex and LuLu. When she got close behind the bull, Lulu stopped all forward motion. Rex, holding on to the bull's nose ring, was almost yanked off his feet by the bull's sudden stop. Not that that seemed to matter to LuLu, who raised his massive head and sniffed the air, got Cara's scent and snorted, tossing his head from side to side. Rex jumped out of the way, yelling, "Whoa, boy."

"I thought that was for a horse." Cara also took several steps to the side, out of the bull's way.

"What's for a horse?"

"Saying, 'whoa boy.'"

"It doesn't matter, horse, bull, what's the difference?"

"The difference," Cara breathlessly said as LuLu charged past her, "is that LuLu's not whoaing!"

"I told you. He wants your hat."

The rain fell faster and harder. "Well, he can't have it. I need it. It's raining." Normally she wouldn't care, but the rain was undoing the hairstyle she'd worked so hard to do. "Why does he want it, anyway? Don't you feed him enough?"

Even with the rain streaming down his face, she could see the uneasy look flicker across his face. "I feed him enough," he muttered.

"Then why does he have to eat this hat?" She stamped her foot. The puddle she'd stamped in shot water all over Rex's jeans.

"Doesn't want to eat it." He was still muttering. "He wants to, to…"

His voice faded away. "To what?"

"Wear it."

"*Wear* it?"

"See," Rex began, "LuLu isn't your usual bull. He's…he's…" The rest of the sentence was inaudible.

"Are you telling me LuLu's gay?" Cara's eyes widened.

"Shh," Rex said fiercely.

"Why should I shush? There's nobody here but you and me and LuLu."

"I just don't like people talking about it."

"Poor thing," Cara said, handing her hat over to Rex. "It must be a difficult world for a gay bull in this redneck neighborhood."

It was Rex's turn to look surprised. Silently he took the hat out of Cara's hand, poked a finger through the straw and slid the hat down one of the bull's ears. LuLu practically purred.

"You're right about that," Rex said. "He tries so hard to attract the other bulls, but it's always a no-go. Maybe with your hat—"

"Well," Cara said, "I'm glad you treat him with such kindness and understanding." She paused a moment. "Are you sure he's not just a transbullsite?"

"What are you talking about?" Rex asked.

"A male bull that wants to dress like a female cow?"

"Hey, who knows my bull better than me? I know my bull."

"I can see that. The question is…" It was really storming now. She couldn't believe she was standing out in the middle of a Texas gullywasher discussing a bull's sexual orientation.

"The answer is no," Rex said, "he won't touch any of the cows. Come on." He grabbed her hand. "Let's make a run for the truck before we drown in this rain."

"It won't be easy in these shoes."

"Take them off."

"I will not. There's yucky stuff in this field."

Rex lifted her off her feet and ran with her to the fence. She knew she was in heaven in his arms. She'd just never imagined it would be so wet and sloppy.

He put her back down to carefully separate the barbed wire fence. She climbed through the space. The back of her crop top caught on one of the barbs and tore. Rex untangled the material from the barb and she was cleared to go to the other side.

When they reached the truck, he pulled on the handle but the door didn't open.

"You have to unlock it," Cara said.

"I never lock the truck."

"You don't worry somebody might steal it?" A stricken look came over her face.

"Who?" Rex said, rivers of rain running through his hair and down his face as he looked around the human-free landscape.

"Somebody. I always lock up. In fact…" She hesitated, but, suddenly aware that they were indeed the only people around, decided there was no point in trying to get out of this one. "I did lock up." She folded her arms over her soaked top and gave him a defiant stare.

"But the keys are in there."

"Well, *that* was a stupid thing to do. You're never supposed to leave your keys in a car."

"Why. The. Hell. Not." He shouted the words over a clap of thunder, shouting them very slowly.

"You have a point," she conceded. "I was just thinking of protecting the truck."

"You protected the truck, all right." Thunder rolled over the top of them. "If we don't get going, it may be too late to protect ourselves."

10

RAIN SLICED against her skin like shards of glass, pounding hard, with no relief. Cara was cold. Her feet, barely contained in the sandals by the thin strap, slipped sideways, frontward and back as she ran alongside Rex, trying to keep up with him.

Rex's arm was around her shoulders and he had her tucked as close to his side as he could under the circumstances. He was at least a foot taller, and her shoes, so sexy when they were dry, had become lethal in the field.

"You're going to break an ankle in those things." He dug his heels in what was quickly becoming a muddy swamp and ordered, "Take off the shoes."

"But the yucky stuff."

"Cattle don't roam on the roads. You're safe."

She tried to pull one shoe off, hopping on the other foot, until he took her hand, placed it on his shoulder and shouted to be heard above the rain, "Don't get all shy on me now. I've seen you under sheets."

"I know, but still..."

"For God's sake, you can't take your sandals off without hanging on to something, and I'm the only thing here." He was laughing at her, his dark hair falling across his forehead and into his eyes. "You hold on to me. I won't let you fall."

Cara didn't need any further invitation to lean into him, placing her hand where his shoulder began and his chest ended. Off went the left shoe. A bare foot hit the grass. It was a cold and icy feeling. She took off the other shoe and he took them from her.

"Where are we going?"

"Back to the house."

"That far?"

"You locked the keys in the truck, Cara. Nothing else we can do except stay here and drown."

He had a point. They walked fast, only her steps didn't match his. "It seemed like we were riding in the truck forever," she mumbled as she fell farther and farther behind him.

He barely heard her complaints. But heard he enough to know they were getting fainter and fainter, until finally he turned around, saw her standing a good fifty feet behind him with her hands on her hips and a glare in her eye. That was one feisty woman.

He liked feisty women. He wanted to smile, swoop her up in his arms and carry her away, she was that adorable. But he liked watching her, too, and he could swoop anytime, whereas the rain and the wet top she had on might be a once-in-a-lifetime experience. He couldn't help it if her breasts were completely exposed to his view through her soaked shirt. Every delectable curve was there for him to see. The dark areolas, the erect nipples. The nipples of a wanting woman. Whether it was because she wanted him or because he wanted her, he felt overpowered by the need to lift her top, take her nipple in his mouth and pull gently until she whimpered.

"How far are we now?"

"Distance is only a state of mind." His voice cracked like an adolescent schoolboy's. He wasn't the kind of guy to throw away an opportunity when it landed in his lap either. Slowly, with deliberate determination, he continued to slosh his way through mud and muck back to where she stood. He didn't hurry, despite the wet conditions. Why should he? He had a great view that was getting better the closer he got.

"I asked you a question," she said, water pouring down her face, her hair clinging to all parts of her. "I'm waiting."

Ah-ha. The stance of a woman determined to get what she wants. And he was just the one to give it to her.

He stopped within a half inch from her. So close her nipples slightly grazed his rib cage. The touch, barely a whisper, sent a ripple of heat straight to his groin. He unbuttoned the first button on his shirt. He heard her gasp. He unbuttoned the next one and the next one, working his way down. Her eyes widened. The last button came undone. Her chest rose and fell in quick bursts of breath.

He shrugged out of the shirt, no small feat considering how wet everything was. He wasn't wearing a T-shirt underneath, nothing to protect him from the rain.

"What are you doing?" she gasped.

"What do you think?"

The wet pellets hit his skin hard, taking his mind off the urge to lay Cara down on the wet dirt and sink into her.

Cara wasn't moving. Her eyes were big brown saucers rimmed with wet lashes. Hair that had swung freely from side to side with pretty, swirly curls only an hour ago was now glued in wet strands to her back and bottom. The wayward piece across her cheek he was able to slide back behind her ear before placing his shirt around her shoulders.

Cara gazed up into his face. The blood was pounding so hard in his ears he didn't hear the words "Thank you," but he could read her lips.

She slipped her arms through the sleeves. Instead of buttoning up the shirt, which would be almost impossible to do as wet as it was, she wrapped the material around her waist, holding it closed with her hand.

"Now we're going to the house," he said.

This time, she simply nodded.

Once again, he placed his arm around her shoulders and pulled her into his side. They ran side by side, her hip rubbing against his thigh, the friction intense. His kept his pace slow so she could keep up with him. Even at a slower jog, his legs were so long that it took her one and a half steps for each one of his.

By the time they reached the house, Rex knew Cara was exhausted from fighting the rain and wind. He held open the gate to the white picket fence and waited for Cara to go through. He took her by the hand, not that he needed to but because it was becoming a habit and he didn't want to think about how it was possible a habit could form in so short a time or what that meant right now. They ran to the porch, where they were finally protected from the rain and wind by the overhang.

"You don't have a key, do you?" Cara asked, unable to hide her disappointment. "They're in the truck on your key ring."

"Of course I have a key. Right here." Rex went over to a clay flowerpot. There wasn't anything in it except some dried-up dirt. He lifted the pot and picked up the key that lay on the wooden porch.

"Isn't that dangerous?" Cara asked, pointing to the spot where the key had been.

"No. The pot's empty, so I'm not going to get a hernia lifting it."

"I'm talking about the key." Was he purposely being obtuse?

"We keep the door locked." He gave her a look as if he thought she was.

"To keep the key under the pot. Anyone can find it. That's the first place that people will look."

"Come on," Rex said, unlocking the door then opening it for her. "I've already learned you're paranoid. All the more reason to consider moving out of evil Erie and into peaceful Pegleg."

At least one hundred bolts of lightning crossed overhead. That wasn't so bad. Until the explosion. Cara screamed and tackled Rex at what she thought had to be dynamite.

He held her tight, rubbing her back, murmuring, "It's okay, little one, it's okay."

"It was a bomb." Her heart almost pounded out of her chest and into his. His hand stroking her shoulder blades in gentle rotation comforted her, made her lean closer into him. She couldn't seem to get close enough.

"It was a transformer. Come on." He only moved slightly away, and even then he kept her right at his side. "Let's turn up the heat, make some coffee. We need to get out of these wet clothes. You're shivering and shaking like a clapboard house in the center of a Texas tornado."

"I am cold." She had to agree. Her teeth were knocking into each other she was shivering so badly. She'd be lucky if they didn't break.

He faced her, both hands on her shoulders, and suddenly gave her a curious look. "I didn't realize you were quite so short," he said.

Those were fighting words. She had been *shortcake* and *shortbread* growing up. No one got away with calling her that now. She shrugged out of his reach. "What's that supposed to mean?" She gave him a certain kind of smile. If he had known her better, he would have known that the smile wasn't a smile, it was a warning.

"It doesn't mean anything. Just a statement. You're

taller in your shoes, that's all. Without your shoes, you're shorter.''

"You see, Doctor," she said, "it's a requirement in the Erie school system that a kindergarten teacher be no taller than five foot three inches. It's so we don't give the five-year-olds inferiority complexes.''

"Really?" He looked puzzled, which didn't surprise her, because even she couldn't believe the crap pouring out of her mouth.

"Oh, yes. Do you know how hard it is to find teachers at or below the height requirement?''

"No, I don't. But it sounds like a good idea. Maybe I'll bring something like that up at our next school board meeting.''

He seemed to ponder the height issue among kindergarten children, which made Cara want to shake some common sense into him. "Oh, for heaven's sake, I was only joking.'' Her shivering got worse and she crossed her arms over her ribs and belly trying to keep warm.

"I knew that." He came back with a smile that bordered on lip-smackingly divine. "I was only playing along.''

"Okay then. Good.'' With as much dignity as she could muster considering that his shirt was now molding to her body, she assessed her surroundings. "I need to get out of these clothes. Where's the heat you promised? Where's the coffee?''

"Right here." Rex flipped the light switch and nothing happened. "Damn." He walked inside the living area, turning on lamps that didn't shine. "The transformer that just exploded must have cut off the electricity.''

"What do we do?" She wasn't panicked. Not yet. There was still some feeble light coming through the windows. But it wouldn't last long, although being alone with Rex in the dark wasn't the most dangerous place she could possibly be.

But it could be the most dangerous place for him given how she could hardly stop ogling his chest. She thought he might be thinking the same thing when he left her standing in the living room, all alone.

She heard the sound of drawers opening, things being pushed around, clanging, rattling, then drawers closing. He came back with several flashlights. "Here, take a few."

She didn't argue. She took two.

"Take off your clothes."

"I beg your pardon?" She couldn't believe he would order her to do something like that. That was a fantasy come true.

"In there." He pointed to a door. "It's a bathroom. You can get undressed in private."

She didn't move. This wasn't good. What happened to the getting-naked-together part? Again, he took her by the hand and led her through the living room, down a hallway and into a small bathroom. He opened cabinet doors, and by the third one, found what he'd been looking for. "Here." He handed her a big white towel. "I'll take one for myself. Get undressed and wrap yourself up in that. You'll be warmer and more covered up than you are now."

She stared at terry-cloth material.

"What's the matter?" he asked.

"Is this all? It's only a towel."

He took it from her, unfolded it and held it up by the corners.

"Okay," she said, taking the towel back. "It's big." Too big. She would have searched for something more revealing, shorter, maybe a little threadbare in all the right places, and maybe a few wrong ones, too. She couldn't now because he'd already seen the size of the towel.

A few minutes later she came back into the living room, the towel wrapped around her sarong-style with one corner tucked in to hold the whole thing together. She'd debated leaving her coins on, but the necklace and bracelet were cold against her skin, so she'd left them on the vanity in the bathroom. Hopefully, that wouldn't mess with her luck. She carried her wet clothes bundled in her arms, holding a flashlight in each hand.

Rex was bending over, leaning into the fireplace. From her viewpoint she only saw his rear end barely covered in the towel, long, muscular legs and that was about it. That was enough. She could hear him striking one match, then another. Finally, the fire caught and flames filled the space, the smell of smoke burning her nose.

When he turned to face her, she nearly fainted. The towel hid nothing. He might as well have been wearing nothing, considering how much of him wasn't covered. He came toward her and she couldn't move. All she wanted to do was fling off her towel, pull his off, too, and have her way with him.

"Rex?" She almost choked on his name. She had to think of something to ask him besides *Do you want to have sex?* "Do you have any aspirin?" That was bland enough.

"Back in the bathroom, in one of the drawers or in the medicine cabinet. You'll find it. Wait, let me get you some water."

He rushed off to the kitchen and came back within a few seconds. He put the glass on a table and took the clothes out of her arms. As he did, her towel caught in his fingers, the corner coming out from where it had been tucked, and fell forward. She immediately grabbed the corner, keeping the towel from falling. She dropped her flashlights on the wooden floor instead, barely missing her toes. She swung the towel back into place and bent down to pick them up, and with a flashlight in one hand and the glass of water in the other, headed back to the bathroom.

She found the condoms in the middle drawer, and shut it quickly. Then reason came over her. She had permission to be there, to look. She hadn't found any pain relievers. Still, condoms could be the start of a very good pain reliever. Orgasms opened the blood vessels in the brain and relieved headaches much the same way as caffeine. Orgasms were very healthy.

The aspirin was in the last drawer along with safety pins. Maybe God had sent the rain to make this moment happen. The moment she could conceive the old-fashioned way. Condoms and safety pins. Rex, Cara and baby. All it would take would be one pinprick in the foil package. She took one of the pins and stuck it all the way through the wrapper and latex. The she stuck it again and again.

She opened the package and unrolled the condom. She turned on the water and filled it like a water balloon, then gently squeezed to see where the water ran through the holes.

If she were a devious, self-serving woman this would be the way to go. But, she thought as she threw the punctured condom in the toilet and replaced the pin, she wasn't.

She flushed, watching the swirling water take away the defective protection. She noticed that no more water came back into the toilet. Now look what she'd done. She'd wasted the single flush on an unused item of sabotage.

Cara swallowed two aspirin, then juggling the glass, condoms and flashlights, she left the bathroom and headed back to Rex.

Rex had placed their clothes over the stair rail and across dining-room chairs to dry. He had laid a blanket on the floor near the fireplace. There was also a bottle of wine, a deck of cards, a cheese board and a battery-powered radio playing soft classical music.

She sat on the blanket and he sat across from her. "What now?" she asked.

He handed her a glass of wine and raised his. She followed. "To you," he said.

"To you, too."

"To your future as a rancher."

"Ah, well… We have to talk about that." A flash of lightning and a crack of thunder rolled over the cottage, shaking the walls. Another warning? "Later, we'll talk. Maybe we can do other things now."

He sent her a very sexy smile. A downright evil grin. "Do you want to play gin rummy, or do you have something more exciting in mind?" he asked.

She wasn't sure what he meant until she realized that she was holding on to the condoms. Nothing like being caught with your innermost desire right there in the palm of your hand.

"Gin rummy. The condoms." She threw them on the floor by the deck of cards. "They'll be used like poker chips."

"Whatever you say."

The rush of heat boiling through her veins had nothing to do with the heat from the fire. Her breath caught in her lungs and she had to take a second before she could speak. He stretched out his leg, and touched her toes with his foot.

His towel crept up on his leg. She tilted her head to get a better look at what was peeking from under the cloth. She had to look away. The silky tip of his penis played peek-a-boo and she couldn't look. Because if she did, she'd grab the towel and toss it away.

Maybe that wasn't a bad idea now that she thought about it. "Strip poker."

"We're stripped. Or haven't you noticed?" He laughed. The sole of his foot stroked the sole of hers.

She had to concentrate on not closing her eyes, because that's what she wanted to do. Close her eyes and not see, just feel his touch.

"Take off the towels."

His grin was wicked. "I like the way you think."

"What I'm thinking is that we'll play strip poker backward. Every time you win, you have to put on a piece of clothing."

"Of course I'll win."

"I didn't mean you as in *you,* Rex. I meant it as in the collective sense. Because I will win."

That brought on a very ungentlemanly snort.

She only smiled very sweetly. "We'll see," she said with confidence.

"I'm keeping my towel on. You keep yours on. Let's have some form of modesty here. You never know who will drop by."

She tried to speak, to say something witty or easternly, sophisticatedly boring, only she couldn't speak. How could one even get a coherent thought, when she'd just offered to get naked and he suggested she leave her towel on? How much more insulting could that be?

She was having nothing of that.

Cara got on her knees, close to him, as close as she could without actually touching him, and slid her hand down his chest, fingers spread wide, palm to skin, sliding her hand lower...lower, until she passed his belly button and touched the top of the terry-cloth towel. She moved her fingers to where the ends came together, on his thigh, and slipped her hand inside, massaging his thigh, feeling the muscle contract, the skin heat under her touch.

She slowly, torturously, let her fingers touch, tease the soft tip of his penis. Silk, that's what he felt like to her. Hard and soft, his erection grew along the side of her hand, even though she wasn't touching him there. She glanced at his face. His eyes were semi-closed. His breath came in short bursts. She slipped her finger along the side of his member, and he groaned, reaching down, touching her hand, making her stop further explorations.

With her other hand, she batted his away and continued to travel the length of him, circling his girth. She took her hand away, and his eyes popped open. She placed her fingers to her mouth, and licked them, wetting them, then brought them back to his penis, sliding her wetness down the length of him. "Do you like it?"

"Yes." The word was more a groan.

He reached for her ankle, pulling her foot toward him until her toes touched his penis. She slid closer, circling him with her toes, feeling the smoothness that seemed to be in direct contrast with how stiff he had become. "I want you, do you know that?" He slid her foot up and down the length of him.

She pulled her foot away and reached for the cards. "What about our game of poker?"

"Forget the poker. I can't see the cards anyway."

"You lit the fire."

"Forget it." He reached over, taking the corner of the towel. "I want you. Now."

"I'd be less than honest if I didn't say I wanted you, too." She did want him. She reached over and touched his face, running her fingers down his cheeks, his chin. Slipping them into his hair. She loved the feel of him. She loved being with him. She was happy. Right now, for the first time in as long as she could remember, she was happy.

Still on her knees, she straightened herself. Taking the ends of the towel, she undid them where they were hooked together, and let the towel fall to the floor, exposing herself to him.

Rex had been erect before, but when she dropped

the towel, he almost lost control of his body, like a teenage boy having sex for the first time. That's how he felt. With Cara, everything seemed like the first time.

Her breasts were full, round and firm. Her nipples erect. She now sat cross-legged on the floor and he had a wonderful view of beautifully shaped thighs, and a peek into the glory of all that made her a woman.

She only gave him a serene smile. He would have concentrated on that smile, but he had so many other things to look at. As she moved a little toward him, her breasts swayed. He reached out, he couldn't help it, and touched her nipple. Her breathing seemed to stop. So did his. Then she arched her back, giving him access, and he took it. His mouth covered her nipple, his tongue circling the erect point, before she pulled away. He looked down at himself. "There's no hiding it, you know. You do that to me."

She blew out air. "That's nice. It's pretty."

"No one ever called it pretty before. Come here, baby," he said. "Let me warm you all over." Cara didn't need a second invitation. All she wanted was Rex. She was having some frighteningly strong feelings for him, but she'd never let him know it. She never would have been this bold if she thought she'd ever see him again. Right now though, all she wanted was him.

No. Not him. His sperm. To fertilize her egg. Her baby.

But, deep down, she had to admit to herself that wasn't the entire truth. What she wanted was him. Just him.

He brushed his lips against her breasts and he gave each enough attention to turn her into a seething mass of wanting more and wanting more now.

Finally, he worked his way down her body, kissing

each rib, lavishing kisses on her belly button, all the while his fingers caressed her woman parts, rubbing her, stroking her, making her legs feel weak. He held on to the back of her thighs and wouldn't let her fall. He put his mouth where his fingers had been and tasted her, sending her into a spiral, but stopping before she could reach her peak. He kissed her then, making her taste herself. Then gently guiding her down to him. He felt wonderful. He tasted wonderful. But she wanted more. She broke away for a condom, ripped open the foil and covered him with the condom. When he was protected, she lay on the blanket and he came to her.

Over and over that night—she lost track of how many times—they made love. Each time was more sweet than the time before. It was almost as if she knew that come morning, once whoever was picking them up arrived, it would all be over. And even if she was wrong, and it wasn't, she would be leaving in a few days.

She couldn't fall in love with him. And if she had already, she was going to have to put a stop to those feelings. A relationship between them would never work. Never. She was leaving. This was a one-night stand for him, and she would be left with her memories. She was glad she had thrown away the sabotaged condom and hadn't perforated another one. She couldn't do that to him. She had taken great care to make sure they were both protected.

She didn't want to have a baby anyway. Not this way. Not with him. Or was that with*out* him? Whatever it was, she was fine with no baby.

And she'd keep telling herself that until she believed it.

11

THE NEXT MORNING dawned gray, but to Cara, waking up wrapped in Rex's arms, the sky was blue, the sun was shining.

She was all warm and secure spooning with him. His face nuzzling her neck, his mouth blowing warm over her cheek. One of his hands held her hip and the other cupped her breast. If it hadn't been for the horn honking outside, she would have stayed this way with him all day.

"Someone's out there," she murmured. "Make them go away."

Rex let go of her and stretched. "Clay. He's come to pick us up. The phone lines were back up a couple of hours ago so I called him."

"It's too early."

"I know." He grabbed her again, turning her to face him, and kissed her lips, running his tongue across her mouth and over her teeth. "I don't want to go," he said.

"I know." She moved closer to him, as close as she could.

The honking started again, more insistently this time.

Finally they got dressed and went outside. "It's about time," Clay said. Despite the cloudiness, he wore sunglasses.

"Nice to see you, too," Rex told him. "This is Cara."

"Nice to meet you." Clay stared at her.

"Is something wrong?" she asked.

"Nope, not a thing."

Rex opened the door to the back seat and she climbed in. He sat in the front, on the passenger side, but leaned sideways so he could see her. After they were heading back to town, Clay said, "Nice jewelry."

That perked her up. "Thanks, I liked your billboards, too. I'm trying to convince Rex not to take them down."

"They're really a safety hazard," Clay said.

"Am I believing what I'm hearing?" Rex asked. "After all the grief you gave me?"

"If you think that was grief, just wait. You don't know grief." Clay's hands tightened around the wheel. "Anyway, I'm not backing down on the fact that it was a good campaign, but you're right. No need to put something out there that's going to cause an endangerment to the public."

"Too bad," Cara said. "I really liked those two animals. Maybe you can store them somewhere, or put them out on the pasture where LuLu is, so when I come back to visit, I can go see the cow and bull. If not for them, I never would have met Rex." She reached over and rubbed Rex's forearm.

Clay turned his head for only a brief moment. Over the top of his sunglasses he glared at her with such venom, she immediately sat back in the seat.

"Are you sure I didn't offend you?" she asked him.

"I don't know you well enough," Clay said. "I do know—" he sent her a smile that should have been charming but chilled Cara instead "—that I really like your gold."

Cara told them about the coins and how she had inherited them. Rex asked a lot of questions, Clay scowled at her. It didn't make for a very comfortable ride home.

Finally, she stopped talking and stared out the window, watching the green pastures turn into more residential areas.

"Someone broke into your lab." Clay, speaking almost under his breath, broke the news to Rex.

"What happened? Who did it? When? Why didn't you come to get me?"

"We'll talk about it later, after we drop Cara off." Clay turned for a second to look at Cara. "We don't want to bore your friend with details."

"WHAT HAPPENED with Dr. Rex?" Kate asked later that afternoon when they met for lunch at Mama Jo's.

Cara smiled with a tiny shrug and didn't answer. The day did turn out to be so sunny and bright that if the rainstorm last night hadn't heralded the most important moment of her life, she'd never have guessed it had rained.

Kate took two rolls of assorted-flavor antacids out of her purse, opened them and placed the small, powdery pills in a straight row down the middle of the table, lining them up according to color.

"I brought this." Cara held up the bottle of liquid antacid she'd bought when she had first arrived. "I forgot you would be bringing relief, too."

"We'll probably need both. The liquid is quicker, the pills are more discreet. We can start on the pills right here, and mainline the liquid out in the parking lot."

The waiter brought the appetizer—nachos el carbon, filled with black beans, fajita beef and chicken, sour cream, salsa, *pico de gallo* and assorted other toppings. They didn't bother using the little appetizer plates. Cara took the nachos on her side, and Kate took the ones on hers.

They were halfway through the dish when Kate apparently ran out of patience. "I said," she said, "what happened last night?"

Cara took a breath and made an "mmm" sound.

"Was that for the doctor or the food?"

Cara put her fork down and looked at her friend. "He was wonderful, Kate. I think I'm in lust." She might tell Kate she was in lust, but she pretty much knew that she had fallen in love. She chewed a green antacid and chased it with a big drink of ice tea.

"I can understand that," Kate said. "He's one good-looking hunk of male. Every woman who meets him wants a piece of him."

Cara popped her head up. "They do?" She'd destroy them all.

"Cara, the good doctor is one hunted bachelor. Women hide out in the men's bathroom hoping to get a glimpse of him." Kate appeared to be serious.

"I'm not surprised." And she wasn't, but the information didn't sit well. "Does he, you know, does he act on those...women who offer him pieces?"

"I doubt it. He's a terrible tease, but I'd bet he's pretty discriminating when it comes to the woman he's fooling around with."

"I hope so, since I'm one of those women."

Kate dropped her fork. "Why, Cara, you little dickens." She smiled a great big smile, showing gorgeous white teeth.

Cara had to smile back. Then she gave a little shiver. "Normally, I would never do anything like that. I just met him. But it was like, what can I say? I mean, he was there, and I was there, and our clothes were wa-a-a-ay over there—" She pointed to some space on the other side of the restaurant. Then she sighed, her thoughts drifting away to the night before.

Kate snapped her fingers in front of Cara's face. "Don't stop."

"You see, it was raining. Was it raining here, too?"
Kate stared at her and didn't say a word.

"Silly question. Never mind. It makes no difference." Cara rushed the words out. "The bottom line is, Rex didn't take the keys out of his truck, and when I locked the truck, we couldn't get back in."

"Why didn't he call someone?"

"He had everything in there, the cell phone, wallet, calling cards, everything. We were stranded. In the rain. Just us. So what could we do?" she asked.

"I don't know, but I'm sure Rex could have thought of something. I heard through the grapevine that he was one imaginative doctor."

Cara could feel her face begin to flame. "He might be, but in this instance we were more worried about hypothermia. We had to run through all that rain to the house and when we finally got there, the electricity was out. I heard the transformer blow. We were soaking wet, so we got naked and were about to play strip poker." She lifted her head and straightened her shoulders. "What else could we do?"

"I wouldn't know," Kate said sarcastically.

"Well, we didn't play."

"Why am I not surprised?"

The waiter took away the appetizer and plopped the main course on the table. Cara took three more antacids, rubbing her tummy in small, circular motions as the cherry-flavored pills made their way down the path. She wasn't sure eating this much was worth all the pain that followed. Although one more bite and she had to say it did.

"And I had to make some very hard decisions." She finally told Kate about her plan to have a baby, and how at first she thought the sperm bank was for humans. How she saw Rex and knew without a doubt that he was the one who would be her perfect donor.

"There he was, naked, and I couldn't help myself. I had to have him. This was the right thing to do."

Kate leaned over the table a little, getting closer to Cara. "He didn't use condoms?" This seemed to scandalize her more than any other part of the scandalous story.

"He did use condoms. And I didn't get pregnant. I didn't puncture the condoms. Well, I did one, but threw it out. I couldn't be deceitful to him. I couldn't. I think I'm in love with him."

Kate sighed. "I don't want you to get hurt."

"I'm not going to get hurt."

"Falling in love with the wrong man?" She raised her eyebrow with the unanswered question.

"He's not the wrong man. It just the wrong time and place." The knowledge about broke her heart.

Later that afternoon, trying to read a book in her room at Mandelay, Cara wondered if that "not going to get hurt" statement was true. Rex hadn't called.

She wasn't going to wait around forever. Absolutely not. She was going to get dressed, go to a movie, a club, dancing, something. She wouldn't be some kind of desperate dolly waiting for her man to call. A man who might not even be *her* man. Maybe she'd been right all along, and this had only been a one-night stand for him. But the way he'd touched her, gazed at her as the night wore on, it was hard to believe he didn't want more of her.

Cara took a deep breath and did her best not to cry. Sometimes life wasn't fair. There was the time she had bought strawberries. They were big and beautiful. But they were also out of season and expensive. She bought them anyway, and put them in the refrigerator. She thought she'd save them for a special occasion, maybe when she had a special date. A week passed with no date and no special occasion. One night she turned on the TV to some old movie and when she brought out the strawberries to eat there was mold growing all over them. That wasn't fair.

Not that she'd compare Rex to a moldy strawberry, but since he hadn't called her, he wasn't much above moldy, either. With that gross thought in mind, Cara plopped down on her bed, her empty bed, and gave herself up for a long, long cry.

REX FELT AS IF the bottom had dropped out of his chest and his heart was floating down there somewhere near his...well, anyway, that wasn't where it ought to be.

Clay, Arthur, Tigger, Clyde, Cathy and Barbara were all standing in the lab. One of Cara's coins was on the floor next to the freezer, another was behind it. He held a third in his hand. Some time between him closing the clinic and picking her up later at Mandelay, she'd managed to break in and steal from him. She hadn't had a lot of time to do it, but she had done it. The proof was right here.

Cara? How could she do this to him? He'd thought she was the one. He wanted her, more than he had wanted any woman, and he'd had visions and dreams of a future between them. He'd never felt this way about anyone else. When he first saw her, he went hard. Every time he saw her, he went hard. Not that a sexual attraction was important in the ways of a heart, but it sure helped. She had a good heart. A wonderful heart. She was a kindergarten teacher. She was warm and loving.

She was a liar, a thief. A traitor, too. He had been played for a fool.

"What do you think we should do?" Barbara asked.

"Call the police."

"No." Arthur was adamant. "Not that. Don't bring them into it."

"Why not?"

"She's such a pretty girl. I'd hate for her to go to jail."

"She can't get away with it," Rex said. He wasn't about to let his personal feelings intrude.

"Call her, talk to her," Tigger suggested. "Maybe it's a mistake. Maybe she was testing out some theory. You're the one who said she had a good imagination."

"That's right," Cathy agreed. "Call her. Go see her."

"I will with the sheriff."

"Don't be such a wimp," Barbara said. "Go see her first, find out what happened, then get the police."

"Do you have an inventory yet on what was taken?"

"Five straws of LuLu's semen."

"That's a lot of money."

"Tell her to give it back and you won't press charges."

Despite the strange hurt he had somewhere near his heart, Rex had his own ideas about how to deal with Cara. And he suspected none of his business partners would approve.

CARA HAD BEEN in such a deep sleep that she had no idea what time it was when the phone started ringing. By the time it registered that the noise was coming from the phone and she'd reached for the receiver, the ringing stopped.

No sooner did she close her eyes when it started ringing again. This time, though, she was prepared. "Hello."

"I want to see you tonight." His voice was deep and seductive.

She was trying very hard not to let the information

Kate had so casually dropped about Rex and his social life affect her. "What time is it?" she asked.

"Eleven."

"Oh." She yawned, pretending disinterest. "I guess you've had a busy day." She was going to ignore what Kate had said about those women who were after Rex. She wasn't going to think about who he might have been with earlier. The person who was more important to him than she was. After all, they might have had one incredible night, but to Rex, she might be just one incredible night in a long list of incredible nights. The night might have meant more to her, but that was her problem and she would have to deal with it.

"I had a wonderful time last night," she said, just testing the waters.

His voice hardened. "I'm sure you did."

The tone of his voice startled her. He was being a womanizing pig, an egomaniacal turkey.

"You have a very high opinion of yourself."

"Yes, I do. At least I have a high opinion of my professional ethics. We have to talk, Cara, right now."

"I'm already in bed. Naked," she added, still trying to get the mood back to the Sunday-night level. Just to tease him, because Sunday would be the last night he'd ever have her. Let him weep.

Only she was the one who was going to weep with wanting. She could imagine him in a big leather chair, leaning back, his fingers over his eyes, holding at bay a tension headache. He sounded that tired. Suddenly she felt very sorry for him. She must have worn him out last night and this morning. She had to smile, a soft secret smile. That was a good thing. "But I could put on some clothes, I guess, and you could come over."

"I'll be there."

"Rex? What happened with the clinic? Something's different. You sound different. You sound so sad."

"I had a bad day, and that was the good news."

"I don't understand. What's the bad news?" In Texas they talked in riddles. Everything he said all seemed to make sense when he said it. Then when she went back and rethought the words nothing made sense.

"The bad news is, it's fixin' to get worse..." He let the rest dangle.

Finally, she could stand it no longer. "There's more?"

"The worst possible news on top of the already bad news, at least to me."

"Can you tell me?"

"We have to talk. In person. I'll be right there."

"Rex? Are you mad?"

"No. Don't move."

Cara jumped out of bed. She didn't have any clothes to receive him in. She threw on a pair of jeans and a T-shirt and waited for him to climb through the window. Her Romeo.

Only he came through the door. And he looked as if he were a bee who got usurped from his hive.

"You took my semen," he accused.

Oh, my, he thinks I used those pinpricked condoms. "No, I didn't. I was thinking about it, but I didn't. There's a difference."

"Yes, you did, and I want it back."

He wasn't being rational. "Rex, you know when you have an orgasm, you can't take that semen and put it back. That's silly."

"Don't tell me it's silly. You hand it back."

"I didn't take your semen. I was going to try but I threw those condoms away."

"You were going to try and take my semen?"

"I wanted a baby, Rex. I thought Noble Sperm Bank was for people when they needed to be artificially inseminated. I didn't know it was about a bull until you showed me the picture of LuLu."

"What about last night?"

She lowered her gaze to the carpet. "I had stuck some pinholes in a condom package, but I threw it away. I couldn't do that to you."

"All last night was about was sex? Having a baby? It didn't mean anything to you?"

That shocked her. How could he say that to her? "Of course it did. What do you think? I realize I don't know you well, but I thought I knew you well enough to think that what we had was special. The way you looked at me. The way you touched me. The way you held me."

"It was special."

"Ha! I had lunch today with Kate, and apparently, what is special to you and me is also special to you and a horde, or perhaps I should say a herd, of other women, too."

"I've had it." He had raised his voice. The look he gave her was full of scorn, and it hurt her. "I'm done with all you and your feminine manipulation. I've had about all I can handle." He stormed out of the room, slamming the door, and it wasn't two seconds that he came back. "Your coins, from your bracelet, were found at the lab where the straws of semen were stolen. I'll give you twenty-four hours to bring them back. After that, I call the police."

He slammed the door so hard it rattled the walls.

12

To anyone looking at Rex Noble, they'd think he was cool and collected. What they couldn't see was how he felt inside, his heart slamming in his chest, his insides ripped apart. Cara had done this to him. How a woman had turned him to this in such a short time, he didn't know. He was hurting. But he'd get over it. He always had before.

The gold coin he had been flipping through his fingers he now placed in the middle of his desk as if it deserved a place of honor. Was there honor among thieves? Hell, no. Yet, in a bizarre way, the coin did deserve its place of honor, because without the coin, he never would have known who had stolen the semen.

Not only bull semen, but possibly his own. His baby. How would he ever know? And if she was pregnant with his child, how could he possibly keep her from going back to Erie?

There was one way—by holding her captive. He doubted, after what he'd accused her of doing, that she'd willingly stay here with him.

The only other way was to make her a prisoner. She deserved to go to jail because of what she had stolen.

He released the condom wrappers he'd found in the trash can at the cottage from his fist, put them on the desk and gently smoothed them out. There were six of them. One had pinpricks through the foil. He had even found the safety pin, still open, in one of the bathroom drawers.

Cathy and Barbara and the old boys had found some of the coins and the police had found several more of Cara's coins near other freezer units.

Rex knew he had been a chump. He'd been set up. Set up by a woman who he thought he loved. No. Make that definitely loved. He had always believed in love at first sight, but until she'd hit him over the head with hot wings, it had never happened to him.

Now she'd made him too mad to be in love. She'd made him look like a fool. No one, not even Cara, would make a fool out of him and get away with it. And any woman who might be pregnant with his child was not going to get away from him either.

He had to call Les Herman, Pegleg's police chief, and report her, hand over the evidence. While no one had told the police officers their suspicions about Cara when they were here, and had pretended the coins near the freezing units meant nothing, now was the time to face the truth. Rex had no choice. Rex cleared the foil wrappers off the desk and hid them in the back of the top middle drawer. The chief could know about LuLu's stolen semen. That Cara had also stolen semen from Rex was between Cara and him and no one else.

Les came in a while later bearing his fingerprint kit. "Come on, Les," Rex said. "Call Houston and see if they'll send someone out with more up-to-date investigative equipment. Don't waste your time with that stuff."

"There's nothing wrong with this." Les dropped the kit on Rex's desk. It made a loud plunk and only bounced once. "It works perfectly fine."

"I hope there wasn't glass in there."

"I don't think so." He only looked worried for a second.

"When was the last time you used it?" Rex asked.

The chief actually turned red. Then with boldness and bluster he said, "It's never been used. There's no crime in Pegleg."

"There is now," Rex said darkly. He told Les his suspicions about Cara. It was one of the most difficult things he had ever done. He handed Les the coins they had collected.

"Why would she do it?" the chief asked. "What's the motive?"

"I don't know. Maybe she's a spy or something."

Thinking about Cara and the way she looked the first time he saw her in her very urban, very un-Pegleg-like clothing made him smile. Not a big smile, mind you, but a smile all the same.

Then he remembered her in the cottage, sitting on the floor, naked. Her breasts, so perfectly formed, firm, and when she'd crossed her legs— He closed his eyes for only a second then popped them open again. Yet, even in that brief second he could see the dark triangle of soft curls, the moist center that he had tasted, touched, entered. An acute desire for her made him hard and very uncomfortable in his jeans. He needed release, and he needed it from her.

Les opened his fingerprint kit, reading the directions while he talked in his monotone voice about why it would work just as well as anything Houston would have. Rex thought about Cara's nipples, which were a lot nicer to think about than some stupid fingerprint kit that wasn't going to work anyway.

Her nipples were sweetness. He could still taste them, feel how they stood up to his touch, grew erect under his tongue. The soft moan she made deep in her throat spurred him on. "Cara," he said, not even realizing he had spoken her name out loud until Les said, "She's a dog, huh?" The chief's question sliced through Rex's thoughts.

Rex snorted. "Not at all."

"She's good-lookin'?" he asked, sounding surprised.

"She's okay, if you like that type."

"I'd still like to know the motive."

He had a sneaking suspicion that she probably got the idea when they were talking about it Sunday afternoon. She may have thought to use that ridiculous cow and cottage story as a cover-up for her real intention. To steal his personal semen. For her own means.

Women were funny about things like that, going the indirect way when there was a perfectly straight line.

He refused to admit to himself that it hurt to know that his feelings for her were deep, and to Cara, he was nothing more than stud service.

By the time the chief left, leaving behind a lot of black dust and probably taking nothing with him, Rex had started receiving the phone calls.

Tony called inviting him to dinner, apologizing for whatever Cara might have done.

Kate called. "You're a cad," she yelled and hung up.

And that was the crux of the difference between men and women. Women were always wrong, and Tony and him had it right.

Tony called back again, "I'm sorry about Kate. She doesn't understand these things. Come to the restaurant for dinner tonight."

"I'll think about it."

"Drinks on me. As much as you want. I'll be the designated driver. Get drunk and let the anger out."

"I'm not angry."

"Good, then my liquor bill won't send me to bankruptcy court."

"I'll think about it, Tony. Thanks."

Then Clay called. "It's all my fault. I never should have put that cow billboard up. It gave her fancy ideas. Why don't you meet me at Tony's tonight and I'll buy you a drink."

After Clay, the calls were rapid, from Arthur, Tigger, Clyde, Cathy and Barbara. "Why do they all think I need to get drunk?" he asked Cathy. "I'm fine."

"Good. Meet me at Donetti's. I have a girl I want you to meet."

That held zero interest for him. So he told her "No, not interested." He couldn't even pretend to himself he wanted to go out with anyone else.

"You're a stupid guy, Rex. Call Cara, kill her with kindness, apologize for being such a mule, and then, when you get her all melted and jelly in your arms, go in for the attack. She'll never know where it came from."

Now, that wasn't a bad idea, Rex thought. It would give him a reason to call her back. Not that he needed one. But maybe he'd get the semen back. And maybe he'd get Les over there to arrest her, and make it impossible for her to go back to Erie until they found out if she was pregnant with their child.

Rex placed the call to Mandelay. Cara answered on the fourth ring. Her "Hello" was all breathless and damn sexy. His mind went blank for a moment and it took a second for him to round up his composure. It took almost a full minute to remember the reason why he was calling. She had that forget-everything-and-only-remember-her effect on him.

"Am I catching you at a bad time?" he asked, keeping his voice cool and controlled.

"Not really," she answered. "I don't want to talk to you."

"Cara, let's not say something you don't really mean."

"I mean it with all my heart."

She didn't sound so sure though and that was a good sign. "What're you doing?"

"I was taking a shower."

He had sudden visions of her sitting on the bed, wet and naked. He knew what she looked like wet and naked and that made his breathing stop. "Are you naked?" He almost choked out the words.

"I may be naked," she said, her accent charming, all eastern and softly clipped. On second thought, maybe disarming was more like it. Her voice was almost lyrical. Everything about her had made him forget what it was he had planned to do, and he couldn't allow that to happen. "Because when people take showers, they usually don't wear blue jeans."

"Go put on clothes."

"I can't."

"You have to," he said with all his charm. "I'm going to take you to Donetti's tonight, and I can't if you're naked."

"I can't go with you tonight."

"We'll talk, I'll apologize, you'll forgive me, and we'll pretend none of this ever happened." He paused. "You can't?"

"Yes. I can't."

She wasn't supposed to say that. It wasn't in his plan. "What do you mean you can't?"

"I have plans tonight."

"You have a date?" He wasn't jealous. Not one bit.

"Not a date really. I'm going with Tony and Kate for dinner. At Donetti's."

"Donetti's?" He had to close his eyes and count to three, taking deep breaths before he could go on. "I'll join you."

"I don't want you to join us."

Oh, she was a coy one, that Cara. "Yes, you do."

"And if you show up, I won't talk to you."

He'd join them all right. "Well, then, there's nothing to talk about, now, is there?" He just wouldn't let on about his plan.

The tone of her voice turned to sugary brightness. "I hope I get to see you soon."

"Liar," he said instead of goodbye.

She only hung up the phone.

Poor Cara, Rex thought. She didn't know it yet, but she was going to be putty in his hands.

CARA AGAIN WORE her hair loose tonight. It had looked good when she left the hotel, but that was a top-down-Mustang ride ago. Now she raked her fingers through the thick mass of tangles and curls, doing her best to make sure it was still presentable, hoping it was, because there was no way she was getting up to use the rest-room mirror, or take one out of her purse. She wasn't going to take her gaze off the man over there by the entry. She couldn't believe Rex was here. After she'd told him not to show up. The nerve of him.

Lipstick? Where was it? Had she even put some on? Her finger glided over her bottom lip and came off pink. That was good. Then she realized she might have taken the cosmetic off the bottom, and her lipstick was top heavy, so she mashed her lips together trying to even out the color.

"Look!" Cara's elbow nudged Kate's arm. Her voice couldn't conceal the excitement and touch of urgency she felt. "Rex." She almost swallowed the name Rex.

"Where?" Kate asked.

"There." Cara nodded toward the entry, tucking stray strands of hair behind her ear.

"Hmm," Kate murmured, kind of dreamy-like.

"He looks real nice tonight. Ignore him. Maybe he'll go away."

"I will. Believe me, he's not going to get near me."

Tony looked at the two women, shook his head and continued to eat his sushi.

"Kate, look over there, that's Tigger, one of the old men who I thought was donating semen. And that's Barbara, the office manager, over there." Cara waved at them. They lowered their heads and ignored her.

Rex immediately found Cara sitting with Kate and Tony. Hell, he was so attuned to her he would have found her even if she were inside and he was outside.

As he walked to the table he saw Tigger and Barbara. Those two were up to something. That Barbara, she was a wild woman. When Tigger started to wave at him, Rex started to head in that direction, but he saw Tony, and Tony was waving at him, too. Not that he didn't love Tig as a grandfather, but Tony had Cara at his table, and there wasn't a contest of where he was heading.

Cara didn't care about any stolen semen. All she wanted was for him to sit next to her so she could rub her hand across his muscled thigh and feel those muscles twitch under her touch.

"I thought you told him not to come here," Kate said. She could barely be heard over the laughter, music and conversations taking place at every table.

"I guess he didn't listen to me. He must be unable to resist my charm."

Kate smiled. "I would bet that's it."

As close as they had been yesterday, Cara still stared almost awestruck as he walked toward their table. She couldn't help it. His jeans were so tight they would be almost indecent anywhere except in Pegleg where peel-on jeans were the uniform of choice for both men and women. What was more, she knew what was underneath those jeans.

He weaved his way slowly through the throng of customers and waitstaff, busboys and wine stewards. The room was crowded and not easy to navigate without stepping on, over or through someone.

Her mouth was dry, her tongue stuck in there, not having enough moisture to move around, or to let her speak in anything other than the croak she heard when she tried to tell Tony and Kate that Rex was coming over.

She reached for the water, but stopped midway, bringing her hands back to her lap. Her hands had betrayed her, getting all clammy.

Rex was halfway to their table, and she had to get some fluid down her or she'd end up making a froggy-sounding fool of herself. She tried for the glass of water again. When her hands slid over the glass and didn't get even a grasp on it, she stopped herself from picking it up. She knew if she pushed it anymore she'd have nothing but a wet mess and probably broken glass.

So instead of drinking water, she just watched him watch her as he walked toward their table. Watching him was so wonderful she almost forgot her heart was breaking because of him. The jerk.

Looking at him made her just want to smile all over. And get naked. And she could swear that he must be thinking the same thing, because his expression was one of a determined predator.

The closer he walked to their table, the more angry he seemed to become. His smile turned into a jaw-clenching frown.

His hands, so relaxed moments ago, were now formed into fists. Muscles that rippled under the cotton shirt, seemed tight and tense. She didn't know what had caused the change, but it didn't matter because he was walking toward her and her universe was now totally focused on him.

"Rex. You're here." She thought she sounded normal, she thought she could be understood. She didn't sound too much like a cottonmouth snake. "I thought I told you not to come."

"I couldn't think of spending a night away from you."

It took the kick on her shin, courtesy of Kate, before she realized Rex had asked, "Room for one more?"

Tony said, "Sure," before Cara could formulate the words "Yes, come sit next to me so I can rub your leg." He sat in the chair opposite her.

He stood halfway up, enough to reach into his pocket, and he pulled out a coin. A coin matching the necklace and bracelet she wore. He dropped it on the table. "Here. I believe this is yours."

The table became silent as they all stared at the coin. Cara reached for it, "Yes, it is. And like I said before, I didn't leave it in your lab."

"Who else could have?"

"You tell me."

"You lied to me, and you know what I'm talking about."

"I have not," she said indignantly.

"Yes, you have. From the very beginning."

"No, I haven't. I just haven't been telling the whole truth."

"That's lying." What was wrong with her?

"No," she said, just as determined to have her say. "You're not seeing the big picture."

"Excuse me." He leaned back in the chair, his arms flung outward. "The only picture I see is your coin by one of my freezers and semen has been stolen."

"I didn't steal your semen."

"What about the pinpricks? And you know what I'm talking about."

Her face turned ash white. Her eyes filled with tears. "I told you I was only thinking about it, I didn't do it."

Kate turned to him and said, "That was low, Rex."

"I'm not the one with the safety pin."

"I didn't do that."

"I found it."

"What's he talking about?" Tony asked.

"Later," Kate hushed him.

Tony, looking confused, shrugged.

"I didn't use it. Or you didn't use it," Cara said, looking straight at him.

"How do I know?"

"You have to trust me."

"Trust you? You lied to me. You've stolen from me."

"No, I haven't. Anyway, if I did, it's your fault. I thought you were a semen bank for babies. Do you think I was going to confess how terribly wrong I was when I went looking for donor fathers and found catalogs of bulls?"

"Fathers?" Now he looked confused.

"Those old men, I thought they were semen donors. I thought I'd have a baby who came out ninety years old."

"What old men?"

"In your semen bank."

"They are donors. They're investors in the company."

She took a deep breath. "I can't believe after all we've been to each other, you'd accuse me of lying and stealing your semen."

Tony laughed. "Cara, you didn't have to steal Rex's semen, he's been known to give it away. Young men only dream of living the life of Rex."

Kate slapped Tony's arm. "Shut up."

Rex saw Cara's face and more tears and tried for damage control. "Tony, you know that's not true. Tell her it's not true."

"I'm not lying."

Now Cara was gulping for air. "All I wanted was to get a donor and to be a mother. I didn't want a husband. I just wanted a baby."

"All women want husbands." Tony and Kate made noises in agreement with Rex.

"You're wrong." Cara was pointing her finger at the trio. "If you saw what my mother was picking out, you wouldn't be saying that."

"Hey," Tony said, sounding insulted. "I was one of those guys."

"You were different. I've known you since before we were born."

He nodded. "That's true."

Rex was a man who had gotten where he was in business and in life by going with this gut. His instincts were usually uncanny. He could spot a person who was telling the truth a cornfield away. Cara may not be lying right now, at least about the baby she wanted and the husband she didn't, but she had totally disregarded the fact that the coin was by his freezer unit. And he reminded her of that fact.

"I don't know how it got there," she said.

"Don't you?" He didn't believe her. He looked at Tony. "What about you? Did you send her to steal the semen?"

"What the hell are you talking about? My own semen was stolen."

Kate grabbed both men by the hands and said, "You two stop it right now. You should be working together." She looked at Cara. "Did you remember losing one of the coins?"

Cara shook her head, wiping her eyes with the back

of her hand. "No. There are so many of them. I know some are loose and one fell off that first time I went to the clinic. I kept thinking I needed to get the bracelet fixed."

Rex took a deep breath. "I'm sorry. Maybe I was wrong."

Her eyes looked stormy. "Just maybe?"

"That's as far as I'll go right now without more evidence."

Cara stood. "I'm going home."

"You haven't eaten," Kate said.

"I'm not hungry."

"We'll see you tomorrow then."

"I'm going home. To Erie."

"You can't leave yet," Rex said, standing up. "You're not leaving until I know if you're pregnant."

"Oh, Doctor, believe me. I'm not pregnant."

"How do you know?"

"In order to get pregnant, you have to have sex, and you and I, we didn't have sex."

Now he had been sucker punched. How dare she say that night of passion, many times, wasn't sex? What did she think sex was, anyway?

"What are you talking about? Of course we had sex."

"You just don't get it. If you had been a gentlemen, you would have pretended I was telling the truth. You saw my humiliation." She started poking him in the chest. "I explained it to you. You, Dr. Noble, should get your name changed from Dr. Noble to Dr. Nasty." With her head held high she walked regally out of the restaurant and would have made it, too, if she hadn't been stopped by Clyde who dragged her back to the table.

"I have a confession to make," he told them. "I stole the semen."

"What are you talking about?"

"I had this plan, see, Doc. I like this little girl." He nodded to Cara. "And you need to settle down, so I thought, if I plant one of her coins—they fall off your bracelet, dear, all over the place—that you two would find yourselves together and get married."

Tigger came up to the table. "It's my fault," he said contritely. "I planted the coin."

Before long, Barbara, Cathy and Arthur had also come to the table. The amazing thing was that none of them knew the others were doing the same thing. They each dropped coins on the table, and each said they were sorry. "Where's the semen?" Rex asked.

Some had put it in other freezer units. Barbara had taken hers home and fertilized her African violet with it. "It died though. It must be too strong a fertilizer. In fact, I think you need to pay me for the dead plant and buy me another."

Rex gathered Cara's hand. "Can you forgive me?" he asked.

"No." She turned and left the restaurant, head held high, back straight, and she didn't look back.

Rex looked from Tony to Kate. "I don't know what she's so upset about. You eastern women are so sensitive."

Kate stood, throwing her napkin on the table. "You deal with him," she told Tony, then hurried after Cara.

Tony shrugged. "Women, go figure."

Rex nodded, looking longingly at the door Cara had vanished through.

Tony signaled the waiter. "Tell the man what you want, Rex. It's on the house."

13

CARA HAD GONE straight from the airport to her apartment. She didn't call her mother, even though it would have been the right thing to do. All she wanted was to go home and be by herself. She still had four days of vacation left, and she wasn't going to tell her mother she was in Erie until the morning she had to go back to school.

As she had driven down the familiar streets toward her home, she realized that Erie didn't feel like home. She didn't know why, it just didn't. When had that happened? She loved Erie.

Now all she could think about was a big bull in Texas and the bull's big owner. The man she loved, despite that he had called her a liar.

She sat at her familiar desk in her office at home. All the school supplies, the teacher's manuals, the how-to books surrounded her. Before, whenever she had come in here, she'd been filled with enthusiasm at the prospect of teaching her little babies. But now she knew they weren't her babies, they were little kindergarten kids who belonged to other people.

When had the little babies in her class stopped fulfilling the need she had? She used to love going to her classroom, loved teaching, loved planning the lessons. She had loved wiping sniffly noses, and watching the kids play and learn. For some reason none of that thrilled her anymore. She knew she would still love her job and love her kids, but the thrill of the job wasn't there. She wanted more. Much more. She wanted Rex. She wanted Rex's baby.

Why was it that life was so complicated? Why couldn't Rex simply understand that? Why did he have to go off about the pinpricks? She told him she hadn't used those.

Anyway, Rex wouldn't even consider marrying her, and she certainly didn't want to marry him. If she did, she'd be giving in to her mom's bet. Of course, it was a nonissue because Rex never gave her any indication he might be interested in marriage.

Besides, where would they live? Even though Erie didn't feel like home right now, she was sure in a week or so it would, and she'd settle right back into her routine.

Even if things had worked out between her and Rex, she couldn't stay in Texas. She had her family and her job and her friends here.

When she had been in Pegleg, Cara thought she had everything figured out. She was a modern woman, she was going to have a baby, raise it on her own, be pen pals with the father. She knew what she wanted and no one could stop her.

Then something had happened between the time she left Pegleg and arrived back in Erie. Time, that's what had happened. Time to think. Time to reflect. Time to contemplate the fact that she didn't have a baby, she didn't have Rex, and probably would never have either.

She wanted him. All she could remember were the moments she had spent with Rex. To remember what it was like to stroke his face. The feel of his temple where the tiny pulse point seemed to accelerate beneath the touch of her fingertips. She'd circled his temple with a softness and gentleness she didn't realize she possessed. The feel of his cheek, the contour of his jawline traveling upward toward the earlobe, then behind the shell of his ear and toward the nape of his neck. Never would she have thought that a cheek could make her body tingle, make her want to drink in the fragrance of his cologne, nuzzle the crook of his neck and never have to raise her head.

What she realized most of all, what she hadn't expected, was the loneliness. The terrible, terrible sense of loss, something that had hit her hard when she had least expected it. The moment she had left Tony's restaurant.

On Sunday night, the phone rang, and she could tell by the ring that it was Cecilia. Only her mother's rings were that persistent.

"Where have you been?" Cecilia shrieked at her. "Don't you know I'm your mother?"

"Yes. How are you?"

"I'm as fine as can be expected being the mother of a daughter who drops off the face of the earth for ten days."

"I'm sorry, Mom. I couldn't stand the matchmaking anymore."

Her mother let out one of her big sighs. "I guess you're right. I shouldn't meddle. After all, I'm sure Brigit's skinny daughter is already married by now and probably pregnant."

"Do you know that for a fact?" Cara hoped Shannon was married. It would sure be a relief to get Cecilia off her back.

"No, she's not married," her mother snapped. "If she were married, don't you think Brigit would be lording the fact over us until we all puked?"

Oh, well, Cara thought. So much for that wish. "Maybe you and Brigit can call it a draw and the two of you can go to the Catskills and leave us alone."

Cara could hear her mother nodding, since her cheek was rubbing up and down on the mouthpiece.

"I was thinking the same thing. There's no point in playing around with your future and your happiness."

"Thank you, Mom."

"Well, I know I shouldn't have done this, since you've been such a terrible daughter, running out on us without a word. But you know, there was this sale, and I did find a beautiful dress for you, and I'm dying for you to come over and try it on."

"Is this a setup?"

"How could it be setup? Did I know you were going to be home? Did I know I was going to see you?"

"No. Okay, I'll be right over."

Ten minutes later Cara was knocking on the front door of her parents' house. Her mother opened it and gave her a big hug. "I missed you," she said, and for the first time Cara knew her mother really meant it.

"Where's Dad?"

"He's in the den. Do you want to go and see him?"

"Sure."

"Good. I'll go get the dress. I hope you like it."

"I'm sure I'll love it."

Cara's dad was sitting on the chair in the den, and for the first time in as long as she could remember he didn't have his head buried in a newspaper, and he wasn't watching television. He stood up and walked over to her, gave her a big hug and a kiss on the cheek. "You had us worried, Cara. Don't ever leave without giving us a number where we can reach you."

"You're right. I'm sorry. It was so wrong of me to do that."

"That's right, it was," said a wonderfully familiar voice. "Do you know how long it took to pry out of Tony where you lived?"

Cara swung around. "When did you get here?"

"Thirty minutes ago."

"Ohmigod. With my parents?"

"That's why your mother called you. I wanted to meet them first before I saw you again."

"Why? To see if I come from good breeding stock?"

"Come on, Cara. You don't believe that, do you?"

"No."

"I asked her to call you because I wanted to see you again. In neutral territory."

"This isn't neutral."

"It is to me." He stood in front of her, gathering her hands in his. "I had to see you again. I had to tell you how much I love you. How sorry I am about what happened."

"Rex." She put her arms around him and melted into his chest. Home. This is where she belonged. The feel of him. His arms around her. His face nuzzling her neck. This is where she needed to be.

"I see you found him," Cecilia said. "Nice boy. If he had been living in Erie, I would have brought him over to meet you."

"I know you would have, Mom." Not likely. Rex was too manly. Cecilia had preferred all the wimpy, skimpy men with no personalities.

"Here," her mother said. "Your dress."

It would figure her mother would have bought her a bridal gown.

Cecilia held it up against her own body. "Do you like it?"

"It's nice." She wasn't going to get excited over lace and silk, no matter how beautiful the dress was. She wasn't getting married.

"I was hoping you'd have changed your mind about that." He pulled one of Cara's gold coins out of his pocket. In the hole where it was supposed to be attached to the bracelet, he had tied a big ring. A diamond ring. "I was making sure the ring and the coins all matched. Wouldn't want you clashing." He took her hand, slipping the diamonds and gold on her finger.

She looked at her hand, then at her mother and father, and finally at Rex. "I love you, you know."

He released a big breath. "You can't possibly love me more than I love you."

"You called me a thief and a liar."

"You did lie and you stole my heart."

"I didn't steal your semen," she whispered.

"We'll talk about it when we can use visual aids," he said quietly.

"I can't hear anything. Did she say okay?" Cecilia interrupted.

"I don't recall hearing a question," Cara said.

"Did you ask her? What's taking so long?"

"I hope you'll marry me, Cara. I love you. I want you. I want to be the father to all your children. I love your heart, your spirit and your kindness. I love your protectiveness, your loyalty and your body." He winked, leaned over and whispered in her ear, "Especially that one particular dimple on your hip, I love to nip it and lick it—"

Cara stepped back, her face heated, her temperature rising. She gazed at the man in front of her. Pure male. How she loved him. "I almost want to say no because of my Mom and Brigit's stupid bet. But I don't want to lose you. I don't want to be apart from you. I only want to be with you always and forever. So it's a yes."

Cecilia started jumping and screaming and singing, "Where's the phone, where's the phone, I've got to call that Brigit. Where's the phone?"

Cara took Rex by the hand. She whispered so only he could hear, "Come on with me, big boy. I want to take you back to my apartment so that you can show me the right and proper way to gather up your personal stash of semen."

Live the emotion™
Anytime. Anywhere.
send for your 2 FREE ROMANCE BOOKS!
See Details Inside....

We'd like to send you 2 FREE BOOKS

and a surprise gift to introduce you to Harlequin Duets™. Accept our special offer today and

Live the emotion™

HOW TO QUALIFY:

1. With a coin, carefully scratch off the silver area on the card at right to see what we have for you—**2 FREE BOOKS** and a **FREE GIFT**—ALL YOURS! ALL **FREE!**

2. Send back the card and you'll receive two brand-new Harlequin Duets™ novels. These books have a cover price of $5.99 each in the U.S. and $6.99 each in Canada, but they are yours to keep absolutely free!

3. There's no catch. You're under no obligation to buy anything. We charge nothing—ZERO—for your first shipment and you don't have to make any minimum number of purchases—not even one!

4. The fact is, thousands of readers enjoy receiving books by mail from the Harlequin Reader Service® Program. They enjoy the convenience of home delivery…they like getting the best new novels at discount prices, BEFORE they're available in stores…and they love their *Heart to Heart* subscriber newsletter featuring author news, horoscopes, recipes, book reviews and much more!

5. We hope that after receiving your free books you'll want to remain a subscriber. But the choice is yours—to continue or cancel, any time at all. So why not take us up on our invitation with no risk of any kind. You'll be glad you did!

GET A *Free* MYSTERY GIFT…

We can't tell you what it is…but we're sure you'll like it! A FREE gift just for giving the Harlequin Reader Service® Program a try!

Visit us online at
www.eHarlequin.com

How To Hunt a Husband

Holly Jacobs

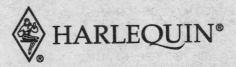

HARLEQUIN®

TORONTO • NEW YORK • LONDON
AMSTERDAM • PARIS • SYDNEY • HAMBURG
STOCKHOLM • ATHENS • TOKYO • MILAN • MADRID
PRAGUE • WARSAW • BUDAPEST • AUCKLAND

Dear Reader,

In *How To Hunt a Husband,* Shannon and Nate (aka Roxy and Bull) embark on a journey of change and discovery. Their little trick to escape their mothers' meddling ends up being a lot more than either one of them ever dreamed about, especially when it ends in love. *How To Hunt a Husband* is a sequel to last year's *How To Catch a Groom.* I hope you enjoy revisiting these characters as much as I did!

Somehow it seems appropriate that this book is about change and discovery, because it's the last of a fantastic series. Though Duets is being put to bed, so to speak, Harlequin's new romantic comedy line is on its way as Flipside. I hope you'll discover Flipside—it's a smart, sassy, single-volume series that will keep you laughing even as you fall in love.

Holly Jacobs

I love to hear from my readers. You can find me online at www.HollysBooks.com, or snailmail me at P.O. Box 11102, Erie, PA 16514-1102.

Books by Holly Jacobs

HARLEQUIN DUETS
43—I WAXED MY LEGS FOR *THIS?*
67—READY, WILLING AND...ABEL?
    RAISING CAIN
84—HOW TO CATCH A GROOM
92—NOT PRECISELY PREGNANT
100—THE 100-YEAR ITCH

SILHOUETTE ROMANCE
1557—DO YOU HEAR WHAT I HEAR?
1653—A DAY LATE AND A BRIDE SHORT

To JoAnn Ross, a fantastic writer,
a wonderful mentor…and a heck of a friend!

A special thanks to Burhenn's Pharmacy!

1

——————

"THAT WOMAN," Brigit O'Malley said.

There was a certain humph in her mother's voice that left no question in Shannon O'Malley's mind as to who "that woman" was.

Tuesday was pinochle day, so "that woman" had to be Cecilia Romano. Even a beautiful March day—and beautiful days in March were rare and treasured in Erie, Pennsylvania—couldn't obscure the black cloud "that woman" had given Brigit O'Malley.

Actually not much could shake Brigit from her Tuesday-evening funks.

"Mom, why do you go play cards every week when you always come home in a snit?"

"I am never in a snit. *Snit*. That's such an undignified word. I am—" her mother paused a moment, searching her thesaurus-like brain for a better word choice "—perturbed. Cecilia perturbs me beyond the limits of what a sane rational human can endure. Why, do you believe she's saying her daughter could—" she sputtered her way to a standstill.

"Cara?" Shannon said. "What could Cara do?"

Shannon didn't actually know Cara Romano, but knew of her, not only through their mothers, but because Shannon's sister, Kate, had married Cara's ex-fiancé, Tony Donetti.

The logistics of their connection were tangled at best, but it was their mothers that made Shannon feel a bond to the unmet Cara. After all, Cecilia Romano seemed as determined to control the fates of her children as Shannon's own mother was.

At least Brigit O'Malley had long ago decided that Shannon was a hopeless cause and had concentrated on getting Mary Kathryn's life in order. But since her sister had moved to Texas with her new husband, Shannon had noticed her mother was around a lot more, dropping in unexpectedly—as she'd done this evening—and taking a sudden interest in Shannon's activities.

Truth be told, all the attention made her a bit nervous.

More than a bit.

A lot.

Her mother stopped sputtering and said, "Cecilia said Cara can find a man before you can, when everyone knows that you are far more beautiful than that Cara Romano is. Why, men are beating down your door, begging to marry you. Aren't they?"

"Not exactly."

Beating down her door? Heck, she could hardly

remember what it was to have them knocking softly.

Shannon hadn't had a date in months. She'd been so busy planning for Mary Kathryn's wedding, then dealing with her parents in the aftermath of her sister's great bridal escape, that she simply hadn't had the time—or inclination—to date. "And, since I'm not looking for a man, Mother, I'm going to assume that Mrs. Romano is right, Cara will probably beat me to the altar."

No, the last few man-free months had convinced Shannon that dating was overrated. Without a man in the picture she'd been able to do exactly what she wanted, when she wanted, without having to consult someone else. She hadn't watched one blood-and-guts testosterone-filled film during the entire time. She'd watched chick-flicks. Lots of chick flicks. She'd drooled over Colin Firth, Ewan McGregor and Hugh Jackman—big-screen men who didn't mind that she hadn't shaved her legs for weeks.

Yes, there were advantages to a man-free existence.

"You're not a—" her mother paused and lowered her voice as if there were hidden microphones in the apartment that might overhear her question "—one of those women who doesn't like men?"

"I like men just fine, at least on a limited basis. *Limited,* Mom. That's the keyword. I'm not looking for anything long-term when I date from now on.

I've decided that I want to see a man only as long as the initial politeness lasts.''

"Initial politeness?"

"You know, that golden time in a relationship when a man will do what you want. When he'll listen to what you have to say as if every word is a treasure. Why, when things are new he'll even see chick-flicks or go shopping. Once that glow is over, I'm done with him."

That was going to be her new rule of thumb. *Use them, then lose them.*

"Shannon Bonnie O'Malley, you take that back."

Shannon suppressed a shudder. "Mother, I hate it when you call me that."

"We've had this fight over and over again. Bonnie is a perfectly lovely name. It was my mother's name and she was a wonderful woman. You're lucky to be named after her."

"You're right. Bonnie is a perfectly lovely name, so is Shannon for that matter. But some names don't go together. Bonnie doesn't go with Shannon. Ichabod and Archibald, they don't go together either."

"Why do you have to be so difficult? Mary Kathryn never complained when I called her Mary Kathryn."

That was the refrain of her relationship with her mother. Shannon had been *difficult* when she'd played soccer rather than join the science club.

She'd been *difficult* when she'd discovered a passion for art rather than something more academic.

Mary Kathryn was the good daughter, bending to her parents' dreams for her. And Shannon? Well, she was the variable in the equation of her mother's life.

"Ah, but Mary Kathryn's not a Mary Kathryn anymore, is she?"

When her sister ran out on her wedding she changed her life completely. New man. New state. New job. New name. A part of Shannon envied her sister those changes.

"She's Kate. Kate Donetti," Shannon continued. "And I think she's happier that way."

Her mother just shook her head. "You are the most difficult, cantankerous girl alive."

"I learned from the best." Shannon leaned over and gave her mother a peck on the cheek. She'd never really seen eye-to-eye with her about, well, about anything, but she loved her.

And though she frequently annoyed her mother, she didn't doubt Brigit loved her as well, even though she wasn't overly demonstrative.

"Here, try this on," her mother said as she thrust a garment bag at Shannon.

Shannon looked at the huge bag. "What is this?"

"It's Mary Kathryn's wedding dress. I asked her to mail it back to me. We spent a small fortune on that dress, you know. I want to see it walk *all* the way down the aisle. Oh, she did some damage we'd have to get repaired, but let's see if it fits you before we worry about that.''

''Fits me?'' Shannon stared at her mother, not sure where she was going with this. ''Why would you care if it fits me?''

''Well, if it doesn't we'll have to find something else for you to wear.'' Her mother put her hand on Shannon's shoulder and started steering her toward the bedroom. ''Come on, try it on.''

Shannon ground her heels into the carpet and faced her mother. ''Wear when?''

Maybe her mother's fight with Cecilia had finally driven her over the edge. Maybe she'd been sniffing just a bit too much formaldehyde in the lab she worked at.

Maybe her mother was totally deranged.

''At your wedding,'' her mother said.

''What wedding?'' Shannon asked, feeling not-very-bright and more than a little nervous.

''The wedding I'm planning. I told you what Cecilia said about Cara. I can't let that woman beat me, so that means I can't let her daughter beat you to the altar. I thought right after school got out. June twenty-fifth. What do you think about that day? That leaves you plenty of time for a honeymoon before you start back to school next fall. Of course, that doesn't leave me long to get the entire thing planned. Less than four months.''

''Mother, I know I seem dense here, but just who is it that I'm supposed to be marrying?''

Shannon had often felt like the not-so-bright family member. Her parents and Mary Kathryn all had a ton of initials behind their names. They lived for academia.

Well, actually, since she'd married Tony, Kate lived for Donetti's Irish Pub and Cooked Sushi Bar, but that was beside the point. She still had initials behind her name, and Shannon was still *just* the high-school art teacher.

Oh, her family never added the *just* to her job description, at least not out loud, but Shannon knew they thought it. They valued those initials, and though she had a B.A. in education and art, she didn't have all those extra, more impressive initials. And she taught art, not a serious subject like science.

Shannon realized her mother was talking again. Something about a wedding.

Her wedding?

Who did her mother think she was going to marry?

"…Seth."

Shannon's attention jumped back into focus. "Mother, you're not suggesting I marry Seth? You went to his wedding to Desi, after all."

"How could I forget. When it was Mary Kathryn's wedding that wedding planner didn't worry at all when I pointed out the cake was too small, but at her own wedding? Why, the cake was huge.

A veritable mountain of cake. Still I never understood why she had Barbies on the top.''

Her mother was quiet a moment, obviously pondering why Seth and Desi had had Barbies for their wedding-cake toppers.

''So what does Seth have to do with anything?'' Shannon finally asked when she couldn't stand the silence any more.

''I called Seth to see if he knew a nice man you could marry…''

NATHAN CALDER sat at the bar in O'Halloran's Bar and Grill. He wasn't drinking anything harder than cola even though it was Friday and he was off tomorrow. He'd simply come by to show Mick how he'd spent his tax return…on his new Harley.

Yep, he was a bad-assed, Harley-riding… pharmacist. A bad-assed, Harley-riding pharmacist who'd only just got his motorcycle license and obviously shouldn't have been awarded it, since he'd stalled the motorcycle three times on the way over to Mick's.

He felt like he was this year's April Fool joke because it was hard to feel tough when you were sitting in the middle of traffic, wearing your new leather jacket…and trying to restart your engine.

Harder still when you flooded it and had to wheel the motorcycle to the side of the road and wait ten minutes for the gas in the carburetor to evaporate before you could try the engine again.

Nate sipped his cola, wondering how he was going to get the bike home without repeating the incident.

He planned to ride the bike to hockey practice this week and let his team "ooh" and "ah" over it, but maybe he should rethink that plan, at least until he'd mastered the art of not stalling.

Nate caught a glimpse of movement out of the corner of his eye and turned. A beautiful woman had taken the seat next to him. A heart-stoppingly beautiful woman. Tall, with reddish hair cut short, but not the least bit mannish. No, this woman was the type who made any man in proximity sit up and take notice.

The kind of woman who made him forget all about his Harley troubles.

"Hey, Mick. Could I have the usual?" she called in a husky sort of voice that made every man within hearing distance who hadn't already noticed her turn her way.

"Sure, thing, Shannon-me-love," Mick said in his patently fake Irish brogue.

"Come on, Mick. Give the lady a break," Nate ribbed his friend. "You know you grew up right next door to me in Glenwood Hills, not in the green hills of Ireland."

Nate shot a grin at the redhead.

The bartender smiled as he said, "Ah, sure I do, Nate, but Shannon likes the brogue for atmosphere, don't you my sweet?"

"Ah, Mick, the Irish apple of my eye, you can

be sure I do. Why, if me mum keeps insisting I get married, I may just take you home and make the poor woman's dreams come true. Why, she'd not only be getting her wedding, but it would include a good Irish boy as well. Ah, she'd never recover from the sheer joy of it all. And I'd be trading the O'Malley last name for O'Hallaran. My initials would stay the same. Yes, you may be the perfect husband material…at least if it wasn't for the wee fact that you're a hound when it comes to the women.''

Mick leaned across the bar and said, ''And though I'd rather be kissing a banshee than marrying anyone, I might just make an exception for you, Shannon-me-love.''

Chuckling, he moved toward the other end of the long bar where a customer was hailing him.

''He's something else,'' Shannon murmured as she took a sip of whatever it was Mick had given her.

''Sure is. Why, his first day of high school he convinced the teachers he was an Irish exchange student.''

Mick's Shannon grinned as she asked, ''You knew him then?''

''Sure did. We've been friends forever. I'm Nathan Calder. Not that he'd ever introduce me to a pretty lady. He likes to keep them all for himself. Selfish, that's Mick.'' He chuckled and added, ''Friends call me Nate.''

"Shannon, Shannon O'Malley."

She held her hand out to Nate and they shook.

If asked, Nate would have testified that there were actual sparks flying off their joined hands. He'd have sworn to it in a court of law. Slightly bemused by the experience, he pulled his hand back as quickly as possible.

As a professional, Nate had shaken a lot of hands, but none that left him feeling as *shaken* as Shannon's did. It wasn't as if there was anything special about her hand. He quickly glanced at it to make sure.

Nope. There was nothing special about it at all. Just five fingers on a nicely shaped palm. One small ring. Short, neatly manicured nails.

What on earth was he doing noticing a woman's manicure? He must be more flustered than he'd thought about the whole stalling-the-motorcycle thing.

He tried to pull his scattered wits back together. "Well, Shannon-me-love O'Malley, if Mick stands you up on that offer of marriage, give me a call. My mother would love nothing more than to hear some woman is making an honest man of me."

"You're mother's on the marriage kick, too?" she asked, sympathy in her voice.

"Not just the marriage kick," he admitted, "but the grandbabies kick as well."

It wasn't that Nate didn't like kids.

Someday he might want one…maybe even two.

But not now. After all, he'd just bought a Harley. Harleys didn't come with baby seats. Plus it was hard to be a bad-assed biker if you were carting around a diaper bag.

Okay, so it was hard if you couldn't go more than three blocks without stalling the motorcycle, but it would be worse with a baby, of that he was sure.

"Oh, mine hasn't started in about grandchildren yet," Shannon was saying. "No, she's just after a husband for me. She's already planning the wedding in June."

"Oh, so you do have a fiancé?" he asked, slightly disappointed. After all, he'd noticed the ring on her hand, but it wasn't on the right finger. Damn. Here was a woman he would have liked to get to know better.

Not in a marrying, baby-producing way, but in a she's-too-hot sort of way.

He'd love to feel her body pressed against his, his Harley rumbling beneath them as they rode through town. And after the ride... Well he could think of a few other places he'd like to take this woman.

"No, there's no fiancé," she said. "But that's not going to stop my mother. Why, she's already set the wedding date and is calling around trying to find a priest who will marry us, since Father Murphy said no. Fortunately, all the rest have said no as well, since there's no groom. Priests have rules about that kind of thing. And my mother wouldn't consider me really married if I wasn't married by a priest in the church, wearing a long white gown with a whole group of her friends watching.''

''You win hands down,'' Nate said. ''My mother just complains about her lack of grandchildren.'' His voice rose and he said, *''And to think of the forty-eight hours I spent laboring with you. The doctors said another baby would kill me, and so you were destined to be my only one. An only child who almost killed his mother.''*

''Oh, she brings out death-guilt? That's a hard battle to fight,'' Shannon said.

''It gets worse.'' Again he altered his voice and said, *''And all those years I slaved away, trying to be the best mother I knew how to be, and all I want from you now is grandchildren before I'm too old to enjoy them. But do you care? No. Every girl I introduce you to you find something wrong with. You're too picky, that's what you are.''*

''Too picky. My mother says the same thing. She's spent the last month fixing me up with…well, between you and me, I don't think she's been *picky* at all about the men she's hooked me up with. Desperate. That pretty much describes my mother's matchmaking.''

She sighed and took a sip of her drink. ''Tonight's date was a prime example. I told her no. No more dates. I have a plan, you see. I want to live a solitary, chick-flick, hairy-legged life. But she invited me out to dinner with her and my father. At least that was the story. They were at the restaurant, all right, but so was he. His name was Neil. He works with Mom and Dad at the college.''

"Doing what?" Nate prompted.

"A philosophy professor. Mom and Dad had a mysterious lab emergency. Have you ever heard of a lab emergency?"

Nate shook his head.

"Me either. Anyway, they left Neil to entertain me while we finished eating."

"You don't look overly entertained," Nate said with a chuckle.

Frustrated. That's how she looked.

Nate could sympathize. His mom had planned her own set-ups these last few months.

"Oh, Nate, you don't know the half of it. Neil spent the rest of the dinner talking about things so deep my head was spinning. It's not that I'm dumb, but he was being pompous on purpose. Then he turned the subject to how Kepler's observations of heavenly bodies impacted our way of viewing the world around us, and added that he'd like a chance to spend more time studying my heavenly body...."

Shannon drained her glass. "Well, I finished my spare ribs faster than anybody should, and I hope Neil was feeling philosophical about my emphatic rejection of his heavenly-body proposal. There was absolutely no way I was *impacting* with him."

"Most men aren't overly philosophical about rejections," Nate pointed out.

"Yeah, he didn't seem very pleased. My mom called my cell phone to apologize for their 'emergency' and to see how the rest of the meal went. I told her that I left right after the entrée because I didn't want to be Neil's dessert. That's when she accused me of being picky, and I said if she didn't watch it, I'd show her how non-picky I could be by picking a man that would fry her butt. I mean a biker, with long greasy hair and tattoos or something. She'd be off my case about marriage quicker than she could light a Bunsen burner."

"Yeah, rebellion has its place. My mother wants me to grow up and settle down, though maybe not quite as bad as your mother wants you to. Mom keeps pointing out I'm thirty and that it's time to become an adult. But to be honest, I don't recall ever having had a childhood, so I've staged my own mini rebellion. I've decided it's time to do some of the things I've always wanted to do but was too busy with school or establishing a career to try."

Nate took a sip of his cola and continued. "I thought about tattoos, as a matter of fact, but I didn't think it would go over well with my customers."

"Customers? What do you do?" Shannon asked.

Nate smiled and replied, "I'm a pharmacist. I can't see my customers being comfortable with me tattooed. And you? What do you do when you're not out on bad dates?''

''I'm a high-school art teacher.''

''Too bad you weren't a stripper or something. I could take you home and scare my mother out of rushing me into marriage.''

''Yeah,'' Shannon said, wistfulness in her voice. ''If only I was a stripper and you were a greasy biker, life would be perfect.''

They both paused and, though he didn't know her well, he could see she realized the opportunity they had in front of them at the same moment he did.

Nate weighed the possibility. After all, he didn't need an actual stripper. He just needed his mother to *believe* he'd brought home a stripper.

''I just bought a bike,'' Nate said slowly. ''A Harley Fatboy.''

''You did?'' Shannon asked, something akin to awe in her voice.

Nate nodded. ''So if we told your parents I was a biker, it wouldn't actually be a lie.''

He didn't mention the fact that he still questioned his abilities to actually ride the bike.

''And I do take my clothes off every night to put on pajamas, so I guess you could say I strip.''

They both laughed and let the idea grow. ''You know, if I took you home disguised as a stripper and told my parents I was in love with you—a woman who takes off her clothes for a living—my mother might get off my back about babies, at least for a while.''

''Your mother would hate a stripper daughter-in-law as much as my mother would hate a biker son-in-law.''

She grinned. ''Oh, it's too perfect. Kismet even. My mother would have to rethink her wedding plans if I brought you in and introduced you as the man in my life. The only man I'd even consider marrying.''

Nate thought his mother was a bit of a pain, but Shannon's mother sounded certifiable. ''Um, you didn't really explain why your mother is already planning your wedding, even though there's no groom in sight.''

''Well, it all started when my sister—the *good* daughter—ran out on her wedding with the best man. She changed her name from Mary Kathryn to Kate, and changed her man from Seth to Tony. She also changed careers.''

''From?'' he found himself asking, even though he wasn't sure he was following Shannon's explanation.

''From research scientist and professor, to an employee and part-owner of Donetti's Irish Pub and Cooked Sushi Bar.''

''Cooked sushi?'' Nate echoed.

Maybe it wasn't just Shannon's mother who was crazy…maybe it was her whole family.

''It's a long story,'' she warned.

"I've got all night. And we'll need each other's full stories if we're going to entertain this plan."

Shannon took a deep breath and started, "Well Mary Kathryn and Seth were best friends who decided to marry because it seemed like the logical thing to do, but they didn't have any passion between them. So on her wedding day, Kate picked up her skirt and hightailed it out of the church before the I-do's were done. She ran off with Tony, the best man. I felt horrible for Seth, but it turns out he fell head over heels for Desi, the wedding planner. So, it was happily ever after for everyone but me and Tony's ex-fiancée, Cara, because my mom suddenly noticed I'm single and made a bet with Cara's mom…"

Nate half listened as Shannon's story unfolded. The rest of his mind was occupied with wondering about how she'd look dressed up as a stripper.

The mental images were tantalizing.

This might be a crazy plan, but desperate times called for desperate measures.

And this mental image of Shannon disguised as a stripper was making Nate feel quite desperate.

2

"NATE, is that you?" Judy Calder called out as Nate entered his parents' home the next morning.

Normally Nate would have had to suppress a groan, knowing the course his conversation with his mother would be taking.

It wasn't that he didn't love his mother. Of course he loved her. Loved her a lot. After all, how could you not love a woman who almost died giving birth to you?

But this week the only thing he was suppressing was a grin.

He followed the sound of her voice into the kitchen. "Yeah, Mom, it's me. Where's Dad?"

His father could generally be counted on to run interference on the grandbaby nagging front, not that Nate wanted too much interfering today. He had the plan, after all.

A delightful plan.

A perfect plan.

A mother-proof plan.

A plan guaranteed to buy him some much-needed respite from his mother's pleas.

"Your father was on call and had to run in to the store," she said.

"I just stopped in to check that little leak you were having under the sink," Nate said from the doorway.

The kitchen was next to blinding. Bright-yellow walls, brilliant-white cabinets, sparkling surfaces. A floor you could probably actually eat off of.

Judy Calder believed in everything being just-so, whether it was her kitchen or her son's life.

She turned from the counter. In her late fifties, his mom didn't look her age at all. Folks might find his mother young-looking, but no one ever took his father for anything but his age. Paul Calder had been gray-haired since Nate could remember, and he blamed his wife for every one of those gray hairs. But after years of watching how much his father doted on his mom, Nate suspected that both of them owed the color of their hair to genetics, because the two of them were obviously meant for each other.

"Oh, honey, that's so sweet of you to stop and see about the sink. But it's okay. I called a plumber. After all, you know you're not any more mechanical than your father is."

He opened the small door off the kitchen that led to the laundry room and grabbed his father's toolbox from the corner.

"Not mechanical? Mom, how can you say that? After all, who fixed the dryer just last week?"

"You kicked it, dear."

"It stopped making the noise right after that."

His mother didn't understand the fine art of home repair. Nate's opinion was, when something worked, don't fix it, and when something didn't work, try kicking it first. In this case, kicking was all that had been called for.

"Why, it was practically purring when I finished," he said as he set the toolbox down on the counter and opened it up.

His mom shook her head and kissed his cheek. "And it started squeaking again about ten minutes after you left. I got out the spray lubricant, unscrewed the back of the machine and sprayed all over. It hasn't squeaked since."

"It was my kick that took care of it." His mother looked ready to contest the point, so he hastily went on, "But, I won't argue. Just let me have a look at the sink. If I don't think I can handle it, we'll just let the plumber come. But do you know how much they charge for a service call?"

Slowly, his mother backed away and gave him room to open the cabinet doors. Nate rolled up his sleeves and slid down and under the sink.

"Probably not as much as the roofer charged when he had to fix your patch job," his mom muttered.

"I heard that," Nate called as he studied the silver U-ish pipe over his head.

"I wanted you to. And speaking of hearing, I

need you to listen. No excuses that you didn't hear me this time. You're coming to dinner Friday night. It's Sunday, so that's five days' notice."

He wiggled the U-ish-looking pipe. "This seems loose. Hand me the big pipe wrench, okay?"

She handed the wrench to him as she continued, "About dinner on Friday. I'm going to invite Jocelyn and her daughter Kay over."

"No."

Too bad he couldn't kick the pipe. He could barely get his torso under the sink. But he gave it a couple good thwacks with the wrench just in case that was all it would take. But the pipe just seemed even looser after that and not fixed at all, so he tried to get the wrench around the big bolt that held the sections together.

"And I'm going to make that pot roast you like," his mom continued.

"I hate pot roast. I like pork roast and sauerkraut."

His mother always forgot what his favorite dishes were. He thought it was some passive-aggressive way of getting back at him for not giving her grandchildren yet.

"And I'll make some of my delicious homemade dinner rolls."

"They're like bricks."

"And you're going to love Kay—"

"Kay? Couldn't her parents give her a whole

name? "Kay. I could never love a woman who's name was just an initial."

"—and maybe she'll be the one you finally marry. Then the two of you will give me grandbabies. Lots and lots of grandbabies. I've met Kay. She's built for babies. Wide hips, you know."

He thought of Shannon. He wouldn't call her hips wide. Not that they were too thin. No, they looked perfectly proportioned to the rest of her body.

His mother would be disappointed.

He grinned—thankful he was hidden under the sink—ready to launch the plan he and narrow-hipped Shannon had devised. "Sorry mom. Kay sounds delightful. But I'm seeing someone."

"Since when?"

He could hear the suspicion in her voice.

Deciding to stick to the truth when possible, he said, "Last night, at Mick's place. They're friends."

"You met her in a bar? Nice girls don't go to bars and pick up men," his mother assured him.

"She didn't pick me up, I picked her up." Mick had practically had to throw them out so he could close, they sat and talked so long. The plan was simple, they'd use each other as weapons to diffuse their mothers' mutual matrimonial designs.

One bad-assed biker and a stripper to the rescue.

"Well, nice girls don't *let* men pick them up in bars," his mother humphed.

"This one did."

He finally got the big pipe wrench to grip the bolt that connected the pipes and turned it.

The pipe fell off with just the first half turn and landed on Nate's nose. "Ow!"

"What did you do to my sink?" his mother yelled.

"Your sink?" he hollered back as he shimmied out from under the cabinet gripping his aching, moist-feeling nose. "Your sink? What about my nose? I think it's sunk into my face."

"I always thought your nose was too big anyway. It could use some sinking. You have your father's nose, and he never did have an attractive one."

"Thanks, Mom." Nate grabbed the towel and held it to his nose, trying to stem the flow of blood. "Can you bleed to death from your nose?"

"No. Now what about my sink? You broke it didn't you? And now the plumber is going to charge me twice as much."

"Mom, I'm dying and you're worried about your sink and money? That shouldn't be the biggest concern of a devoted mother. My bleeding to death should be."

She folded her arms across her chest, obviously not feeling overly devoted. "What did you do to my sink?"

"The bolt that held the pipes together was obviously loose, which is probably why it was leaking and the explanation for the fact it fell off so easily. I'll just tighten it back down and you should be fine.''

"That's what you say. But I remember that time you were going to cut down that tree in the backyard. You broke my chain saw.''

"Mom, I'd cut almost all the way through that branch and was trying to pull it down when that big one over top of it fell instead…you're lucky it crushed the saw, not your son.''

"Well, I was rather partial to that saw,'' she said with a mischievous grin. "Let's face it, honey, though I adore you, you're not Bob Vila. Actually, you're not even Tim-the-Toolman Taylor.''

"Gee, your faith in me makes me feel special. And speaking of feeling special, I've got a new girl now, so you can cancel Friday night's dinner with the wide-hipped initial girl.''

Maybe just mentioning a new woman would be enough to get his mother off his case for a while. If it was, they wouldn't have to move on to the second part of their plan.

"No, I won't cancel dinner,'' she said. "Though I won't invite Kay. Instead you can bring this bar floozy to meet your mother.''

She lifted the towel and peeked under it at his nose. "I think it stopped bleeding, but you're going to have quite a mark.''

Nate gingerly felt his nose, and though it seemed swollen, it didn't feel as if he'd broken it.

"Wonder how the floozy will feel about your new nose," his mom added.

"She's not a floozy, exactly. She's a nice girl."

"Who got picked up in a bar."

"Mom, our first official date's Friday. You don't take a girl to dinner at your mom's on the first date."

He grinned. Arguing with his mother was a part of the plan. After all, if he gave in too easily, she'd suspect something. She was a sly one, his mom.

But he was slyer.

Much slyer.

Why, if he hadn't become a pharmacist, he probably could have been a spy he was so wily.

"Maybe you should bring over more first dates. After all, you've never brought one here before, and I still have no grandbabies. Maybe if you bring this girl here now, she'll realize you're serious about this relationship."

"You said she was a floozy. Why would you want me to be serious about a girl like that? And who said I was serious? It's our first date. We just sat at the bar and drank last night, so that doesn't count. If I bring her here for dinner she'll think I'm—"

"—a nice guy," his mom interrupted. "She'll think you're a nice guy. Dinner will be at seven. Don't be late."

She leaned over and glanced under the sink. "Now fix my sink."

"Oh, I'll fix you…I mean your sink," he said with a grin.

If he'd become a spy instead of a pharmacist he'd name his missions. He thought of the possibilities as he started to reattach the pipe.

Operation Meddling Mothers. Yeah, that was perfect.

Operation Meddling Mothers was about to begin.

"Mom?"

Shannon had already agreed to Sunday dinner with her parents—and no one else—before she met Nate. She had expected to find the ordeal trying. But now, despite her mother's new marry-off-Shannon campaign—or rather because of it—she was looking forward to the evening.

"Oh, Shannon there you are. I have so much news. I've been busy," her mother said as Shannon walked into the house at promptly four-thirty.

"Me, too," Shannon said, kissing her mother's cheek.

Her mom patted the chair next to her. Shannon sat as her mother exclaimed in an excited, breathless voice, "I'm sorry that your dinner with Neil didn't work out."

"Mom, you have to stop setting me up. I'm not interested."

As if Shannon hadn't even spoken, her mother continued, "I've got you a date for next Saturday night! A nice boy. His name is Shelby."

"Sorry, Mom, no can do."

"Now, Shannon, there you go, being difficult again. I know you have name issues and you think I haven't thought about how Shelby and Shannon sound together. But I have. It's not a Shannon Bonnie thing. Oh, I know, I know you're going to say that whenever someone says your names together, other people with think they're being shushed, but really, dear, that's a very narrow view. A man is more than his name."

"Mom, really it's not his name—"

"And I know that you think this entire wedding thing is just about my bet with that woman, and maybe that's what instigated it, but Shannon, dear, let's face it, you're not getting any younger. It's time you settled down and found happiness. Why, your father has endowed my life with such joy. I want you to find a man as endowed as he is."

Shannon started choking. "Mom—"

Her mother, obviously unaware of what she'd just said, continued, "And I realize that you like to buck the system. That you hate to do anything I suggest because…well, because you're just a tiny bit difficult, dear."

Shannon was about to argue, as usual, that she might be difficult but she'd learned from the best. And not only was her mother difficult herself, she was certifiable. But she didn't get to say all that because her mom held up her hand, stopping her before she started.

"Uh-uh-uh. You know you are. All I'm saying

is don't say no to meeting Shelby just because I suggested it. I'm not saying marry him tomorrow—"

"No, you're saying marry him in June."

"At the end of June," her mother corrected. "That gives you plenty of time to get to know him. But that's not what I'm worried about. I'd just like you to meet a nice boy. Shelby's a podiatrist. He's—"

"Mom, if you'd take a breath, I'd tell you I can't go out with Shelby because I'm already seeing someone. It's not because of the name issue, though you're right, that would be the pits."

"See, I knew the name thing would be an issue," her mother muttered.

"It's not the name thing. It's simply that I've thought about what you said the other day, about me always fighting your wishes, and decided you were right. If you want me to consider marrying, I will. As a matter of fact, I've found a man I really like. We have a date next weekend."

"Really?" Her mother looked suspicious.

"Really," Shannon assured her. "Mom, we might not always see eye to eye, but I never lie to you. Yes. I met a man after I ditched Neil. His name is Nathan Calder and I like him."

That wasn't a lie at all. She did like Nate. Oh, there was a physical attraction. After all, the man gave new meaning to the phrase *tall, dark and handsome*. But it was more than that. He genuinely seemed like a nice guy. Easy to talk to. Down to earth.

Why, they'd sat at O'Halloran's and talked most of the night away. But they'd made good use of their time. They'd devised a plan to take care of both of their mothers' nagging.

If Shannon was looking for a man—which she wasn't, she was sticking to her motto, use them and lose them—but if she was, Nate might warrant a look, or even two.

"I think you'll like him," she said.

Silently she added, *if you met the real him.* But if things went the way they'd planned, Brigit O'Malley wasn't going to like Nathan Calder at all.

"You'll bring him by?"

"Yeah. Next weekend sometime, maybe? Let me run it by him and I'll get back to you about when."

Shannon spent the rest of the visit basking in her successful first step. Her mother was about to learn a valuable lesson. *Be careful what you wish for...it just might come true.*

Oh, yeah. Her mother wanted her to find a significant other, and Shannon was about to do just that.

Only she doubted that when her mother envisioned her riding away, duly wed, she pictured her on the back of a Harley.

SHANNON BONNIE O'MALLEY, who would have thought?

Shannon asked herself the rhetorical question as she stared at her reflection in the mirror.

She was rather awed by what she saw.

Oh, Shannon had realistic views of herself. She wasn't gorgeous, but she wasn't so ugly that her mama tied pork chops around her neck to get the dog to play with her when she was a baby. She was comfortably in the middle most days.

But now?

Well, who knew that the right undergarments could make such a difference? After she'd hatched her plan with Nate the other night, she'd made an emergency trip to a lingerie store to prepare for their date and had left herself at the mercy of a sales clerk.

The woman and her underwear—not *her* underwear, but the underwear the store sold—were amazing.

Panties that sucked things in.

And a bra that stuck things out—things she never even imagined she owned.

Actually, the bra was the most interesting contraption she'd ever seen. It had a little pump and she could actually inflate it until she'd achieved just the right size breasts.

Oh, they were fake breasts, but—she checked the mirror again—no one would ever know. Instead of a flat drop from her neck to her feet she had a long channel of cleavage exposed from the daring cut of her new red dress. A new red dress that would give her mother a heart attack and convince Nate's mother that pushing for grandchildren might not be such a great idea, at least not if Shannon was the woman in the running for becoming their mother.

She backed up so she got a good look at the entire effect. Though the hemline fell to her knees, the slit up either side practically showed off her new body-sucking panties.

Oh, yeah, this was good.

She finished applying her makeup with a heavy hand and studied the results.

Yes, she believed she could convince Nate's mother she was a stripper.

No, she took that back.

Not *stripper*.

If she was a stripper, she'd find the term insulting. Degrading even.

Even if she was taking off her clothes for money, she hoped she'd still retain her sense of dignity.

Exotic dancer.

Yep, that's the term she'd prefer if she was a stripper…*exotic dancer*. It sounded so much more dignified.

Her doorbell rang and she checked her watch. Nate was prompt. She liked that in a man.

She slipped on her stiletto-heeled boots and zipped them all the way to her knees, then hurried to the door.

She opened it and immediately looked to Nate's face for his reaction to his exotic-dancer date.

His slack-jawed, ogling response was just what she'd hoped for.

"I take it you approve?" she asked.

"Oh, honey, I do, but my mom will absolutely faint. She told me only floozies allowed themselves to be picked up in a bar and when she gets a look at you, she'll rest her case, but she won't rest easy. As a matter of fact, after seeing you, my mother might try to make me move back home so she can protect me."

"Do you think you need protection?" Shannon asked with her throatiest voice. She figured if she was an exotic dancer, she'd have that kind of sexy bedroom voice and had been practicing all week.

"I don't think any man in his right mind would want to be protected from you. But I do think every man's mother would want to lock her son up rather than let a stripper like you—"

"Actually I prefer the term *exotic dancer,* if you don't mind," she said, pleased she'd managed to keep a straight face.

She'd managed, but Nate didn't.

He burst out laughing.

"Oh, that's good. Real good. You know, you could have been an actress instead of a teacher."

"Well, it won't be good if you laugh like that. How are we supposed to convince your mother you're head over heels in love with me if you can't stay in character?"

"Sorry." He crossed his heart. "It won't happen again."

"It had better not. It's not just that I'm worried you'll blow the charade with your mom. That would be *your* problem, after all. It's that I need to know you're going to be able to convince my mom when we meet her tomorrow."

"I don't know if I'm ever going to be able to look as good as you do."

"I'm going to take that as a compliment."

"You should. But can I point out that Shannon isn't a very good stripper name."

"Oh, I thought about that. When I dance—I'm an exotic dancer, not a stripper, I'll thank you very much to remember that—I use the stage name Roxy."

"Oh, Roxy is good." He laughed. "I think you're having just a little too much fun with this."

Shannon drank in the sight of him—and oh what a sight it was. Nate had that Cary Grant-ish sort of look—the kind that was born for a business suit, but could as easily carry off just jeans and a T-shirt.

She wondered what he'd look like in a tux.

She tried to picture it.

Oh, yeah, Nate Calder would look mighty fine in a tux. His shoulders were broad and the jacket would hang ever so comfortably from them.

As a matter of fact, she thought she'd tuck quite comfortably under those arms, given a chance. Not that she expected to be wrapped in Nate's arms, not unless it became necessary as part of their act.

But if she did get tucked into Nate's arms, she thought she'd fit well.

Wrapped in Nate.

The mental image of him holding her so tightly that she could hear his heart popped when he said, "So let's go. We don't want to be late for my mother's dinner. Though I hope you heeded my warning and ate something already. My mother might be known for her lobbying for grandbabies, but she's not known for her cooking—especially her pot roast."

"That bad?" Shannon asked.

"Worse."

Nate's Harley was parked outside her apartment building waiting in all its regal splendor. "Oh, wow, this is a great bike."

He puffed up. "It's a classic. A Fatboy. I can't believe how lucky I was to find one."

He handed her a silver helmet. "Will it mess up your hair too much?"

"No. There are advantages to short cuts. I'll just spike it back up when we get off."

"Then let's go."

Climbing on the back of a motorcycle wearing stiletto heels was more difficult than Shannon had imagined. She used Nate's shoulder to steady herself.

He stood and pressed down on the starter.

The engine turned over, but didn't catch.

He did it again.

And again.

Nate turned around and offered her a sheepish grin. "Sorry. I just got my license, and I haven't quite got the hang of some parts of motorcycle riding yet."

"Would you be insulted if I offered to start it?" Shannon asked.

She didn't want to hurt his feelings. Despite their bravado, men tended to have rather fragile egos. "I've been riding motorcycles since high school. I dated Johnny Palmer, the school's resident bad boy and he taught me."

That wasn't all Johnny had taught her. One night when he got a bit too presumptuous and Shannon had slugged him hard in order to convince him that no meant no, she'd learned to hitchhike because Johnny had up and left her on the side of the road.

"You ride motorcycles?" Nate asked.

"I don't own one, but I do know how to ride."

"Can you start one in those heels?"

She grinned. "Let's see."

Nate climbed off the bike and stood next to it as Shannon slid up into the driver's seat.

She stood and pressed on the starter. The motorcycle hummed to life with a Harley's belly-rumbling sound.

"There you go," she said, her voice loud in order to be heard over the noise.

"Why don't you just drive?" he asked.

"Are you sure?"

She peeked at his face and he seemed serious. Most men she knew wouldn't be caught dead buzzing around town on the back of a motorcycle driven by a woman.

Women might have come a long way, but Shannon had found that not all men had.

"Sure I'm sure. I tend to stall it…a lot. And mom will have a fit if we're late. But maybe later you could give me some lessons?"

Oh, Shannon could think of a lesson or two she'd like to give Nathan Calder, but she didn't share that bit of information with him.

Their dates were completely for show. They were cohorts, nothing more. And of course, she wasn't looking for more. She wanted to revel in her chick-flick-watching, hairy-legged, single status.

Not that her legs were hairy tonight. The dress was too high-cut for that. But as soon as they'd derailed their mothers' wedding plans, she was going back to not shaving…at least not too often.

"Let's go," he said.

She simply nodded, and let him crawl onto the bike.

Nate's arms wrapped around her stomach. The top of his right hand grazed the bottom of her enhanced breast. Shannon found herself wishing there wasn't a balloon full of air separating her breast and his hand. She'd like his hands—

She cut off the thought. She wasn't in a real relationship with Nate. They were conspirators. Associates. Despite his Cary Grant-ish looks, she had to remember that.

"Here we go," she called as she pressed the pedal, put the Harley in first gear and took off down the street, ready to begin the game.

3

"Mom, we're here," Nate called as he opened his parents' front door and walked into the living room with its lime-green walls and slate-gray carpet.

Over the years Nate had gotten used to his mother's loud color choices and rarely gave them a second thought. He actually kind of liked things bright and a bit wild. But he saw the surprised look on Shannon's face and wondered if she preferred something more sedate.

No, she didn't look like the sedate type in that dress. She looked like a pin-up girl…a fantasy woman.

Not that she looked like *his* fantasy woman. No, she looked like every man's fantasy. That dress—

He forced himself to concentrate on the job at hand, which was convincing his mom to lay off the wife-and-baby stuff.

Shannon's dress was a means to an end, that's all.

"Mom? Dad?" he called. "They must be in the kitchen."

Shannon stood and nervously smoothed some invisible wrinkle in her skirt.

Gone was the illusion of an exotic dancer named Roxy, and in her place was an art teacher who was feeling nervous.

"What's wrong?" Nate asked softly.

She sighed. "They're not going to like me."

"They're not going to like me dating a stripper."

That was the plan. His parents wouldn't like her, her parents wouldn't like him. No more marriage talk.

"Exotic dancer," she corrected, as if she'd been doing it for years.

Then, softer, she added, "People normally like me."

"Shannon-me-love," he said, using Mick's pet name for her, "we don't have to do this. Come on, it was a crazy idea anyway."

This was supposed to be fun, but Shannon didn't look as if she was having fun. Not at all.

She gave herself a little shake and said, "No, no, I'm okay. Just chalk it up to a case of stage fright. It's not a crazy idea...well, maybe it is. But we have crazy mothers, and it's sort of like fighting fire with fire...fighting their craziness with a crazy plan of our own."

She straightened and smiled at him. "Let's go."

"Shannon, really you don't have—"

"Come on, big guy. Roxy never misses an entrance."

She smiled and Shannon the art teacher was replaced by a stripper—an exotic dancer, he corrected himself—named Roxy.

"You're sure you can pull it off?" he asked.

"You just watch and learn, biker-boy." She patted his cheek. "I'm going to show you how it's done. Don't forget, you'll be putting on your own performance tomorrow."

He turned and heard noise coming from the kitchen. "Well, I'd say it's show time."

His mother rounded the corner.

"Nate," she said, spying him, her face one big happy smile…until she spotted Shannon.

The smile disappeared rather abruptly and was replaced by something that looked as though it could be called terror.

But Nate would give his mother credit, she held out her hand, stuck a fake-looking smile on her face, and said, "You must be Nathan's new friend."

Shannon took the hand and shook it a bit too enthusiastically. "Oh, it's so nice to meet you, Mrs. Calder. I mean, most guys don't take me home to meet their moms even after we've been dating for a long time, but Nate here, he's brought me on a first date. You know, the minute he walked into the bar, I knew he was something special."

"Ah, yes, the bar," his mom said, just as his father walked into the room.

"Paul, this is Nate's friend—"

Nate was pretty sure he heard a tone akin to horror as she said the word *friend*.

"—uh, dear, I'm not sure I caught your name."

Shannon laughed, a throaty sort of laugh that made a man's thoughts turn to sex.

Raw, hot, steamy sex.

Nate wondered if it was part of her act, or just her normal laugh. He couldn't tell and wasn't about to ask. He preferred to think it was part of the act.

"Shannon, ma'am. Shannon O'Malley, although at work I go by Roxy."

"At work?" his mom asked.

"Yeah. My boss, he says Shannon doesn't give a man the right sort of mental image, and mental images are our specialty."

"Just what do you do, Shannon?" Nate's father asked.

Nate stood back, waiting for the shoe to drop.

Shannon grinned. "Why, I'm an exotic dancer. Didn't Nate tell you?"

"What?" his mother gasped.

His father didn't say anything. He just stood, looking from Nate back to Shannon.

"An exotic dancer," Shannon repeated.

"A stripper," Nate explained.

Shannon elbowed him...hard. "I told you I don't care for that term. It sounds dirty. I do what I do because I'm good at it, because I need to earn a living. It might not be the Rockettes, but it's not raunchy."

"A stripper?" his mom said weakly.

"It's a nice place, ma'am. The owner, well, he doesn't let anyone mess with the girls. He looks after us. Hey, we even get medical insurance, and you know how expensive that can be. My friend Candy—her real name is Patricia, but the boss says that doesn't create a good mental picture either, so she's Candy at work—why, she's got two kids. Her deadbeat husband left her, and doesn't pay child support or anything. So she works the morning shift—"

"Strip joints have a morning shift?" Nate's dad asked.

"Ours does," Shannon said, her head bobbing as she nodded. "Twenty-four hours a day, seven days a week."

"Uh," Nate's mom said. "Dinner is ready, so why don't we all go in and sit down?"

Nate took Shannon's arm, and they followed his parents into the dining room.

"You're doing great," he whispered.

"Yeah, I am," she whispered back and shot him a grin.

Nate could see his mother's immediate baby plans fading fast. She would never want a stripper for her grandchild's mother. Yep, Shannon was doing a great job, playing the stripper to the hilt.

But as the meal went on, Nate realized things weren't going quite the way he planned.

Shannon went on talking about the strip club,

about Candy and her two kids, about Marcy, the exotic dancer who was working her way through grad school. She wove intricate tales that had the entire family hanging on her every word.

Hell, Nate hardly noticed the charbroiled nature of the roast his mother served, or the huge lumps in the mashed potatoes. He was as caught up in Shannon's stories as his parents were.

"Why," she said, leaning across the table, exposing cleavage Nate hadn't noticed at the bar the night they met—and he was man enough to always notice cleavage, so how had the fact that Shannon had some escaped his notice?—"one night, I was up doing my number and was down to just panties and tassels, when this guy comes in and jumps up on stage. Now, my boss, he doesn't let anyone bother us, and no one is allowed on stage, so Bruno—he's our bouncer. I asked once and his name really is Bruno, which seems a bit too stereotypical to me, but it's his last name, not his first. His first name is Kyle, which isn't bouncerish at all. Anyway, Bruno—he'd kill me if I called him Kyle—he jumped up and grabbed the guy before he could touch me. And the guy lunges forward and makes a grab anyway, but all he grabs is a hand full of tassel, which means I was left there exposed…"

She paused for a moment, and if Nate didn't know it was an act, he'd have sworn she was truly embarrassed by the incident, as if it had really happened.

"Oh, dear, what did you do?" his mom asked.

"Well, of course, I covered myself. I mean, I strip, but only to tassels and panties—we don't strip all the way—and here I was one tassel shy of a complete outfit. And then, this guy he tosses me up his jacket, and before you know it, there was a pile of jackets and shirts at my feet. I just picked one up, slipped it on and finished the dance. You should have seen my tips that night."

"Why, the men were gentlemen," his mom said, a note of approval in her voice.

If Nate didn't know better, he'd have thought his mom was almost impressed.

"Most of the guys who come in are gentlemen. Sort of lonely. Part of the job is going out between sets and visiting them. Most of them are just happy to have us there, talking to them. I feel sort of bad for them."

Man, she was playing this as the stripper-with-a-heart, not the heartless stripper.

Nate glanced at his mom. She'd always been a soft touch, and one look at her face told him that she'd fallen for Shannon's—aka Roxy's—story.

"Dear, I never thought of it that way. Why else would a man go to someplace like that? Of course he goes because he's lonely."

Nate could swear he heard his mother sniff.

Shannon had his mother believing that not only

was she a stripper, but that she was a stripper with a heart of gold, dancing to help a bunch of lonely, sweet gentlemen.

"Not all the guys go there because they're lonely, Mom," he felt obliged to point out.

"Of course that's why they go," his mother said.

"The poor men just don't know how to interact with women," Shannon, the armchair psychiatrist, said.

"Well, maybe we should start some sort of support group. Men who visit strippers—"

"Exotic dancers," Shannon corrected.

"Exotic dancers," his mother agreed. "We could see if we could find a therapist, and you could take brochures to work and hand them out to the men. We could teach them how to deal with women in the real world. How to meet nice girls."

"Hey, we're nice girls," Shannon said.

"Why, of course you are, dear. But you're already dating Nathan, and the one girl's in grad school—between that and work, she doesn't have time for a relationship—and the other one has young children and a nasty ex. The gentlemen at the club have problems. We need to introduce your friends to men who don't have too much emotional baggage of their own—someone who can help them deal with theirs. We can—"

"Mom, you'll put the club out of business if you reform all its customers and save all its dancers,"

Nate said. He gave Shannon a little kick under the table.

"Nate's got a point," she said. "My boss is a nice guy and runs a clean club, but I don't think he's nice enough to let us lose all his business for him. I'm sure he wouldn't allow me to pass out brochures."

"I guess you're right," his mom said with a sigh. "But I think I'll talk to some people in town about setting up a support group, anyway. We won't target just your club, that should work, shouldn't it?"

"I—"

"Honey," Nate's dad said, "I think you're putting Shannon on the spot. This is her first dinner with us, after all. There'll be more."

"You're right, Paul. Shannon, we'll talk about this later, next time you come. Right now, let's talk about dessert. I made Nate's favorite, key lime pie."

Nate forced himself to smile as his mother looked at him expectantly. "Great."

Great. Just great.

His mother had implied she expected to see Shannon at dinner again, which meant she liked her.

His mother liked Shannon in spite of the fact she thought she was Roxy, the exotic dancer.

And, in addition, they were having his *favorite,* key lime pie, for dessert.

Nate hated key lime pie.

"...YES, MOTHER." Shannon sighed heavily, on purpose, so that the sound would carry over the telephone wires.

"I heard that, young lady."

"Heard what?" Shannon asked, though she knew the answer. It was better to play this out. After all, her mother had to believe she was reluctant to bring Nate over to the house.

"That sigh," her mom said, right on cue. "Is it so much to ask that I meet this man? You said last week you'd talk to him about stopping in."

"Talk to him. I didn't say we'd stop in for sure. If you just wanted to meet him that would be one thing, but you want a wedding and you're assessing his ability to play the groom—that's another thing entirely."

"Now, Shannon, you know that I only want what's best for you and—"

"Have you talked to Kate this week?" she asked.

If she was really trying to get out of bringing a man to meet her mother, she'd try to sidetrack her.

"You're changing the subject," Brigit accused.

Shannon was glad her mother couldn't see her broad smile. It was useful to know someone so well, especially when trying to put one over on them.

"No, no I'm not," she denied. "I just wondered if you'd talked to her."

"No." Her mother's voice was laced with suspicion. "I was going to call her after I talked to you."

Shannon smiled. Her strategy was to keep her mother off balance and she had a bombshell all ready to drop and topple her. She fired. "It seems Cara's in Texas."

"Cara's in Texas?"

"Yes."

"Now, why do you suppose she's down there? Are you saying you think it's something to do with her mother? That Cecilia sent her down there? Maybe she thinks Cara will have luck finding a cowboy. Goodness knows the girl wasn't finding a man here in Erie."

"If Mrs. Romano is taking this bet as seriously as you are, I wouldn't be surprised if they're up to something."

Shannon didn't add that she didn't think Cara would be any more happy about this bet than she was.

"After all," she continued, "if they tried something in Erie, you'd certainly find out. But Texas…that's a big state. Who knows what the two of them have cooked up."

"Well, I suppose I'd better call Mary Kathryn—"

"Kate," Shannon corrected her mother.

"Kate," her mother said with a sigh. "I'll call her and see if she knows just what's going on."

"That's great. Goodbye, Mom."

She didn't get the phone a millimeter from her ear before her mother yelled, "Oh, no. You might have given me something new to worry about, but I haven't forgotten that I expect you to bring the boy—"

"Man."

"—to the house for dinner tonight."

"Mom, we just met. It's just a date."

"Good," her mother said. "Dating is good. Bring him by and we'll find out all about him together."

"I'll bring him along if you promise not to start talking about weddings with him."

Silence.

"Mom?"

"Fine. I won't mention the word *wedding*. Now, be here at five. I'm calling Mary…Kate."

"Five it is, Mom."

"I look forward to it," her mother said right before she hung up.

"So do I," Shannon murmured to herself as she hung up the phone.

At least she hoped she did. After all, last night hadn't gone the way they'd planned.

She'd admitted it was her fault.

She'd apologized to Nate, and though he'd accepted her apology, he'd still been a bit put out when he'd dropped her off at home.

Shannon knew where the problems stemmed from. It was a curse.

She liked to be liked.

She blamed genetics.

Women were trained to be likable, to be easygoing. They were genetically and socially predisposed to want to be accepted.

No, that might sound good and scientific, but unfortunately the theory just didn't play out.

Look at her mother. She obviously didn't have an overwhelming compulsion to be liked. Not that Shannon didn't like her mom.

She did.

But *easygoing* wasn't a word that people used to describe Brigit O'Malley.

Overbearing.

Pushy.

Opinionated.

Competitive.

But not *easy-going*.

And frequently not *likable*.

No, wherever this need to be liked stemmed from, she couldn't blame her mother or her mother's genes.

But she could blame her mother for the fact she found herself in this absurd situation at all.

Her musings were interrupted by a sound that could only be a Harley Davidson. Loud and rumbling, the Harley drew closer, and Shannon's heart sped up.

Not that she was excited about seeing Nate.

Of course she wasn't.

Her accelerated heart-rate probably had to do with the fact that she was nervous about him being mad at her.

Not that she'd blame him if he was.

A tiny part of her had been afraid he wouldn't show up today. Not that she cared on a personal level—they hardly knew each other after all, though she was inclined to like what she did know of him. No, the only reason she was concerned about his not showing was because she needed him to get her mother off her back.

And now, he had shown up, even after she'd mucked up last night. Maybe he'd only shown up because his mother had invited her back to dinner next weekend. Well, she'd use that time to try to undo the damage she'd done last night. She was going to carry her exotic-dancer routine as far as she could and try to shock his mother into disliking her.

She wasn't going to examine the fact that knowing she'd be seeing Nathan again next weekend wasn't any particular hardship.

He was a nice guy. But that didn't mean she wanted anything more than the friendly partnership they'd formed. After all, she liked her chick-flick-watching ways.

Shannon waited for him to knock, even though she knew he'd arrived. Heck, with the amount of noise the Harley made, the whole neighborhood knew he'd arrived. But she didn't want to appear too…excited? Anxious?

Whatever. She just didn't want him thinking she was too pleased to see him. She was playing it cool, despite the fact her heart was racing and her palms were sweating.

She heard the knock and had the front door opened a split second after his knuckles had tapped the wooden door.

Nate jumped back half a step, obviously startled that she'd opened the door so fast.

So much for her cool act.

"Hi, Nate," she said, trying to gauge his mood.

"Shannon." He didn't smile and her name came out rather terse.

He was still upset.

Darn.

"Aw, come on, Nate, I said I was sorry. I swear, by the time dinner is over next weekend, your parents will be begging you never to see me again. Your mom will declare she can wait to be a grandmother, at least until you find an appropriate woman. I'm really sorry that they liked me."

His hard expression evaporated and she saw a hint of a smile. "Well, it was kind of funny to hear her go on about starting a support group for guys who frequent strip clubs."

Shannon chuckled. "By the time I was done describing the place, I almost believed I was talking about other exotic dancers, and not just adapting stories about teachers I know from school. I never realized I had a gift for telling stories.''

"Blarney," Nate said.

"What?"

"Mick would say you have the gift of the blarney. A fine Irish tradition."

"Well, if anyone knows blarney, it's Mick. I can see why you've kept him around all these years. He's a great guy. I'm not much of a bar person, but after all my mom's fix-ups, I always seem to end up there. Mick's doesn't seem like a bar, but rather just a place to hang out with friends."

Something in Nate's expression changed slightly. Oh, he was still smiling, but there was some difference that Shannon couldn't quite identify.

"So are you ready for our lesson?" he asked, not sounding overly enthused.

They'd agreed it would be better if Nate was the one driving the motorcycle when they pulled up to her parents, so she'd suggested they spend the afternoon practicing.

Shannon figured if she could teach kids to appreciate art, she could teach Nate to ride a Harley without stalling...at least she hoped she could. That way when the charade was over he'd not only have his mother off his back, but he'd be able to actually ride his motorcycle.

"I'm all set," she said. "I thought we'd go over to the school parking lot. It's virtually deserted most weekends."

"Fine. You drive there, I'll drive back."

4

HE'S A great guy.

An hour and a half later, Nate was still stewing about Shannon's comment about Mick.

It wasn't as if he didn't agree. Mick *was* a great guy.

Funny.

Intelligent. He'd been working his way through school for years. Balancing his school work with owning his own business—so you could add independent to his glowing list of *great*nesses.

Yeah, Mick was a great guy, and all of a sudden, it bothered Nate and he wasn't sure why. Oh, he might suspect, but he wasn't sure and wasn't about to examine his level of annoyance until he was sure. He was afraid of what he might find.

Because there was no way he could be jealous.

That flood of *some feeling* that overtook his system every time he thought of the casual friendliness Mick and Shannon had displayed the first night had to be something else entirely.

A great guy.

Ha.

He could tell Shannon some stories about great

old Mick that would make her spiky hair stand
on end. But he wouldn't, because who Shannon
thought was *great* made no difference to him. It
wasn't as if they were anything more than partners.
He had no real claim on her.

Why, he hardly knew Shannon.

They were just helping each other out of their
mother-marriage woes.

She could date whomever she wanted. Not that
she was dating Mick.

At least, he didn't think she was dating Mick.

Maybe he should talk to Mick and make sure
Shannon wasn't dating him.

Not that it mattered.

It wasn't as if Nate was looking to date Shannon
in any way except their *fake* way.

He eased the motorcycle into her driveway and
cut the motor. She unwrapped her arms from
around his waist.

He sort of missed the feeling of her pressed
against him.

"That was great, Nate," she said as she climbed
off the bike.

She pulled her helmet off, set it on the back of
the bike and ran her fingers through her short hair
as she grinned at him. "You made it all the way
home without stalling it once. I think you've got
it."

"Thanks to you." Nate put down the kick-stand

and leaned the bike gently against it, then took off his own helmet.

"Nah. You would have got it on your own. You just needed practice, that's all."

"What time are we supposed to be at your parents?" he asked.

"Five. We've got time."

"Time for what?" he asked. There was a certain gleam in her eye that made him nervous.

They'd talked about motorcycle lessons and dinner, but they had no other plans for the day, of that he was sure.

"Time for me to take you to see my friend, Emilio."

Emilio?

How many men did Shannon have hanging around?

"Is he a great guy, too?" Nate asked.

The moment the words were out of his mouth he wished he could suck them back in.

"What?" Shannon asked, shooting him a piercing look with those beautiful green eyes.

Beautiful green eyes? Man, next thing you know he'd be waxing poetic about her emerald gaze, or some such nonsense.

"Never mind," he said, his voice sharper than he intended. "So, why are we seeing this Emilio?"

"Because you're getting that tattoo you wanted," she said with a grin.

"I don't think so," Nate said, feeling a hint of regret.

It's not that he hadn't toyed with the idea of a tattoo, but it certainly didn't fit his daytime persona and...well, he didn't like needles.

It wasn't a very manly concern, so he didn't confess it to Shannon, but there it was. It wasn't just a small dislike, but more of a minor phobia.

Okay, maybe a major phobia.

Yeah, he was not meant to be tattooed.

"No. No tattoos."

"Trust me," Shannon said.

"So what do you think?" Nate asked as he climbed off the motorcycle he'd parked right on her parents' perfectly manicured lawn.

Oh, her mom would hate a Harley on the lawn, which is why she'd told Nate to park there.

Shannon stood at the side of the motorcycle, dressed in the most preppy and innocent-looking outfit she could manage. A pale-blue oxford shirt, a dark-blue pair of jeans and white tennis shoes. She'd wanted to dress in stark contrast to Nate's outfit.

She'd helped him pick it out and thought they'd done a great job of transforming her professional-looking pharmacist into a bad-assed biker.

Nate was dressed in a black T-shirt with its arms cut off, under a black leather vest.

Okay, so his hair wasn't long by anyone's standard, but he'd done something to it. It looked wild.

He'd put on dark glasses that shaded his warm brown eyes. Well-worn, faded black jeans and black leather riding boots finished the ensemble.

Well, almost finished.

"So?" He flexed his arm and the mermaid on his right forearm undulated in a suggestive sort of way.

It was fake, but no one would know it.

Emilio was good. Fantastic, actually, she thought with a great deal of teacherly pride. She'd been working with him privately for a few years. He was one of her best students, ever.

The crowning glory of her year was getting him an art scholarship. It felt like a validation for all the time and effort she gave both to her school students and her private ones.

She loved teaching kids to appreciate art, while she worked with people who not only appreciated it, but created it. Occasionally there was one of those rare students who had the type of raw talent that just begged to be developed.

Emilio was one of those.

"My mother's going to freak out," she said, admiring Emilio's work. "Mom's not into guys with tattoos. She's hoping for a professional for me. Let's see, she's fixed me up with her banker, her accountant, and even tried to fix me up with her gynecologist...I drew the line with that one. Ew. She thinks I need someone who will settle me down."

"So, she's hoping for a professional. What are you hoping for?" Nate asked from the other side of the motorcycle, suddenly serious. He peered over the top of his dark glasses, waiting for an answer.

"Someone I can love." The words were out before she could stop herself. She could feel her face heat up. What a stupid, stupid thing to say. "I didn't mean to say that."

"You're embarrassed," Nate said. "Why would wanting to love someone embarrass you?"

"It sounds so...I don't know, juvenile. But it's the truth. I want someone special. I'm not settling for less than love just because my mother might lose a bet. I want what she has with my dad, what Kate found with Tony."

"Good for you." They walked toward the front door.

Before they reached the steps, she stopped. "And you? What are you looking for?"

"I don't know. I don't think guys spend much time thinking about stuff like that."

"If you don't think about it, how are you going to know what you want?"

"I guess I'll figure it out when the time comes."

Shannon found his answer less than satisfactory, not that it mattered what Nate was looking for in a woman. Didn't matter a bit. All she was worried about was this meeting with her parents.

"What you're looking for doesn't matter tonight. What does matter is that you're looking to be as shocking as possible. I want my mom to send that dress back to Kate. I want her not to weigh every man she meets as potential husband material for me. I want her to cancel the church and stop hounding local priests.''

''I'll do my best,'' Nate said with a grin.

They walked up the steps and onto the porch. The boards creaked as they walked to the door.

Shannon knocked, rather than just unlock it with her key and walk in. She was staging a grand entrance, after all. It wouldn't work unless someone was there to witness it.

''By the way, Roxy,'' Nate said with a devilish grin, ''I have a new name, too.''

''Oh?'' She looked up and could see that it was going to be good. ''What is it?''

''Bull.''

Shannon snorted. ''Oh, that's good. Very biker-ish.''

''I thought you'd like it. I—''

Nate was interrupted as the door flew open.

Shannon's mom stood there, a smile on her face…a smile that slowly faded when she saw Nate.

''Shannon?'' she asked, still staring at Nate as if she couldn't look past the biker on her steps to see if her daughter was indeed present. She didn't even notice the motorcycle on her front lawn, she was so horrified by Shannon's date.

''Hi, Mom,'' Shannon said brightly, pleased with

her mom's reaction. "This is my friend, Nate, Nate Calder."

"But call me Bull," Nate said. "That's what my friends all call me. I think it fits my personality better than Nate ever did."

"Bull?" Brigit asked weakly.

"Yeah."

Shannon saw the moment her mother spotted the motorcycle. If anything she looked even more disgusted.

"And is that your…vehicle?" she asked, her voice even fainter.

"My bike? Yeah. Isn't she a beaut? A bike is like a woman, they each have their own personality, their own style. It takes just the right man to ride them. My bike, like Shannon, is a lady. A classy ride. I can't figure out why either of them like me, but I'm glad they do."

He looped an arm over Shannon's shoulders and pulled her toward him.

She'd been right when she'd figured that she'd fit easily within the confines of his embrace.

"Oh, Bull," she murmured as she batted her eyelashes in what she hoped was a lovesick manner. "You do say the sweetest things."

"They're not always sweet," he said with a suggestive lilt to his voice.

"No," she said with a grin that suggested a private joke. As if she suddenly realized her mother was there, she added, "Oh, Mom, I'm sorry. It's just that Bull makes me forget myself."

"Oh" was her mother's flat response.

"Are you going to invite us in?" Shannon pressed.

"Certainly. Certainly. Come in." Brigit didn't add *make yourself at home.*

As a matter of fact, she wore an expression that said she wanted to go lock up all the valuables before Nate came into the house.

Somehow Shannon kept a straight face. Nate did as well. He was doing a fantastic job. She'd have to do as well next week when they went to his parents to redeem herself for yesterday's little like-me fest. She had a week to learn to be as difficult and as unlikable as possible.

"Your dad's out back grilling some steaks," her mother said, as she led them through the living room and into the dining room. "You do like steak, Mr.—"

"Bull. Just call me Bull, ma'am. And of course I like steak. A real manly meal, that is. I was afraid we'd be eating some highbrow sort of meal, like couscous or sushi. Give me a big steak any day of the week. Rare, if that's okay."

"Rare. I'll tell Sean," Brigit said as she hurried out. "Shannon, make your friend at home."

The minute her mother was out of the room Shannon started laughing.

"Bull. Just call me Bull, ma'am," she mimicked. "You're good, Nate. Very good."

"I thought she was going to pass out," he said.

"Me, too. She went to get reinforcements—my father. That's unusual. Normally Mom likes to run the show unimpeded. You must have her flustered if she's going for help."

Shannon got Nate settled at the dining-room table and brought him a beer.

"I don't like beer," he said.

"Drink it. It's part of the persona," she whispered, just before her mother came back into the room, her father in tow.

"Bull," her mother said, barely hesitating on the name, "this is my husband, Sean. Honey, this is Bull, your daughter's date."

Oh, Shannon had truly upset her mother if she was being referred to as "your daughter." The only time that happened was when she or Mary Kathryn were really in the doghouse.

Shannon watched as her father set the steak down and her mother fussed with drinks. They kept shooting each other looks. It was that strange "couple-speak" that some couples—couples who were truly connected and meant for each other—had. Those kinds of looks carried more meaning than words.

Shannon knew that she'd never marry for less than what her parents had. She wanted someone who could read her looks, who understood her, who would support her.

She wanted someone who would love her.

Why couldn't her mother understand that?

Her parents had set the relationship bar extremely high. But Kate—the perfect daughter, the daughter who even when she rebelled managed to retain her perfect status—had emulated her parents' relationship when she'd married Tony Donetti.

Sure, maybe they didn't seem to have as much in common as her parents did—at least not on the surface—but it didn't take much to see that they fitted together perfectly.

They'd given each other looks like those her parents shared when they'd come home for Seth and Desi's wedding. Shannon had noted those looks and envied each one.

No matter how hard her mother tried to marry her off to an acceptable man, she was going to hold out for an *exceptional* one.

The dinner was quiet for a while, then obviously Brigit couldn't stand it any more because she said, "So, Bull, what do you do for a living?"

"Oh, a little of this and a little of that," he said in a noncommittal way around the bite of steak in his mouth.

"Which means?" Brigit pressed.

"I only work when I have to. And I've done a bit of everything. A bouncer. Mechanic. A few jobs I don't think I'd better bring up." He chuckled as if he'd said something funny, but Shannon's parents didn't even crack a smile.

"So…" her father finally said when the silence at the table grew too weighty, "…how did you two meet?"

Shannon looked to Nate, giving him the floor.

He obviously caught her meaning, because he said, "We were introduced by a mutual friend at the bar, then we went to an art show and that's when I knew Shannon here was the woman for me."

Shannon figured her parents would totally freak out at the bar comment, but instead her mother zeroed in on the second part of his statement. "An art show?"

Shannon was glad her mother had asked, because she'd love to know just what Nate had in mind with that little tidbit.

"Yeah. There was a local show of biker art."

"Biker art?" her father echoed.

"Yeah. All the tattoos this local artist has done over the years…he'd taken them all and copied them onto canvas collages."

"Tattoos?" her mother said weakly.

"Yeah. I have a lot of them, though this mermaid," he flexed his arm, causing the mermaid to wiggle suggestively, "is the only one that shows unless I take off my shirt," he paused half a beat and then added, "or pants."

"Oh, no," her mom said in a rush, "that's fine. The mermaid is beautiful."

"Yeah, I think so. As a matter of fact, Shannon here is thinking about getting a tattoo with me. Matching hearts with each other's name in 'em. Maybe we'll do that as an engagement thing. What do you think, babe?"

"Engagement?"

Her mom just kept repeating what Nate said, clearly too shocked to think of anything original to say.

"Yeah," Nate said as he reached over and patted Shannon's hand on the table. "Shannon here, she told me about how you need her to get married in order to win a bet, and of course, I'm willing. I mean, if anyone understands how important winning a bet is, it's me. I've probably won, and then lost, a million dollars over the years. I'd like to see to it that you won because, let's face it, that's a lot more fun than losing. After all, you'll be my mother-in-law soon, so your honor is tied to my honor and I wanta see you win."

"But married? Why, you only just met," Brigit protested.

"Shannon said you had everything reserved for the end of June. That leaves us plenty of time to get to know each other."

"But…but…" her mother stuttered.

Shannon stared, mouth slightly agape. Her mother was stuttering. That never happened. Her mother was always in control, always had a plan, always had some contingency, always got the last word.

Nate had totally silenced her mother!

He was her hero.

She reached under the table and gave his knee a squeeze of thanks.

"Shannon," her mother said with a tsking noise. "Are you two teasing? Married? Already? Oh, you two. I want Shannon to marry for compatibility, stability—"

"Love?" Shannon added.

"Of course, love. I would never want you to marry so I could win a bet."

Shannon managed not to scoff.

Bull smiled. "Well, Shannon and I were sort of set on the idea of a June wedding, but we could put the final decision off for a while, if that would make you feel better. Just don't go canceling anything 'cause I can't see me changin' my mind."

"Definitely put off a final decision for a while," her mother echoed. "It wouldn't do to rush into things."

"But Cara's in Texas and Mrs. Romano—" Shannon said.

"Shannon, the ideas you get. I was just kidding about the bet."

"But Kate's dress?" Shannon asked.

"You'll have it when you need it, but I don't want you to rush into anything."

"But—"

"So, Bull, why don't you tell me more about—" her mother hesitated as if searching for a subject she thought was safe "—your motorcycle."

"Well…" he said, and launched into a long monologue on the joys of Harley Davidson motorcycles. As he talked he gave Shannon's hand another squeeze.

She just sat back and watched her mother's wedding dreams evaporate.

It was a good night.

5

"GOOD NIGHT," Nate, aka Bull, said when they arrived at Shannon's house a few hours later.

Shannon was riding a high because they'd defeated her mother.

She'd won!

"You could come in for a while, if you like," she said.

Nate looked surprised to hear the invitation, which is exactly how Shannon felt to hear herself issue the invitation.

She wasn't sure why, but she was sure she wasn't ready for the night to end.

"I don't have work tomorrow," he said, slowly, almost hesitantly.

What was with him?

Nate had been quiet since they'd left her parents' house. Not that it was easy to talk on a motorcycle, but still, he seemed…well, distant.

"Never mind," she said. "Forget I asked."

She was just asking him in to celebrate their victory and you'd have thought she was asking him to get his teeth drilled.

"No, I mean, yes, I'd like to come in." He might

have said the words, but they didn't sound overly sincere.

Did she have cooties or something? She'd been sweating bullets at the beginning of the evening, but she didn't think she smelled.

"Really, never mind. It was just an idea," she said as she unlocked the door and stepped inside.

She would have shut the door in his face, but he caught it before it shut and pushed it back open. "Shannon, I'd really like to come in."

She shrugged and started walking into the foyer, leaving the door open for him to follow if he wanted.

She didn't turn around, but heard the door shut, and then his footsteps against the hardwood floor as he followed her into the house.

"Make yourself at home," she said, gesturing toward the couch.

This room was the reason she'd bought the house. Big, with dark, original woodwork, a huge stone fireplace and hardwood floors. She loved nothing better than to curl up on her couch and just enjoy the comfort of the room.

But tonight, with Nathan standing in it, the room didn't feel big, or comfortable.

"Do you want something to drink?" she asked after he'd taken a seat.

"I'm okay. Those couple beers were plenty."

She wished he had wanted something so she would have an excuse to leave the room and collect herself. For some reason, she was feeling a bit breathless and she wasn't sure why.

She sat opposite him on the couch, leaving as much space as possible between them.

Silence weighed heavily on the room.

Shannon tried to think of something to break it and finally said, "Um, I don't suppose you're hungry?"

"Nah. Your mom's a much better cook than my mom is, only don't tell my mom I said that. I'm quashing her grandbaby plans, I don't want to take everything away from her."

"Okay."

Silence again ruled the room for what seemed like an eternity.

Finally, Shannon said, "This is silly. Just go home. It's okay."

"No it's not okay," he said. "I'm not sure what's going on. Even that first night, we didn't have any trouble talking to each other. I felt an immediate connection—as if we'd been friends for years. So why all the awkward silences now?"

"Maybe it's because before, we had a plan. We were working toward a common goal. That first night we were plotting out strategy, a couple of nights ago we were carrying out act one, and tonight act two. It's over now. We don't have anything else to talk about, at least until I come to dinner at your parents' again next week. It's not as if we're friends, or as if we're really dating."

"Maybe we should," he said abruptly.

"Should what?" she asked.

"Really date."

"Why?"

"Why not?" he said.

Shannon clutched her chest and laughed. "Oh, be still my heart. *Why not,* he says. Now, those are words to warm a girl's heart. *Why not?* It's sort of like saying, 'Do you want a cheeseburger' and having someone answer, 'Sure, why not?'"

"Come on, Shannon, that's not what I meant," Nate protested.

She continued talking, as if she hadn't heard him. "I mean, if this is how you sweet-talk women, it's clear why you're not married and your mother is pining away after a grandbaby."

"Hey, that's not fair," Nate said. "I sweet-talk women just fine."

"Oh, yeah?" Shannon slid closer to him and looked him right in the face. "Say we were dating for real. Pretend I'd invited you in, and we were sitting next to each other on my couch. What sweet nothings would you whisper in my ear?"

His face was a hand's length away from hers. She looked right into his dark-brown eyes. No, not quite brown. That was too plain a word to describe the rich color. They were the color of coffee. A perfect mug of Colombian coffee that had been hand-roasted to perfection.

"Come on, this isn't fair," Nate protested. "You're putting me on the spot."

"Ha. I rest my case. You, Nathan Calder, are no sweet-talker. A man who is used to using smooth words on women wouldn't have any problems coming up with something on the spur of the moment."

"Hey, I can *smooth* as well as the next guy," he said.

"Let me just say, ha, again."

"Stop ha-ing me."

"Ha. Ha. Ha. Okay, I'll give you that you talk as smooth as the next guy, but only because guys don't talk smooth at all, unless it's in the movies. And then they only manage it because it was probably a woman writing the script. Men wouldn't know a sweet word if they had a giant thesaurus in front of them."

Nate actually shook a finger at her as he said, "That's a totally sexist thing to say. Men don't need a woman's help to smooth-talk a woman."

"That was a rather convoluted sentence, don't you think? And you shook your finger at me as though I was some kid that needed scolding."

He dropped his hand on his lap. "I did not."

"Hey, I know a finger-shake when I see one and you definitely shook."

"Shannon, I don't shake fingers."

"Ha. You're a finger-shaking, non-sweet-talking…man."

"There you go, ha-ing me again."

"Finger-shaker."

"Ha-er."

They both paused, faces inches apart and, as if on cue, they both burst out laughing.

Nate managed to stop laughing long enough to ask, "Why are we fighting? We've done it. We totally freaked your mom out, and even though my mom loves you, we'll get her next time. So why are we fighting?"

"Why not?" Shannon said with a huge grin.

His smile was a mirror image. "You know, you're a rather annoying woman at times. But then, I think that's a feminine trait. Annoying men."

"Oh, yeah, that's sweet talk if I ever heard it." She batted her eyelids and sighed, "Your melodic prose sets my senses aglow."

"You want sweet and smooth? How about this? You're eyes are like…" He paused, and the pause dragged on until it had become silence.

"Oh, you smooth-talking, sweet-worded man, you."

"Hang on. Give me a second to put this together." He took a deep breath and said, "Your eyes are your most striking feature. When people meet you, they probably think it's your hair—that fire-engine shade is an attention-grabber. But anyone around you long enough knows it's not the hair. You're eyes they…sparkle. They show your every emotion. They grab hold of a guy, like some sort of charm, and don't let go. I've seen those eyes, your eyes, in my dreams every night since we met.''

Shannon laughed, but it sounded forced even to her ears. ''Okay, that's enough.''

''What? You don't seem amused any longer. Is this making you nervous?'' he challenged.

''Why would I be nervous?''

Shannon asked the question because, to be honest, she didn't have a clue why Nate was making her nervous, but he was. Her heart was pounding, her palms were sweating.

Maybe she was sick?

Maybe she was having a heart attack?

It would serve him right if she was. After all, he was the one making her feel this way. Elevating her blood pressure to such a degree that some vessel was bound to give way.

''Maybe you're nervous because I'm looking at your eyes and it makes me wonder what it would be like to kiss you.''

''Why would looking at my eyes make you wonder about kissing me? You'd think my lips would do that.''

There. She'd told him. Eyes didn't make people think about kissing, but lips did, and looking at Nate's lips, Shannon was pretty sure kissing him wouldn't be a hardship.

''No, just like you'd think your hair should be your most striking feature, but it isn't, it's your eyes, not your lips that makes me think about kissing you. Looking into your eyes, I feel as if I've known you forever, and I feel this surge of desire and that's what makes me want to kiss you. Desire. A soft, sweet need to connect.''

"Okay," she said, her voice soft and breathy to her own ears. "That was a pretty smooth line."

"It wasn't a line," Nate said, inching closer, closing the slight distance that separated them on the couch. "I'm serious. I want to kiss you."

"But, this is all pretend. It's not as if we're really dating, or anything."

"Who says we couldn't?" he asked.

"Couldn't kiss, or couldn't date?"

"Both."

"Me. I say."

"Why?"

Looking at his lips so close, so tempting, Shannon almost wanted to say "why not?" and just kiss him. But she resisted the urge and said, "Listen, I'm not ready to settle down. I like my life. I like sappy movies and not having to shave my legs. I like doing what I want and not worrying about someone else."

"Me, too."

"You like watching sappy movies?" she asked.

"No. Not that part. But I do like my life the way it is. Uncomplicated. That's the beautiful thing about our…well, whatever it is we could have. We're coming into it knowing what we want. Uncomplicated. If I ask you out and you don't want to go, you can feel free to say no. And vice versa.''

"So what you're suggesting is we date, but not really.''

"We'd date enough to keep our moms off our backs.''

"So, more than just a couple dinners. An ongoing casual dating thing? That's what you're suggesting?''

"Yeah,'' Nate said. "As if we were friends.''

"Buddies.''

"Pals.''

"So-o-o,'' Shannon said, dragging the word out. "If I were to ask if you wanted to watch a movie tonight?''

"Then I'd say I'd much rather kiss you.''

"And if I did kiss you?''

"Then I might be tempted to try something more.''

"Okay, so let's not take a chance on tempting you,'' she said. "At least not yet. Let's just watch a movie.''

If Nate was annoyed that she was avoiding kissing him he didn't show it. He simply smiled and asked, "What movie?''

"*Terms of Endearment*?''

"No way. That's too sappy for any self-respecting man.''

"*Steel Magnolias*?''

"Even more no way.''

"Are you too manly to watch a chick-flick?" she asked with a grin.

"Yeah. Just call me Bull, ma'am. If it don't got blood and guts, I don't watch it."

"*Terminator*?"

"*Terminator*?" That stopped him. "You've got a copy of *Terminator* in with all those girly films?"

"When you get down to the core of the movie, it's a love story."

Shannon had always admired the sweet poignancy of the couple's love in the midst of such horrible odds.

"No way is it a romance," Nate protested.

"When's the last time you watched it?"

"I don't know, but I know Arnold doesn't make chick-flicks."

"*Terminator* it is, then."

NATE LOOKED at the woman curled in his arms. Shannon had fallen asleep sometime before the end of the movie. He hadn't noticed right away. But gradually, she'd leaned his way, pressing her warm body against his.

Leaning closer and closer.

He'd wrapped an arm around her and had enjoyed the sensation of just holding her.

The credits rolled and he smiled.

She'd been right, *Terminator* was a romance, though he'd never thought of it that way.

His smiled faded.

What on earth was he doing?

He was cuddled on the couch, a sleeping woman in his arms and he felt…almost content.

He'd never even kissed her.

They'd talked about kissing, but hadn't.

Instead they'd simply enjoyed watching a movie together. Shannon had made them popcorn and they'd sat on the couch like some old married couple watching a movie.

He noticed a stray piece of hair falling over her eye. It just barely touched her eyelid because her hair was so short.

Normally he liked long hair on women, but on Shannon…well, the short cut worked. It fit her personality. It sort of said, "wild and free-spirited." But what her hair didn't say was "sweet." No, that's where her eyes came in.

Thinking of her eyes made him think about all the stuff he'd said. Sweet, goopy sort of stuff. Where on earth had that come from?

It was well after midnight—well past the time for him to leave—and yet he'd stayed. He didn't know why, but he couldn't bear to wake her. He just wasn't ready to go yet.

The phone rang, jarring him from his musings. Who would be calling her this late at night?

Shannon didn't even move.

Without thinking, Nate grabbed the phone which was on the end table next to him.

"Hello?" he asked in a hushed whisper.

"Who is this?" a female voice asked.

"Who are you trying to reach?" he countered.

"Shannon. Shannon O'Malley."

"She's sleeping right now. Could I take a message?"

"Is this Bull?"

"Yes," he answered slowly.

Who was this? He was sure it wasn't Mrs. O'Malley. He'd recognize her voice. "With whom am I speaking?"

"*With whom?* That's pretty classy speech for a biker. I'm Shannon's sister, Kate, by the way."

"Ah, Kate. The runaway bride." He kept his voice soft, not wanting to wake Shannon.

"She told you?" Kate asked, surprise evident in her voice, even through a phone line.

"You'd be surprised how much she's told me," Nate said.

He wasn't sure if he was supposed to carry out his act for Shannon's sister, but he wasn't going to take a chance. If she wanted to explain their relationship and ruse later, that was up to her.

"Well, she hasn't mentioned you to me," Kate said.

If he wasn't mistaken, she was annoyed now.

He grinned. "I'm not surprised. We've only known each other a short time."

But it didn't feel like a short time. Other than their short awkward period tonight, Nate felt as if he'd known Shannon a long time. A very long time.

"Tell me about yourself," Kate said. "I got a

phone call from my mother, all frantic that Shannon brought you to dinner. You've got Mom totally distressed, you know. Something's up.''

"I don't know what you mean. I'd give the phone to Shannon and let her answer your questions, but she's sleeping. Would you like me to leave her a message?''

"You're answering her phone after midnight because she's sleeping?'' Kate asked slowly. "That in itself says a lot. No, don't leave a message. I'll call back tomorrow.''

"Great. Good night.''

He started to set the receiver back on the charger when he heard Kate say, "Hey, Bull?''

He put the phone back to his ear. "Yes?''

"If you hurt her, you'll be mincemeat.'' Her voice was serious. Very serious. "Shannon likes the world to think she's tough, but underneath all her bravado, she's not so tough at all. She's totally soft and vulnerable. I won't have you toying with her.''

"Thanks for the warning,'' he said.

"I mean it.''

"I know.'' He paused and added, "It was nice talking to you, Kate.''

"It was interesting talking to you, Bull.''

He hung up and glanced at the woman still sleeping in his arms. The video had turned itself off and there was some late-night infomercial about some kitchen appliance on the television.

Nate didn't need to slice or dice anything bad enough to pay $29.99 for it.

He should go.

It was late.

And yet, he didn't move. He went back to studying Shannon and wondering what he was doing here, and why he was so reluctant to leave.

SUNLIGHT TICKLED its way beneath Shannon's eyelids, rousing her slowly from whatever she'd been dreaming about.

It was one of those gray, gauzy sort of dreams that she couldn't quite pinpoint, but she did know that it had left her feeling warm. Not in a heat sort of way, but in a comfortable sort of way.

She lay in that fuzzy state between sleep and wakefulness and realized something wasn't right.

She kept her eyes closed and tried to decide just what was amiss through her sleep-fuzzed brain.

It took a minute to realize what was out of place. That it wasn't a pillow cushioning her head. No, it was something harder, warmer. Something that rose and fell in a rhythmic sort of way. Something like…

A body.

More specifically, her head was cushioned on someone's chest.

Her eyes popped open as the realization struck with full force. She was on the couch in her living room sleeping on Nathan Calder's chest.

How had that happened?

The night came flooding back at full force.

They'd put one over on her mother, come home, talked about kissing and a casual dating relationship, then watched *The Terminator*. Only she didn't remember the end of the movie. She remembered sharing popcorn and sitting next to him....

And now she'd spent the night with him.

She grinned.

Oh, that would twist her mom's skirt.

She chuckled at the thought. It was enough to shake Nate from his sleep. She felt the change in his breathing pattern and knew he was awake before his eyes even opened.

"Good morning," she said brightly.

He sat up and pulled back, distancing himself from her. "Shannon, I'm so sorry. I meant to get up and go right after the movie, but you were sleeping so peacefully, then your sister called—"

"My sister? Kate called here?"

"And we talked for a while, then I was going to go, but I sat a moment and next thing I knew...well, this was the next thing I knew. I'm sorry."

"Nate, it's okay."

"No, it isn't. I've..." he paused, obviously searching for the word. "Imposed. Yeah, imposed. I didn't mean to."

"Nate, really it's fine." She didn't want to tell him that she sort of enjoyed waking up next to him. That she liked the warmth of his body. She could tell him there was something rather comfortable about snuggling next to him. She could, but she wouldn't.

She simply repeated, "It's okay."

"But—"

"No harm, no foul. I mean, it's not as if you compromised my virtue." She didn't add that compromising with Nate was starting to look sort of appealing.

She sat up and ran her fingers through her hair, knowing that *appealing* wasn't quite the word she'd use to describe her morning look.

"I guess you're right," he said slowly. "After all, I didn't even kiss you, so your virtue is still very much intact."

"There you go. See, no problem. Tell you what, if you give me a couple minutes to grab a shower, I'll even play hostess and offer you breakfast."

"Yeah?" he asked with a grin.

"Yeah."

"Does your hospitality extend to letting me grab a shower as well?"

"I'm pretty sure that the book on etiquette my mother gave me when I turned sixteen would demand that I—"

"Offer a guest a shower?" he filled in.

"Yeah."

Nate laughed. "You're nuts. Go get your shower and I'll make myself at home. I'll even make the coffee since you're making the breakfast."

"Oh, you are a true gentleman, Bull."

"Yeah, Roxy, I try."

Shannon scampered off to get her shower and Nate watched her disappear down the hall.

He'd just spent his first night with her.

And he realized he didn't want it to be the last night they spent together. Not that he was looking for anything permanent, nothing like his mother envisioned. But more nights with Shannon, that he could handle.

Nate poked around in her kitchen, locating the coffee in the freezer and the filters in the cupboard over the coffee maker. It was a small kitchen, bright, without all the loud colors his mother favored. No, this was softer with a lot of whites and pale yellows.

It suited Shannon.

He'd just got the coffee ready and had pushed the button to start it when he heard the front door open.

"Shannon?" a voice called.

A voice Nate recognized immediately.

Well, Shannon wanted her mother to believe they were an item, and it appeared she was going to get that wish answered in spades.

He walked out of the kitchen into the living room where a very annoyed-looking Mrs. O'Malley stood.

"I saw your motorcycle in the drive," she said, disapproval evident in her voice.

"Yeah. I didn't plan on staying the night or I'd've put it in the garage. I don't like letting my baby stay outside all night."

Last night Mrs. O'Malley had been knocked off guard, but she'd had time to regroup. Her stance would do a three-star general proud. Her tone left no doubt that she was back in control. "Where is my daughter?"

"In the shower. I was just making coffee. Could I offer you a cup?"

"No. I'm on my way to Mass and stopped to see if Shannon wanted to join me."

"Want me to go ask her?" he asked, smiling as if he didn't have a clue why she'd take offense at the question.

Mrs. O'Malley sputtered a moment, looking as if she'd swallowed a cow whole. "I...I don't think so. Tell her I'll call her later."

"Sure thing."

"And Bull?" Mrs. O'Malley said, moving a few steps closer.

"Yes, ma'am?"

"If you hurt her, you'll be mincemeat."

Some of the humor left the situation. Nate raked a hand through his hair. "You're the second O'Malley to tell me that in less than twenty-four hours. What is it that makes you all think Shannon couldn't take care of me herself if I hurt her?"

Her sister and mother might not think so, but Nate suspected Shannon was more than capable of standing up for herself. From what he could see, all the O'Malley women were formidable.

"Shannon's too soft-hearted for her own good," her mother said. "She believes in fairy tales. I think that's why she enjoyed planning her sister's wedding so much. But I know that romance isn't enough. That people need more than a good shot of lust to make a relationship work. I don't think the two of you could possibly have that much in common. Odds are, this will end badly. I don't want her hurt."

"And yet, you're willing to see her married off just to win a bet," Nate said gently.

Mrs. O'Malley heaved a sigh and shook her head. "No. I want to see her married off because Shannon is the type of person who's meant to be married. She needs someone to love, someone who in turn will love her to distraction. This bet…well, it simply presented an excuse to introduce her around."

"Someone to take care of her, you mean?"

"I say what I mean, young man." Mrs. O'Malley's voice was once again sharp and in command. "I raised both of my daughters to be able to take care of themselves, but I also think life is more meaningful if you share it with someone."

She paused a moment and added, "Do you think you're the man Shannon should be sharing her life with?"

"Maybe. Maybe not. But I know that none

of the guys you've set her up with are him,"
Nate said.

"So do I."

Her admission surprised him. "And yet, you
continue to do it."

"In hopes that the next man would be the right
man. The one she's been waiting for."

"And you're sure I'm not him?" he asked.

"As sure as I can be. Shannon needs a good guy.
Someone who will come home every night after
work. She needs the little things, trading stories
about their days, eating a quiet meal together.
Something as simple as watching a movie together.
Someone with common interests. I don't think
that's you."

"Maybe you're right," Nate said. "Maybe I'm
not her Mr. Right, but I am her Mr. Right-now, so
I'll thank you to forget about setting her up with
anyone else for a while."

"Fine," Mrs. O'Malley said with a short nod.
"Tell her I'll talk to her later."

"Sure."

She started toward the door, then abruptly turned
around. "And Bull, remember what I said."

"Don't worry, I don't intend to hurt her."

Mrs. O'Malley turned and left, shutting the front
door with a soft thud.

Nate went back to the kitchen and poured a cup
of coffee for himself as he pondered his confron-
tation with Shannon's mom.

Mrs. O'Malley was right. From the little Nate knew about her, Shannon was special. He'd known it that first night in Mick's bar. And now, having spent time with her, he was even more convinced.

He thought—

"Hey, a man who makes me coffee in the morning, that's my kind of man," Shannon said, as she came into the kitchen, her hair still wet. She was wearing jeans and a t-shirt. Her feet were bare. She didn't have a speck of makeup on.

She looked as far removed from Roxy as a woman could.

And yet, this look was ever so much sexier.

He forced himself not to think about how much sexier as he handed her a mug of coffee.

"I believe you said something about breakfast," he reminded her.

She grinned. "Sure did."

"So what are you making me?" he asked.

"Nothing. We're going to get on your motorcycle, and drive down the street to Perkins. There, I plan to order a huge stack of pancakes, and drown them in syrup. How about you?"

"So, I made the coffee, and you're allowing me to take you to Perkins?"

"Hey, it's my treat."

"I wanted to try your cooking," he said. "After growing up with my mother, well, let's just say, I like to know how a woman cooks right up front."

"In this case, you don't."

"That bad?" he asked.

"Uh, you know your mom's roast the other night? That looked good in comparison."

"Thanks for the warning then. Perkins it is."

"I thought you might see it that way," she said with a laugh.

"Do you mind if I get that shower before we go?"

"Help yourself."

"Thanks."

"And Nate?" she called as he started toward the bathroom.

"Yeah?"

"I'm glad you spent the night."

"Me, too," he said, then turned and hurried down the hall. He liked being here with Shannon, liked holding her last night.

He just plain liked her.

And he didn't have a clue what to do about it.

6

___

SHANNON HELD the phone away from her ear and looked at it, as if it could provide some answers.

She put it back to her ear, and said, "The dress?"

"Yes. I need that dress back. When you get married, you'll have to find your own dress. I've decided Mary Kathryn's—"

"Kate," Shannon corrected automatically.

"Kate's dress doesn't suit you."

She'd won.

Her mother might be saying the dress doesn't suit, but what she meant was that Bull didn't suit.

Her mom was done trying to marry Shannon off to just any man.

Shannon was free and clear.

Why wasn't she feeling elated?

"Honey, I want you to find the right man when the time's right. You don't have to rush anything."

"What about the bet?"

"Don't you worry about that. I love you and just want you to be happy."

"Mom," Shannon said. She sniffed.

A moment.

She'd just had *a moment* with her mother.

"Mom," she said again.

Brigit O'Malley was not one for big demonstrations. "Get that dress ready. I'll pick it up later."

"About Bull," Shannon said, ready to confess all, to tell her mother her nefarious plan.

"Not one more word. This was a good conversation and I'll not have it ruined by fighting about your boyfriend. I'll stop by later this week and pick up the dress," she said, hanging up abruptly.

Shannon was victorious!

Her mom was off her back.

She could let the hair on her legs grow so long she would be able to braid it.

She could go on a week-long chick-flick fest.

There was a world of opportunities in front of her.

But what she really wanted to do was call Nate and share her victory.

Truth be told, she'd wanted to call him after he'd dropped her off on Sunday. She thought about calling to say hi. Maybe to see how the ride home had gone.

Had he stalled the motorcycle?

But she didn't call. Didn't want him to think she was reading more into their *casual* relationship than he was.

She didn't call and hoped he would.

He didn't.

He didn't call Monday either.

Neither did she.

As much as she wanted to call him, she just couldn't. She must have picked up the phone a dozen times, but always slammed it back down.

She wasn't sure why it was so hard to call him. She had the perfect excuse, to share the news about her mom. But she didn't call, and neither did he.

Wednesday was a repeat performance. Look at the phone. Think about calling. Even go so far as to pick up the phone. Set it back down. Don't call.

Thursday she didn't pick up the phone at all. Oh, she thought about it, but since he hadn't called her, she wasn't about to call him.

She realized just how juvenile she was, but wasn't able to stop herself. Something about Nate made her feel as if she was back in high school, giggling with girlfriends over boys.

Friday she woke up with a light heart. She and Nate were having dinner at his mom's again tonight. She'd see him after school.

She practically danced through the day. Even Robbie Pembrooke, a student who could try the patience of a saint, couldn't faze her happiness.

Of course, she did inform him that graffiti didn't qualify as an art project...at least not in her class. She made him miss math—his favorite class—to clean his "project" off the side of the school and write a letter of apology to Mrs. Appleton, who, to the best of Shannon's knowledge, did not, nor ever had had an affair with the janitor.

No, even Robbie Pembrooke couldn't faze her good mood.

Shannon noticed that Robbie had stopped scrubbing and was simply standing in front of the wall.

"Robbie," Shannon hollered.

He turned and said, "My arm's killing me," with that teenaged whine that would one day grow into a fine man-whine.

"Tough," she said.

The boy turned back and started scrubbing again. And Shannon smiled.

"You look awfully happy," her friend, Patricia, said, as she took a seat next to Shannon on the bench. "So, what's up?"

"Maybe it's just a happy sort of day. It is Friday, after all."

Patricia shook her head. "I know a Friday-smile when I see one, and this is something more."

"Well, it just so happens I have a date."

She didn't admit that it wasn't exactly a date.

"Oooh, do tell. Does it involve candlelight and a new outfit?"

"Yes, to the new outfit." Shannon had gone shopping yesterday and was pretty sure her outfit was going to scandalize Nathan's mom.

Yes, one look at those pants and Mrs. Calder was going to be so scandalized she'd beg Nate to stop dating Roxy.

The thought should have made her feel victorious, but instead, she felt a bit let down.

"Yes, new clothes, but not candlelight. Just a quiet dinner. Not much to tell. Just me, on a date."

"That's it?" Patricia asked, sounding a bit skeptical.

"Yep."

"Hmm," Patricia said, studying her.

"Robbie, you missed a spot," Shannon called, ignoring Patricia's scrutiny. She smiled as Robbie grumbled, not because he grumbled, but because she was going to see Nate in just a few hours.

"So, how are the kids?" she asked. And even as she listened to Patricia talk about her kids, she couldn't help but smile.

She'd see Nate tonight.

"OH, SHANNON, dear, I'm so sorry," Mrs. Calder said as they entered the house that evening.

Shannon didn't have to ask just what it was Mrs. Calder was sorry for. There was a distinct smell of burnt—well, she wasn't sure just what it was, but whatever it had been, it was charcoal now.

"I made the most lovely veal for dinner—"

Ah, veal, that's what it was.

"—but there must be something wrong with my oven."

"Or with your cooking," Nate muttered low enough so that only Shannon caught it.

She stifled the laughter that bubbled just below the surface. She'd felt giddy since Nate had shown up on her doorstep. He was wearing jeans and a polo shirt...looking positively good enough to eat.

"That's okay, Mrs. Calder," she assured Nathan's mom. "Really."

"No, dear, I promised you dinner and you're getting dinner. Why, I don't imagine you get to eat right at the club you work at. I think they're more interested in drinking than good food. So, let's go."

"Go?" Shannon echoed, realizing that this burnt meal could be a problem.

A big problem.

"We're going out to eat." Mrs. Calder started to gather her purse.

"But…" Shannon looked down at tonight's exotic-dancer outfit.

Tight pseudo-leather—pleather—pants, a bright-red blouse and stiletto black heels. Add to that that she'd slicked her hair back with goop and piled on the makeup, and she definitely didn't want to go out in public looking like this.

"But…" she stammered.

Nate hadn't said a word. She elbowed him hard and looked from him to her outfit, then back at him. She saw the dawning of understanding on his face.

"Mom, really, that's okay," he said in a rush. "We'll come back to dinner tomorrow, and you can try again."

"Ah, son, I know you love my cooking."

Nate shot Shannon a look and she knew exactly what he was thinking…his mom was the worst cook alive.

"But, really darling," Mrs. Calder continued. "I

enjoy a night off now and then as well. So, let's go."

"Pizza," Nate said. "Let's just order in pizza."

"Now, will you two stop fighting? We're eating out. Paul," she hollered.

Shannon didn't have to be her child to realize that was that. Mrs. Calder wasn't going to be dissuaded.

Mr. Calder ambled into the foyer. "Shannon. How nice to see you again. I assume you heard about our change of plans."

Nate nodded. "Where do you want us to meet you?"

"I was hoping we could all ride together," his mom said.

"You don't like my motorcycle," Nate accused.

"It's not that..." his mom started, then shrugged. "Okay, it is that. I don't like it. And if you were to crash on the way out to dinner, I'd never get over the guilt. You'd be maimed because I can't cook. You don't want to put your mother through something like that, do you? After all, you're the only child I could have and the suffering I went through to get you...why, you couldn't willingly subject me to any more, could you?"

"Mom, that's ridiculous. I'm a grown man and—"

"We'd love to ride with you, Mrs. Calder," Shannon interrupted.

"Thank you, dear, for understanding."

"No problem."

His parents walked out the door and toward the Calder's blue sedan.

Nate hung back and held Shannon back as well. "Why did you do that?" he whispered.

"Because she worries about you. There's nothing wrong with that."

"Not when it's my mom doing the worrying," he said, obviously put out. "But when it's your mom, then it's another story."

"My mom doesn't worry. She bosses. There's a difference," Shannon said.

"She bosses you around because she's worried about you," Nate countered.

"Since when did you become and expert on my mother?"

"Let's just say that maybe I have a bit more objective insight than you do."

"Let's not and have you explain."

"Just leave it alone, Shannon."

"Are you two coming?" Nate's mom called from the car. She paused and said, "Is something wrong?"

"No, of course not," Shannon said as she shook her arm free of Nate and walked toward the car.

"Good," she said with a smile. "Then we're off."

NATE POKED at his dinner salad as he listened to Shannon and his mother chatter away happily.

Shannon was making a mess of things again. His

mother seemed to enjoy her as much tonight as she had last week. At the rate Shannon was going, he was going to be married off and the father of four.

Somehow the thought didn't send the familiar jolt of terror down his spine. Not that he was thinking of marrying Shannon. But if he had to get married, she'd be number one on his list.

And thinking he'd even have a list of women he'd marry totally freaked him out and he kicked her leg under the table and shot her a get-on-with-it-already look.

He knew she caught the gist of his meaning because she winked at him and said, "I've been thinking about changing jobs."

"Really, dear, that would be wonderful. Not that what you do for a living affects our opinion of you. After all, you're such a sweet and caring young lady."

"Why, thank you, Mrs. Calder." Shannon smiled sweetly at the praise.

Of course, the loud red color she'd painted on her lips should have made smiling sweetly very difficult, but Shannon pulled it off.

"So what are you thinking about doing?" his mom asked.

"I'm going to—"

"Shannon, it is you," someone interrupted her.

Nate looked up and saw a petite brunette and a tall skinny man standing next to their table.

"Patricia?" Shannon said weakly. She glanced down and blushed.

Nate realized that she obviously knew the couple, and it was just as obvious that she was embarrassed to be caught in her Roxy get-up.

"What are you two doing here? And where are the kids?" Shannon asked.

"Kyle was sweet enough to invite me to dinner and I left the kids with a sitter. Are you going to introduce us?" Patricia asked.

Shannon smiled, and Nate suspected he was the only one who noticed how forced it was.

"Patricia Leonard and Kyle Bruno, this is Nate Calder and his parents, Paul and Judy."

"These are your friends from work, dear?" Mrs. Calder asked.

Nate suddenly realized that these were the friends she'd based her little strip-club stories on and suppressed a groan.

Their plans were about to tank, all because his mother was a lousy cook.

He knew what he was getting her for Christmas…cooking lessons. She didn't have to be a cordon bleu chef, but man, you'd think at her age she could broil a hunk of meat without ruining all his plans in the process.

He'd be the first man in history forced to walk down the aisle because of a burnt meal.

"Why, Shannon," his mother said, "you didn't

tell us Candy here was dating Bruno. That's wonderful.''

"Candy?" Patricia asked.

"She prefers to be called Patricia," Shannon corrected.

This time Nate didn't try to suppress his groan. No, he let it out, knowing that if his mother noticed it would be the least of their worries.

Shannon had told his mom that Patricia stripped under the name Candy and of course his mom— the woman who could forget about dinner until the smoke alarms went off—didn't forget little things like Shannon's fictional account of her fictional job at the fictional strip club using her real colleagues' fictional stripping names.

"How come you didn't tell me you two were dating?" Shannon said.

Nate could tell she was trying to head off further questions from her friends, but he could have told her that the way his luck was going, it wasn't going to work.

"We didn't really want anyone to know," Patricia said. "It's all so new and you know how it is at work. Everyone knows everyone's business."

"Tell me about it," Shannon muttered.

Nate could tell she was thinking about everyone at school knowing this particular business on Monday.

It occurred to him that reading her was getting

easier and easier, and he wasn't quite sure how he felt about that.

"I suppose people in your line of work tend to band together," his mother said. "I mean, it's wonderful to have friends who understand what you do and why. People who don't judge you," his mom said.

"Oh, you're so right," Patricia said. "So many people just hear the bad stuff, how tough it can be. They don't understand that there are good things involved with the job. That the good things far outweigh the bad."

"Shannon was just telling us about it the other night. Would you like to join us?" his mom said. "I'd love the chance to get to know Shannon's friends better now that she and Nate are so close."

"Sure. We'd love to," Patricia, aka Candy, said as she pulled up a chair from a neighboring table. "So, Nate, how long have you and Shannon been seeing each other?"

"A while," he said as noncommittally as he could manage. He turned to Kyle, aka Bruno the Bouncer. "How 'bout those Pirates?"

"Yeah. How 'bout them?" Kyle countered. "I think they can go all the way this year." He turned to Nate's dad and said, "You?"

"An Indian fan through and through."

Nate worked at keeping the conversation turned to sports. He figured if they were talking balls and strikes loud enough his mom couldn't start to cross-examine Shannon's friend about *work*.

"Patricia..." his mom said.

"And what about the Otters still being in the play-offs?" Nate said, hoping to out-talk his mom. He should have known it wouldn't work. "It's so great to still have hockey games so far into the spring."

His mom shot him an evil glare and continued, "So, how long have you worked at...well, with Shannon?"

"Oh, it must be three years now, right Shannon?" Patricia said.

"Yeah," she answered, sounding as morose as he felt.

"I've been to all the home games," Nate said. "I play amateur hockey with some friends."

"Me, too," said Kyle. "A bunch of us at work got together and formed a team. We've got games through July. I love baseball, but hockey, now that's a tough sport."

Nate's mom picked right up on that. "The people you...work with are on a hockey team?"

"Co-ed. It's just for fun. Work can be so stressful, there are just so many demands, we need somewhere to unwind. And there's no better way to de-stress than skating around an ice rink hitting pucks."

"I imagine you do need an outlet given the circumstances,'' his mom said. ''It's good that all the women at work have you to look after them.''

Kyle grinned at Patricia. ''I look after some a little more closely than others.''

''Well, I'm sure you're a gentleman. Shannon told me that you've been her hero on more than one occasion.''

''Oh, yeah. There was that time the Pembrooke clan got together and...

7

"WELL, NOW, that was an interesting night," Nate said as they walked from his car up to her porch.

Interesting was going to be the discussion in the teacher's room on Monday, trying to explain what had happened...yeah, that would be interesting.

For the life of her, Shannon couldn't think of a way to explain her outfit.

Somehow they'd made it through the meal without having Nate's mom see through their deception, but it had been a near thing more than once. Thank goodness for the Erie Otters being in the play-offs. The guys had kept that conversation going for quite a while.

"Interesting," Shannon repeated. "Yeah, you can say that again."

She stood, staring out at the street lights wondering if she could bribe Patricia and Kyle into silence. Oh, her date was going to be all over the faculty room on Monday, she just knew it.

"That was..." Nate left the sentence hanging, smiling as he stood next to her.

"Funny, Calder. Real funny. Let's see how

funny you'd think it was if some of your customers from the pharmacy saw you all bikered up.''

His smile faded abruptly and he laid a hand lightly on her shoulder. It was meant to be comforting, not something designed to arouse her...but arouse her it did.

The slightest touch, the smallest gesture could heat her blood stream, at least they could if it was Nate doing the touching or the gesture.

''You're really upset,'' he said, softly.

She nodded. Though she wasn't nearly as upset about dinner as she was by the power Nate seemed to have over her. ''Yes, I am.''

''Hey, I'm sorry.''

She shrugged. ''It wasn't your fault.''

''I should have refused to go out with my mom. I just don't know how to tell her no sometimes.''

''Tell me about it. It's not your fault I'm in this absurd situation. It's my mother's. You not being able to say no to a dinner is far more understandable than me not being able to say no to a wedding.''

''I know you don't want to hear this right now,'' Nate said slowly, ''but I have to confess, I'm sort of grateful to your mom.''

''Grateful?'' Of all the things she'd expect to hear him say, that wasn't one.

''Grateful?'' she repeated.

''Yeah. I mean, if your mom hadn't come up with that bet and started throwing you at men, you wouldn't have ended up at Mick's. If you hadn't ended up at Mick's, then I wouldn't have met you. If I hadn't met you I wouldn't be standing here on your porch, with a full moon blazing overhead, thinking about doing this—''

There was no time to think, no time to prepare, though even if there had been, Shannon would have been defenseless as Nate stopped talking and moved toward her. He turned her gently until she was facing him and then lowered his lips to hers.

She could have turned her head. Could have backed away. Instead, she met the kiss.

Hot. Hard. Demanding. Any thoughts of ruined reputations or overbearing mothers were immediately lost in the sensation of kissing Nate.

The smell of him, the taste of him, the firmness of his lips, the warmth of his body pressed to hers…it all merged into one throbbing blaze of desire. Shannon was swimming in a sea of sensations—drowning in them.

The kiss eased, and slowly their lips parted, but neither of them released their hold on the other.

''Wow,'' Nate said as he released his breath.

Shannon laughed. ''Oh so eloquent, as always, Mr. Calder.''

''How's this for eloquent…I want you. Not just some kiss on your porch, but all of you. I want to take you inside, into your room and—''

''Nate,'' she said, interrupting his description because it so well matched her own thoughts…her own desires. "I don't know. I don't want to take our charade, our partnership, and try to turn it into something that it's not. Something it can't be. What we have is fiction. Even our casual dating agreement isn't a real relationship."

"I'm not suggesting marriage. I'm suggesting that this could be good. Very good. I think over the last two weeks we've developed something more than fiction...we've become friends. We both understand that we're not ready for a lifelong commitment. Why can't that friendship extend to what we both so obviously want?"

"Nate, I've come to value your friendship. I know we haven't known each other long, but you mean something to me. Something I'm not willing to lose. Do you really think we could be intimate and still just be friends?"

"Why not? A friendship that extends into the bedroom." He paused. "Bedroom buddies."

"Why not?" she repeated with a laugh. "Yes, you are eloquent."

"You want something more eloquent? How about this." He paused a moment, then said, "I haven't been able to get you out of my head since that first night at Mick's. I like being with you. I like laughing with you. I liked holding you in my arms while you slept last week. Hell, I didn't even mind watching a chick-flick with you."

"You said *Terminator* wasn't a chick-flick," she pointed out with a laugh.

"I lied. You were right. It's a romance."

"And this? What will this thing between us be, Nate?"

"We're friends. Friends who desire one another."

"And that will be enough?" She was asking the question of Nate, but really, it was meant for herself.

Could it be enough to be just intimate friends with Nate?

What had he said? Bedroom buddies. Friends who occasionally slept together, but had no real commitment?

Could that work?

She didn't know the answer.

"It could be enough, I think. At least for me," he said. "What about for you?"

"I don't know the answer to that. I'll confess, I've had boyfriends in the past, but no one I've wanted the way I want you. No one I felt this sense of friendship...this sense of connection with."

"Is that enough?" he asked softly as he pulled her close, tighter within the shelter of his arms.

"For now," she said, nodding as she answered her own question. "Yes. It can be enough for now."

Decision made, she didn't want to think or analyze any more. She just wanted him—immediately, if not sooner.

She tore herself away from his embrace, and

fumbled through her purse for her keys. Two tries later, she couldn't contain the tremor in her hand long enough to get the key into the hole.

"Let me," Nate said.

He unlocked the door and swept her inside, slamming the door behind him. He dropped the keys, and they landed on the tile with a clank.

"I—"

"Shh. We're not talking. We're…"

His lips met hers again, stoking intoxicating desire that rose and grew to new, heady proportions. He steered her backward down the hall, without ending the kiss.

Shannon was just getting the hang of walking backward and kissing when she thwacked to an abrupt halt, her back pressed against her bedroom door, her front pressed against Nate. She reached behind her back, fumbled with the knob and they both practically fell into the room as the door swung inward.

They stood at the end of her bed and she wrapped her arms around his neck. The hunger of their kiss grew until it threatened to overwhelm her.

Shannon pulled back and tried to catch her breath, but Nate didn't seem to want to oblige. His hands were tugging at her shirt, pulling it up and off. And suddenly she was helping him, needing to remove any barriers between them. As he slid off his own shirt, she unbuttoned her pants and tugged downward.

They didn't budge.

Not even an inch.

She tried again. But, unfortunately, pleather seemed to have a lot of the same characteristics as leather. It didn't slide well on hot, sticky skin.

And even more unfortunately, Shannon was definitely hot…and not because of the temperature, but because of the man standing next to her, watching as she tugged at the waistband of the pants. The fabric moved a millimeter toward her feet and then stuck again, as if superglued.

"Problems?" Nate asked, tossing his shirt on the floor.

She stared at his naked chest. It was a sight to behold. Firm, without being overworked. He looked like a man who was active enough without being obsessed by his body.

"Shannon?" he said, reaching for the snap on his jeans.

"Yes?" she said, her voice practically a whisper.

She knew he was asking her something, but she was mesmerized by the sight of him and had lost track of what she'd been doing and what he was asking. She reached out and grazed a line down his chest with the tip of her finger.

"Shannon, you stopped. What's wrong?"

Stopped? Her mind was fuzzy. She felt almost drunk on the sight of him.

"Stopped?" she echoed.

"Stopped undressing." He slid the zipper on his pants down with maddening slowness.

"I, uh…" What were they talking about? She didn't have a clue. She stood, frozen to the spot, watching every movement Nate made. Feeling a little more…just a little *more* with each movement.

"Shannon-me-love," he crooned, his face lowered and just a breath away from her own.

His lips grazed hers again. She felt frenzied with desire. With need. A need that had to be met.

Her bra stood between her and his naked chest. She reached behind her back, trying to undo the clasp, but couldn't get her hands to stop trembling enough to work the small hooks.

"Allow me," Nate said against her lips, not really pausing the kiss at all, but speaking into it.

The bra was unclasped and before she could draw in a breath, it was gone. Her chest pressed to his, her heartbeat melded with his.

Thump, thump.

Thump, thump.

It was as if there was no separation between them. They were one.

One breath.

One heartbeat.

One entity.

His hand reached between their fused chests and touched her nipple, just a soft brush. Shannon heard herself groan.

"Here, let me help," he said as his hands hooked onto her waistband and tugged.

The pants didn't move.

Suddenly she remembered what she'd been doing when he removed his shirt.

She remembered the fact that she was stuck in her pants.

Nate's lips left hers and he looked down, studying the problem.

"Uh?"

"They're fake leather," she said as she joined his tugging. "They say it's like leather, but maybe they should say it's like a chastity belt. Parents all over the world would buy pseudo-leather pants for their daughters."

They both tugged and the pants slipped down another fraction of a millimeter.

"Maybe if you sat down on the bed and I pulled," Nate said.

Shannon nodded. She was starting to feel a bit claustrophobic about being stuck in her pants. What if they couldn't get them off?

She sat on the edge of the bed and gripped the footboard.

Nate pulled. Hard.

She was glad she'd held on, because her pants didn't move at all, but her body practically flew off the bed. Suspended between the footboard and Nate's grip on her pant-legs, she hung like a suspension bridge.

Nate let her settle back down onto the mattress and Shannon could have sworn she heard a chuckle, but when she checked he looked serious.

"I don't think this is working," she said. "I should have taken them off before I got so..."

"Hot?" he supplied, unable to continue his fake seriousness. He was grinning.

Leave it to a man to find the idea that he'd got her so worked up that she was stuck in her pants a compliment.

"It is warm out tonight."

"I don't think that's why you're all hot," he said as he reached out and gently touched her nipple. It stood at attention. "No, I don't think it has a thing to do with the weather."

"You're enjoying this." He reached for her again, and she moved back. "Let me think a minute."

"Are you saying this," he touched her nipple again, "disturbs you?"

"You disturb me even when you're not touching me. This just makes it worse." She paused and added, "A good worse."

"Do you have any powder?" he asked.

"Powder?"

"Maybe if we shake a little into your pants it will help."

"You want to powder my pants?" She giggled. "Ah, Bull, you are a kinky man."

"Ah, but you love it, Roxy."

They both burst out laughing: Full, deep, catch-your-breath-when-you're-done sort of laughter.

When she could breath again, she said, "You know, this has never happened before."

"Getting stuck in your pants?" He gave the waistband another little tug, but it didn't move at all.

"No. This. Laughing like this when I'm…" she paused, looking for the right word.

"When you're what?"

She found the word. "Aroused."

"So, you're aroused, huh?" he asked, a macho sort of tone in his voice.

"Yes." She would have sworn in a court of law that his chest actually puffed out. "Don't let it go to your head, but if we don't get my pants off me soon, I just might explode with wanting you."

"I like your way with words," he said as he wiggled his eyebrows.

They both burst out laughing again.

Maybe it was nerves, or maybe, just maybe there was something special about her relationship with Nate. Something more than just friendship. Something that bore reflection.

But she'd reflect tomorrow. Right now, she just wanted to get her pants off.

She found a bottle of powder from her vanity and sprinkled some liberally into her pants, reaching down her thighs and rubbing it as far as she could.

Nate sat on the edge of the bed, watching her every move. "Want help?"

"If you help I'm bound to get hotter, which will ultimately defeat the purpose. Stay there."

"Are you sure?" he asked. The laughter had died from his voice. Now she heard something else, something thick and hot.

"Yes, I'm sure."

"So, basically, you want me to stay over here and watch you...strip."

"Yeah. Remember, no touching."

"Your boss has rules, right, Roxy?" he asked. There was humor in the question, but underneath that was desire.

"Right, my boss has rules."

He leaned back on his elbows and watched. "Ah, Roxy, I'm a lucky man."

"And don't you forget it, Bull."

She worked the powder a little farther and pulled again. The pants moved. Slowly, bit by bit, she eased them down. Once clear of her hips, they came off.

Free at last.

"Hey, Roxy, I like the undies."

Shannon blushed, knowing he was looking at her thong underwear. "I bought them to go with the outfit. They made me feel sexier."

He pulled her toward the bed. "I think you should wear them all the time."

"Really?" she asked, her voice a whisper.

"Really. Thinking of you in your powder-blue oxford shirt, jeans and sneakers, so proper on the outside, but knowing you have these on underneath, and that I'm the only one who knows about them...I think I'd like it."

She was sitting next to him, and his hands were moving all over her, as if he was trying to memorize every inch of her body.

"Move a bit closer," he murmured, pulling her next to him, so that their thighs touched.

She was falling back under his spell...falling hard. "I don't know, Bull. Mama says bikers are dangerous," she murmured.

"Yeah we are. We live on the wild side."

She reached out and ran her hand down his naked torso. "Now, where were we?"

"I think we were doing this..." He swept her into his arms and kissed her. All the fun and laughter was cast aside in a wave of longing.

They kissed, they touched. The world outside the bedroom door was long forgotten. The questions were gone. In their place was just this man. This time. The feel of him. The scent of him.

Shannon was high on the wash of sensations that flooded her system.

"Nate," she whispered as his lips left hers and continued their course of exploration.

Lower, lower. He reached the thong underwear, but rather than removing them, he simply caressed beneath them and through them.

The effect was like spontaneous combustion. Shannon felt as if something burst as she squirmed beneath his probing until it was almost too much.

"Your turn," she murmured, realizing he hadn't removed his jeans.

"I'm not finished."

"I know, but still, it's my turn with you."

She began her own study, trying to learn everything about him. Soft skin, hard muscle, downy hair...different textures, different feels, but all adding up to Nate.

She fumbled for her nightstand drawer and removed a small foil package. She'd never found condoms very sensual, but as she slowly slid this one in place, firmly fitting it to the length of him, she realized they could be. That with the right person, every movement was part of the package and could become an erotic part of making love.

She shuddered with need.

Nate moaned, and in one fluid movement, flipped Shannon on her back, removed her panties, and plunged into her depths. She met his every thrust, needing to feel him as deeply as possible. Needing to drive this frenzy to fulfillment.

Needing.

Needing.

And suddenly it wasn't need. His driving rhythm sent her over the edge of desire to completion. She screamed with the power of it. And at that primal sound, Nate too groaned, as his movements slowed, n stopped. He was still buried deep within her, mbedding himself fully within her, branding himself on her skin. Still joined, he sank on top of her, his body fused with hers.

Just as she thought she might run out of oxygen, he rolled slowly to one side, but held her, rolling her as well, so she was facing him.

''Wow,'' he said with a smile.

Nate Calder might not be the most eloquent guy around, but this once Shannon couldn't think of a better way to put it.

''Wow,'' she repeated as she snuggled into his embrace.

NATE HELD SHANNON as she slept. He was too keyed up to sleep himself.

What they'd just shared…

He couldn't quite figure it out.

He'd wanted it to be just sex. Two friends sharing a moment together.

Bedroom buddies, he'd told her.

But it wasn't just sex.

Sex was easy. This wasn't.

They'd laughed together over her pants dilemma.

He'd never laughed in the middle of becoming intimate with a woman. That in itself was new and different. Maybe the situation should have pulled him from the moment, but it hadn't. If anything, it had intensified his need. Added a new dimension to his desire.

He touched a spiky strand of hair.

Shannon O'Malley was different from any other woman he'd ever had a relationship with. He wasn't sure just what that difference was, but he was sure it was addictive.

After what they'd just done, he should be thinking of leaving, of going home. He'd never spent the night with a woman, unless you counted the other night when he'd fallen asleep with Shannon.

Even then she was different.

He knew that unless she kicked him out, he was staying tonight. Staying as long as she'd let him.

He gently rolled out of bed, and went into her bathroom, then quietly slipped back under the covers and pulled her into his arms.

In her sleep, she cuddled into his chest and sighed. And Nate knew he could finally sleep as well. Maybe in his dreams he could figure out just what was different about Shannon *Roxy* O'Malley.

8

SHANNON WOKE UP to the sensation of warmth and weight. It took a moment for her sleep-fogged mind to register just what that meant.

Somebody was in her bed.

More specifically, Nathan, aka Bull, Calder was lying next to her, hogging the covers.

Even more specifically...she liked it.

This was the second time she'd woken up next to him.

She smiled as she inched closer to him until the length of him was pressed against her back. He shifted in his sleep, wrapping his arms around her.

She'd slept with Nate, both figuratively and literally.

The thought kept chasing itself around in her brain. It was easier to acknowledge the sleeping part than the part that came before they slept.

This was just a friendship that extended to the bedroom.

Which made it hard to classify what they did as *making love,* but making love is exactly how it felt to Shannon even if she couldn't call it that. She wasn't sure what to call it.

Sex sounded too raw and hard.

She thought of the terms she'd overheard kids at school use. Most sounded worse than sex. Then she hit on *boinking* and smiled. It sounded light and fun, sort of like what they'd done.

If what they'd done wasn't making love, then it was, by its very definition, light.

Light and fun.

She'd boinked Nathan Calder.

He wasn't her boyfriend. He was a friend who was male. A partner.

And so they weren't lovers, and they were no longer just friend and allies.

They were…boink-buddies.

She laughed.

"What's so funny?"

She turned and looked at the man next to her. "Sorry. I didn't mean to wake you."

"You didn't," he assured her. "I've been awake for a while now."

"Why didn't you get up?"

"I was just enjoying the scenery."

"Scenery?" You couldn't see out the window in her room from her bed. Suddenly his meaning occurred to her. "Oh."

He grinned. "So, why were you laughing?"

"I was just trying to define…" she hesitated, "Well, this. What we have between us."

He shifted slightly, reminding Shannon she was naked in bed with him.

"And did you?" he asked, his voice low and...well, sexy.

Shannon didn't feel sexy. She felt naked and more than a little rumpled.

"Did you, Shannon-me-love?"

"Did I what?" she asked, unsure what they'd been talking about, but totally sure that whatever it was, it wasn't nearly as enthralling as the naked man next to her.

"Did you decide how to define us?" he asked.

"Yep. You said bedroom buddies, but I have a much better term."

"Are you going to tell me?" He reached out and toyed with her hair. Whether he was smoothing it out, or mussing it up, she wasn't sure, but the feel of it made her want to purr like a kitten. She wanted to arch her back and let him continue to run his hands anywhere he wanted.

This was definitely better than hairy legs and chick-flicks.

"Shannon?" he murmured. "What's your new term for us?"

She grinned. "Boink-buddies."

"What?" he asked.

"Well, I couldn't quite define us as lovers."

"Why not?"

She'd expected to hear laughter in his voice when she'd revealed her term for their relationship. That didn't sound like humor, but more like annoyance. She shifted slightly, putting space between them.

"Why wouldn't you define us as lovers?" he pressed.

"Because we're not. You don't love me. I don't love you. We like each other. We're partners in crime. Friends. A friendship that extends to the bedroom. Remember?"

Nate remembered all right. After all, he'd been the one spouting that nonsense last night. And last night it had sounded perfectly logical and completely desirable to just be bedroom buddies.

But this morning?

He didn't want logic.

He didn't want to be just friends who slept together.

And he didn't want what he'd done with Shannon reduced to such a frivolous term as *boink-buddies*.

What they'd done had been…magic. He winced at the word. It sounded way too sentimental for him to be using, but it was accurate.

Magic.

What they'd done together had been so much more than anything he'd ever experienced, and Shannon was doing her best to minimize it.

"Nate, what's wrong?" she asked softly.

"Nothing," he said, though he knew that for the lie it was. There was something more than just *boinking* between him and Shannon.

Making love?

It certainly sounded more accurate than boinking.

Normally using a phrase like *making love* would be what made him grimace. But not this time. Not with Shannon.

Yet, he didn't point the fact out to her. Why? Because using the term out loud would give it a power he wasn't sure he was willing to give.

She moved farther away from him.

"I think I'm going to grab a shower, if you don't mind," she said. "Obviously you're not a morning person."

"What makes you say that?" he asked.

He heard the sharpness in his voice, but was annoyed enough that he didn't try and temper it.

"You're grumpy and quiet. I'll just let you wake up while I get dressed."

"Fine."

She wrapped the top blanket around her, and took it with her as she got out of the bed. He wasn't even going to get to enjoy the view.

Great.

What had looked like a promising morning suddenly looked as if it couldn't get any worse.

SHANNON HAD her shower, then headed to the kitchen. The atmosphere was oppressive.

Nate was still quiet and Shannon wasn't sure if it was indeed just a morning mood. He seemed put-out about something.

Maybe he regretted what they'd done.

Maybe he thought she'd suddenly start placing all kinds of girlfriend demands on him. Well, she thought as she dug around in the cupboard for a coffee filter, she wasn't about to do that.

She didn't want a significant other any more than he did.

They were friendly allies and boink-buddies, nothing more, nothing less. That didn't give either of them any rights to make demands. Actually, a demandless relationship was what they'd planned, so if that's why he was mad, well he could just get over himself.

Granted, last night was the best boinking she'd ever had.

Having a man who could make her laugh even as he made her quiver with desire…well, that was rare and special. A man like that was to be treasured.

But treasuring didn't mean owning.

"Do you want anything to go with the coffee?" Shannon asked the silent, grumpy man sitting at her counter.

"You can't cook, remember?"

"I can make a bowl of cold cereal," she assured him.

Okay, so cooking wasn't her forte, but it wasn't as if she couldn't pour some milk.

"Are you sure? I—"

The doorbell interrupted him.

After the way the morning had started, Shannon

figured things couldn't get worse…then the door-bell rang again.

"Shannon? Open up. It's your mother."

Things had just gone from worse to *worse-r*.

"Oh, rats." She stayed in the kitchen, hiding in case her mother peeked through the door's small window. "Do you think I can wait her out?"

"Shannon, I know you're in there," her mother called.

"Nope. I think she knows you're here. And since my Harley's out front, I'm betting she knows I'm here as well," Nate—ever the optimist—said.

"Rats."

"Want me to get it?" he offered.

If she wasn't still annoyed with his less than pleasant mood this morning, she might sigh and think something like, *my hero*. But she was annoyed.

He regretted last night and that was what accounted for his attitude.

Well, fine. Let him regret it.

It wasn't as if she'd built any hopes on a forever sort of relationship with him.

"Shannon, do you want me to get it?" he asked again.

She gave her head a little shake. "No. She's my mother. My problem. But be prepared. You know what she's going to think."

"That we're sleeping together…oh, no, what's the term you used? *Boinking*." He practically sneered the word as he said it. "She's going to think we're boinking."

"What's with you this morning?" Shannon asked. Enough was enough. "You've been in a mood since we first woke up. Maybe you're regretting last night, but you don't have to worry. I won't be making any demands on you. You set the ground rules and I'm more than happy to live by them. A quick tumble in bed isn't going to change my desire to remain independent."

"Go get the door, Shannon. I'll finish making the coffee, and we can talk about my mood and your potential demands after your company leaves."

"Fine." She walked to the door with all the enthusiasm of a woman walking to the guillotine.

Nate was regretting last night. He was probably going to tell her he wanted out of the charade and out of their friendship.

She could get by without ever playing Roxy again, but if Nate left for good…she'd miss him.

Darn.

And if that weren't enough of a problem, her mother was here.

What else could go wrong today?

She opened the door, suddenly very aware of her bare feet. Why having bare feet should embarrass her, she wasn't sure. Odds were her mother had seen her feet bare thousands of times. But there it was.

Bare feet spoke of comfort...of being relaxed.

Her feet were bare and Nate was in her kitchen making coffee.

No, the day wasn't looking overly bright.

"Good morning, Mom. What's up?"

Brigit pushed her way into the foyer. "Shannon Bonnie O'Malley, that man is here."

"Yes, he is. I think he's in the kitchen finishing making coffee. Would you like a cup?"

"No. It's eight o'clock on a Sunday morning and there's a man in your kitchen making coffee. Do you see what's wrong with this picture?"

"Yes." Shannon nodded, trying to look appropriately serious. "I know what's wrong with this picture, Mom. I'm not in the kitchen drinking that coffee, and you know I function better with a jolt of caffeine coursing through my veins."

"Now, Shannon, I realize you're a grown woman—"

"Do you, Mom?" Shannon asked softly.

"Do I what?"

"Realize I'm a grown woman?"

"Of course I do. You and your sister are both grown women, and you know the last thing I want to do is interfere in your lives."

"Then why are you here yelling about a man in my kitchen? Why have you spent too many weeks trying to find me a husband? Why—"

Her next why would have to wait. There was another knock on the door.

"Did you leave Dad outside?" Shannon asked.

That would be just like her mom. Leaving her father outside left Shannon without an ally. Her mother liked to use every advantage.

"No, I left him at home. He doesn't know that you and Nate are practically living together. It would break the poor man's heart to know that his daughter is shacking up with a man."

"I'm not shacking up. But if it's not Dad, then who…" Shannon left the question trail off as she opened the door and found herself face to face with Nate's mom.

"Mrs. Calder?" she asked weakly.

"Shannon, dear. Is Nate here?"

"Nate?" Shannon's mom said. "Oh, you mean Bull."

"Bull?" Mrs. Calder echoed, obviously confused.

"Nate's biker name," Shannon's mom supplied.

"That darned motorcycle," Mrs. Calder said as she walked into the house. "I hate it. He's going to get in an accident and kill himself on that thing. Why, he almost did himself in fixing my sink. A man who could injure himself under a sink is a man who shouldn't be tooling around town on a motorcycle. Really, I hate it."

Her mom nodded. "I imagine you do. Look at the slippery slope it dragged Bull down."

Mrs. Calder shot Mrs. O'Malley a strange look.

Shannon felt like Alice having slipped down the

rabbit hole and confronting Tweedle Judy and Tweedle Mum.

Her mom thought Nate was a biker, his mom thought she was a stripper.

If last night's dinner meeting was ill-met, then this morning's gathering was absolutely insane.

"Let me go get Nate," Shannon said softly.

She needed help here.

He might be upset, but one half of their mom problems was his mom problem.

Where was he? It didn't take this long to make coffee. He was probably hiding. Well, he could just un-hide because while she might be willing to face her mom on her own, no way was she taking on his as well.

"Why don't you both make yourself at home, while I go find Nate."

"No need," he said as he walked down the hall. He'd obviously helped himself to a quick shower. He was wearing his jeans from the night before, and one of her old T-shirts. What was a big sloppy T-shirt on her was tight on him and emphasized every muscle on his chest.

Now that Shannon had firsthand knowledge of that chest, the memory made her blood heat up.

"Mom," he said, "and Mrs. O'Malley. It's a bit early to come calling don't you think?"

"I tried calling your cell phone," Nate's mom said, "but all I got was your voice mail."

"How did you know where Shannon lived, Mom?" Nate asked.

"I looked it up in the phone book," she said, then turned to Shannon. "Don't you think it would be wise to have an unlisted number, honey? Given what you do for a living?"

Shannon reached out and took Nate's hand. Whatever annoyance was between them this morning was forgotten as they joined forces to face their common enemies.

Two enemies at once—before coffee—was too much.

He gave her a reassuring squeeze.

"Shannon," her mother said, "Bull's mother is right. I didn't realize you were listed. Any of your students could call you at home."

"Students?" Mrs. Calder echoed. "Students. That's a good thing to call them, I guess. They all have so much to learn, which is why I want to start—"

Nate interrupted her. "Mom, what did you need me for?"

"Oh, yes. Mick called. He said you were supposed to meet him this morning at seven for some fishing thing?"

"I entirely forgot." He turned to Shannon. "We had a fishing date with a bunch of college buddies."

"They're waiting for you down on the bay," his mom said.

"Now, about that coffee," her mom said.

"That sounds lovely," Mrs. Calder said. "I'd love a chance to get to know you."

Shannon didn't want her mother and Mrs. Calder sharing confidences over coffee, but they were moving toward the kitchen. She tried to think of something to stop them and cleared her throat, sure that some great idea would come to her before she finished.

"Ec, ec," she coughed, stalling for time.

No great idea appeared.

She tried again. *"Ec, ec."*

Still nothing.

The women stopped in their tracks.

"Shannon, are you all right?" her mother asked.

"Ec, ec. I think something's caught in my throat." She started to hack and sputter, along with the coughing. *"Ec, ec."*

"Shannon?" her mother said, rushing to her side, Mrs. Calder at her heels. "Honey?"

"Nathan, do something," his mother said.

"Ec, ec, ec, ec…" Shannon continued.

Nathan smacked her back.

"Ec, ec…"

It was working. Both mothers had forgotten about visiting over coffee. They looked concerned as they watched her choke. *"Ec, ec."*

"Nate!" his mother cried.

He smacked her back harder.

"Ec, ec…"

"Nate, I know you think hitting things is the answer to any problem, but I don't think it's working."

Shannon's throat was feeling quite raw, so she stopped hacking and said, "I think it's better. You saved me, Nate."

"See," he said, shooting his mother a rather superior look, "Smacking things does work."

"Honey, are you sure you're okay?" her mom asked.

"Just let me catch my breath," she said hoarsely.

As Shannon bent over, trying to appear as if she was recuperating from her choking spell, she noticed that not only was Nate's tattoo fading, it had a few huge streaks through it.

It was obviously a fake and only a matter of time until her mother spotted it. Spotting details was something her mom was good at.

"Listen, I'd better get down to the bay before the guys leave without me. Thanks for letting me know, Mom," Nate said, herding his mother toward the door.

"About that coffee?" his mom asked.

"I think you two should take a raincheck. I need to get going, and Shannon had better go gargle with something."

"What if she starts choking again?" her mom asked.

"Oh, whatever it was, Nate's smacking dislodged it. I'm fine. We'll all just have that coffee another time.''

Nate, her hero, was ushering their moms toward the door. ''I'll call you this week, Mom.''

''Me, too,'' Shannon assured her mother.

''But—''

''Thanks for stopping,'' they both said in unison and Nate practically pushed both moms out the door.

Shannon shut it before they could protest.

''Phew,'' she said.

''Yeah, phew,'' he echoed.

''So, you better get going if you're going to meet the guys to go fishing.''

''Are you sure you don't mind?''

''Mind? Why would I mind? The idea of our being together is that we don't have any real claim on each other. We're together when its convenient. This is uncomplicated, remember?''

''Yeah. Boink-buddies,'' he said, a hint of that something had returned to his tone—it sounded almost like annoyance.

''Yes,'' she said. ''Boink-buddies. Now, get out of here.''

''Fine. I'll call you, okay?''

''Sure.'' She kissed his cheek, a smile on her face.

She kept it plastered there until he left and then allowed it to slip. She had no idea what was wrong with her. This was the perfect relationship.

Uncomplicated.

Dating, but not really.

She could have her chick-flicks and a good boinking now and then, too.

Add to that her mom was off her back.

This was good.

Great even.

So, why was she feeling as if things were a total mess?

9

SHANNON TOOK her break outside on Monday afternoon, just like every other teacher. Winters in Erie were long and cold, and spring days were meant to be treasured.

Nate had got in from his fishing weekend late last night, but he'd called.

Shannon hadn't expected him to, and had felt pleased...too pleased.

Because if she'd felt that happy hearing from him, how would she feel if she hadn't heard?

Miserable.

She was pretty sure that you weren't supposed to feel miserable if you didn't hear from a casual boink-buddy.

After all, the whole point of their dating relationship was that they had the luxury of not calling.

So what was wrong with her?

She didn't have the time to figure it out because she had other things to deal with. Patricia was making a beeline toward her, looking determined.

Shannon knew that she was going to be grilled about the scene in the restaurant. She'd known it was coming and had tried to prepare a plan. She'd decided to go on the offensive. Rather than try and explain her outfit, she would attack.

The petite brunette with the big load of curiosity approached the bench, but before she could start her interrogation, Shannon asked, "Patricia, how could you?"

"How could I what?" Patricia looked confused as she sat down next to Shannon.

"How could you not tell me that you and Kyle are dating? I mean, we're friends and friends are supposed to share things like that."

"Well, you were so excited about your date that it just slipped my mind," Patricia said.

It sounded plausible, but Shannon caught the look of guilt that flitted across Patricia's face.

Oh, it was brief, but she saw it.

"Ha! You were hiding the fact you two are dating, even from me."

"Well, let's talk about hiding things," Patricia said. "You made out like you were just excited about a date, when in actuality, you were so happy because you were going out with the man you love."

She paused, as if expecting Shannon to respond, but Shannon couldn't think of a thing to say. She'd expected to be interrogated about her outfit, not about being in love. Because she wasn't in love.

Of course she wasn't.

"You're in love," Patricia repeated as if she could hear Shannon's mental denial. "And you didn't even tell me.'' She added a huge *humph* to the end of the sentence for punctuation.

"I...'' Shannon found it hard to finish the sentence.

The words didn't seem to want to come out, but she forced the issue and hoped Patricia didn't hear the strain in her tone as she finished, "I am not.''

Patricia laughed. "Are too.''

She shook her head. "You're mistaken. Nate and I are buddies.''

Boink-buddies, she thought, but she didn't say that part out loud. There was no reason to give Patricia any more fuel to add to the fire she was building.

"Buddies? I saw how you looked at him. That was more than a *buddy* look.''

What had happened to her offensive?

Time to get this back on track. "Listen, about you and Kyle—''

"Uh-uh-uh. I'll tell you all about me dating Kyle, but only after you fill me in on what's going on between you and this Nate. And that explanation had better include why you were dressed in those leather pants.''

Ah, here was the outfit comment she'd been expecting.

"They weren't leather,'' Shannon admitted. "*Pleather*. And I highly suggest avoiding the material at all costs, at least when you're going out on a hot date.''

Remembering her pleather experience, she smiled.

"Aha!" Patricia shouted. "There it was. You were thinking of him."

"What?"

"That smile. It says, *ooh look at me I'm in love.*" She leaned closer to Shannon and said, "So, spill it."

And though it was the last thing she'd planned, Shannon did. By the time their break had ended, she'd told Patricia the whole story.

"Wow. That's romantic," Patricia said with a small sigh. "And more than a bit ironic."

"Ironic?" Shannon echoed.

Moronic.

That's how the tale sounded as she told it.

After all, she was an adult. Why on earth would she need to go to such elaborate lengths to foil her mother's plans?

The truth was, she hadn't needed to.

So why had she agreed to this zany plan with Nate?

Because there had been something about him. They'd laughed as they shared their horror stories about their moms. They'd laughed even more as they'd plotted their mutual escape. Being with Nate had felt right.

More than right, it had felt—

"You and Nate got together to avoid just this."

"Just what?" Shannon asked, her attention snapping away from her feelings for Nate and back to her friend.

"This. Falling in love." Patricia heaved a mighty sigh and actually put her hand on her chest.

"You've got it all wrong. We didn't want to avoid falling in love, we wanted to avoid our mothers' plans."

"And you fell in love instead," Patricia maintained, punctuating the sentence with another sigh.

"We're not in love."

"Listen, *Roxy,*" Patricia said with what sounded suspiciously like a giggle. "You can deny it all you want, but I know love when I see it, and you're in love."

"But—but—" Shannon sputtered.

She didn't love Nate.

After all, they'd only known each other a few weeks.

Of course, she liked spending time with him. From that first meeting she'd felt somehow connected to him.

And maybe she missed him more than a bit when they weren't together.

Then there was the fact she hadn't been able to stop thinking about him, and even worse, dreaming about him. Hot, X-rated dreams that didn't even begin to compare to the actual heat of making love to Nate.

But that didn't mean she was in love.

Did it?

"I'm not looking for that kind of relationship," she said.

"Shannon, love isn't something you can plan on," Patricia continued. "It just is what it is. You love Nate."

"I love Nate?" Shannon whispered, weighing the way the words felt as she said them.

They felt almost good.

Right.

She loved Nate?

She loved Nate!

How on earth had she not known that she'd fallen in love with him?

"I love Nate," she stated rather than asked.

"Yes, you do," Patricia said with a grin. "So what are you going to do about it?"

Now, that was a question.

She loved Nate, a man looking for an uncomplicated relationship.

And suddenly what they had together was looking more than just a bit complicated.

NATE LOOKED frazzled.

More than that, he looked ready to pull his hair out as he listened to something someone was saying on the phone.

Shannon stood at the counter, waiting for him to notice her. When he did, he smiled and held up a finger for her to wait.

"No, ma'am. It's not meant to be taken orally. It's a suppository. It goes...

He finished his explanation and Shannon felt a stab of pity for him. After all, it had to be an uncomfortable thing to explain.

He hung up and gave Shannon a weak smile. "Hey."

"Bad day?" she asked.

"You don't know the half of it. I'm used to odd questions and can handle most without blinking an eye, but today it's been one strange thing after another. I had to explain that birth control pills have to be taken *every* day, not just on days you have sex. And then there was the couple who—" He stopped. "No sense in scaring us both. So, what brings you in today?"

"Maybe I have a prescription?" she asked, teasing in her voice, hoping to make him smile. Then she added, "Or maybe I just wanted to see you."

That was the truth.

Since the moment the light bulb had gone off this afternoon, she'd been anxious to see him and decide if she was right, if she really loved this man.

She stared at him and tried to measure what she felt…and she couldn't. It was so big and all-encompassing, that it couldn't be quantified.

It was limitless.

Only one emotion could be that big. Love.

Yes, she loved Nathan Calder.

So now what?

Did she blurt out *I love you,* or did she wait and try to simply work it into a conversation?

Hey, Nate, you never stall your motorcycle any more…and by the way, I think I love you.

She groaned.

No, she was simply going to have to wait to tell him until she could think of a better approach.

"Is something wrong?" he asked. "Did my mom come back?"

"No, nothing's wrong, exactly. I thought maybe you'd like dinner?"

Dinner.

She could tell him at dinner. After all, it was better to just say the words and get it over with.

She wasn't going to worry about form or style. She wouldn't even worry about changing the rules. She would just say those three words, *I love you* and trust that it would all work out.

Yes, she'd tell him tonight at dinner.

"Dinner sounds good. I need a quiet night more than you know. The idea of a quiet, uncomplicated evening is so appealing."

Shannon almost flinched at the word *uncomplicated.*

She was pretty sure saying she loved him wouldn't constitute an uncomplicated night. After all, loving him changed everything. And everyone knew that change was always complicated.

She wasn't going to tell him.

Maybe he'd simply sense it. After all, how could he miss it? She felt as if she had a sign flashing over her head…*I love Nathan…I love Nathan…*

How could he miss something like that?

She'd make long, slow love to him and he'd know. Ah, now that was a plan. Even if he didn't sense it, she'd still get to make love to him.

She smiled at the thought and said, "Well, we'll have to see if we can find something to do that will relieve your stress."

"Oh, that sounds like a plan," he said, and murmured a few specifics in her ear.

"Nate," she whispered back, feeling breathless and tingly all over.

If she let him do what he was planning to do, she could whisper the words *I love you* in his ear.

Maybe he'd even whisper them right back.

She could only imagine how much more breathless and tingly she'd be over that.

That's it, she was going to tell him.

"I'm so glad you stopped by," he continued. "I mean, everyone wants something from me, all day long. It's Nate this, and Nate that. Give me something as undemanding as what we have and life is good."

Undemanding.

That was as horrible a word as *uncomplicated.*

If she said *I love you* maybe he'd feel obligated to say the words back.

That would definitely be demanding.

Damn. She wasn't going to tell him.

At least not tonight.

She wanted the perfect moment to say the words. The perfect night.

Tonight didn't sound like the time.

No, she wasn't going to tell him.

Before she could answer, someone called, ''Nate.''

'''Scuse me,'' he said, hurrying toward the back of the pharmacy.

She watched him go, the feeling in her chest growing, beating to get out, and she wondered how she could go through an entire night looking at him, listening to him, laughing with him and not tell him how she felt. The feeling was that big.

Even if she didn't plan on telling him, it might slip out.

Then things would get complicated, and he'd feel as if she was demanding, and then he'd never say the words back.

It was an excuse and she knew it, but even if she'd figured out she was in love with Nate, she wasn't quite sure what to do with those feelings.

She had to sort things out.

Feeling decidedly like a coward, she looked at the clerk and said, ''Just tell Nathan that I...''

She hesitated, trying to think of a plausible lie, and settled for a half truth.

''Tell him that I can see he's busy. Tell him to forget about dinner and go relax. I'll talk to him...soon. Tomorrow.''

She hurried out before Nate could come back and

find her and ask questions. Because she didn't feel that she had any answers.

NATE HAD BEEN disappointed Monday when he came out of the back room and found that Shannon had gone. Seeing her had made his day from hell brighten considerably.

But she'd run out and canceled dinner.

Why?

Maybe his bad mood had scared her off. After all, they had an informal relationship, one based on fun. His mood wasn't fun. But it had been such a stressful day, and talking with her had made him feel better.

Just seeing her walk in the store and smile had been enough to make him feel better.

Then she'd left.

It wasn't just that it was one of those days when things went wrong, it was one of those days where nothing went right.

When Shannon left, things went from bad to worse. He needed her. It was a feeling that was growing by leaps and bounds.

He was addicted to her, he decided.

And it wasn't an addiction he was looking to break.

Her boink-buddy comment had annoyed him because it wasn't accurate. They were more than that, even if she didn't want to admit it.

At least, she was more than that to him. He hoped he was more than that to her.

How much more?

That was the question that had been plaguing him.

How much more was she to him? How much more did he want to be to her?

He'd called her that night hoping he could convince her he was in a better mood. He was eager to see her, to explore just what they had become. But Shannon said she had to go to her mom's.

He asked if she wanted him to come as well, but she'd said no. She had it under control.

Tuesday he had hockey practice, so he'd left a message on her answering machine suggesting they get together Wednesday night.

Wednesday she left a message on his machine saying she had a PTC meeting, whatever that was. He figured it had to be like a PTA meeting, and when he tried to call back she wasn't there, so he couldn't ask.

Thursday they'd talked a few minutes, but couldn't get together because she'd promised to go out with her friend Patricia. He'd found out that PTC was indeed like PTA.

But to be honest, that wasn't the question that was nagging him. No, he was worried about why she was avoiding him, because he was pretty sure she was.

He wasn't taking any chances on Friday.

He hadn't seen her since Monday, and on Monday it had been a brief glimpse at best. Not nearly enough.

He missed her.

Which is why on Friday he parked his Harley in front of her house and hurried to the door.

He hadn't called first. Mainly because he was tired of talking to her machine, and hearing her voice on his, or simply grabbing a few seconds with her.

Oh, he knew they'd set the ground rules. This was supposed to be an easygoing sort of relationship. One where they saw each other when they had the time and the inclination. There were no strings.

But he'd had the inclination all week, and would have made the time, but Shannon had been busy.

Too busy for him. Not needing to see him as much as he needed to see her.

To hear her.

To touch her.

He was thinking about touching her as he rapped on the door.

She opened it, wearing as anti-Roxy an outfit as she possibly could. Well-worn gray sweats, a battered T-shirt, short spiky hair wild…and he'd never seen a woman look more lovely. More tantalizing. More…

He'd planned on at least saying, ''Hi, Shannon,'' and playing it casual, following the absurd rules they'd set down, but when he drank in the sight of her, the only thing he wanted to do was…

He pulled her into his arms and kissed her.

Not just some little peck-on-the-cheek sort of greeting.

No.

It was long and hot with desire.

Hungry with his need.

He'd kissed her before, but still there was a sense of discovery and wonder as his lips devoured hers.

Or maybe her lips were devouring his, because in their meeting he felt her own need answering his.

He kicked the door shut with his foot, and pulled his jacket off, without breaking the contact.

She helped him, then her fingers moved to the buttons on his shirt. He could feel the slight tremble in her hand as she tried to manipulate the buttons. Finally she gave up and just pulled. The buttons pinged onto the floor.

She broke the kiss, looked down at the floor and said, "I can't believe I did that. I'm sorry. I—"

Before she could finish, he grabbed her shirt, tugged it over her head and said, "Forget the buttons. Forget anything but this."

He stopped her from apologizing by resuming the kiss, as he eased her around the corner and into the living room.

He turned and let himself fall onto the couch, pulling her along with him.

She landed on his chest.

"Nate, is this going to be big enough?"

Even though his brain was muddled with the feel

of Shannon, he knew she was asking if the couch was big enough to hold them both, but he deliberately misconstrued the question. "It was big enough last time."

"But we didn't do it here..." she said, then let the sentence fade off as she caught his entendre and started to laugh as she said, "It was more than big enough. It was huge. It was massive. Oh, I shouldn't go on like this, or I'll give you a swollen head."

"Too late," he said, as he burst out laughing. They both laughed until they were breathless with it.

Their quips were funny, but not quite that funny. For Nate, the laughter was just a giddy sort of release. He was here, with Shannon, where he belonged.

This.

Just that one word summed up why he'd spent the week missing Shannon.

This.

He felt complete, holding her, laughing with her.

And as he showed her that a couch could indeed be *big enough,* he knew *this* was much more than boinking.

This wasn't uncomplicated, as they'd planned.

As a matter of fact, he suspected *this* could be quite complicated. He didn't mind the complication at all, and hoped he could convince Shannon not to mind as well.

As he made love to her, the feeling of certainty as to what *this* was grew.

Her name rolled off his lips like a chant to the rhythm of their bodies.

And when she whispered his name in return, he lost all control and took them both over the edge. They tumbled over together.

They twisted and somehow managed to snuggle on the couch afterward.

"Nate, I—" Shannon started, then stopped herself short.

He waited for her to finish the sentence, but instead of the two little words he longed to hear, that he'd hoped she was going to utter, she said, "I just wanted to say, you were right, it was plenty big enough."

She laughed then, and gently ran a finger along his jawline.

It was just the smallest of caresses, but it was enough to stir Nate's desire.

"Maybe we should go get a shower and then finish discussing how big is big enough," he said with a chuckle.

"Now, that's an offer a girl can't refuse."

They raced to the shower, laughing like a couple of kids.

Nate knew he'd have to tell her that things had changed for him, that he didn't want to be boink-buddies, he wanted more.

He wanted it all.

In the morning, he told himself as he ran his soap-filled hands all over her luscious body.

Tomorrow morning he'd tell her everything.

10

"GOOD MORNING," Nate murmured in her ear.

Shannon wiggled closer to him, not saying anything, mainly because her first impulse was to blurt out those words she'd decided not to blurt—at least not until she could figure out just how to say them right.

If she said them wrong he might leave. After all, love wasn't what he'd signed on for…uncomplicated was.

Nate was toying with her hair as he held her tight.

She liked the way it felt.

Wrapped in Nate.

Waking up on a Saturday morning with him in her bed.

She'd missed him so much last week, but had stayed away because she was afraid…afraid she'd blurt out the words and ruin everything.

The words were right there on the end of her tongue, but she valiantly held them in, not wanting to scare him off.

"Are you just going to lie there all morning?" he asked with a chuckle.

Pushing the words to the back of her mouth, she managed to squeeze "Maybe" out past them.

She congratulated herself for not saying them.

Maybe she could be with him and not say them, at least not until there was a chance he'd say them back.

If she could just give him more time maybe he'd love her, too.

"Are you hungry?" he asked.

"Yes."

Aha, she'd managed another word and hadn't let those three little ones slip.

She was getting good at this.

"Do you feel like taking a chance on my making pancakes?"

"I love—" she bit the words back and filled in "—pancakes. I'm more than willing to take a chance on your cooking."

Sneaky, sneaky little words.

Almost as sneaky as the feeling that had stolen into her heart and wouldn't let her shake it.

Nate looked almost disappointed for a split second. Maybe he'd hoped she'd offer to cook them?

The look passed quickly, and in its place, he smiled. "Maybe after we fortify our strength with breakfast we could come back in here and…"

He whispered his plans in her ear. Soft and low, his voice tickled her senses.

She hoped he could make his pancakes fast, because his offer sounded very, very tempting.

She nodded, saying, "I love—"

Darn. There they were again. "—I'd love to."

How on earth was she going to have breakfast and then make love to Nate again and not say them?

Maybe she could handle not telling him how much she loved him, not telling him how cute he was on the back of his Harley, how much she liked hearing about his day, how much she loved spending an evening arguing about what constituted a chick-flick, and how much she loved the sight of him dressed as a Harley rider or as a pharmacist.

She couldn't tell him how much she liked watching him with his parents, how much she loved waking up next to him, how much she loved…just how much she loved.

She pushed back the words and the thoughts, and pulled back the blanket. She gave a small yip. "It's cold in here."

Nate didn't yip as he crawled out of bed, but she could see goose bumps covering the skin she'd grown to know so well.

Shannon reached in her closet, pulled out her favorite fleecy robe and wrapped it around herself. It might be a bit ratty, but it was still warm.

"Here," she said, handing him a second robe, the one her mom had bought her for Christmas and she'd never worn. Her taste didn't match her mother's in robes—or much else, for that matter.

She could have offered him something else, but

one of the other things she happened to love was teasing Nate.

"It's pink," he grumbled, almost on cue, holding it with two fingers as if the color was somehow contagious.

"So?" she countered.

"Real men don't wear pink."

"Well…if you're really that insecure about your masculinity, I'll find you something else."

"I'm not insecure." He slipped it on. "But I mean, if I were really Bull, I'd deal with the chill without resorting to this," he muttered as he knotted the belt.

What was a huge robe on her, stretched to its limits across Nate's much broader shoulders.

Looking at him, his hair sleep-mussed, wearing her pink robe, Shannon was awash with the need to say the words.

Just to let them out.

Forget planning.

Forget perfect.

She was going to be brave and simply say them. She loved so many things about Nate, that she simply couldn't contain it another minute.

Tell him.

That's all she could do. That and pray he wouldn't walk right out the door, but would stick around long enough to learn to love her, too.

Ah, but he was wearing a pink bathrobe. He'd never walk out the door in that.

He was trapped.

This was the perfect time.

"Nate, there's something I have to tell you. I've spent the week trying to decide how, and finally have come to the conclusion that there's no right way. It's something important…" The words that had been aching to come out, hung back.

"Yes?" he said, when the silence hung in the room a few seconds too long for comfort.

Shannon garnered her strength, and said, "I love—"

The doorbell rang.

Who on earth would be ringing her doorbell at eight o'clock on a Saturday morning, interrupting her perfect moment?

"Mom," she muttered. Who else could it be? "I'll get rid of her."

Shannon Bonnie O'Malley, aka Roxy, had had enough. She wasn't going to play dodge-the-wedding-bullet with her mom any more.

She wasn't going to try and find a perfect way to tell the man she loved that she loved him.

She was going to be bold and take charge. She was kicking her mom out and then she was going to talk to Nate. She was going to tell him she loved him and he was just going to have to deal with the complication.

"You want help?" he asked.

"No. You go start the breakfast, I'll get rid of her."

He kissed her cheek. "Good luck."

He went to the kitchen and Shannon marched to the front door.

Enough was enough.

She pulled the door open and just stared.

"Good morning, Shannon, dear," Mrs. Calder said.

Her mother leaned over and kissed her cheek. "Good morning, sweetheart. Judy and I met in the driveway. You know what they say, great minds think alike. I brought donuts."

"And I baked some homemade muffins this morning," Mrs. Calder said.

Shannon decided both moms visiting again was scarier than the thought of Mrs. Calder's home-made muffins.

She tried to think of something to say, "I…uh…"

Her resolve might have been enough to let her deal with her mother, but no amount of resolve could help her deal with both mothers.

She needed reinforcements.

She needed Nate.

"Come on in, Judy," her mom said as she and Mrs. Calder walked past Shannon and into the house.

"Is Nate still in bed?" her mom asked, without waiting for an answer.

Shannon heard Nate say, "Mom," as the two women walked into the kitchen.

Knowing there was nothing to do but follow, Shannon did just that. She realized that her feet were bare, but she couldn't even work up any embarrassment about it.

She simply had too much on her mind and three little words just dying to be said, but there was no way to say them with both their mothers here.

"Shannon, your mom brought donuts and mine made us muffins," Nate said, a grim mock-smile pasted on his lips.

"Yes, they told me."

"So, what brings you both out this early on a Saturday morning?" he asked both mothers as he poured coffee into four mugs.

"I came to tell Shannon she had to quit her job," his mom said. "I worry all the time. This can't go on, and I'm sure her mother agrees with me."

"Quit her job? Of course I don't agree with you. At least Shannon has steady work and a steady paycheck. While all your son does is ride around on a motorcycle all day."

"I hate that motorcycle," his mom confessed.

The phone rang and Shannon automatically picked it up. "Hello?"

"Shannon," Kate said. "I'm thinking I should come home. Mom says that this Bull guy is trouble and…"

The argument about motorcycles and quitting jobs continued.

Kate poured out her worries across the phone line.

Nate stood there looking as lost as Shannon felt.

Shannon realized that telling Nate she loved him couldn't possibly get any more complicated than this.

The teacher in her came to life. Shannon put her fingers to her lips and let out a shrill whistle.... *Zwwwwwippppp.*

Three sets of eyes were immediately focused on her. She'd known they would be. She'd used the whistle for years to get unruly students' attention.

"Enough!" she said.

She put the phone to her ear and said, "Kate, I'll call you back later. Don't come home. Everything's under control.

"Mom and Mrs. Calder, I'm done playing games. Things aren't the way they seem. This is..."

She looked to Nate and saw him give a small nod of agreement. "It all started at Mick's bar, just like we said. It was after one of the horrendous dates you fixed me up on, Mom. I'd had enough."

"Me, too, Mom," Nate said. "All that, *And I almost died giving birth to you, and all I want is a grandbaby*...stuff. And fixing me up with some initial girl."

"Kay," his mother supplied.

"Yeah, fixing up," Shannon echoed. "Remember Shelby, Mom? Shelby and Shannon. At least if someone said Nate and Kay it wouldn't sound like you were being shushed in a library.''

Nate laughed. ''I hadn't thought of that, but you're right. You aren't destined for a Shelby.''

''Shannon has definite ideas about what names go together,'' her mother said. ''Nate and Shannon. Those go well, don't you think, dear?''

Shannon couldn't begin to tell her mother just how much she agreed...at least not until she told Nate how much they went together.

''That's our point. Shannon and Nate do really go together, at least not the way you two think.''

''Or Roxy and Bull,'' Mrs. Calder said. ''Those two names go well together, too, don't you think, Brigit?''

''I certainly do, Judy.''

They knew.

Their mothers knew the truth.

Shannon saw it in their eyes.

''But as much as my daughter focuses on names,'' her mom continued, ''I have to say, I prefer focusing on careers, on personal traits. And I'd say a pharmacist and a teacher go together about as well as—''

''A biker and a stripper—''

''Exotic dancer.'' Nate corrected his mom before Shannon could.

Shannon reached out, took his hand and gave it a squeeze. ''So you both know this is just an act.''

''Of course we knew. We're bright, capable

women who saw through your little charade," his mom said.

Shannon's mom gave her a funny look. "But it's not all an act."

"What do you mean?" she asked.

"Why, look at the two of you, united against us. Holding hands, sleeping over. You two are in love," her mom said, her voice practically cooing. She sounded just the way Patricia had.

"I can't speak for Nate, but what I feel for him isn't something I'm going to discuss with the two of you. As a matter of fact, it's time you both left. You've meddled enough. Nate and I will work things out on our own."

"But, honey, there are just some things that a girl needs her mother for."

"You're right, Mom, but this isn't one of them." She steered both protesting mothers to the door. "Thank you for stopping by."

"But—" her mother and Mrs. Calder said in unison.

"But nothing. Nate and I are adults. Whatever is going to happen next in our relationship is up to us."

"This isn't about the bet, you know, honey," her mom said softly. "I want you to be happy. I think Nate's the man for you."

"I know that, Mom." She kissed her mother's cheek.

Shannon shut the door on both of the moms, then headed back to the kitchen.

She hoped that when she said the words Nate would admit he loved her as well, or that he was willing to give them a chance.

''They're gone?'' he asked.

''Yes.''

''Phew,'' he wiped his brow. ''We may be able to handle keeping things uncomplicated, but our moms certainly try to make things interesting. Do you think they'll stay off our backs now that they know the truth?''

''No,'' she said with a small smile. ''They'll probably both start in again tomorrow.''

''So…'' he paused, obviously looking for something to say, ''Do you still want those pancakes?'' he asked.

''No, I don't think so.''

''You said you wanted to talk about something?''

''I…'' She was chickening out. There he was, standing in the middle of her kitchen, and all she wanted to do was run over to him and shout the words, *I love you.*

She gathered her courage.

Before she could get the words out he said, ''Just because they know doesn't mean our…'' he hesitated, obviously looking for a description of their relationship.

''Our dating-but-not-really relationship?'' she

asked. "Our boink-buddy-ness? Our *uncomplicated* thing?"

"Yes. There's no reason we can't keep seeing each other. I enjoy being with you. What we have is good."

Talk about being damned by faint praise.

Here she was ready to spill her heart out to him, to tell him she was finding it hard to breathe when he wasn't around and he says that he enjoys being with her?

Of course he thought what they had was good. It was uncomplicated.

Shannon hated that word at this point.

She hated this stupid charade.

She'd just say the words, and when he dumped her she'd pick herself up and move on.

Maybe she'd agree to go out with Shelby. After all, he might not be complicated-phobic.

"I don't think things can continue the way they've been going," she started. "After all, part of our reason for being together is gone. Our moms know."

"Still, what we have works, Shannon-me-love…"

"Don't you Shannon-me-love me," she said. "Here I am, ready to tell you that I love you and you're still harping on about our stupid deal, our *uncomplicated* plans."

This time she was the one shaking a finger, she shook it right in his face as she continued, "Well,

I want complicated. I want it all. I want someone who calls me every day, not just when he feels like it. No, I take that back, I want a man who *feels* like calling me every day. But you don't want that. That would be messy. Well, that's fine. Just fine. I'll go find a man who doesn't mind a bit of complication.''

''You think you can replace me that easily?'' he asked, softly, moving closer.

''Sure.'' Which was a big lie. She doubted she'd ever replace Nathan.

''You think you'll find another guy who doesn't mind wearing a pink bathrobe and watching chick-flicks, who knows how to pry you out of pleather…who loves you like I do?''

''I'm sure there are men out there who are more than capable of wearing pink and watching chick-flicks. As for pleather—'' she stopped, unsure she'd heard what she thought she heard.

''Say it again.''

''I know how to pry you out of pleather,'' he said, a big grin on his face.

''Not that part.'' She grabbed the fluffy pink material and pulled him close.

''I don't mind watching chick-flicks if they have at least a bit of blood-and-guts. I may wear pink, but I like blood-and-guts.''

''Nope. Not that part either.'' She felt as if she was going to explode with joy.

''Oh. I love you?'' he asked with a smile.

"Yep, that's the part."

"I do." He kissed her then and she could feel it.

He did—he loved her.

She broke the kiss and said, "But you were just going on about how you wanted uncomplicated…"

"You didn't want love, you wanted to be boink-buddies."

"No, I didn't. I thought that's what you wanted. I realized the other day that what I feel for you went further than I ever expected it to. I came by the pharmacy to tell you."

"But you ran out on me," he said with a frown.

"You were tired and rattling on about needing things uncomplicated, and I knew saying those words would complicate everything, so I didn't."

"Shannon, nothing in my life has been uncomplicated since I met you. As a matter of fact, this is the most complicated, convoluted relationship I've ever been in…and I couldn't be happier. Or rather, I could be if you did one little thing."

"What's that?" she asked. She'd do anything for him—for the man she loved.

"Say the words. You still haven't said them, you know."

"Really? How negligent of me. Nathan Bull Calder, I love you. I think I loved you from that first time we talked at Mick's."

Suddenly she was wrapped in Nate, her face

pressed to a fuzzy pink bathrobe. She felt as if she could burst, she was so happy.

"So, you know what this means?" he asked.

"What?"

"Your mom's won her bet."

"No, no she hasn't. The bet was that I'd get married…" She looked up and saw his intent in his eyes. "Oh."

"One more word, that's all I need from you."

"Yes."

"Should we go call our moms? They're probably still in the driveway trying to decide what to do next."

"Later," Shannon said. Her mom would be absolutely beside herself with excitement—and totally unbearable to live with as she tried to plan the wedding.

Shannon remembered how bad it had been when her mom had tried to plan Mary Kathryn's.

"My mom will just have to wait a while longer. There's something we have to do first."

"What would that be?" He ran a finger along her cheek.

It was the slightest touch, but it left Shannon decidedly weak in the knees and more than a bit breathless.

"Have I ever mentioned I find men who wear pink very sexy?" she asked, her voice a soft whisper.

"Is that so?"

"Almost as sexy as bikers named Bull..."
Laughing, they forgot their moms.
They forgot all about complications.
All they remembered was love.
After all, that was all that really mattered.

Epilogue

"MAY I PRESENT, the brides and grooms," Father Murphy boomed as two couples walked into Sabella's for the reception.

"Kiss. Kiss. Kiss. Kiss," the crowd chanted.

Brigit O'Malley watched as her daughter—her beautiful, talented daughter—kissed her brand-new husband.

She sniffed. It was a dainty sniff...quiet and refined.

Not at all like the big honking sniffs Cecilia was making as Cara and her Texan kissed as well.

Cecilia had called weeks ago and told her Cara was getting married. She'd rattled on and on about her wedding plans...plans that never came to fruition.

A part of Brigit had felt bad when she'd heard that Cara and her Texan had eloped. She'd almost resigned herself to losing the bet. Then Brigit realized that just a civil ceremony didn't count. She'd technically won.

But for some reason, Shannon felt a bond to Cara, although to the best of Brigit's knowledge the two had never met. Kate and Cara had become friends, and through her, Shannon and Cara had formed a bond. They ended up talking and coming up with this diabolical plan.

Cara and her Rex had shared today's ceremony, having their civil marriage blessed at the same time Shannon and Nate married.

The girls had suggested they felt drawn to each other because both their mothers were meddlers.

A meddler?

No way.

Brigit knew she was just a loving, concerned mother.

As was her good friend, Cecilia.

Brigit sighed as the couples moved onto the dance floor. She spotted Kate and Tony. And there was Desi, that delightful wedding planner, and Seth. Everyone was here.

She sighed again.

"We did good, didn't we?" Cecilia asked.

Brigit looped her arm around the shorter woman's shoulders. "Yes, we did. They all look so happy."

"Speaking of happy, about the bet..."

Brigit nodded. "Yes, I know having two ceremonies today makes it a draw. The girls planned it that way. Our children are trickier than I ever gave them credit for."

"They take after their mamas."

Brigit smiled. "Yes, I guess they do."

"But I was thinking, maybe we should go."

"Go?"

"To the Catskills together. I talked to Rachel and Jessica-Marie. Rachel's going to be away on business, but Jessica-Marie would love to come. And I thought maybe we'd ask your son-in-law's mama, that Judy Calder, to fill in for our fourth."

"Fourth?"

"Well, we need someone for pinochle. A long weekend. Think of the games we could have."

"The four of us in the Catskills?" Brigit hugged her friend.

Her best friend.

The kind of friend that only came along once in a lifetime. "Oh, Cecilia, that would be lovely. We'll have so much fun. And we deserve a vacation, after all the work the girls put us through."

"And do we get any thanks?" Cecilia asked.

"No. Why, all I asked for was a dignified service and just look at these cakes. They're not what I would have chosen."

Brigit personally thought that despite the fact they were not quite dignified, Shannon's was ever so much nicer than Cara's.

Why, Cara had a bull on hers.

Brigit wasn't sure she'd want a bull on top of a cake, but Cara said that it was a bull that had brought her and Rex together and then laughed. Brigit didn't get the joke.

But she did get Shannon's cake toppers. A Harley Davidson with two Barbies that Desi and Seth had loaned them. The Ken doll was dressed in black and had a small tattoo on his forearm, and Barbie had on tight red leather pants.

Every time she looked at those pants, Shannon laughed, though she wouldn't explain it to her mother. But Brigit did understand the rest of it.

Instead of saying Shannon and Nate it said Roxy and Bull.

The stripper and the biker.

Brigit hugged Cecilia. "Yes, after all the work we've gone to, making sure the kids are happily married, I think we need a break. The Catskills it is."

"Great, because soon I won't be able to get away."

"Why?" Brigit asked.

"Because I'm sure my Cara and her Rex will be giving me a grandbaby soon."

"Nate's mother was just telling me that she plans to be a grandmother early next year, something about Nate owing her a baby since he almost killed her. She seemed positive, so I'm sure I'll be a grandmother before you."

"You want to bet?" Cecilia asked.

Brigit looked at the reception room full of people she loved. Now that both her girls were happily married, it was time to add to the family again.

She smiled. "You're on…"

* * * * *

*Harlequin Flipside
is coming next month!*

*Please turn the page for a taste of
acclaimed author Millie Criswell's*

STAYING SINGLE

For romantic comedy lovers everywhere!

1

IT WAS A BAD DAY for a wedding.

Francie Morelli gazed down the red-carpeted aisle toward the altar, where her handsome husband-to-be, all smiles and nervous perspiration in a black Armani tux, awaited her arrival, and knew this with a certainty.

Unlike him, Francie wasn't nervous, just panicked. The kind of panic you get when you can't catch your breath, or you feel like you might throw up.

Okay, so maybe she was a teensy bit nervous.

Though she'd done the wedding thing twice before and knew what to expect. Not that she had ever actually made it all the way to the altar and said her I do's.

And it didn't look like she would get that far this time, either.

Swallowing with some difficulty at the dangerous thoughts going through her mind, she tried to ignore the ''Run, Francie, run!'' mantra currently playing through her head to the tune of ''Burn, Baby, Burn,'' the disco song so popular in the 70s.

The choice of music was a bad omen. Burning

in hell was a definite possibility if she didn't go through with this wedding, which was probably the lesser of two evils, because she knew Josephine Morelli's punishment would be far worse.

The devil had nothing on Josephine Morelli.

Through her blush veil, she could see her mother, hands locked in prayer and supplication, pleading with the Almighty to give her daughter the courage to go through with the ceremony this time. The older woman's tear-filled eyes—Francie knew there were tears because her mother liked to make a good showing at public events (funerals were her specialty)—were fixed on the massive gold crucifix hanging above the altar, as if by sheer will alone she could command God to do her bidding, as Josephine had commanded Francie so many times before.

Fortunately for the world at large, God seemed to have a stronger backbone than Francie.

A hushed silence surrounded her, as those in attendance waited to see if she would actually go through with the ceremony. Aunt Flo was biting her nails to the quick, while Grandma Abrizzi had her rosary beads clacking at top speed.

Francie's sixteen-year-old brother, Jackie, had taken perverse delight in explaining that several of the male guests, her uncles, in particular, had placed bets on the outcome of today's event. The odds were five to one that she would never see her wedding night.

Not that Francie had anything in particular against matrimony. It just wasn't right for her. She had no desire to become an extension of a man, with few interests of her own, except family and meddling in her children's lives.

Meddling, like marriage, was another one of those M-words that Francie hated—meddling, marriage, menstruation, menopause, Milk of Magnesia—Josephine's remedy for every childhood ailment. No, M-words were definitely not good. She'd have to remember that the next time she dated, if there was a next time. At the moment, that seemed remote…remote, redundant, ridiculous.

She would not allow her mother to bully her again.

Standing beside Francie, John Morelli clutched his daughter's arm in a death grip, trying to keep her steady and on course. But she knew, just as he did, that it wouldn't. She was in collision mode and there was no way to avoid it.

Still, he had to try. His wife would expect no less. And John, like most of the Morellis, wasn't going to buck Josephine's wedding obsession. Not if he wanted a moment's peace.

Francie's toes began to tingle—a surefire indication that flight was imminent. She wiggled them, hoping and praying the urge to flee would pass. If not, the white satin shoes she wore, like Dorothy's ruby slippers, would whisk her away from the solemn occasion, to her favorite place of refuge,

Manny's Little Italy Deli, where she knew he would be waiting for her with a pastrami on rye and a large diet soda.

Okay, so stress made her hungry!

Her roommate, Leo Bergman, suitably armed with a packed suitcase and a train ticket to an as-yet-unknown destination, would also be there to offer moral support and a stern lecture. Leo was almost as good as Josephine when it came to offering opinions and advice that no one wanted, only he did it with a bit more finesse.

Patting his daughter's hand reassuringly, John leaned over and smiled lovingly.

"Don't be nervous, *cara mia.* Soon this will be over and you'll be married and settled down. It's the right thing to do, you'll see. And it will make your mother very happy. You know how she's waited for this day."

The second coming paled by comparison!

Francie adored her father and wanted to agree with him; she wanted that more than anything. But words of reassurance stuck in her throat like oversize peanuts, and all she could offer up was a gaseous smile and a deer-in-the-headlights look.

"I'm sorry, Pop, but I don't think I can go through with this. I'm just not ready to get married. I'm not sure I'll ever be ready."

John's eyes widened momentarily, then he looked down the long aisle to where his wife was sitting in the first pew, the smile on her face suddenly melting as she noticed his resigned, worried expression.

"Your car's out back. I gassed it up, just in case, and left some money in the glove box."

Warmed by the gesture, Francie kissed her father's cheek. "I love you, Pop. Thanks! I hope Ma doesn't give you too bad a time of it."

Then she turned and hightailed it out of the church and into the warm September sunshine.

COMING NEXT MONTH

HARLEQUIN flipside™

#1

STAYING SINGLE by Millie Criswell

"Engaging men" are lining up for Francesca Morelli, thanks to her interfering mother! She's arranged three weddings so far for her twenty-nine-and-pushing-it daughter. Unfortunately, all three have gone off, uh, *without* a hitch, because the only vow Francesca's taking is to stay single! That is, until former best man Mark Fielding steps onto the scene.

#2

ONE TRUE LOVE? by Stephanie Doyle

Corinne Weatherby believes everyone has just *one* true love. Okay, so the one she's picked is a shallow, inconsiderate womanizer—nothing a good breakup scene can't fix. There's a drama queen lurking just below her financial-controller surface. Her "I'm leaving you!" will turn the boy around. But her office buddy Matthew overhears her performance and decides to go for it, determined to prove *he* is her real one and only.

Clever, witty and unexpectedly romantic!

HFCNM0903

Is your man too good to be true?

Hot, gorgeous AND romantic?
If so, he could be a Harlequin® Blaze™ series cover model!

Our grand-prize winners will receive a trip for two to New York City to
shoot the cover of a Blaze novel, and will stay at the luxurious Plaza Hotel.
Plus, they'll receive $500 U.S. spending money!
The runner-up winners will receive $200 U.S.
to spend on a romantic dinner for two.

It's easy to enter!

In 100 words or less, tell us what makes your boyfriend or spouse a true romantic
and the perfect candidate for the cover of a Blaze novel, and include in your submission
two photos of this potential cover model.

All entries must include the written submission of the contest entrant, two photographs of the model
candidate and the Official Entry Form and Publicity Release forms completed in full and signed by
both the model candidate and the contest entrant. Harlequin, along with the experts at
Elite Model Management, will select a winner.

For photo and complete Contest details, please refer to the Official Rules on the next page. All entries
will become the property of Harlequin Enterprises Ltd. and are not returnable.

**Please visit www.blazecovermodel.com to download a copy of the Official Entry Form and
Publicity Release Form or send a request to one of the addresses below.**

Please mail your entry to: **Harlequin Blaze Cover Model Search**

In U.S.A.	In Canada
P.O. Box 9069	P.O. Box 637
Buffalo, NY	Fort Erie, ON
14269-9069	L2A 5X3

No purchase necessary. Contest open to Canadian and U.S. residents who are 18 and over.
Void where prohibited. Contest closes September 30, 2003.

HARLEQUIN® *Blaze*™

HBCVRMODEL1

HARLEQUIN BLAZE COVER MODEL SEARCH CONTEST 3569 OFFICIAL RULES
NO PURCHASE NECESSARY TO ENTER

1. To enter, submit two (2) 4" x 6" photographs of a boyfriend or spouse (who must be 18 years of age or older) taken no later than three (3) months from the time of entry: a close-up, waist up, shirtless photograph; and a fully clothed, full-length photograph, then, tell us, in 100 words or fewer, why he should be a Harlequin Blaze cover model and how he is romantic. Your complete "entry" must include: (i) your essay, (ii) the Official Entry Form and Publicity Release Form printed below completed and signed by you (as "Entrant"), (iii) the photographs (with your hand-written name, address and phone number, and your model's name, address and phone number on the back of each photograph), and (iv) the Publicity Release Form and Photograph Representation Form printed below completed and signed by your model (as "Model"), and should be sent via first-class mail to either: Harlequin Blaze Cover Model Search Contest 3569, P.O. Box 9069, Buffalo, NY, 14269-9069, or Harlequin Blaze Cover Model Search Contest 3569, P.O. Box 637, Fort Erie, Ontario L2A 5X3. All submissions must be in English and be received no later than September 30, 2003. Limit: one entry per person, household or organization. **Purchase or acceptance of a product offer does not improve your chances of winning.** All entry requirements must be strictly adhered to for eligibility and to ensure fairness among entries.

2. Ten (10) Finalist submissions (photographs and essays) will be selected by a panel of judges consisting of members of the Harlequin editorial, marketing and public relations staff, as well as a representative from Elite Model Management (Toronto) Inc., based on the following criteria:

Aptness/Appropriateness of submitted photographs for a Harlequin Blaze cover—70%
Originality of Essay—20%
Sincerity of Essay—10%

In the event of a tie, duplicate finalists will be selected. The photographs submitted by finalists will be posted on the Harlequin website no later than November 15, 2003 (at www.blazecovermodel.com), and viewers may vote, in rank order, on their favorite(s) to assist in the panel of judges' final determination of the Grand Prize and Runner-up winning entries based on the above judging criteria. All decisions of the judges are final.

3. All entries become the property of Harlequin Enterprises Ltd. and none will be returned. Any entry may be used for future promotional purposes. Elite Model Management (Toronto) Inc. and/or its partners, subsidiaries and affiliates operating as "Elite Model Management" will have access to all entries including all personal information, and may contact any Entrant and/or Model in its sole discretion for their own business purposes. Harlequin and Elite Model Management (Toronto) Inc. are separate entities with no legal association or partnership whatsoever having no power to bind or obligate the other or create any expressed or implied obligation or responsibility on behalf of the other, such that Harlequin shall not be responsible in any way for any acts or omissions of Elite Model Management (Toronto) Inc. or its partners, subsidiaries and affiliates in connection with the Contest or otherwise and Elite Model Management shall not be responsible in any way for any acts or omissions of Harlequin or its partners, subsidiaries and affiliates in connection with the contest or otherwise.

4. All Entrants and Models must be residents of the U.S. or Canada, be 18 years of age or older, and have no prior criminal convictions. The contest is not open to any Model that is a professional model and/or actor in any capacity at the time of the entry. Contest void wherever prohibited by law; all applicable laws and regulations apply. Any litigation within the Province of Quebec regarding the conduct or organization of a publicity contest may be submitted to the Régie des alcools, des courses et des jeux for a ruling, and any litigation regarding the awarding of a prize may be submitted to the Régie only for the purpose of helping the parties reach a settlement. Employees and immediate family members of Harlequin Enterprises Ltd., D.L. Blair, Inc., Elite Model Management (Toronto) Inc. and their parents, affiliates, subsidiaries and all other agencies, entities and persons connected with the use, marketing or conduct of this Contest are not eligible to enter. Acceptance of any prize offered constitutes permission to use Entrants' and Models' names, essay submissions, photographs or other likenesses for the purposes of advertising, trade, publication and promotion on behalf of Harlequin Enterprises Ltd., its parent, affiliates, subsidiaries, assigns and other authorized entities involved in the judging and promotion of the contest without further compensation to any Entrant or Model, unless prohibited by law.

5. Finalists will be determined no later than October 30, 2003. Prize Winners will be determined no later than January 31, 2004. Grand Prize Winners (consisting of winning Entrant and Model) will be required to sign and return Affidavit of Eligibility/Release of Liability and Model Release forms within thirty (30) days of notification. Non-compliance with this requirement and within the specified time period will result in disqualification and an alternate will be selected. Any prize notification returned as undeliverable will result in the awarding of the prize to an alternate set of winners. All travelers (or parent/legal guardian of a minor) must execute the Affidavit of Eligibility/Release of Liability prior to ticketing and must possess required travel documents (e.g. valid photo ID) where applicable. Travel dates specified by Sponsor but no later than May 30, 2004.

6. Prizes: One (1) Grand Prize—the opportunity for the Model to appear on the cover of a paperback book from the Harlequin Blaze series, and a 3 day/2 night trip for two (Entrant and Model) to New York, NY for the photo shoot of Model which includes round-trip coach air transportation from the commercial airport nearest the winning Entrant's home to New York, NY, (or, in lieu of air transportation, $100 cash payable to Entrant and Model, if the winning Entrant's home is within 250 miles of New York, NY), hotel accommodations (double occupancy) at the Plaza Hotel and $500 cash spending money payable to Entrant and Model, (approximate prize value: $8,000), and one (1) Runner-up Prize of $200 cash payable to Entrant and Model for a romantic dinner for two (approximate prize value: $200). Prizes are valued in U.S. currency. Prizes consist of only those items listed as part of the prize. No substitution of prize(s) permitted by winners. All prizes are awarded jointly to the Entrant and Model of the winning entries, and are not severable - prizes and obligations may not be assigned or transferred. Any change to the Entrant and/or Model of the winning entries will result in disqualification and an alternate will be selected. Taxes on prize are the sole responsibility of winners. Any and all expenses and/or items not specifically described as part of the prize are the sole responsibility of winners. Harlequin Enterprises Ltd. and D.L. Blair, Inc., their parents, affiliates, and subsidiaries are not responsible for errors in printing of Contest entries and/or game pieces. No responsibility is assumed for lost, stolen, late, illegible, incomplete, inaccurate, non-delivered, postage due or misdirected mail or entries. In the event of printing or other errors which may result in unintended prize values or duplication of prizes, all affected game pieces or entries shall be null and void.

7. Winners will be notified by mail. For winners' list (available after March 31, 2004), send a self-addressed, stamped envelope to: Harlequin Blaze Cover Model Search Contest 3569 Winners, P.O. Box 4200, Blair, NE 68009-4200, or refer to the Harlequin website (at www.blazecovermodel.com).

Contest sponsored by Harlequin Enterprises Ltd., P.O. Box 9042, Buffalo, NY 14269-9042.

**Madcap adventures of bull hijinks and reforming bad guys, with a little love thrown in!
Join author Colleen Collins as she takes you from the Colorado Rockies to the Florida Keys with two heroines determined to get their men.**

Don't miss these two new stories!

Let It Bree
Can't Buy Me Louie

Colleen Collins

September 2003

Available at your favorite retail outlet.

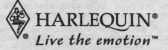